Katherine Kingston
Arianna Hart
Dawn Madigan

Pleasure Raiders

'Cause it's All About the Booty

Ellora's Cave
Romantica Publishing

What the critics are saying...

Pleasure Raiders

"Congratulations, ladies, on creating a rare treat where all the gems in the treasure chest are diamonds!" ~ *Ecataromance*

Checkmate

5 *Stars* "Checkmate is a highly entertaining, erotic, romantic, Gladiator and Survivor meets Temptation Island. A definite keeper!" ~ *Just Erotic Romance Reviews*

5 *Angels* "A well-written story and a continuation of Ms. Kingston's line of great releases." ~ *Fallen Angels Reviews*

Concubine's Revenge

"An enjoyable sweet revenge story full of emotions and humanity. Thanks Ms. Hart!" ~ *Just Erotic Romance Reviews*

An Ellora's Cave Romantica Publication

www.ellorascave.com

Pleasure Raiders

ISBN 9781419954474

Edited by Briana St. James and Heather Osborn
Cover art by Syneca

Electronic book Publication November 2005
Trade paperback Publication May 2007

Content Advisory:

S - ENSUOUS
E - ROTIC
X - TREME

Ellora's Cave Publishing offers three levels of Romantica® reading entertainment: S (S-ensuous), E (E-rotic), and X (X-treme).

The following material contains graphic sexual content meant for mature readers. This story has been rated E–rotic.

S-*ensuous* love scenes are explicit and leave nothing to the imagination.

E-*rotic* love scenes are explicit, leave nothing to the imagination, and are high in volume per the overall word count. E-rated titles might contain material that some readers find objectionable—in other words, almost anything goes, sexually. E-rated titles are the most graphic titles we carry in terms of both sexual language and descriptiveness in these works of literature.

X-*treme* titles differ from E-rated titles only in plot premise and storyline execution. Stories designated with the letter X tend to contain difficult or controversial subject matter not for the faint of heart.

PLEASURE RAIDERS

CHECKMATE

Katherine Kingston

Chapter One

"Captain, we have a problem!"

Devonne sighed. Without taking her eyes or attention from the viewscreen port, she asked the Personal Care Droid, "What now?"

"A seam has come loose in your only remaining dress uniform." The PCD made an annoying huffy sound before adding, "And the refresher just tore a button off it."

Devonne made a mental note to get the programming adjusted to remove that huffing noise from the droid's speech system. "Fix it."

"Captain, I beg your attention. Those seams have been—"

"Captain?" Another voice cut through the droid's complaint. The combination of surprise, alarm and doubt in the single word warned Devonne that fate was about to throw a monkey wrench into their carefully worked out plans.

Ignoring the PCD, which continued to babble on about clothes, she turned to face her first mate. Reed stared at a screen in front of him. "What have you got?" she asked.

He frowned and tugged on his earlobe. "If I didn't… I swear it looks like someone had the same idea as us and got to the Denogrenian ship first."

"What?" She spoke so loudly it startled the two other crew members in the room into looking up from their panels.

Reed pointed to the screen that showed two blinking blips. Devonne studied the data readouts. "Magnify."

Reed pulled the direct link from his face and disconnected it from the panel. Devonne repeated her order to magnify the display.

Sure enough, another smaller blip clearly approached the large blip that represented their target. A wavery yellow line shot out between them.

"Damnation!" Devonne clenched her fists and clamped her lips shut. She wanted to scream her frustration as she watched the evidence of a tractor beam hauling her prize toward a rival. When she reclaimed some measure of control, she said, "Identify secondary target." She already knew but needed to hear it confirmed anyway.

"Identifying," the computer's soothing male voice responded. "Target identified as KCS *Fool's Quest*, registered out of Kalima, Prox G-04, number 668940435453545435. No official standing listed."

"What the hell is *he* doing here? Damn. Shit! No official standing, indeed."

"Captain?" SueBelle, the newest member of the crew, looked up at her, eyebrows raised.

"Reginald Jameson Jernigan. Commonly known as Raje. Or Prince Reginald. The son of a bitch."

"You know him?"

"For my sins."

"How?" Navigation Officer SueBelle asked.

Reed spoke at the same time. "What's he doing?"

"Beating us to the prize." Devonne's fists clenched again. "But why? I thought he was out of the game. Unless he had another fight with his uncle. But even then…"

She needed this cargo. Her exiled clan, now more than five hundred strong, was hidden in an obscure corner of an even more obscure planet and rapidly outgrowing their hiding place. They needed a bargaining chip to finally gain a place where they could settle permanently. Interstellar piracy had a limited life span and she had neared the end of it. This was her grand finale, her swan song, the move that would end her life of crime and let her retire in peace. She wasn't about to give it up to an arrogant jerk who viewed life as a game and stolen cargoes as his ticket to personal wealth and power.

"I'm *not* going to let this go. CC, can you calculate the combined mass of both those ships?"

"Can do, Captain," the ship said.

Reed threw her an incredulous look. "You can't be thinking of trying to snag both of them?"

"Why can't I?"

"You're going to play chicken with *him*?"

"Why not?"

The computer came back and gave an answer. The number wasn't as low as she'd hoped, but it might still be possible.

"That's why," Reed said. "I know all the reasons you don't want to lose this one, but still... Why not wait until he releases...never mind. He can still run faster, can't he?"

"CC, how much acceleration can we generate if we divert every bit of power to the engines?"

"Including life support systems, Captain?"

"Everything but critical systems."

The rest of her crew, SueBelle, Reed and Nathan, looked at her as though they feared she'd lost a critical neural system or two herself.

The computer's answer came a few seconds later and gave her pause. It might be enough. If... "How long can we maintain that level and still have enough fuel to get back to Esketan Station?"

"With present fuel levels, a maximum of thirty-six hours."

"Captain, you can't mean to try to hold them both!" Reed challenged.

She gave him her sharpest, sternest look. "I don't mean to try. I'm going to do it. Reed, take us in just the way we'd planned. Nathan, prepare to activate tractor beam as soon as we decloak. SueBelle, fine-tune position coordinates to give us maximum grapple on both ships."

They trusted her enough to follow her commands. She'd taken a few strange gambles before and they'd paid off. She hoped she could do it again one last time.

* * * * *

They'd just decloaked and were preparing to activate the tractor beam when the computer announced, "Incoming message. Marked 'Urgent'."

"Source?" SueBelle asked, without looking at the display or lifting her hands from the controls.

"KCS *Fool's Quest*."

They all looked up at that.

"Open channel," Devonne said.

"Video link requested," the computer announced.

"Open video link."

A man's face appeared on the screen at the side of the cockpit. Without greeting or any other polite pleasantries, he said, "Devonne, what the hell do you think you're doing?"

She stared at the figure on-screen, looking for changes wrought by the six months since she'd last seen him. She didn't find any. His hair was still as black, his face just as strongly chiseled, his mouth hard and sensual, cheekbones high and sharp. His eyes were still that strange light yellow-green color. She expected anger, but instead his expression looked more amused.

"Greetings to you, too, Raje," she said. "Or should I say, 'Your Highness'? It's been a while since we last met."

"Nearly six months," he snapped back. "And you don't appear to have developed any more sense in the interim."

"You always did say the nicest things to me."

"Can it, Dev. What's going on here?"

"You can't guess? You used to be smarter than that, Raje. And, by the way, why are *you* here? I thought you'd gone respectable, *Your Highness*."

He ignored the last part of her question. "Okay, it's not the 'what' it's the 'why'?"

"Which part of 'Royal Denogrenian Treasure' don't you understand?"

He closed his eyes for a moment and shook his head. "The part where you think you can take it away by holding both the Denogrenian ship and mine in trac."

"Thirty hours. I can hold it for thirty hours. About how long it will take a fleet of Denogrenian warships to get here."

He looked startled. "Then we both go down."

"Right. Want to talk about it? The thing is, I have nothing left to lose, and you do."

"Ridiculous. If you don't care about your own life and freedom, what about your crew?"

He had her there and they both knew it.

Amazingly it was SueBelle who spoke up first. "We're with Captain Devonne all the way." Reed and Nathan nodded agreement.

"Devonne, this is ridiculous," he said. "Will you meet me to talk about it?"

"Just talk?"

His black eyebrows rose. "I'm open to all sorts of…communication. But whatever you want."

She ignored the suggestion in the words. At least she tried to ignore it. But his deep, sexy voice slipped past all her defenses and worked its way into her blood, warming it, making her too aware of him. Worse yet, he was doing it deliberately, putting in that low gravelly rumble, because he knew what it did to her. Her body remembered what the rest of her wanted to forget. The familiar low pressure began to gather. Damn it.

"I want the Denogrenian ship." It came out a bit sharper than she intended, betraying the emotions roiling through her.

"Hmmm… That is a bit of a problem. I want it, too. And I got to it first."

"But I'm getting to it last. And while you may have it, you're stuck here until I decide to let go."

"But you are as well," he pointed out. "Stalemate, Devonne. Let's talk about it."

"Permission to board extended, *Your Highness*," she said. "But come alone."

"Of course. I figured you'd want me all to yourself."

"Don't flatter yourself," she growled, annoyed because her heart was thumping too hard and her hands were shaking.

"I'll be there in twenty minutes." He signed off.

"Wowza." SueBelle's stare mixed admiration with envy. "If you don't want to keep him, can I have him? All that sexy good-looking man and he's a prince to boot?"

"You don't want him. He's an arrogant jerk."

SueBelle shrugged. "I'll take my chances."

The PCD droid came over and said, "Captain, you must dress appropriately to welcome the Gambrian First Heir and commander of *Fool's Quest*. Please come and change. I'll have the seam repaired quickly."

Devonne sighed. The droid was right. "Go fix the seam. I'll be there in a moment."

She waited a moment to be sure no hitches would arise, but it appeared the trac hold was stable. She slowly made her way back to her cabin, unable to contain the memories Raje brought.

* * * * *

Two Years Previous

The marooned, sentient flotsam of a dozen or more worlds crowded into the cozy bar. Its location next to the most discreet and therefore expensive unofficial repair dump for space-going vessels ensured it had steady business. As usual, the smell in the bar nearly knocked her down when she entered. After several years of sporadic patronage she shouldn't be startled by it. But the aromas of bodies from various planets, beverages from even more different corners of the universe, and several kinds of smoke drifting on the air combined into a reek so strong it had nearly physical force. By the time she'd settled down with her first drink she wouldn't notice it anymore, and she'd forget all about it before the night ended, until the next time she came and it caught her again.

Devonne made her way through a cloud of smoke so dense it obscured the far end of the room. It stung her eyes and nose and left a bad taste in the back of her throat. When she reached the bar, she had to squint to see at all. She found a pair of open stools and climbed aboard the one next to a Vingistian of indeterminate gender. They had no interest in contact with humans except to trade for tobacco and alcohol.

Unfortunately a man, human from the appearance of his hands, walked up within moments and took the other open stool.

Not too surprisingly, the panel directly in front of her didn't work. She looked for the barkeep.

"Gin," she told the critter, when he extended a tentacle to ask. She would actually have preferred beer but even if you asked for a name brand, the result was often problematic.

"Taking the safe route?" the man on the next stool asked.

Devonne shrugged, hoping that would discourage him. For good measure she added, "I generally do."

"Somehow I doubt that." The wry humor and sexy undertone in the words made her turn for a better look at him.

Through the dim light, further obscured by the smoke and tearing it caused, she saw a shadowy human form. The masculine face appeared to be comprised of lean, beautifully molded lines and sharp features. The eyes were light, but she couldn't tell their color.

"Why?" she asked, curiosity trumping caution.

"You're in here, aren't you?"

"I said generally."

"This is one of your occasional exceptions?"

It was anything but chilly in the bar so that couldn't account for the shaking of her hand as she picked up the mug the barkeep slid toward her. The man's voice was deep and a bit rough. Nothing about the words had any sexual edge, nor did his tone, exactly. But the combination washed over her like a touch running from her throat to her groin.

She hadn't had a man in way too long.

Was this one a possibility? She glanced at him again and took in the lines of his face. Lean, sharp, very attractive. Did she want him to be a candidate, though? She preferred a series of old acquaintances where she knew what she'd be getting, but she hadn't run into any of them in months.

"My adventurous side is on the loose tonight."

Oh, dear skies, had she really said that? The words had slipped out while she was still considering a response. She couldn't have made the invitation much more blatant.

He didn't react in any way she could read. His expression didn't change and all he said was, "Except when it comes to the drinks."

"Adventurous isn't the same as stupid. I put the line right between 'tastes bad' and 'makes me ill'."

He laughed lightly and the sound rolled over her bare skin like a warm, tingly shower. It felt as though every nerve ending in her body stopped for a moment to pay attention, then buzzed in reaction.

"What do you do with 'tastes *good* and makes me ill'?" he asked.

"The most dangerous trap of all. I avoid it whenever I can recognize it."

"What about 'tastes bad and *doesn't* make me ill'?"

"What's the point?" she said.

"True. But that limits you to 'tastes good and doesn't make me ill'?"

"There's something wrong with that?"

"How do you know in advance? Or do you just keep to what you do know?"

"I told you I generally played it safe."

"But not tonight." He tapped the panel in front of him. "I'm taking the liberty of ordering another gin for you."

"What are you drinking?" she asked.

"Synthlan beer. I'm in a reckless groove tonight."

"Uh-oh. Maybe I'd better get out of your way."

"Why?" He took the beer and gin from the split tentacle that stretched toward him holding the glasses, and passed the gin on to her. "Which part did I fail? Tastes bad or makes you ill?"

"Neither. Yet. I just don't know."

"What happened to your adventurous side?"

Devonne's head buzzed. The combination of a surprisingly potent gin, the smoke in the place and the effect of an attractive man so close put her off balance. Once again the answer slipped out without her consciously framing it. "It's considering exploring some exotic tastes."

"Drat," he said.

"What?"

"Let's me out. I'm not an exotic taste at all."

"I think I disagree with that." Damn, she was coming on to him. This wasn't her. She didn't do stuff like this...except after a long hard month of trying to make it through a good run with a limping ship, living with celibacy while two of her crew members were screwing each other almost daily, followed by too much gin on top of too little food.

"I'm just another human male," he answered.

"Not just another..."

"Better looking than most?" He made the question sound so dry she could tell it wasn't vanity but curiosity that sparked it.

Devonne shrugged. "Maybe, but that's not what I meant. More interesting. Sharper. Not many with your wit as well."

His grin showed appealing grooves bracketing his mouth. "Some people think that puts me in the 'tastes bad' category. Or maybe it's the 'bad taste' category. Never quite sure which."

"Not me. I like astringent."

"So do I."

"Got a name? I'm Devonne."

"Raje. I've always thought—"

A Sangari male, warrior class judging by his size, squeezed his huge, furry body between them, growling to get the barkeep's attention. In the process he jolted her arm, making the remnants of the gin in her glass spray onto his fur.

Devonne's pulse leapt. Sangari were notoriously vain about their lush, gleaming pelts, grooming them constantly and meticulously. They also had hair-trigger tempers.

The creature hissed its displeasure and raised an arm to swipe at her.

"I don't think so, pal," Raje said, putting his hand on the Sangari's arm to stop the motion and draw his attention.

An angry roar preceded the warrior-male's effort to swing again, at Raje this time. Raje jumped down from his stool to avoid the blow and the seat fell onto its side.

A chaos of cheers and jeers accompanied the clatter. Other crashes resulted from people diving off chairs and under tables nearby.

"You don't really want to start something," Raje told him.

The Sangari disagreed vehemently with Raje's assessment of his state of mind. His growling speech made the words nearly incomprehensible when he answered. "Pelt is damaged."

"Oh, I doubt it." Raje looked at the thick, matted fur on the upraised arm, then yelled, "Barkeep! Got a wet rag back there?"

"That won't fix the damage!" The creature's roar rose several levels in volume. "Pay for cleaning."

"You're joking right? This some kind of con you work on cadets around the space academies? Or planning to work, so you're practicing it here? Not a good choice, pal."

"How you want to pay?"

The barkeep handed Raje a damp cloth. Raje tried to swipe it over the spots the gin had made on the Sangari's thick, sleek pelt. The warrior-male took exception to the effort with a growl that vibrated through the room. He pushed Raje away from the bar.

Chapter Two

People raced for the exits or fell back toward the walls to leave room for the fight they saw coming. A couple in a corner started taking bets.

Shock rattled through Devonne's system. The Sangari wouldn't be placated and Raje's attitude wasn't helping. "Shit," she yelled and jumped off her own stool. Before she could make any other move, though, a large human woman stormed into the room from somewhere in the back. "Oh, no, you don't," she shrieked. "Not in my taproom. This is a respectable establishment." She managed to make that pronouncement with a totally straight face, so she'd either practiced it or managed to delude herself into believing it. "No fighting in here."

Neither the Sangari nor Raje paid much attention to her. The Sangari swung one of its massive fists toward Raje, who ducked at the last moment. His obvious hope, that the other creature would become unbalanced by the effort, didn't pan out. Devonne doubted he'd expected the maneuver to work, but it was worth a try. Her pulse jumped and her throat tightened as she watched Raje sidestep a series of bone-crushing punches.

Raje was a tall man, but also a lean one, with tough muscle but not much bulk. He moved quickly and gracefully. Only his fast reflexes kept him from being tromped and stomped by the Sangari, who stood almost a foot taller and weighed probably twice as much.

The woman who was either owner or manager continued to yell at them to stop and warned of charging for damages, but she made no attempt to step between them or otherwise halt the fight.

Raje had a pistol holstered on his hip, but the Sangari had a dart tube on his left arm. If Raje made any move for the gun, he'd have a projectile in his chest or eye before his own weapon cleared the holster.

The Sangari had all the advantages in this fight, yet Raje's calm suggested he had some sort of ace in the hole. A weapon she couldn't see?

She wondered if the other male honored some obscure code that barred use of weapons if the opponent didn't reach for one first. More likely he was just enjoying the prospect of beating up on the human. The two danced around in slow circles on the cleared space near the barstools, occasionally knocking over a chair or table that got in the way. They feinted toward each other, the Sangari swinging freely and occasionally landing a jolting blow, while Raje managed to connect only once or twice, with punches that had no discernible effect on the warrior-male.

As she speculated on what he was trying to do, admiration for him also roused. Raje looked cool, confident and collected, even while facing a much larger, stronger opponent. His lean shape moved with power and grace, though his blows didn't have much impact. The way his gaze flicked around as though he searched for something in the room suggested he had a plan. She just couldn't figure out what it might be.

What the hell was he up to?

The Sangari was almost directly between them when Raje's eyes met hers with just a bare flick of a glance. It hit her then and she felt like kicking herself. If she hadn't been so busy admiring him, she might have picked up on it quicker. He had an ace in the hole.

Because of her slowness, she had to wait for them to make another complete rotation. The Sangari landed a punch to Raje's shoulder that sent him reeling backward. He crashed into a few cheering bystanders who eagerly steadied him and launched him back into the fray. When he was three-quarters of the way around, having suffered another couple of blows, she managed to catch his eye and nod.

He wasted no time in maneuvering his opponent so that she was directly behind him, her body shielded from view of most of the crowd by the Sangari's bulk. Would it be considered poor sportsmanship, she wondered as she reached carefully for her own weapon. It shouldn't. The creature had attempted to assault her first. He'd then chosen to pursue a more interesting course, taking on what he considered a more worthy opponent. Too bad for him. He'd have to eat his own stupidity in disregarding her.

She wrapped her fingers around the pistol and used a finger to slide the lever down to the stun setting. When she had a clear shot, she yanked the gun from her holster, leveled it at the broad back and fired.

A brief, focused bolt of blue-white light coughed from her weapon, hitting the creature dead square in the middle of his back. The Sangari went down hard, folding up like a puppet whose strings had just been cut. A four hundred-pound puppet. The thud rattled the building, knocking a few glasses off the shelf.

Raje studied his fallen adversary for a moment then shrugged and looked up at her with a wry grin. "Nice work. But it took you long enough."

"Didn't want to cut the fun short too soon."

"Gotcha." He sauntered over to the bar and lifted his drink, draining it one long swallow. His eyes glinted in a way she could see even through the smoky haze in the room. He looked around briefly and grimaced before he brought his gaze back to her. "You hungry?"

"Depends on what kind of hunger we're talking about."

His dark, angled brows rose. "Food." He kept the straight face for a moment before a wry grin crooked his lips. "First. Dessert later."

"Food sounds good."

"Come on." He pressed his thumb against the panel to pay for their drinks and wrapped an arm around her shoulders.

She appreciated the gesture as they threaded their way through the crowd. A few people—human and otherwise—stepped forward to congratulate him or nod acknowledgement, but most just cleared out of their way.

Outside, the cooler air hit her with a bracing blast.

"You aren't hurt, are you?" she asked. "It looked like he landed a couple of good ones on you."

"I'll have some bruises. You got any medicine for them?"

"Maybe later."

His fingers tightened around her shoulder in response. "Thanks for taking care of him."

"Thanks for giving me the opportunity. You didn't have to. I appreciate it."

"Ulterior motives. Been to Mack's Chops?" he asked. "It's not far."

"Never been. I hear the food's good. And expensive."

He shrugged. "I had a good haul. I'm celebrating."

"Honored to help you then. So, how'd you come by a name like 'Raje'?" she asked as they swung around a corner, heading for the restaurant.

"Reginald Jameson Jernigan. When I was growing up, the kids I hung out with pronounced it 'Ray-zhi-nald'. Eventually it got shortened to Raje."

"Cute."

"Not terribly."

She waited for him to explain, but instead he pointed at the front of the restaurant, a few doors down. "We may be in luck," he said. "It doesn't look too crowded tonight."

They discussed the traffic on the street and the contents of display windows in the shops they passed, most of which had already closed for the night, until they reached the place and were seated in a quiet, cozy corner. She noticed Raje pass a credit chip to the man seating them and wondered how much it cost him to get this prime location away from the busiest part of the dining area.

Once they'd ordered their meals, he leaned forward and studied her, so she felt free to do the same. Although the lighting was soft, it wasn't as dim as in the bar.

She had to restrain her galloping pulse and the urge to sigh. The general outlines of his face had suggested he was attractive.

The reality was so much more. Only a couple of old scars—a light burn at the temple, and a thin white line running from the side of his cheek down to his jaw—kept him from being almost classically beautiful. Strong lines of cheekbone and jaw, perfectly shaped and sized features and large, bright eyes combined into a form that suggested he shouldn't ever need to resort to piracy to make a living. The eyes were an unusual light yellow-green color that leaned toward the yellow.

Apparently he recognized her reaction to his looks. "Don't say anything about it, please. I can't help it. I was born with it."

"What?"

"The face. I know what it looks like, and most people think I bought it. I didn't."

"I'll bet you fool most people."

He shrugged. "It has its uses. I can be seriously charming when I need to be and that comes in handy."

"With women like me?"

He stared hard at her. "How much did you pay for yours?"

"You think I'd pay someone for this?"

"Why not? It's very appealing."

She laughed harshly. "I look in the mirror occasionally. It's far from perfect. And it looks a bit…lived-in."

"Perfection is boring." He reached across the table and ran a finger down her cheek and jaw to her chin. "This is much more interesting." Tingling erupted where he touched, bursting into a trail of fireworks along the side of her face.

Heat from it rushed all through her body. Her cunt swelled, wanting him. It had been way too long and he was the sexiest man she'd seen in years. She made an effort to collect herself and tamp down the reaction. At this rate she'd be bursting into flame or dragging him under the table for a quick hump before their dinner arrived.

"So what are you doing here?" She hoped it didn't sound rude, but she had to change the subject, and quickly. Besides, if he couldn't deal with her bluntness, they had no future.

Future? Where had that come from? She'd known the man for all of two hours and had no clue to what he might want other than a night's entertainment.

He gave no indication her forthright question bothered him. "My ship's getting some repairs."

A servoid appeared with their food, and they waited while it set the various dishes before them.

She questioned him about the circumstances of the damage, but he managed to sidestep any specific answers. He hadn't really answered her original query either.

While she was framing her next question, he forestalled it by asking, "I know it's not polite, but I can't help but wonder. What's an attractive intelligent woman like yourself doing in this business?"

It was practically the same question she'd tried to ask him. She considered her answer carefully, wondering how much she could safely tell him. For a moment she watched his hands as he maneuvered the food from dish to his mouth. Strong, capable hands with long, graceful fingers. His skin was several shades darker than hers, a warm coffee-with-cream brown, and she envisioned those fingers touching her… Damn! She had to make an effort to concentrate on the conversation.

"There weren't too many choices. Subsistence farming in a place that barely supports life or…redistribution of goods."

The grin showed a pair of attractive grooves bracketing his mouth. "Redistribution of goods. I'll have to remember that."

Oh Flames and Stars, but this wasn't good. She wanted to see that grin again and again. She wanted to kiss that sensual-looking mouth. She wanted to strip off his clothes and…*no*!

He questioned her carefully while they ate, learning about where her people were, though not in terribly specific detail or why they were there. They discussed their families and upbringing, again wording everything cautiously so that neither offered enough information to endanger anyone else.

Raje ordered a fine Zegobrian wine to accompany the meal and they drank it with the respect due an expensive vintage.

She was sure the food was good, but she had no idea what she ate. Somehow most of it disappeared. The smooth, light burn of the wine and the distant hum of conversation in the room made a backdrop to her awareness of Raje and her desire for him.

They sat at the table talking for some time after they finished the meal. She declined dessert or further drinks once the servoid had cleared away their dishes. He paid the tab and they left.

"Walk a bit?" he asked. "I need to tamp down some of that food. There's a river through the old part of the city that I understand is very pretty at night. They light it up with all kinds of stuff."

She nodded. The evening brought a cool, bracing breeze as they made their way along a street that sloped downward toward the riverfront.

"There's a transport a block or so over, if you prefer," he offered. "But it's not that far to walk to the river."

"No."

They discussed some of their more interesting business dealings and exciting runs while they went. Devonne couldn't help but be more aware of the hand that held hers than the words they exchanged, though she found the mere sound of his voice touched her somewhere deep inside.

The riverfront was every bit as intriguing and lovely as he suggested. Where it cut through the city, the banks had been built up to contain the water's flow, and paved walkways lined a section of it.

She'd been on this world and in this city several times before to get repairs done on her ship, but she'd never come down to this part of town.

Restaurants and small shops crowded beyond the walkways on either side of the river. To attract attention, most had arranged colorful arrays of light on their shops. Strings of small bulbs defined rooflines, doorways and windows, while other establishments sported huge embellishments made of light tubes, in the shapes of flowers, amulets, historical monuments of dozens of worlds, knotwork and every other decorative element a sentient mind could conceive. The lights reflected in the dark running water of the river, doubling the show.

But the bridges overshadowed even the light display on the buildings.

There were dozens of them. It appeared that each shop and restaurant insisted on building its own span to ensure customers on either side of the river could reach them. And they vied with each other in making each bridge more elaborate, fanciful or beautifully decorated than the rest. High arches with elaborate stone or brick-work sat next to sleek polychromate carbon spans with built-in sparkling lights or deep, radiant kaleidoscopes.

A gigantic stone bridge strung with ribbons and garlands of tiny winking lights formed the backdrop for their first kiss.

He stopped her beside the entry to the span and pulled her off the walkway into the shadow of the structure. It gave them some privacy, but reflections of the lights still sparked off his face and glittered like fireworks in his light eyes as he dragged her into his arms.

Not too far away, a band performing in one of the restaurants played lively dance music.

Although he was several inches taller, she fit nicely against him. The scent of the smoke in the bar earlier and the food from the restaurant still clung to him, mixing with the remnants of an expensive, designer fragrance embedded in his clothes and the essential male aroma of Raje.

When his mouth came down on her, the world rocked. At least if felt that way to her. The warmth of his lips seeped into hers and spread along every inch of her skin. His lips teased hers, rousing a fountain of heat deep in her gut. It pumped a lava flow of desire through her body. No man had ever kissed her like that, or maybe she'd never felt so close and connected already to the man kissing her. Whatever the reason, the experience was a revelation.

He didn't hold her for long, and she moaned lightly when he pulled back and released her.

The lights danced in his eyes when he said, "I have a room at a hotel a little ways down. But I plan to stop and kiss you at every bridge between here and there. If you want."

"Is that a promise?"

He studied her face for a moment and his grin broadened into a smile. A great smile, with wicked grooves bracketing the sensual mouth. "Oh, yeah," he said.

The next bridge was only twenty feet away. The plain brick arch had so many strings and bunches of lights draped over it, there were no dark, shadowy places around it. Oblivious to any potential audience he stopped near its edge and kissed her anyway. It was no safe peck either. He drew her to him and rubbed his lips back and forth over her mouth, sucked her bottom one between his and nibbled at it until she opened, inviting him farther in. Their tongues touched and tangled. It felt as though a part of him flowed into her through that contact and filled all the empty places in her heart and soul.

By the time he drew back she could barely stand. Her legs had begun to wobble and the heat inside her became a fire, while her cunt swelled and oozed moisture. It made walking a challenge.

Next to a fantasy concoction of dancing figures of light that ran along the tops of the rails, he kissed his way across her cheek to her ear, nibbled on a lobe and teased the tender skin beneath it.

The next span had a more gothic theme, since it led into a mock horror house. They stood beneath eerily lit skeletons and dark ghoulish shapes. He ran a finger around the joint of her shirt and trousers to release the tape that fastened top and bottom together. The fabric parted at her waist, letting him reach under her shirt and rest his hands on the bare skin of her sides. Warmth and tingling shocks drove into her where he touched. She waited for him to go higher. Her breasts ached for it, but instead he pulled back again.

"The hotel is right over there," he said, pointing to a five-story building looming on their right. "Just two more bridges before we get to it. Or would you rather go back and circle around again?"

"No." It came out as a breathy protest and he grinned at it.

"Good."

At a span that looked like a series of puffs of cotton, rising higher and higher until they peaked and sank again, he licked, kissed and nipped at her throat. She couldn't keep her hands off him this time and managed to draw his shirt loose from the trousers. She worked her fingers up his chest, almost melting with the feel of his warm, firm skin and the light coating of hair.

Her breath heaved in and out in huge gulps by the time he pulled away again.

"I don't know if I can do one more without dragging you to the ground and ripping your clothes off right here in public," he admitted.

"Good. Forget another bridge. Let's go."

They joined hands and ran toward the hotel. As they sped up toward it, he suggested, "You might want to straighten your uniform. This is a respectable establishment." His tone took on a bit of a mocking edge on the last words.

"I'm very respectable," she told him.

"Well damn that's disappointing."

"Depending on how you define the word."

"Ah." He restored his shirt to its neat tuck into his trousers, and she followed suit.

If anyone paid attention to them Devonne wouldn't have noticed. All her concentration belonged to the man beside her and the effort to get to his room before meltdown occurred. She was on fire, the mass of her body under too much pressure and threatening to explode.

The stiff way he carried himself and a slight hitch in his breath suggested he coped with the same problem.

When the lift doors opened, depositing them on the fourth floor, he pointed left and they raced down the hall.

They made it into the room, ran across the floor, kicking off boots and shedding clothes as they went and landed together on the bed. He stretched out beside her. She had time for a quick glance at his form and liked what she saw. Liked it a lot.

As she'd noted earlier, he was tall but on the slim side, with no extra bulk. Broad shoulders topped a hard chest, then narrowed down to a slim waist and hips. Lean muscle and smooth skin wrapped the strong bones into one very appealing package. His cock stood at attention, nicely filled out and eager for her.

His mouth found hers again, for a long, dazzling kiss that made her blood fizz and her womb throb. His hands bracketed her face, then slid down along her throat and chest to her breasts.

Electric sparks ignited everywhere he touched.

Devonne reached for him in turn, running her fingers into the silk of his dark hair. He pressed against her. Rivers of heat streamed from every place his flesh met hers. The hard length of his cock dug into her belly. She moved to position it closer to where she wanted it.

He had other ideas and drew back a few inches. "Not yet," he said, between placing nipping kisses all along her throat. The delicious tingly ache of those drew a sigh and then a moan from her.

"I don't… I'm going to explode," she warned him. "Soon!"

"Beautiful." Lips nuzzled her breast. A raspy tongue circled it just outside the areola, then spiraling inward until he brushed across her nipple. The sharp pleasure drew a louder moan from her. "You're so beautiful," he sighed as he moved from one breast to the other. "And so responsive."

"You're setting me on fire."

She felt like a volcano with the magma building up inside, threatening to erupt in heat and flames. Delight sparkled in his eyes as he watched her reaction. When his gaze met hers, though, he stilled for a moment. It felt as though their souls brushed together in that brief instant as they looked at each other.

"Please…" she groaned as his clever mouth dipped again and his tongue drew lightning bolts of sensation from her other breast. When he sucked the nipple into his mouth and tongued it hard, she screamed.

A hand slid down her belly and delved into her hot, moist cunt.

"You're ready for me." He withdrew the hand and held it up, showing his fingertips gleaming with the evidence of her desire for him. One finger went to her lips, letting her smell and taste the fruit of her longing.

She lifted her head to kiss his lips, cheeks, chin and mouth. Fire burned sweetly into her, forever branding his shape, his taste, his smell, the feel of him on her soul.

He shifted, lifting himself up and over her. When she parted her legs further to make room for him, he pushed against her cunt, his cock probing for her entrance.

It had been so long since she'd had a man, she'd almost forgotten the vibrant sting of being stretched and filled. He took care as he pressed himself into her, watching her face to be sure she could handle his length.

Their harsh breaths mingled in a syncopated rhythm of delight as he pulled back and them pushed hard into her again and yet again. The volcano inside her shook and jolted, pulsing closer and closer to eruption.

Tension drew her body into hard knots. With her fingers on his back, she felt the muscles of Raje's body bunch and harden as he strained toward completion. The rhythm of his plunges into her sped up. Each time he slammed home, the fireball inside her swelled closer to release.

Devonne sobbed and clung to him until he drew back one last time and paused for a moment. Then he plunged deep into her. It set off the explosion. She screamed as it rumbled through her, wave on fiery wave of pure pleasure. And as she bucked and jolted with the spasms, he roared, slammed into her again and stiffened with his own orgasm.

Once the fierce jolts had subsided, she drew him down on top of her, wrapping him tightly in her arms and holding him close. She'd had orgasms before, but no man had ever brought her to this level of joy or reached so deeply into her soul in the process. She'd worry about that later, but right then it just felt intensely right to be joined with him in the most intimate possible way.

"I knew it." He spoke next to her ear and his breath tickled. "I knew it would be like this when we talked in the bar."

"Be like this?"

"Hot, hard, gut-wrenching. The best sex that's ever happened to me."

It had been for her, too, but she didn't dare admit it. "The best sex you've ever had? Isn't that always the sex you *just* had?"

He laughed but drew back so he could look her in the eye. "Not necessarily. I've had crappy sex. The bang-bang-done-gone variety. Bodies in heat."

"That wasn't what this was?"

"Hell, no. And the next time's going to be even better."

"The next time?"

"Starting in about…five minutes, I hope."

"You're in a hurry?"

His wicked grin worked its way into her like a treacherous bolt of lightning. "Oh, no. Unless you really wanted to get some sleep tonight?"

"Plenty of other time to sleep."

He pulled out and rolled onto his side on the bed, facing her. "Want to check out the bathing facilities here? They're pretty spectacular—one of the reasons I got the room."

Chapter Three

"You planned to pick up a woman and bring her here all along." Devonne heard the note of accusation in her voice. "Sorry, I have no right to—"

He stopped her with a finger across her lips. A wash of color stained his cheeks. "I did plan to pick up a woman. Hell, it's been weeks since the last time. But, then, weren't you at least halfway looking for the same thing yourself?" He waited for her nod but stopped her when she began to say something. "The thing is, I wasn't looking for you. I'd about given up hoping you were out there and I'd someday run into you."

"Me? Have we ever—"

His smile was tender and a bit sad. "No. But you're the one I've been looking for. The woman who's enough like me to stay with me and unlike enough to challenge me. Pretty enough to be intriguing but not hopelessly vapid. Has a sense of humor that understands mine. Smart enough and bold enough to make life interesting." He shook his head slowly. "There aren't many like you around. The only other one I've met was old enough to be my grandmother."

"Did you sleep with her anyway?"

His grin crooked into a more wry humor. "Yup. Game old girl. We had a good time. I learned a lot from her."

She looked into his eyes. Despite the self-deprecating humor, he was serious. "You still see her?"

He shook his head. "She retired to her garden and her great-grandchildren on Xanthee's Stake a couple of years ago. I've been kind of missing her. Until you."

"You're an unusual man, Raje Jernigan," she told him.

"Yeah, a few others have said so, too. Sometimes they use cruder language, though. 'You're a weird bastard, Jernigan'. Heard that a few times. And 'crazy son of a bitch'. Been called that more than once."

He helped her up off the bed.

The facilities were every bit as impressive as promised. In addition to the standard waste disposals and sonic array cleaner, there was an old-fashioned, glass-enclosed shower with jets at three levels. Beside it sat a whirlpool tub big enough to hold both of them easily. A dozen jets sprayed water from its walls.

"Oh, wow! I've never been in a real whirlpool. Does it actually have hot water?" She did some blushing herself when she realized how naïve and unsophisticated that sounded.

"Real hot water." He pressed a button and water hissed from three of the jets. It started to pool on the bottom of the white composite tub.

"It'll take a few minutes to fill. Want to give the shower a try while it does?"

"Sure. Both of us?"

His grin broadened, grew purposely sensual. "We can wash each other's…hair."

There wasn't a lot of extra room in the shower with both of them in it, but that didn't mitigate the sensual delight of hot water running down her body. She turned her back to the spray and had the added pleasure of being able to look at Raje.

Even with the water plastering his dark hair to his head, he was beautiful. Every inch of him, from the gorgeous face down to his long, bony feet, appealed to her.

He reached up, made a selection from a panel showing soaps and shampoos and pushed a button. Fragrant white lotion poured into his cupped hand. "Turn around," he said and proceeded to rub the shampoo into her hair, massaging her head in the process.

She'd never guessed her scalp could be an erogenous zone, but it felt so good it made her legs shaky, forcing her to lean back against him.

After he'd thoroughly shampooed her hair and helped her rinse it, he gathered a puddle of soap in his hands and began scrubbing her shoulders. He moved down her chest and sides and finally to her breasts. His big hands covered her mounds, his brown skin an interesting contrast with the silvery foam bubbles and her paler flesh. It was the most erotic thing she could ever remember seeing.

He washed down her belly and along her legs. His hands moved up the insides of her thighs to just below her slit, where he stopped.

When she sighed he reminded her, "We're taking it slow this time."

She nodded. "Your turn, then." She spun him around and gathered up a handful of shampoo before she realized his greater height might be a problem. "Do you think you could kneel?"

"For you, love, anything." His tone made it only half joking, and he did sink to his knees, facing away from her.

She had a great view of his very nice ass as she bent over him to massage the suds into his hair. When she finished with that and rinsed it, she washed him as he'd done her. Gobs of soap smoothed the way, letting her hands glide sweetly over his chest. She circled around the hard pectoral muscles before stroking down to his flat abdomen.

Moving around to his back, she soaped his shoulders and ran her hands over his taut, firm butt. The feel and smell of him set her blood frothing almost as briskly as the shampoo. To reach his legs, she had to ask him to stand again and turn. When she bent down, she found herself confronted with his lovely, firm cock, standing at glorious attention.

How could she resist an invitation like that? Devonne wrapped her hand around his hard shaft and began to test its firmness and texture with her fingertips. He drew in a sharp breath and then panted as she explored even lower, testing the delicate firmness of his balls. No man had ever allowed her to play with his body in this way.

He tolerated her exploration for a while, but then carefully removed her hand. "If you continue like this ten seconds more,

I'm going to explode in your palm," he warned. "It might be interesting, but there are other even more fascinating things to do. I expect the tub is full enough by now."

She had to force herself to release him and to get out of the wonderful, sensual warmth of the shower. The whirlpool tub provided its own reward for the sacrifice, however. Following his lead, she climbed into the tub and sat, immersing herself up to her neck in the heated water.

"Merciful stars! I've died and gone to heaven."

"Good isn't it?" Raje stretched out so that his legs were on either side of her and he leaned back against the side of the tub, arms outstretched along the top of it. "One of the few things I miss when I'm aboard ship."

They spent some time just relaxing in the warm water. After a few minutes, his foot shifted just enough that he could caress her hip and backside with it. Since her legs were inside his, she found his balls with her toes and began her own exploration.

He tolerated it for a while then he reached over and dragged her toward him, sliding her up along his legs until she straddled his upper thighs. His full, hard cock probed at her abdomen. Her breasts pressed against his chest, nipples gently abraded by the coarse hair there.

His kisses were slower and sweeter, less harsh and demanding now that the most urgent needs had been met. They still went to her head as fast and hard as the gin had earlier.

She leaned into him, reveling in the feel of his skin on hers and the sweet fire he roused in her blood. They teased each other's lips, earlobes and nipples.

A quick lift and adjustment of her position brought her down on his cock, with it sinking deep into her cunt. A gasp escaped from her as he filled her solidly, the tip connecting with the uniquely sensitive place deep inside that made her senses jangle.

"Are you all right?" he asked.

"Stars around us, if I get any better, I'll melt and you'll need a shovel to get me out of here."

He had to help lift her up and down but started at a slow, easy pace that let her savor the feel of him. It felt good in ways she'd never guessed anything could.

* * * * *

She woke with the first rays of the sun beginning to penetrate around the barrier at the window. Her ship should be ready to go shortly. If they hurried they could grab breakfast together, or…

Raje still slept, but the rhythm of his breathing changed as she stirred. He'd kicked off the sheet during the night. She couldn't help but admire his marvelous body. The brown skin was smooth and unblemished but for the sprinkling of dark hair over it and a few small scars.

She levered herself up cautiously, then leaned over him. Taking care to touch with nothing more than her tongue, she licked delicately at his hip, thigh and then his cock, which hung limp between his legs. His skin still tasted faintly of last night's soap combined with a more masculine essence.

He jerked awake sharply as she tongued her way up his cock to the tip. The hard shaft of it began to fill and rise. "You—what are you doing?" The words were thick with the remains of sleep.

"Way I figure it, we've got time for one more before I have to go. I've always wanted to do this."

He sighed and leaned back, spreading his legs to give her easy access to all of him. "Feel free."

She did. She ran her hands over his thighs and balls, riding the flesh between his legs back along the ridge to his anus, then sliding back over the surprisingly delicate male sac. Exploring his cock with fingers and tongue, she learned every graceful inch of him. "It's really not fair," she told him. "Even your penis is beautiful."

"Too bad there's not a contest for prettiest penis. I might even be able to retire on my—ooph!" He started and groaned when she took the entire tip of it into her mouth and began to suck gently. His breath caught on a hitch as she massaged his balls at the same time. He moved her so he could get his hands around her breasts while she took him as deep into her throat as she could manage.

"If they…had a contest…for cleverest use of a mouth…" He had to stop and pant for a moment. "You'd win easily."

She was getting turned on herself just listening to his moans and cries, feeling him swell and throb under her attention. The pulsing in his cock changed and he pumped more quickly, pushing deeper into her throat. When she gagged, though, he withdrew.

Instead he flipped her over and moved on top. He tested her readiness with a finger, found plenty of moisture and plunged in. Their bodies knew each other at some visceral level. They moved together in a dance that needed no words, only a small nudge or a gleaming look for a cue.

A knot formed inside her, growing bigger and more complex with each stroke of his cock inside her. She dug her fingers into his back, clung to him as it tightened until she could barely stand it.

Their pace grew frantic as he pistoned in and out of her, driving her into a frenzied, groaning tension. She couldn't stand it for long. After a few more thrusts, the knot inside her burst. Spasms of release surged through her, making her buck and pant. At the top of a thrust he paused then rammed himself home and came as well.

When it was over, they lay together, holding onto each other, loath to move. They'd both have to get on with their lives soon, but for just a few moments they had peace and complete contentment in each other's arms.

She wanted to keep him with her forever. It couldn't happen—they each had obligations and separate lives—but she indulged a pleasant dream of building something lasting between them.

His thoughts ran along similar lines. "It doesn't end here," he said.

"No?"

"No." He said it firmly. "This is too special, too impossible to let go. We can arrange meetings, coordinate maintenance schedules and rest stops. Devonne?"

He rolled off her and lay at her side, waiting. She looked into his odd, light eyes. She still wanted him more than any man she'd ever met, but was it a good idea to try to continue what they'd had that night? They knew little about each other, aside from the fact that their bodies seemed in tune. Their minds and instincts were, too, on some level, since they'd worked together well during the fight in the bar. Did she dare try to build some future with him on the strength of that?

"Yes," she answered.

* * * * *

Over the next year, they actually did manage to meet about once a month. Several times they coordinated their ships' maintenance times to bring them together. They also worked their schedules to bring them close enough periodically to let them shuttle to some nearby world for shared leave time. Some spectacular vacations together ensued, and sometimes they did even go check out the local scenery. Climbing mountains, paddling rivers in long canoes and watching blazingly colored lava explosions from a fancy restaurant deepened their understanding of each other beyond the sexual needs. On a world called Blaise's Keep, they joined some traditional dance group to learn a set of intricate steps for something called rondels. They ended up dancing the entire night.

She had to tell her crew what was going on. They ribbed her about it, of course, but they also supported her completely and went out of their way to make sure she could make rendezvous with him.

At the end of the year, though, her relationship with Raje changed some more. When the hail came, she and her crew were just finishing up the successful delivery of a cargo of smuggled Asgenish brandy to Latrovsky's Pier. A city full of connoisseurs of fine liquor there had been denied their enjoyment of it by a nobility that decreed some things were intended only for the upper classes. Devonne's arrival with half a hold full of the beverage had caused rejoicing and brought her crew a nice reward.

Raje asked for a meeting and she agreed. They met on the closest planet with shuttle docking facilities and made love, of course, but he had more than that on his mind.

"I've gotten word of a shipment of arms from Duneen to New Yorkland. I know the route they'll have to take. I've figured out a way to stop them and reduce their cargo problems. The thing is…it will take two ships to pull it off."

"You have a buyer for the shipment?" she asked.

He nodded. "I'll even advance a piece of the profit as a good-faith sign. You'll need it to upgrade your cloaking for this anyway. You interested in a partnership for this one?"

She asked him a few more questions about the size of the shipment, the weapons being transported and the armament of the transport vehicle. She'd planned to go home for a week or so of rest before looking for another job, so the schedule was open. His careful answers intrigued her without revealing any of the important details.

"I'm in," she told him, after considering it for a couple more minutes.

He had a good plan for carrying out the lift. Devonne added a couple of suggestions. With the two of them considering all possible issues, they managed to devise a procedure that worked without a single hitch. The profit let her make some further much-needed improvements to her ship.

During the next few months, they did several more operations together and discovered they worked remarkably well as a team. They understood how each other thought and were able to anticipate each other's actions if there were any problems or hitches.

On another occasion he ran into trouble in what should have been a routine contraband run and called for help. Luckily, she was close enough to get to him in time to assist him out of the jam.

They met often for more personal reasons, as well. The sex got better each time, and they had fun together exploring exotic locations and trying out the tourist traps of a dozen or more well-known resort cities.

It was a great ride. Until she found out who he really was.

It happened by accident one morning while they were drowsing together in a replica Nouveau-Victorian boudoir, nestled among the silk and *soverell* pillows, partly draped in satin bedsheets. His p-comm buzzed and before he could reach it to put in private mode, a voice shouted out, "Your Highness! You're needed on board soonest."

He picked it up from the nightstand and said. "I hear. Be there in twenty minutes."

The "twenty minutes" honked her off enough, since she figured that gave him approximately six minutes to dress and say goodbye, and he wasn't all that fast a dresser. But…

"*Your Highness*?" she asked. The sarcastic note wasn't entirely deliberate, but she didn't regret it, either. "I've never heard a space-faring crew address their captain that way unless he really was…"

He drew in a deep breath and let it out on a long, sad sigh as he pulled on his trousers. "Yeah. I'm afraid I am. Sort of. It's a long story."

"And you've only got another minute or so to spare for me."

He winced. "If it had been your crew…"

"True," she admitted. "Quick question then. Honest answer."

He sucked in another deep breath. "All right."

"Who are you? Really."

His face tightened. When he hesitated for a heavy second, Devonne's stomach clenched and twisted. "My name really is Reginald Jameson Jernigan."

"I hear a 'but' there."

Again there was a brief, but frightening pause. "I'm better known as Prince Reginald of Gambria. My uncle is the Grand

Emperor." He looked at her, watching her eyes widen. "I may be technically a prince, but the reality is I'm nothing but an exiled nuisance." In her shock, she barely heard the bitterness of the last few words.

"*Gambria!*"

He paused while strapping on the p-comm and went stiff, as though bracing himself. Well he might, too.

"You..." She couldn't find enough air to get out the words as she all but choked on her emotions. "Son of a bitch. You wouldn't happen to remember a small world in the Vishnin system, would you, *Prince* Reginald? Altraia? I know you do, since I've mentioned it to you more than once. You Gambrians weren't interested in bargaining for mineral rights on Altraia. You just took the whole place by force. Divided the population into two groups. Let those who agreed to work with you stay; kicked the others off into exile. I guess now I know why you didn't want to talk about yourself or your background."

He drew a sharp breath. "We need to talk, Devonne. I had nothing to do with that. I hate it, but I *have* to go now. Can we talk, later? Please?"

She pulled together her scattering wits. "I don't know, Raje. This is a shock." Another thought intruded. "Wait a minute, you're the emperor's nephew... The Rebel Prince? The one reported killed at Scanson. Rumors of your death were a bit exaggerated, I take it."

He nodded. "I never—"

But the other latch had just clicked into place in her mind, sending a wave of pure, white-hot fury through her. "Those arms shipments I helped you lift. You had a buyer for them, all right. You son of a bitch. You've been using me."

"No. It's not like that. Not exactly, anyway. Please, wait until I can tell you more. I'll be back as quickly as I can. Wait here for me?"

"I can't. We're scheduled for another run. If I don't leave in an hour or so we'll miss a rendezvous." Not that she would have waited anyway. Not with the way she felt right then. She didn't trust herself not to kill him on the spot.

"When can we get together again? Next week?" he asked.

"I don't know. I'll have to get back to you."

"Will you?" he asked.

"When I'm ready to."

"Please don't make it too long." He gave her a quick kiss, squared his shoulders and left.

She was probably being unreasonable in not giving him a chance to explain, but she couldn't right then. Even if she didn't have to leave right away, she wasn't ready to deal with his explanations. He'd known. He'd known about her background and what his relationship with the Gambrians would mean to her. He didn't tell her. He'd deliberately hidden that information from her. Worse, yet, he'd used her for his own ends. Thinking they were in a partnership for financial gain, she'd helped him gather arms for his own rebellion. Damn, she'd been gullible.

And she'd just begun to admit to herself that she was in love with the man. Wasn't that a sick joke?

She needed time and space to work it out.

The irony of it just about killed her. That she should unknowingly fall in love with a man who should be her worst enemy. Even if he wasn't truly part of them, as he'd protested, he'd felt guilty enough about it to hide the truth. And he wasn't above using her feelings for him to get what he wanted.

She couldn't know that fate was about to compound the irony.

Chapter Four

She stomped around the ship in the mother of all bad moods for the next week or so. The crew mostly avoided her for fear of being snapped, growled or roared at. Devonne alternately raged at the man for his deception and grieved for the relationship they'd had.

He hailed the ship several times, requesting a private line, but Devonne refused. The more she thought about it, the madder she got.

She loved him, even if they'd seemed destined to have only a sporadic relationship. It hadn't mattered. What they'd had would have been enough for her. But now... The Rebel Prince had used her help to get arms and equipment for his people. Maybe he did actually care for her, though she had to doubt it. But even if he did, what future was there for her with the Gambrian second heir? He would likely end up either as the emperor, since his uncle had no children of his own, or dead. He wasn't popular with current government. Either way there was no place for her in his life.

The next run was another routine brandy delivery that went off as smoothly as usual. She'd planned to return home for a short stay afterward to check on everyone's welfare.

The return trip did not go according to the book.

About three L-secs out from Latrovsky's Pier, the ship's alarm warned of the approach of another vessel. The other ship failed to accept hails or inquiries but drove steadily toward them. When they finally got in visual range, something about the craft seemed familiar, though she couldn't quite recall...

"Evade," she ordered when she recognized the Sangari ship.

Had there just been the ship they saw, they probably could have avoided and outrun it. But when two more decloaked on either side, the possibility of escape diminished quickly.

Devonne debated trying to turn and run as she watched the three ships close in, but the odds didn't favor it. Better to see what they wanted. "Buzz them," she said to Nathan.

"Response on private channel," he said. "They want to speak to you, Captain. Privately."

"Switch to my line, on private."

"Captain Devonne," the voice from the other ship boomed in her ear. It was acknowledgement of her name, nothing more. "This is Captain Grisskinnsini of the Sangari federated fleet, representing the Supreme High Sangari Ruling Quint."

"Captain Grisskinnsini," she responded, struggling to recreate the sounds of the Sangari's name.

"Captain Devonne, as an authorized officer of the Supreme High Sangari Ruling Quint, I'm charged with informing you that criminal action has been laid against you before the Quint, alleging you assaulted a Sangari officer and inflicted bodily harm."

"I what? You mean that incident a year and a half ago on Pargain, when a Sangari warrior knocked my arm and some of my drink splattered on him?"

"I believe that is the incident noted," the other officer answered. "You're also charged with using a stunner on him, resulting in a fall to the floor that abraded his pelt, creating a bald patch, and extensive bruising."

"You are kidding me, right? Whose idea of a joke is this?"

"We find nothing humorous about the incident. My charge is to bring you back to Sangaria to answer the charges at Tribunal."

"That's absurd. Your boy started all the ruckus by knocking my arm."

"That's irrelevant. You'll have a chance to answer the charges before the Tribunal."

"Why do you think I would come with you?"

The other captain's voice took on a sorrowful note. "My duty is to take you back and not permit you to escape. I should hate to have to destroy your ship and your innocent crew to prevent it, but if that is what is required, I'll do what is needed."

"You'd destroy my ship and kill my crew just to get me to answer these ridiculous charges to your Tribunal?"

"That is my duty, Captain," the Sangari said.

Devonne swore to herself and considered her next move. There weren't really many options. The Sangari's calm implacability and what she knew of their race suggested he would do exactly what he said.

"If I agree to come with you, you'll let my crew go?"

"Yes, Captain. We have no quarrel with them. We seek only you."

She sighed. "I'll come with you."

Her crew reacted with the expected disbelief and anger on her behalf. They tried to argue her out of going, even maintaining they wouldn't let it happen. She headed off a near-mutiny by offering a few convincing half-truths that sounded reasonable enough to be believed. It was just a simple bit of bureaucracy she needed to take care of. A bit of diplomacy and a larger bribe should settle it. She did ask them to contact her attorney and have him to meet her at Sangaria, or at least send a representative. Then she gathered up her things and grabbed a shuttle to the Sangari ship.

The trip to their world took a little more than a day. The Sangari didn't try to restrain her or confine her to a cabin, but it would hardly have made any difference. The living space of the ship was so cramped and crowded she could barely move without banging into things anyway. She took a long nap for most of the journey.

Once on Sangaria, they escorted her to quarters so spartan it might as well have been a cell. Again no locks barred her from leaving the room, but aside from wandering the corridor of a block of living spaces, there was nowhere to go. The building sat on a slab of plasticine, in the middle of a stretch of desert. Crews manning the place came and went via a series of hovercrafts that arrived and left every half hour.

She spent only a few hours in the quarters before a group arrived to escort her to some sort of official preliminary hearing. Before three impassive-looking Sangari, she recited her version of events and waited while a translator relayed it.

Her view of the crime didn't impress them much. The translator informed her that she would be facing the Tribunal the next day. Afterward they led her to a small cubicle where she was left to wait for a couple of hours.

When the door opened again, two Sangari flanked a much smaller human man. By then, the sight of her lawyer sent a wave of relief through her. The sheer scale of the room, geared for the larger Sangaris, was starting to intimidate her. The lack of communication other than the formal charging process also worked on her nerves.

"You've gotten yourself into a bit of a fix this time, haven't you?" Grayson Whetlock, her attorney, asked as he took the only other seat in the room. "Not exactly what I expected, though. I had to do some fast research on Sangari codexes on the way here. Couldn't you have picked a fight with a Mascrind or a Johnsonian? Some race with a more straightforward and simple set of laws?"

She shrugged. "More billable hours for you, no doubt."

Whetlock sighed. "Yes, well. This is a bit of a mess. Technically, under their laws, you are guilty of assault, and they're not amused by it. There are a few options we're looking at right now. I've talked to the lawyer for the other guy they've charged and we're working on some things. He's such a political hot chip that even the Sangari are a bit intimidated."

"The other guy? Raje? They captured Raje, too?"

"Raje? Is that what they call him? Reginald Jernigan? Exiled prince and second heir of the Gambrians?"

"That's him."

"You picked up an interesting one there. It should help you, though. Like everyone else in this quadrant, the Sangari have an uneasy truce with the Gambrians and they don't want to risk it. Of course, even they're trying to figure out just what the Gambrians would actually want them to do with Prince Reg. He's been so openly outspoken against the current regime and most of its policies that there's some feeling they'd be just as happy to be rid of him. On the other hand, he's still the second heir, and there is no clear-cut third. He's also exceptionally popular among his own people, where the current emperor is not. They've come close to civil war more than once. The current Gambrian government might not mourn if he had an accident, but they can't afford to *let* him be imprisoned or executed."

"And how does that help *me*?"

"Just a moment," he said, and looked at his p-comm. "Yes." He pressed a couple of flat buttons on the device. "Good."

"What?"

He turned to her. "We've worked out a deal. Prince Reg has agreed to it, if you will. I really think this is the best we can do here, and it should work out just fine."

Her stomach twisted a bit. "Tell me."

"Okay." He drew a breath. "If you're convicted of all the charges the Sangari have laid on you, it could mean up to twenty years in their labor prisons." He paused briefly. "You really don't want to go there." Another pause. "There is an alternative, though. The Sangari love games and entertainment."

"As in?"

"Just about anything and everything you can think of."

"They like fighting," Devonne added.

"Yes, that certainly. But also contests of strength and will and perseverance. And, well, almost anything."

"So how does this affect me?" She fought to control her impatience and nervousness.

"If you'll agree to enter a challenge match, the Sangari will dismiss all charges against you."

"Wait a minute. This presupposes that I think I would lose my case at the Tribunal. The damn Sangari started the whole thing. He knocked my arm, and then he tried to hit me. I was defending myself, damn it!"

Whetlock looked lugubrious. "I know, but it doesn't matter. Under the terms of their judicial code you'll almost certainly be found guilty."

"I will." She felt like grabbing a weapon and doing something worth being found guilty of. "Blackmailing SOBs. This whole business is really about getting new meat for their 'challenges', whatever those involve. Isn't it?"

The lawyer shrugged. "Perhaps. But the fact remains, you face the possibility—"

"I get it." She stood up and paced across the room and back a couple of times. "But my choices are fairly—wait a minute. Why did I have to agree before Raje would? What's he got to do with it?"

The lawyer licked his lips. "Um...well, you see, they want a *pair* of humans in this particular challenge match."

"What? Why? What does 'this particular' challenge match involve?"

He shrugged. "I have no idea. I just know they specified that the two of you would have to agree to enter as a team."

"A team. Raje and I. Oh, that's rich." She made no attempt to keep the bitterness out of her voice.

"I gather you and he didn't part on the best of terms after your last meeting?"

"You could say that." She sighed deeply. "I don't suppose I have much choice here, though."

"Not much," the lawyer agreed. "I really can't recommend trying your luck with the Tribunal. They don't have much regard for aliens."

"No shit. I really would like to know more about what this 'challenge' would involve."

"So would I," the lawyer answered. "But they refuse to tell me anything specific. I've looked over the previous cycle's schedule of challenges, and they seem to encompass everything from foot races to knife fights to the death."

Devonne swung sharply to look at him. "To the death? Raje and I might have to try to kill each other?"

"It's not all that common. More often they have you fight to first blood. Or fight other things. They're um...also quite fascinated by...sexual matters, including some rather...how shall I say this? Some rather kinky human proclivities."

"Things? How many 'challenges' are we required to do? I thought it was just one?"

"Just one challenge. It's ten rounds. One a day for ten days is their usual procedure."

"Ten rounds." She sighed. "Would I be fighting Raje through all of them?"

Whetlock shrugged. "Or having sex with him? I don't know. I doubt it. Sometimes they have people fight animals or machines, sometimes they're contests of throwing or hitting things or eating things that... Well, you can guess."

"It's likely to be the least of my issues, but I'd rather not think about it, thanks." Devonne continued to pace the room, too upset to settle down. "I don't believe this. I just don't friggin' believe this." She pounded a fist down on the room's only table. "Damn. Can I talk to Raje?"

"I'll see if it can be arranged."

He tapped buttons and sent messages. After a few minutes he looked up and said, "They'll be here shortly."

"They?"

"Prince Reginald and his attorney."

"Of course."

It took them almost half an hour to arrive. Devonne wondered how she would feel about seeing Raje again and how he would react to her. When the door opened and the two men entered her heart lurched at the sight of him.

"You didn't go with them as peacefully as I did," she said directly to him, studying the dark bruise under his right eye, the abraded patch on his temple and a swelling cut on his lower lip. He moved stiffly, suggesting other injuries hidden by his clothes. "Are you all right?"

He shrugged and nodded. "No serious damage." He watched her. His gaze held concern, plus hunger and longing, just barely kept in check. "They didn't hurt you."

"There wasn't any fight. They threatened to destroy my ship and crew, so I turned myself over to them."

"I was in dock on Alster. They grabbed me on the street." He drew a deep breath and looked at the two lawyers. "Can we speak privately for a few minutes?" He nodded toward Devonne.

Whetlock threw a quick questioning glance at Devonne. She nodded to him, and he turned to the other lawyer. "I believe we need to discuss strategy for a few minutes." The two of them left.

A hush filled the small room for a moment after they departed. Raje crossed the room to stop close to her. "I'm sorry," he said.

"For what? It's not your fault we're both here."

He shrugged. "I fought with the Sangari. I baited him."

"He tried to slug me. Would have, if you hadn't been there. I'm the one should apologize. If you hadn't tried to defend me, you wouldn't have been involved."

He winced as he smiled with the undamaged side of his mouth. "But then I would have missed out on the best year of my life. If this is the price for that year, it's still worth it."

"Raje—"

"I'm sorry. But I'm not lying."

"About this maybe."

He winced and made an odd sort of shrug, half acceptance and half impatience. "We need to have a long talk, but we don't have time for it now. Let's deal with the matter at hand and worry about the rest later."

She drew a long breath to steady herself and nodded. "What do you know about this "challenge" thing?"

"Not much. It seems to be a series of contests. Different things. Sports, fighting, sex, eating, whatever takes someone's fancy. Pretty much if you can imagine it, they'll have someone do it."

"We may have to fight each other."

"That's a possibility."

"To the death."

"I doubt it. And if that's what they want, we'll figure out a way around it," he said.

"Are you always this optimistic? I missed that about you."

"Only under serious pressure. It keeps me sane. Devonne, I think we ought to do the challenge. My lawyer has consulted with some Sangari sources. He's pretty sure the Tribunal won't be sympathetic to our story and he's entirely sure we don't want to spend any time in their labor prisons."

"My attorney said the same thing. I just wish I knew what they'd ask us to do in this challenge thing."

"They don't give out the agenda in advance."

"I know."

"Do they play fair?"

Raje lifted his shoulders. "According to my lawyer, basically yes. You might not like what they ask you to do, and there's no telling what it could be. But if you do satisfy them they'll acknowledge it and reward it."

. He moved closer to where she stood, stopping just a step away. Her hormones reacted to him as they always did, going info overdrive, driving up her pulse and her breathing, rousing the pressure of desire in her core. Something else overlay it, though. Concern and fear for him woke, bringing with it anger about his injuries and a desperate desire to touch him, to reestablish the close connection they once had.

He reached out and put his hands on her upper arms. Heat exploded where he touched but she controlled the urge to flinch back. His expression was serious. "Devonne, we can do this together. Whatever the challenge might hold. We always worked well together as a team. We'll manage whatever we have to do to beat this thing."

He had a point. They did work well together. If they could just get past the hurt and anger—check that—if she could get past the hurt and anger, they had a decent chance of winning. He showed no sign of resenting her for walking out on him and ignoring all his subsequent attempts at communication. No doubt he did, but the man had formidable self-control, and he realized they'd be better served to put off dealing with their personal problems until they'd solved the legal issues. It made sense. She just wasn't quite as good at burying her feelings. If that was what it took to survive, she'd attempt to match his control.

"All right. We'll tackle the challenge together."

Chapter Five

His smile nearly broke her heart. It reached into her gut and tangled with all her nerves. She still wanted the man in her life. Wanted him for sex and companionship and laughter and shared adventure. She couldn't imagine that she'd ever stop wanting him. How could she let him back in, though, when she couldn't trust him? She still wanted to believe that he truly felt something for her and hadn't just been using her.

"Do you think—"

Unfortunately her question was interrupted when the lawyers rapped lightly on the door and entered. "You've decided?" Whetlock asked.

"We're taking the challenge," Devonne answered.

Both lawyers smiled. "A good choice. To make you feel better, we're negotiating to get some safeguards put in place for you."

A group of Sangari entered right behind the lawyers, indicating their time together was up. They separated the humans and escorted them to their quarters. Devonne had no idea where they took Raje or the lawyers. They brought her back to the bare room in the enormous, sterile, blocky building she'd been in earlier.

She languished there for three long days, with no visitors, no communications and no word from anyone. The only other living creatures she saw aside from a few scurrying things on the sand outside her window were the Sangari guards who delivered meals and jugs of water periodically. She asked them for vids or books but they just gave her blank stares in return.

To keep from going insane, she went through her normal daily exercise workout twice the first day and three times on the second. In her head she plotted courses through asteroid fields and did the basic equations for wormhole geometry the computer normally handled. She thought far too much about Raje and what he might be doing.

Finally, early on the morning of the fourth day, a group of three Sangari came for her. They loaded her into a transport and headed west to the same city they'd taken her before. They didn't go to any justice building, however.

Even from a distance she could tell that the enormous, round structure they headed toward was some sort of sports arena. Thousands of tall, single-person transporters parked around it and Sangari of all shapes and sizes streamed toward the many entrances to the circular coliseum.

She fought to keep her pulse steady and her stomach from clenching as muscles tightened all through her body. It took an effort to stop her breath from growing quicker and her hands from shaking as she wondered what kind of contest they'd be pitched into.

Her escort hustled her out of the transport and into the building through a door around the back, away from where the crowds streamed in. They traversed several long, dingy stone corridors, before one of her guards pushed open a door and led her into some kind of enormous locker room.

The room stretched on for some distance to the left, the walls curving to follow the circular footprint of the building itself. She turned that way when she heard voices in the room, so far down the speakers were out of sight. The guards followed her but didn't move to interfere.

She walked alongside racks of garments hanging from bars a foot or so above her head. Those mostly seemed to be costumes, of every type, style, color and fabric, in a range of sizes so wide some would be too small for a human child while other garments were too big for a large Sangari. A series of closed chests lined the other side of the long, narrow, curving room. Occasionally a surge of noise reached her from beyond the inner wall.

Devonne threaded her way through the clutter and finally joined a pair of men hunched over a dark slate board. They looked up when they heard her coming.

"Where's Raje?" she asked the two lawyers, scanning the area around them.

"In another staging area," Whetlock said. "They apparently don't want the two of you conferring before this match."

Another explosion of noise from beyond the wall drew her attention. "Are there other acts on the program today?"

"I believe there are half a dozen matches or tests on the schedule for today. You're the fourth. The first began a few minutes ago."

Devonne went to the wall and slid back a panel. The heavily barred window behind it offered a view directly out onto the field at the center of the coliseum. A pair of Sangari fought each other with weapons that looked like short, heavy pikes, studded with wickedly pointed barbs and ending in double-sided, saw-toothed blades. Both combatants had blood matting their fur in several places.

"You might not want to watch this," the other lawyer warned. "It's a blooding and likely to get ugly."

"A blooding?"

"A grudge fight. To the death. With short-bladed and pointed weapons to help ensure the battle will take a long time and be suitably gory."

"Lovely." Devonne drew the wood panel back across the window. "They're not going to make us do something like that, are they?"

"Nothing like that. What you saw there is more a traditional Sangari thing. Combat for control of a clan enclave or to settle a debt of honor."

"Do we know yet what we will be doing?"

The two men looked at each other. Devonne's stomach clenched even tighter. "What?"

Whetlock hesitated before he said, "You have armed combat today. Knives. But only to first blood."

She let out the breath she'd been holding. "We can manage that."

"Raje said so too," the other lawyer added. "I've been doing some research on this whole challenge thing. It looks like the main thing you want to remember is that it's *entertainment* for these people. Since you're fighting each other today, you can't really lose, but if you want to improve your chances of the judges siding with you later, you want to put on a really good show. Make it last for as long as you can and have lots of close misses before one or the other of you finally draws blood. The prince thought you and he could manage it."

He paused when another roar from the crowd all but drowned him out. After it had settled again he continued, "Be careful what you do and say to each other. They have cameras and microphones to transmit holovids of you. They'll hear if you try to talk each other through faking it. Prince Reg suggested some hand signals and words for you to use as cues for each other." The lawyer took out a stylus from a pocket and held it out. "If this is the knife, when Reg moves his finger on it like this, it means he's going to feint to the right. If he curls it like this, he wants you to lunge toward him..." The lawyer went through a series of things. Most of them made logical sense. Devonne hoped she could remember them all.

More crowd noises suggested irritation and impatience this time.

"One more thing," the lawyer added. "The prince asked me to tell you this. 'Remember the dance at Blaise's Keep.' He said you'd know what he meant."

She knew and understood. A dance. Their match would be a dance.

A buzzer sounded nearby.

"That means it's time for you to get ready. I had to get one of the Sangari to help me figure out where your outfit was, but we managed to find it." Whetlock lifted the bundle from a table and handed it to her. "We'll leave you to change. Someone will come get you when it's time. They'll give you your weapon then."

Both lawyers wished her well and departed.

Devonne unfolded the clothes provided and was relieved to find a shirt of sturdy fabric with elbow-length sleeves and dark pants of the same fabric, held up by a leather belt. A tunic of heavy leather went over the shirt. There was an odd headpiece like a leather cap that pulled down over the ears and fastened across the chin. The outfit wouldn't win any fashion awards but was practical for a knife fight where no one was supposed to get seriously damaged. Thank the stars. She'd had visions of some seriously impractical, diaphanous thing, especially since a couple of vid stars had recently done shows where they cavorted on amazing "adventures" wearing ridiculously tiny, sheer outfits.

Moments after she'd stepped into the heavy leather boots and strapped them down to fit her feet, the nearest door opened and a pair of Sangari guards escorted her out. They traversed a dingy, curving corridor around the coliseum until they reached a tunnel that led out onto the field.

The equipment on the central part of the grounds had been reorganized a bit since the "blooding" she'd looked out on earlier. Mesh fencing cordoned off a ring about fifty feet in diameter in the center of the field. Low-growing bluish plants covering the ground felt squishy underfoot.

A large Sangari warrior-male approached and handed her the knife he held. "Your weapon." She took it from him, tested the grip and studied it. A ridged handle fit securely into the palm of her hand, while a crosspiece guard prevented her fingers from slipping onto a serrated blade ten inches long. It wasn't made of metal but of some other hardened plastic material nearly as heavy as steel would have been.

They led her out across the field to the ring. Masses of Sangari filled the seats. She hadn't realized their pelts came in such a variety of colors. Most ranged from a pale honey brown to inky black, but a few orange, yellow, pale green and lavender ones stood out in places. On the field, the noise was near deafening, swelling further when the crowd noted the humans being escorted to the ring.

Scanning the area, she finally found Raje approaching from the opposite side. He wore clothing similar to hers. A spark of resentment flared when she realized he had an escort of four Sangari, where she had only two. Then she laughed inside at the absurdity of it. But Stars and Flames, the man looked good. Tall, slim, graceful, he moved with supple power and control.

His stern expression lightened only slightly as he drew close enough to lock gazes with her. He held a knife similar to the one she carried, though his arm hung loosely at his side, the weapon pointing at the ground. His eyes looked more green than yellow under the light of Sangaria's orange sun.

Their guards brought them into the ring and left them facing each other in the center. All but one of the Sangari retreated to take up positions around the outside the fenced-off area.

The remaining alien stood next to them and said, "Neither of you leaves the circle before one has drawn blood. Raise your weapons." When they did so, he backed off two steps and added, "Start."

She watched Raje warily for a moment, trying to gauge what he wanted to do. She understood what he'd meant about the dance, but she hadn't been very good at it then and wondered if she could adapt it adequately now. He'd better lead as well this time as he had then.

Raje took a step to the right, then another. He moved forward, brandishing the knife toward her but not lunging or slicing with it. Devonne circled to the right around him. She kept her gaze locked with his, the movement of his blade in her peripheral vision.

After a few more steps her body started to recall the footwork of the dance, and she was able to match him step for step. Cheers and yells of encouragement rang from the stands, but she pushed them to the back of her awareness. Her concentration stayed fixed on her partner-opponent.

Then the dance brought them together, and he made the move more of a lunge, signaling it to her in plenty of time to let her parry it. He closed with her so their chests pressed together.

Despite the time, the place and the crowd watching, awareness of him slammed into her like a fist into the gut. An adrenaline-fueled burst of exultation jolted through her. This was an amazing experience, doing an exotic and elemental cross between a mating dance and a duel. The first tingles of arousal prickled in her cunt.

When he whispered into her ear, his breath fluttering against the delicate tissues there, it sent a fire of need and desire coursing through her. She had to force herself to pay attention to the words.

"Next reverse. Lunge from the right." It was an order rather than a statement. She nodded as he backed away, still following the footstep pattern of the dance. They circled, lunged, feinted, parried and watched each other until her internalized rhythm of the dance told her it was time for the reverse.

She dipped her right shoulder a bare fraction before she took three fast steps toward him, bringing the knife around from the right. Though he was half turned from her, he saw it and whirled in a blindingly fast move to parry and push both blades away, even as the momentum of her charge took her straight into his side. With his superior reach and speed, she wouldn't have a prayer against him if this were the real thing.

Her blood pumped even harder as she clung to his body for a moment. She panted from the exertion, but desire added its own acceleration.

"Good," he whispered to her. "I'll come underneath…next." The low, intimate sound of the words made them almost a sexual promise. Her body reacted with swelling and moisture in her cunt. She tamped it down to concentrate on the action.

He executed the promised maneuver. With the adrenaline pumping and her muscles warmed up, she did a better job of selling her reaction as a frantic parry. She warned him with a finger gesture before she closed on a rapid series of swipes and lunges that he turned away with more effort than required.

They continued to dance around each other, back and forth, lunging and feinting until exhaustion began to overwhelm the effects of the adrenaline. She had no idea how long they'd been at it, but it seemed like more than an hour. Muscles in her legs and chest began to burn.

She might not know how to judge the Sangari's reactions properly, but the noise level had grown and become more enthusiastic throughout their match. Surely they thought it a worthy match by then.

Raje's breathing was so ragged he could barely whisper the words when next they came together. "End it. Leave you an opening. Left arm. Twist right."

It annoyed her that he'd unilaterally decided she should win the match. But someone had to do it and there was no time for debate. She watched for the betraying twist.

When she saw it she lunged forward with the knife held out in front and stabbed at his left arm. It struck him a few inches above the wrist. She didn't think the blade went in deeply but blood immediately ran down his arm.

He dropped his weapon and slapped a hand over the wound. The Sangari who'd started the match stepped into the ring and declared it over. The injury worried her. It shouldn't be deep or serious, requiring nothing more than a plastiseal bandage to heal it. She hoped. When she questioned him with her eyes, he made a tiny thumbs-up motion to reassure her.

Devonne continued to watch Raje, even as others moved between them. She wanted to go to him but dared not.

Instead her Sangari guards escorted her back to the same room she'd been in earlier and told her to change into her own clothes. She asked about a shower but apparently that wasn't happening. She'd have to wait for a bath when they returned her to her cell.

As the adrenaline began to wear off, she started to shake. For most of the trip back in the transport, she felt unsteady, though she managed to walk back to her own room without assistance. Fortunately the sanitary facilities they provided included a small bathtub and sufficient hot water to fill it. Devonne stripped down and stepped in for a long soak.

After nearly falling asleep in it, she washed her hair, climbed out and toweled off. Someone had left a meal tray while she was in the tub. She ate every bit of it then settled back on the bed and promptly fell asleep.

Waking early, she did some gentle exercise to loosen muscles that had stiffened overnight, ate and waited impatiently for the guards to come get her. Speculation on what the next test would entail kept her occupied until they arrived.

The lawyers weren't there to meet her in the locker room of the coliseum as they had been the previous day, but they arrived a few minutes later. Both smiled and congratulated her on the job she and Raje had done yesterday.

"The Sangarians loved it," Whetlock said. "You two registered high respect levels. Great way to start."

"What about today?"

"We're a bit puzzled about today's match," he admitted. "They call it 'Find a Way.' As best we can tell, it involves making your way through a maze together, but I'm thinking there must be more to it than that. They couldn't or wouldn't tell us, though."

Devonne shrugged. "A maze doesn't sound too bad."

Unlike the previous day, they brought nothing particular for her to wear. When the guards escorted her to the field, she found the ring gone, replaced by a large, multi-sided, roofless structure with no windows and a single door. Raje entered the arena from the opposite side and joined her in examining the building.

"The maze, I presume?"

Devonne shrugged. "I guess."

The Sangari guards escorted them to the door. "Go in," the nearest one ordered. "Find another exit."

As soon as they'd entered, the guard slammed the door shut behind them. Devonne had no doubt it was locked as well.

"There's another door on the other side," Raje told her. "I'm assuming we just have to find our way to it."

"Want to bet it's not quite that easy?" Devonne scanned the space, noting the cameras mounted at intervals along the walls, no doubt to track and show their progress to the crowd. Otherwise the surfaces were completely smooth and unadorned.

"No takers. Let's get moving."

There was only one way to go, a corridor that led straight into the heart of the maze. But some twenty feet farther on, an opening offered the choice of turning to the right or continuing straight. "Votes?" Raje asked, stopping by the intersection.

"Right," Devonne said.

Raje nodded and they turned into the new passage. All of the corridors were so narrow they had to walk single file with Raje taking the lead. Ten feet on, the passage made a sharp right-hand bend. Several things happened at once as they cleared the turn. Raje shouted in surprise and backed up a step. She slammed into him and felt something cool and wet spraying on her. They both backed up a few more steps.

Laughter burst from the crowd in the arena, some of whom could look down on them directly. The rest watched the action on screens fed by the cameras along the walls.

Once Devonne and Raje were out of range, the jets that had sprayed the liquid onto them stopped and receded back into the wall. Raje squeezed a few drops from his damp hair onto his fingers, sniffed at it and tasted cautiously. "Water."

Devonne pushed a wet strand of hair off her face. "Somebody's got a second grade sense of humor."

Raje grinned and pushed back wet hair that flopped into his eyes. "Keep that in mind. I'm betting this isn't the only booby trap."

Because they were careful, they managed to avoid the slick spot in the floor, though Raje had a foot on it before he recognized the danger. A rain of feathers poured over them a little farther on. They let them gather in a pile on the floor ahead before they proceeded. To avoid a spot where electrical sparks shot from one side of the corridor to the other from knee height to just over their heads, they had to get down on their bellies and slither along the ground.

Nothing could have gotten them past the swarm of biting insects without losing a few bits of flesh. They had no repellant with them and could find no way around the area that didn't dead-end. Since they saw the bugs ahead, however, they did race past and thus got by with only a few annoying bites. More laughter rose from the crowd along with some applause.

By Devonne's calculation, they had to be getting close to the end when they met with a nastier obstacle. They made a ninety-degree turn to the right, and then another just a few feet beyond. As Raje cleared the second bend, Devonne heard a solid *whack* and he shouted in surprise and pain. When he backed up, Devonne stopped and waited for him.

"What—" She leaned around the corner and got her answer.

A lone Sangari warrior-male stood there, armed with a pistol in one hand and a narrow, two-foot-long rod in the other. The pistol moved from its aim on Raje to focus on her when the Sangari saw her. He took up more than half the width of the corridor.

Raje rubbed at his thighs and swore with enthusiasm. Devonne looked back the way they'd come. "You think it's even worth trying to find another way?"

"What have we got to lose?" he asked.

"A few more pounds of flesh to the bugs?"

"Votes?"

"Let's try," she suggested.

"My vote, too."

They retraced their route and tried alternate turns. As Devonne expected, each of them ended abruptly at some point, leaving them with only the option of braving the armed Sangari.

"Stay close behind me," Raje suggested as they prepared to pass him.

"Hey, thanks for the gallantry, but you've already got a bruise from him once today."

"I can handle it."

He didn't have to, though. The Sangari let him go by without making any attempt to swing his rod. She wished the same were true for her. He couldn't reach the front of her body since she followed so closely behind Raje, but as they passed, the Sangari struck her a backhanded blow right across her buttocks. She jumped and swore at the sting. The crowd cheered and roared with laughter.

"You all right?" Raje turned around to check.

"Okay. The stupid Sangari decided I needed a spanking."

"Got a heavy hand, too, doesn't he?"

"Yeah. Let's get out of here before he decides he isn't finished."

They couldn't manage to avoid the rain of dirt that sprayed down on them at one point on the trip but raced through it quickly enough to come out with just a few sprinkles on them instead of the thick layer they might have acquired.

At the next intersection some change in quality of light and shadows indicated that corridor would be the last. It wasn't until they made a sharp turn, though, that she saw the last challenge before they reached the opening at the far end of the passage.

The corridor widened for its final hundred feet. The last half of that length was lined with Sangari on either side. Each one held a thin, whippy staff.

"Transport them all to a supernova and let them burn," Raje growled through clenched teeth.

"I second the motion."

"I'm sorry," he said. "I wish this whole thing hadn't happened."

"Me, too, but it's not your guilt. Anyway, I've tackled worse than this." She drew a deep breath. "Let's get it over with."

He nodded. "Just make sure you stay on your feet."

It wasn't fun and it wasn't always easy to stay upright as the flailing sticks landed on her shoulders, back and rear end, but they fought their way through it to the end. Once back out in the open, Raje embraced her, holding her close against him. It felt good to be there. Entirely too good. He was a Gambrian *prince*. Still, she had him for now. No point in not taking what she could.

"Okay?" he asked again.

"A few new bruises. Nothing a few plastrons won't take care of in an hour or so. You?"

"Same." They clung to each other for a while. Gradually the cheering and applause worked its way into her awareness. Several Sangari guards showed up to separate them and take them back to the dressing rooms. They also supplied plastrons at her request.

When she arrived on the third day, both lawyers awaited her. They looked uncomfortable.

"Well done again yesterday," Raje's attorney said. "Your respect levels are very high."

"That's something, I guess. What's today's agenda?"

"Um..." Color flushed his cheeks. "It's sex."

"Sex?"

The lawyer sighed. "Sex. You and Raje. On center stage. It could be worse. I'm told they like variations, too. Group sex. Kinky sex. Practically every variation of sentient reproductive activity. They do find the human variations particularly fascinating. They're partial to chains and leather and whips, I'm afraid, although that doesn't seem to be on today's program."

"Thank the Five Faces of God for small mercies."

Chapter Six

"Don't thank her too quickly," Whetlock advised. "There are seven more rounds to go. I feel sure some of it will come up."

"I'll worry about today's problem today. I hate to ask, but…have they assigned me something to wear?"

The two men looked at each other. "I fear so."

She sighed. "Just hand it over. I'll do what I have to."

He handed her a pile of fluffy, gauzy stuff that would obviously cover nothing. "You put this over it," he added, passing something of a heavier material.

Devonne shook out the lighter fabric to find harem pants, tied together with ribbons at hips and ankles, and a tunic top also fastened with ribbons at shoulders and sides. It was all in shades of pale pink and green. "Yech. Somebody's got really terrible taste. And pink is not my color at all. I hope it doesn't put Raje off."

The lawyers looked at each with a shade of relief lightening each face. They really had been worried about her reaction. Then his attorney grinned. "I don't think you need to worry about *that*."

"Well I hope not. He's got the tougher job today. I can hardly wait to see how they've outfitted him."

"It's…interesting," Whetlock said. "I think he may be more embarrassed about it than you."

She shrugged. "I haven't gotten into this mess yet. I haven't exactly got a holovid model figure."

Both men looked her up and down. Whetlock said, "You'll look fine in those things."

The buzzer sounded, warning her to prepare. The men left.

Devonne had to draw in a deep breath to steady herself. She wasn't nearly as complacent about putting on that gauzy stuff and performing sexually in public as she tried to act.

Her irritation grew as she struggled to get into the mess of transparent fluff and tied the prissy ribbons holding it together. There were no shoes and the material covered nothing. The heavier cloak did provide cover, but she figured that was just to make her unveiling all the more dramatic.

They escorted her out to the field to a swelling roar of approval from the crowd. Instead of the maze from yesterday, the center circle contained a raised circular dais. In the center of it sat a padded platform with posts at all four corners but no curtains hanging from them. A sheet of white material lay on top of it. Halfway there, one of her guards stopped her.

"Give me the cloak," he ordered.

The crowd went wild when she removed it. Her figure wasn't even slightly obscured by the gauzy garments.

"Go," the guard said, nodding toward the platform bed.

Devonne squared her shoulders and marched toward the platform. She froze when she saw Raje approaching from the other side of the field. Damn, but the man looked good no matter what he wore. Even this. The skintight, red leather leggings accented his long, strong legs and narrow hips. The slit in the front allowed his erect penis to poke through, showing off its proud length and graceful shape.

Before he reached her side, he stopped and gave a cheeky wave to the crowd. They roared their appreciation back at him.

"Show-off," she said, not caring if the microphones caught the words. "You always did want to take that pretty penis into a contest."

He shrugged and gave her a wry smile. "This is undoubtedly the closest I'll get. Might as well enjoy it."

"Unleashing your inner flasher?"

"Whatever it takes. Speaking of which, I like that outfit, but I wish they'd got it in a different color. Blue would be much better on you. Not that it matters. It won't be on you all that long anyway."

"Red definitely works for you," she said as he took her arm and helped her up the one step onto the dais.

"Shows off my green eyes and pale penis to good effect," he agreed. He pulled her into his arms and claimed her mouth for a long, hard, deep kiss.

It fired her blood into steam and sizzled along every nerve in her body. She wanted him so badly it was all she could do to keep from jumping on him right then and impaling herself. Even in public. The man had the power to make her forget everything else but him.

"Fire and Ashes," he said and then echoed her thoughts. "I thought I was going to come when we did the knife dance, and then again yesterday. Now seeing you in that...I don't know how to make this last. We need to give them a good show."

She kissed along his throat while his hands slid down her back to cup her buttocks and pull her against his straining cock. "Twice," she said. "We do it twice. Fast and rough the first time, then long, slow and tender."

He sighed as she nipped at his neck. "We have to talk when this is over. I can't stand it."

"What?"

"Not having you to talk to. And other things. I miss you."

"We'll talk, but don't get your hopes up. Now get romantic."

He jerked his head back so he could her in the eye. "I thought I was."

"You're right. I should have said stop being romantic and start being rough. I'm so hungry for you anyway, I'm ready to eat you."

"I think that's on the second half of the program."

"Stop talking and start ripping this stuff off me," she ordered.

He grinned. "Yes, ma'am!" He set to the task with considerable gusto, roughly yanking open the bows she'd tied. He started with the top ones until the two pieces of the tunic came apart. They slid down her body to puddle on the floor, leaving her bare from the waist up. A shiver that owed nothing to any breeze rippled along her spine. Pure desire to be joined to him as closely as possible shook her. He leaned down to take first one, then the other nipple into his mouth. He lapped them with his tongue and sucked hard until she had to put her hands on his shoulders to support herself.

She squealed and wriggled. Experience had taught him what she liked.

He kissed his way back up to her mouth, but stopped at her ear to say, "You might want to get a bit louder with those moans and groans. The occasional scream would be good, too."

"Make me."

"You've got it."

He lifted her in his arms, to a chorus of cheers from the crowd. For a moment, Devonne had forgotten about the onlookers. Raje swore quietly, then placed her on the bed and knelt beside her.

He kissed her on the mouth almost brutally, tangling his tongue with hers, until she forgot about everything else but him and the rush of heat surging through her. Her cunt throbbed with need, oozing moisture.

He nudged her legs apart and tested her readiness with a finger. Satisfied, he moved over her. His cock protruded hard and ready from the slit in the front of the leather leggings. The slick surface of the leather made an odd sensation against her when he entered her.

He filled and completed her. As always it seemed her mind and soul recognized him at some level so deep only sex could reach it, and then only for too brief a time.

He pounded into her hard and fast, deeply, almost savagely. No buildup, just the abrupt intrusion planting sparks in her. They matched rhythm with practiced ease. Sex was always so easy and so right with him. It never had been that way with any other man, no matter how long she'd known him. A star swelled inside her, growing and threatening to explode as its forces pulsed hotter and harder.

Devonne sobbed and moaned and strained to take him even deeper, ever faster. It took just a few more desperate, violent plunges until the blazing ball of heat inside her went supernova, exploding with a force that shook her body to its core. She screamed in joy and triumph. A couple more pushes and Raje came as well, with a roar that echoed through her head.

He collapsed against her. Wrapping her arms around him, she held him close. For the moment his lying and betrayal were forgotten. Tenderness for him filled her.

After a bit, though, the noise of the crowd filtered into her awareness. Some cheers came from them, but there were many impatient calls for more.

Raje rolled off her. Using a corner of the fabric that covered the platform, he cleaned her, then himself.

"Got another round in you?" he asked.

"With you? Yes." Ouch. The words gave away far too much about her feelings.

"Slow and gentle this time."

He did slow and gentle just magnificently. Using fingers and tongue, he embarked on a languid exploration of every fold and crevice of her body. The heat roused more slowly this time, but he knew just how to touch, lick and pinch to fire up the pressure again. Gentle strokes on cheek, nipples and abdomen alternated with harder tugs and squeezes.

She let him work on her for a while, then she pushed him onto his back and levered herself up on an elbow. "My turn," she said, brushing her fingers along his chest and down to his stomach.

The presence of the crowd weighed on her more in this position, while pleasuring him. She forced herself to focus her awareness on Raje, but even that had its own discomfort in her mixed emotions toward him. She had to bury the hurt for the time. Touching him brought back so many memories that tears threatened.

She leaned over to kiss him, moving her lips on his mouth, sucking and nipping. He opened for her and let her explore. His taste reminded her of glorious dinners, exploring new worlds and adventures in space piracy. Heady and intoxicating. So much so, she had to pull back and let her lips wander over his cheeks and the rest of his face, across to his ear and down his throat.

A stop at his chest let her explore that territory, tasting the skin beneath the light mat of dark hair and licking at his nipples. He groaned loudly when she closed her mouth over one, swiped it with her tongue and sucked at it. A surge of elation shot through her. She could rob this strong man of his formidable control. The power of that knowledge went to her head like a drug. He continued the moans and pants as she moved lower, kissing down his abdomen. When she got to his cock and swiped her tongue along its erect length, he roared his pleasure. He tasted of salt and essential masculinity.

It shocked her when he reached for her and pulled her up to their faces were together again. "Sixty-nine? They'll appreciate it. If you're willing?"

She considered it for a second or two. "Not happy but willing. Sides?"

"Sides are good."

He twisted and rolled, while she shifted. They ended up on their sides, with their heads at opposite ends of the bed and their knees at each other's eye level. He leaned forward, lifted her upper leg onto his shoulder and rested his head on her thigh. All she had to do was duck her head and lean in to get her hands on his balls and her mouth around his cock.

Knowing she'd take longer to come, she went slow with him, massaging and kneading his balls, exploring with her fingers the smooth path behind them, tracking around his anus and then up his penis. She dipped into every crease and crook. Fascination with his body drove everything else from her mind for a time, even the presence of an audience.

Meanwhile his tongue did wicked things to her. It roved, hot and slick, up and down her thigh, across the labia and then plunged inside to find her clit. She squealed and groaned deliberately making the sound louder than she normally would have. A piercing shriek forced its way out when his clever lips closed over the bud and began to roll and squeeze it. The man had the most versatile mouth.

The aroma of his sex surrounded her. The feel of him beneath her fingers and the strange vulnerability of it lent a further enticement. She was drowning in him and couldn't imagine wanting to do this with anyone else. With him it was perfectly right, no matter where or when or who was watching.

Then the building pressure in her cunt drove out all thoughts. The explosion almost caught her by surprise as she suddenly came apart in a huge jerk. It drew from her a full-throated scream.

While still jerking from the shock of it, she took him deep in her mouth and sucked, hard. He roared, too, and his cum spurted.

By the time they'd each calmed enough to be aware again, Devonne couldn't handle the emotion anymore and burst into tears.

Amidst the cheers and foot-stomping of the crowd, Raje twisted until he could enclose her in his arms. "Too much for you?" he asked quietly, brushing away a tear.

"I'm just a bit overwhelmed." How could she tell him that she remembered she loved him and didn't believe they could have any future? How could they, when he'd lied to her, abused her trust and used her assistance to further his own personal agenda?

"Me, too." He hugged her closer. "But we're getting through this, and then we'll see where we are."

The next day, Whetlock told her they'd be fighting treckles. As far as he'd been able to determine, treckles were small creatures with nasty bites. Devonne and Raje were outfitted in plain shorts and sleeveless T-shirts with ankle boots. The Sangari handed her a five-foot-long pike with a point at the end. It also had a broad blade about a foot long and six inches wide below the point on one side and a hook on the other.

The center of the field held no ring or platform that day, nothing at all to break up the circular expanse of grayish green vegetation on the ground. Once she'd met Raje in the middle of it, several doors opened in the wall, releasing packs of six-inch-tall, six-inch-wide creatures that each looked like a cross between a crab and a large spider. The treckles moved quickly in any direction on eight spindly legs. A tough carapace protected the upper surfaces of their bodies and heads. They also had nasty, sharp teeth. Due to their size, a single bite wouldn't do much damage, but in a mass they could strip the flesh from a man if they overwhelmed him. Devonne guessed there might be two hundred of them.

Based on the way they charged straight for the middle of the field, toward them, she suspected the creatures were either hungry or regarded them as intruders on their turf. Or both.

Because they ran toward them from all sides, she and Raje stood back to back, waiting.

"Don't try stabbing them," Raje suggested. "You won't be able to keep up. Sweep the weapon at the pack like this." She turned to watch him demonstrate. He held the staff out, angled down toward the ground. The flat blade was nearly parallel with the field surface and the end just a couple of inches above it. He then made a sharp, side-to-side motion. "Cut out their legs and it should disable a bunch of them at a time."

It made sense to her and it worked almost as well in practice as it did in theory. The creatures scuttled out of the way with surprising speed. Each swipe of the blade took out a few but not as many as they'd hoped. It did drive back the ones not disabled or killed. For a while, anyway.

It wasn't the hardest of the challenges they faced, since the creatures weren't particularly smart. They just kept charging with no change in tactics and no coordinated strategy. The animals' only advantage was their numbers. Though Raje and Devonne swept with the pikes and poked and stabbed occasionally at some that got too close, it seemed like the more they disposed of, the more gathered at the back of the pack to take the place of the fallen.

Devonne hacked and slashed until her shoulders and arms ached. For a while she really did think it hopeless. A few managed to reach her long enough to sink sharp little teeth into the bare skin of her shins above the ankle boots, leaving a nasty sting. Mindlessly, she kept skimming the treckles with the pike, taking out one batch after another and impaling stragglers that got too close.

By the time she could barely move her arms from exhaustion, she looked up and realized there weren't more than a couple of dozen left. It gave her a small burst of energy and she swung at them with renewed vigor until no more charged forward. Dismembered carcasses littered the field. Many of them still rocked and struggled, banging against each other in a weird cacophony of clicks.

Around them, the Sangari cheered their victory. By then the last surge of adrenaline had worn off. Devonne couldn't summon any emotion beyond a nauseated horror and disgust.

The Sangari did bring a medical person to clean up their wounds before they took her back to her quarters. She spent a couple of hours soaking in the tub that evening before she felt clean enough to finally fall asleep.

The next day's "match" was the most shocking and trying one yet.

The lawyers were both plainly unhappy and embarrassed as they told her about it. They blushed and stammered while explaining what was expected. When she finally understood, the anger that had been building up through the four days of trials so far exploded.

Chapter Seven

"You can't be serious," Devonne shouted. "*They* can't be serious. Another couple? We're supposed to have sex with another couple?"

Whetlock blushed an even deeper red. "I know it's…awkward," he admitted. "But that is the requirement for this match. Specifically, each of the four of you must be brought to an orgasm through the combined efforts of the other three persons. However—and I think you'll appreciate this—penetration is not required."

"This is ridiculous!" She paced around the dressing room area. "Bad enough that Raje and I had to entertain them that way. At least we lo—had a prior relationship. To do this with strangers? Including another woman? I can't do it. I won't!"

"Devonne, we don't have much time. Are you sure you won't do it? If so, I have to tell people. And we'll both have to go back and see what alternatives we can negotiate with the Tribunal." Whetlock looked at the other attorney. "Maybe they'd let the prince continue on his own?"

"I doubt it, but I'll see what I can do." Both men rose and went toward the door.

"Wait." Devonne forced herself to calm down. "I'll do it. Hell, we're nearly halfway through this. Why blow it now? I was just letting off steam."

Both men turned around, relief spreading across their features.

"I wonder what they'll be asking for next, though?" she speculated, then forced herself to put it aside. "Do they have anything exotic for me to wear today?"

"It's actually not terribly exotic." Whetlock handed her a pile of fabric, all bleached brilliantly white. She shook out a plain, short tunic top and knee-length, loose skirt. "This isn't so bad," she admitted.

As she walked onto the field, ahead of the ever-present Sangari guard, she at first had eyes only for Raje, approaching from the opposite side of the field. As always, he looked stunningly handsome. He wore a plain outfit also, similar in cut to her own, with a loose shirt and trousers. His were a pale blue. He waved an arm in greeting to the crowd and the audience responded with a roar of approval.

To her right, a slight young woman with reddish hair and alabaster complexion approached the center. She wore the same clothes as Devonne, only in a pale green color. A man entered on her left. Blond and blue-eyed, he was taller than Raje but younger and more slender, almost thin. He moved with an awkward, coltish gait. His outfit was a light yellow.

The round raised dais sat in the middle of the field again, with a bed twice as large as the previous one taking up more than half of the surface. Room for all four of them to cavort. Her stomach clenched into a tight knot as her anger rose.

They met on the dais and came together in the small area not covered by the bed. For a moment they studied each other in silence, then Devonne introduced herself and Raje.

"I'm Alden Banner," the man responded, "and my wife, Elissa. We're a bit… Look, we're…we've never done anything like this before, and we're not sure what to say or do here."

"Makes four of us," Raje answered. "Let's just view it as a job to get done. We perform for them. Nothing personal. Who wants to volunteer to be the first victim?"

"I will," Devonne offered. Her stomach clenched painfully even as she said the words. Might as well get it over with.

"Good. Anyone tell you they appreciate a good show?" Raje asked the question of the other couple softly, hoping the Sangari wouldn't hear.

The man nodded. "We've been trying, but we're not exactly..."

"Flamboyant types?" Devonne asked. "Neither am I, but I think I can fake it better. And we've got him." She nodded to Raje. "Mr. Show-off there. So let's put on a hell of an act for them. Follow our lead. Raje, you want to start undressing me?" Despite her sarcasm, she was grateful for Raje's exhibitionist streak. He'd be carrying them on in this performance.

She tried to keep up the brave—even audacious—front, but it took some effort. This was way outside her comfort zone.

"Group hug, first," Raje suggested and grinned at the silliness of it. "Remember, it's all about the show."

The way the crowd whooped and hollered as the four of them snuggled into a tight bunch indicated he was right. It reminded them to go for any dramatic embellishments they could manage.

They broke apart and shifted so the other three surrounded her, each one touching and stroking her. The woman, Elissa, confined herself initially to brushing fingers through Devonne's hair. Devonne tolerated a kiss from Alden but found it almost repulsive. It didn't affect her the way Raje's kissed did at all. Alden's brought an unpleasant, shivery feeling, though the man himself seemed nice enough and wasn't bad looking.

Raje pulled her tunic top up and over her head, released the fastening on the skirt and let it slide down her legs, then spent a few minutes kissing her and running his hands down her sides to her breasts. The feel of his mouth and fingers against her flesh helped relax her. *Focus on that, on Raje, on his touch,* she told herself. Alden helped guide her when Raje tipped her back onto the bed. She slid to the middle to let the other three kneel around her.

Even though she tried to narrow her awareness only to Rage, it was still one of the most bizarre experiences of her life. This was just pure sex, almost completely dissociated from the emotions it usually roiled in. Even when she'd made love with other men before, they'd been people she at least cared for. To do this most private and intimate act with strangers made her feel like some kind of doll. There was a certain weird excitement about it, perhaps in the sheer novelty. She wouldn't ever want to repeat it though.

Raje placed himself between her legs and signaled the other couple to lean in over her. He said, "Each of you take a breast. I'll handle down here. Elissa, if you're not comfortable just fake it but try to make it look good. Alden, she's the love of my life. Make it good for her."

The words jolted her right down to the deepest recesses of her soul. He couldn't really mean it. He was an accomplished liar. It had to be part of the performance. Didn't it? She raised her head.

Alden turned to stare at Raje for a moment. Devonne could just barely see Raje's face beyond the other man and woman. His expression was deadly serious when he met her gaze for a brief moment.

Alden nodded and turned to look down at her breast, blocking her view of Raje. The words kept rattling around in her brain, though. *The love of my life.*

Alden skimmed a gentle hand along her cheek, jaw, throat and chest, reaching her breast and cupping it hesitantly. Elissa leaned over her other breast, letting her long, straight hair slide forward to hide what she actually did. Smart move.

Then Raje began to brush his tongue up and down the insides of her thighs. She moaned loudly and closed her eyes. By not watching, she could convince herself that Raje was not just the mouth moving up her thighs and into her slit but his also were the hands that massaged her right breast and the mouth that blew on her left. The attention soon had her squirming on the bed as the pressure inside built to another supernova.

Raje flicked her clit with his tongue, licking and sucking. She kept her eyes shut and thought only of him, picturing him in her mind since she couldn't actually see him. Tension grew, hard, heavy, tightening rapidly. Then he scraped his teeth over the bud and the stars burst in a shower of fireworks while spasms of release had her bucking and shouting.

Raje rubbed her thighs gently and Alden caressed her breast until her breathing calmed and she opened her eyes. After a few minutes, she sighed and said, "You're a talented group."

They all looked at her, Raje with pride, Alden with something that might be reserved respect and Elissa with an expression she couldn't read at all.

"Alden next?" Raje suggested. The man colored lightly but nodded and stood. Devonne rose with the others, trying not to worry about her lack of clothing. She'd been nude in front of this crowd before.

Alden removed his shirt but then seemed paralyzed with his fingers in the waistband of the pants. Elissa went around the bed and pushed the pants down his legs, revealing a pretty impressive erection. Points to Elissa. The color in Alden's pink cheeks deepened, standing out against his otherwise pale skin. Possibly to help with his discomfort, Raje removed his own clothes.

Alden's penis wasn't as pretty as Raje's, though about the same size. His was thickly veined and had a slight crook to one side. Elissa put her arm around him and held him for a few minutes, then they moved together to the bed. The tenderness and care of the gesture struck Devonne a blow. Once she might have done the same for Raje, though she couldn't remember a time when he'd needed that sort of reassurance.

Raje and Devonne took up positions on either side of Alden's chest. For the first time Raje looked seriously uncomfortable and hesitated. Given her thoughts of just moments before, the irony made her smile. She tried to offer a reassuring glance. Maybe he didn't understand it, though. When Devonne leaned over to kiss Alden, Raje sent a furious glare her way, then sighed and nodded. To improve the show, she stretched out beside Alden, positioning herself so that her breasts were against him, one lying visible atop his chest. Alden stiffened, then relaxed.

Elissa glowered at Devonne until she reminded the woman in a low voice, "It's a show." Elissa bent down to press her lips to her husband's cock, resigned but not happy about it. Devonne brushed her hand up and down Alden's chest. Taking his cue from her, but just as unhappy as Elissa about the situation, Raje also stretched out alongside Alden, letting his cock be squeezed between his stomach and the other man's side. His erection flew at half-mast by then, probably due to his discomfort.

Caressing Alden brought Devonne a surprising revelation. She found affection for the man growing, though she'd met him less than an hour before. Perhaps the very act of being so physically intimate induced it, though surely the man's courage and affection for his wife played a part.

Mercifully, it didn't take long to bring him to orgasm, most likely because Elissa knew exactly how to please him and set about making it happen as quickly as possible. Devonne had to remind him to groan aloud. She sucked on his nipple, intrigued by the difference between it and Raje's more substantial one, and even nipped lightly. Alden did yell strongly as his cum spurted over the hand his wife had wrapped around his cock onto his chest. The watching crowd cheered.

Elissa went next. Fear or disgust made her go rigid as her husband helped her undress. She lay back down, but it took a while to get her relaxed. Raje noticed her discomfort and backed off a few critical tenths of an inch. To the crowd it looked as though he touched her, but no part of his body actually made contact with hers. When she remained stiff and unresponsive, Devonne also moved away. After a minute, Alden asked to take Raje's place at her side and then suggested Raje get behind him.

Neither man was comfortable with the result since it meant much closer contact between the two of them, but Elissa gradually relaxed with only Alden pressing any skin to hers. He leaned over to nip at her ear for a few minutes while his hand slid down into her slit.

Devonne's hair wasn't long enough to hide her face but she tried to look as though she put her mouth on the other woman's breast without actually doing so.

Elissa began to groan and squeal, even shrieking occasionally, as she grew more excited. Who'd have guessed she'd be so noisy? It added nicely to the show, however. She also bucked and wriggled violently. The crowd roared its approval as the woman's back arched up off the bed. When Elissa came, it was with a long, shrill scream. Amplified by the microphones, it resonated throughout the stadium. Alden kissed and held her as she continued to spasm for some time.

A few minutes later, Raje looked at them all and said, "I'm last. Let's try to finish with a really grand finale. So give it all you've got with me. Whatever you want."

"He means it," Devonne assured the other couple when they looked skeptical. "He's a natural exhibitionist. 'Shy' and 'modest' got left out of his tool box. Stand up." She directed the last at Raje.

He complied with just a single raised eyebrow.

"Elissa, get behind him and put your arms around his chest. Alden, behind her." The other woman colored again but did as she asked, getting behind Raje and wrapping her arms around his chest. Her husband stood behind her and reached forward to put his hands on the Raje's sides. Devonne shifted Elissa's hands so they covered the man's pectorals and nipples, then moved Alden's hands down to just below the waist.

"You two mostly just need to hang on and brace yourselves. Don't let him fall or wiggle away."

They both nodded. She met Raje's eyes for a moment. The glint of appreciation and admiration jolted into and all the way through her. They understood each other so well. She'd never experienced such a deep connection with another human being, almost as though they were two parts of the same whole. The idea intimidated and excited her.

It didn't keep her from plastering herself against him, stomach to stomach, chest to chest and face to face, even though it meant her breasts pressed against Elissa's hands.

Holding his face with her fingers, she kissed him thoroughly, aggressively, plunging her tongue into his mouth and exploring all its heated corners. He tasted so good she didn't want to stop, but she finally forced herself to pull back. She slid down his body and dropped to her knees in front of him. Breasts slithered down his abdomen, enclosing his cock along the way. Her knees hit the wood floor harder than she'd anticipated, but with the scent of Raje filling her nostrils and his penis in front of her she could ignore the ache.

A roar went up from the crowd when she leaned forward and closed her mouth over his shaft. She wound her arms around his thighs to steady herself.

The taste of him roused too many memories. Their first night…the hotel on Dariuscon Eight where she'd… *Better not to go there. Concentrate on the show right now.*

He was so close to the edge, she had to take it slow and stop four or five times to keep him from coming too quickly. Alden and Elissa held him tightly because he bucked hard as she stroked his balls with her palms and sucked his cock. Raje begged her to do it faster, between moans. Finding a cruel streak she hadn't known was there, Devonne deliberately slowed for a time, keeping him on the edge. The crowd performed some sort of chant that mixed in with their cheers. It seemed to urge her on.

Still she refused to hurry. Payback for some of his lies. Groans and moans poured out of him until he was all but sobbing as she stroked the insides of his thighs up to his anus. Eventually the crowd's roar reached some sort of crescendo. Time.

She squeezed his balls, tongued the head of his cock and sucked hard. It took only a moment of that until he jerked and came into her mouth. His shout went on for some time and the spasms of release continued for a couple of minutes. Devonne pressed her face into his abdomen, wanting to keep the intimate contact for as long as possible. She wanted to hang onto him forever.

But the others began to break apart, and Raje reached a hand down to help her to her feet. She clung to him for a moment, watching while Alden and Elissa helped each other get back into their clothes. The cheers and stomping of the crowd made a distant background to her desire to hold close to Raje and stay with him. He indulged her by not moving and putting his arms around her.

When the Sangari guards approached, however, they separated and hastily donned the clothes they'd left.

Devonne wished she could have some time alone with Raje. Bringing him off had made her want him even more.

* * * * *

"It's sex again," Whetlock told her the next day. "A different sort of kink this time."

"Hell, now what?"

"You ever messed around with domination and whips and that sort of stuff?"

Devonne shrugged. "Tried it out. It can be exciting if it's done right, with the right person, but it's not really my thing. How nasty do they want this to get?"

"I think that's pretty much up to you and the prince. And really, I think it's still more about giving them a good show."

"Is there some sort of scenario for this?"

"You'll have a word. He's supposed to get it from you by using the equipment provided and whatever other methods he chooses. I think the longer you can hold out, the better."

"We can work that, I think."

"That's what he said, too. He also said to tell you he'll mostly follow your lead on it."

She nodded. "What kind of kinky outfit do I get to wear for this one?"

"Same as yesterday." He handed the clothes to her.

"Could be worse, I guess."

And of course it did get worse. When the Sangari guards came for her, they slapped leather cuffs around her wrists and ankles, as well as one around her neck. They used a fastening embedded in the cuffs to hold her wrists together behind her back. "Your word is 'constellation,' the Sangari told her before leading her out onto the field. "Do not give it to him easily."

Raje had gotten the really kinky outfit this time, something that seemed to be comprised mostly of straps of black leather. They crisscrossed his chest, belted around his waist and hung down to cover his abdomen and groin. Black leather sandals were held on with laces that laddered up his legs. A black leather mask hid the upper part of his face, leaving only his unusual eyes shining through the holes provided.

It gave him an eerie and rather frightening grimness, but as usual he seemed perfectly at ease even in that bizarre costume. It showed off his lean, strong body to good advantage. And Raje, as she'd already noted, wasn't shy about displaying himself.

He was a prince, a royal heir. He'd likely grown up in the glare of public spotlight, so naturally he'd be comfortable with it. Putting on a good show would have become second nature to him at an early age. With his acting skill, it was no wonder she'd never suspected he was more than an average space pirate and didn't realize he was using her. Still, she was about ready to cast all her reservations aside just for the pure pleasure of being with him.

She's the love of my life, he'd said. Could he possibly have meant it?

The Sangari guard delivered her to Raje, who escorted her onto the platform. It didn't have a bed on it this time. A chair, a low bench and a frame higher than her head and wider than her outstretched arms occupied the dais. Chains hung from the metal top and the side bars of the frame. Both the chair and bench had various straps and fasteners attached as well. A rack held an assortment of whips, straps, paddles and other things she didn't recognize. The Sangari had done their research.

"You okay?" Raje asked. "You look a bit pale."

Devonne drew a deep breath. "Okay. This is just a bit too…real, I suppose."

He laughed softly and said, even more quietly, "It's all show. Or mostly anyway. I'll have to use some of these things, and it will probably sting a bit. If any of it's too much for you, though, just say that. 'Too much.' They won't know it's a signal but it'll tell me to back off."

She tipped her head enough to acknowledge it. "Some sting might be interesting. Do we get to fuck again?"

"I'm counting on it. Prepare for a bit of sexual torture along with everything else."

"Let's get on with it, then."

He started by freeing her wrists and sitting her in the chair, where he fastened the hooks on her ankle and wrist cuffs to rings embedded in the arms and legs.

"Now, madam, I understand you have some information I want." He said it loudly enough to be picked up by the field microphones and amplified around the stadium, and with surprising conviction. "Why not save us both some unpleasantness and just tell me now?"

Devonne wasn't sure how to answer or if she could manage to be as convincing in her refusal. Stubborn silence would serve the purpose just as well.

"Nothing to say? I guess I'll have to be more convincing." He pulled open the fastenings on her shirt and released her wrists just long enough to let him strip it off, leaving her bare to the waist. Then he refastened the wrist cuffs and went to the rack, where he picked out something that looked like a short whip with a triangle-shaped piece at the end. She dug the identification out of a long forgotten memory of a picture she'd seen. An old-fashioned riding crop.

Her stomach twisted with a combination of fear and excitement. BDSM had never been her cup of tea. Now she felt, deep in her gut, why it worked. Being bound and at his mercy but believing he wouldn't hurt her too much was a kind of gift. A gift of love and trust.

Of course, he could have made his own private deal with the Sangari. She might be playing into his hands. Instinct said he wouldn't do that. He'd use her in other ways to further his own ends but not an out-and-out betrayal. Was that the same instinct that believed he loved her right up until the day she'd learned who he was?

He brushed the triangular end of the crop across her breasts, teasing her nipples with it. A thrilling curl of dread mixed with the tingling the rough edge of the leather roused each time it brushed over the areola and peaks. He pulled it back and flipped it forward to slap lightly against her right nipple.

It didn't strike hard enough to hurt, producing just sting enough to be arousing. Heat and pressure began to gather in her cunt. A few more slaps followed, getting somewhat sterner each time until it burned a bit. It wasn't a painful fire, however. More of an arousing burn, the kind she got when he pinched the nipple or nipped at it.

"Ready to talk?"

She just stared at him in response, struggling to look more pained than lustful. He released her from the chair and dragged her over to the bench, where he pushed her facedown along its length. The wrist and ankle cuffs were attached to chains embedded in the legs. She could move her arms and feet only a couple of inches. He removed her boots and then flipped up her skirt. The resulting helplessness made her uncomfortable. Had she ever realized before how much she liked being in control?

The crop slapped down on her unprotected butt. It stung, but not very much. A few more and a light burn started to fire back there. Oddly, it dug deep into her, blazing a trail across the short internal distance from butt to cunt.

He smacked her bottom a few more times, then bent down close to her face. "Are you ready to talk?" he asked loudly. More quietly, he added, "Help me out here. Scream. Yell. Protest."

Devonne shook her head in dramatic refusal but she answered softly, "Okay."

When he tapped her with the crop again, she yelled. Long and loud. It brought some jeers and stomping from the crowd. Over the next half hour or so, he switched the crop for several other items, paddles of various sorts, straps, floggers. After a while her bottom and thighs burned but not nearly as badly as her screams and protests would suggest. In fact, the damn beating was turning her on so much she was more distressed by the building desire than by the little bit of pain.

He stopped and asked her about the word again. When she refused, he released her ankle restraints long enough to pull off her skirt, then fastened them to the bench again, with her legs spread widely.

The openness disturbed her, considering a camera was probably stationed to look right up her legs. Within moments, though, the throbbing in her cunt drove it from her mind. She wanted, needed, ached for him. The dominance thing had possibilities she'd never considered before. Some other time, they might—but there couldn't be anything more for them.

A leather paddle slapped against the insides of her thighs. It startled her into a yell since he'd smacked hard enough to hurt. He rubbed the area where it had hit. The pain changed into electrical tingles of need. He brushed up her leg and into her slit. Within the constraints of the bindings, she wriggled an invitation to him. Still, she shouted in surprise when a finger stroked along her labia and dove between them to find her clit.

The real torture began then. He alternated hard smacks from the paddle with soft swipes of his finger on her bud. He dipped into her cunt and stroked until she was bucking and yelling with the need to climax. Need tightened every muscle in her body. Every nerve cried out for the release he denied her. As soon as he felt her getting close, he backed off and let her cool down. Two times, three times, and even a fourth he brought her to the brink of orgasm and stopped.

She hated him.

After the second time, she moaned and groaned and yelled at him. By the fourth time his life was in danger. "You son of a bitch, Raje Jernigan, let me come. Stop torturing me!"

He leaned over and blew lightly in her ear. "You know what you have to do."

He straightened. The paddle came down on her buttocks and his finger began stroking again. Devonne cried and yelled with the frustrated need. When he stopped just short of letting her come again, she howled. "All right. All right. Constellation. The word is constellation. Now finish it, damn it."

She wasn't sure exactly how he managed it in that position, but he straddled the bench himself and lifted her hips so that his cock could enter. She screamed in delight as he filled her with his hot, hard length. It was Raje in her, making her body sing with the special delight only he could bring. He plunged and pulled back, then rammed into her again. She was so tight, so close to the edge, it didn't take long. She jolted hard as the spasms of the too-long-delayed climax made her jump and shout in triumph.

* * * * *

The seventh day brought a different sort of challenge, although Whetlock could give her only sketchy details. "It involves fighting a machine or a group of machines. I wasn't clear on which. Anyway there's apparently some way of disabling it or them but you have to figure it out."

Devonne shrugged. "Nice change from the sex stuff. Any special costume for this?"

"Nope. I think it's come as you are."

The Sangari guard handed her a yard-long metal pole with a rubber handgrip, but he failed to tell her what she should do with it. There were no rings or platforms set up on the field. Raje entered from the other side as usual and joined her in the center of the field. The Sangari guards withdrew.

Moments later a pair of barred gates rose. Three machines rolled out of each opening. About four feet high, black and shaped like an elongated pyramid, they moved faster than she would have expected, homing right in on the two humans. Raje and Devonne moved a few steps to the left. Each line of machines altered course to continue toward them.

This might not be easy but at least it didn't involve public sex.

"Heat-seeking or motion-sensing," Raje said. "Any idea what these are for?" He held up a rod identical to hers.

"Smacking them?" She looked at it again. "I wonder about the rubber grip. An insulator?"

"Could be. Let's see if they're programmed with any sense of strategy. Move apart."

She nodded and they each took a few steps in opposite directions. The robots paused then began to fan out into a circle around them. The farther apart the humans got, the more the robots spread out. When Raje and Devonne reached twenty feet apart, the robots began to separate into two groups that moved together again. A smaller group closed on each of them. The two humans sidled toward each other. The robots regrouped into one unit and fanned into arcs again.

"Some sense of strategy, anyway," Raje commented. "Let's see what else they've got." He charged toward a machine that was marginally closer to him than the others. As he approached, all of the machines pivoted. A small tube emerged from the side of each, all pointing at Raje. A few steps farther, the one closest to him and the one next to it both emitted humming sounds and then burped more loudly. Raje yelped and jumped backward. "Yeoowch."

"What happened? Are you hurt?" She charged toward him.

"They bite."

"What?"

"They throw off some kind of charge. Electrical, I guess, since it feels like a shock. Not serious, but it stings."

They watched the machines for a few moments, wondering what to do. But the robots themselves made the next move. They began to roll toward them again. Not wanting to be shocked, Raje and Devonne retreated toward the one side that wasn't blocked off. After a few steps Raje stopped. "They're trying to force us back to the wall where they can corner us against it."

"Not a good idea. Guess we see how bad they can zap us."

"Let's go."

Running together they sprinted for the nearest gap between two of the machines. Devonne was still surprised by how quickly they turned and aimed, but only the two on either side of the gap fired at them. A burning spot on her leg signaled where a beam had connected with her. It would take quite a few of those to cripple her.

The machines turned and came after them, of course. The two humans spent a few minutes running around the field being chased by the robots. The crowd cheered and jeered.

"We need a better strategy," Raje said as they stopped to gather breath. He looked down at the rod he held. "They gave us these. There must be something we can do with them."

"Smash the things? They look pretty resilient."

"Yeah." Raje studied the machines and then the questionable weapon he held. "There's got to be a reason these are metal. I'm guessing there's some place you can touch on those machines that will make them arc and short out."

"Finding it won't be fun. Take turns?"

"I was going to suggest you try to divert them."

"No way and it won't work."

He shrugged. "Ladies first then? I'd suggest starting low."

Devonne took the first try, lunging toward the nearest of the robots and quickly scanning the surface for any place that looked like a possible weakness. She jammed the rod toward a seam in the plating as the machine zapped her. The touch of the rod had no effect on the machine.

She expected it to work on the very first try? Well, yes.

She jumped backward before it could shock her again. Raje had no more success on his first foray.

Ten minutes into their efforts, the shocks grew stronger. They'd also tried out every likely spot on the bottom two-thirds of the machines. Those zaps could get bad enough to cause serious trouble if they didn't stop the machines soon. Raje's expression turned grim.

In fact, it took almost fifteen minutes before Devonne found the vulnerable spot on the machines, almost by accident. After a jolt knocked Raje off his feet, she ran forward to help and used her rod to knock away the turret turning toward them. The pole slid down the bottom of the protrusion and knocked against the opening in the casing below it. A loud buzzing and a shower of sparks preceded the machine shutting down entirely.

"Damn," Raje said. "Good shootin', Tex."

"Thanks. It's right beneath the little turret that fires at us."

They wasted no time in disposing of the rest of the machines and accepted the applause of an appreciative audience afterward.

* * * * *

The next day was a repeat of the sixth day, but with the roles reversed. She got to be the dominatrix this time. Instead of a word to get from him, her goal was to induce him to crawl across the platform, bringing her a shoe—in his mouth. She laughed out loud at the mental image the words conveyed. He wouldn't like it. She did. The dominant role suited her much better than the submissive one.

Devonne loved the outfit they provided for her this time—all black leather, with solid, body-hugging pants, spike-heeled knee boots and a top that was nothing but a few straps just barely covering her breasts.

"Look out, Raje, here I come," she said to herself as she stepped out onto the field. The sight of him approaching drew a sharp breath from her. "Oh, my." He wore nothing but a thong and the same cuffs circling wrists, ankles and neck she'd worn when playing the submissive role. As she'd expected, he didn't look happy about it, but that might have been in the interests of the show more than letting his true feelings come out. She suspected his reactions were more real than he'd let on. The exhibitionist showman didn't care for being anyone's whipping boy, and it showed, though he tried to make the performance flamboyant anyway. Giving up control didn't come easily to him.

The equipment provided was the same as the day she'd played submissive. She ignored the chair and led him straight to the metal frame where she released his wrists so she could lift his arms and attach the hooks to the chains dangling. "Are you okay?" she asked him quietly in the process.

"Hell no. But I'll manage. Feel free to hit as hard as you like. Might be good anyway. All for the show."

"Same deal as last time. 'Too much' makes me pull back."

He gave a small nod. Devonne went to the table and picked up one of the more sensuous looking floggers. It had a handle with a fall of a dozen or so leather tails eighteen inches long. She tried it on her own palm and found it less stinging and more just tingly than she expected.

She couldn't resist kissing him and running her hands down his body before she did anything else. The tiny scrap of fabric that covered his erection bulged in a way that proclaimed his arousal clearly enough. She loved the solid feel of him, the body that had pleasured hers so often. She loved the man, too, with all his strengths and weaknesses. Too bad some of those likely stood in the way of anything more between them.

Having him at her mercy like this aroused her, bringing the heavy tension to her cunt. She could have him in any way she wanted, do anything she wanted with him. A dizzy shiver passed through her as she considered the power she had. Might as well enjoy it now since it was destined to be very temporary.

That thought brought enough frustration to lead her to step back and try an experimental slash with the flogger across his chest. He watched her steadily with no show of reaction, not even a jerk or wince, though the tails left faint pink trails on his flesh. Several more slaps brought little more emotion. He winced when one of her strokes caught his nipple.

She stopped and said, aloud, "You know what service you're supposed to do for me?"

He nodded. "Something about crawling to you."

"And bringing a shoe. Are you ready to do it?"

His smile combined anger, disbelief, and defiance with a pure erotic challenge that left her breathless. "Not likely."

"Then I'll have to be more convincing," she answered.

"If you can." The challenge was open and deliberate.

It's all about the show, she reminded herself. It didn't stop the frisson of annoyance and determination that made her straighten her back. *If I can, indeed.*

She struck him harder across the chest, leaving a few light welts. Moving behind him, she assailed his back and buttocks until the flesh there had a pink tinge as well. The crowd roared approval.

She set down the flogger and tried one of the leather paddles. It made a much louder *crack* when it hit the skin and raised welts easily. The noise and its effects on him concerned her. Despite his goads, she worried about actually hurting him. She needn't have.

"Is that all you've got?" he jeered after a few more smacks of the paddle. "You'll be a long time convincing me to do anything." It drew cheers and laughter from the audience.

She recognized what he was doing and still reacted. She put back the paddle, picked up the crop and swung it hard. It made a nasty *thwack* on his buttocks and left a pink line that rose into an impressive weal.

Raje actually sucked in a sharp breath. "Closer," he said. "But still not there."

He really wanted her to hit him harder? It had to be hurting him now. Memory teased her. When the positions were reversed, he'd combined the pain with sexual teasing. It had brought her to the point of madness.

Payback was going to be fun.

She set aside the crop for a moment and plastered herself up to his back. Reaching around, she played with his nipples for a bit, tweaking and twisting them until he groaned. The uniquely personal aroma of Raje filled her nostrils, and his silky dark hair brushed against her face. Her own internal temperature level was climbing. His breath hitched when her hands slid down his chest and along his stomach to his groin. She cupped the bulge under the front of the thong and worked it with her fingers.

It took an effort to make herself stop when she realized he was on the verge of coming.

She moved him to the bench and laid him on it, faceup with his arms and legs pulled down at the sides and held there by chains linked to the cuffs. Using a knife she found—rather alarmingly—on the table, she slit the band of the thong and pulled it off him. His cock spring free. Devonne selected a heavier looking flogger than the previous one and approached him, eyeing his erect penis. A sharp breath sounded almost like a sob. It wasn't acting, either. He hadn't bargained on this.

"Are you ready to consider crawling?" she asked.

"Only after you." He tried for cocky and didn't quite bring it off this time. The genuine worry in his tone indicated concern about what she intended. His erect cock showed he was turned on by it as well.

"You'll do better than that." She moved to stand over him.

The expression on his face slammed into her with devastating effect. Light green eyes met hers, and in them she saw apprehension…and trust. His lips curved into that wicked, goading grin. "Make me."

She held the flogger over his chest and let the ends trail over his pectoral muscles and nipples. The leather strips brushed along his abdomen to his cock. He sucked in a harsh breath as it moved down to his balls, left open to her touch since his legs were spread apart by the bench.

Elation surged through her yet again. The crowd began to chant something, apparently becoming impatient.

She raised the flogger and slapped it down across his chest. He drew a sharp breath. A network of pink weals formed. She leaned over him with the pretense of licking his nipples but took the opportunity to tell him quietly, "Less stoicism. More yells." Acknowledgement came as a slight nod.

The next time she struck his belly with the flogger, he did indeed shout. It wasn't terribly convincing to her but the crowd bought it. They cheered gleefully.

Moving down, she flicked the insides of his thighs, then rubbed the pink spots left with her palm. He groaned and squirmed—much more naturally this time. She trailed the ends of the flogger over his penis. Sweat had begun to form on his face and strain pulled his features tight. She touched the top of his cock and ran a finger down it to his balls. It drew a loud moan.

"Are you ready to crawl yet?" she asked.

"No."

She sat in the chair for a couple of moments, doing nothing, letting him cool off. Then she rose and picked up the crop. His eyes widened and he drew a deep breath as she ran it down his chest to his cock. The tip of the crop brushed up and down its length. She raised it and slapped it down on the inside of each thigh, then again, moving higher each time. It left a ladder of pink welts climbing each leg. His fingers curled into fists and his body tensed. He groaned and yelled. Then she tapped his balls with it, just a light slap, but he shouted—as much from fear as pain.

Several harsh breaths made his chest heave when he saw her next target. She struck his abdomen, just above the tip of his cock and held the crop poised a couple of inches lower for several seconds before she flicked it down. He bucked and shouted. She followed it up by leaning over and tonguing the area she'd hit.

"Ready to crawl yet?" she asked, straightening.

He shook his head.

Annoyance mixed with admiration for his courage. How far would he push her?

More torment for him. Bending over, she put her tongue on the inside of one knee and began to nip and kiss her way up the hairy expanse of his inner thigh to his balls. She licked the marks left by the crop and bit between them. Just before she hit the soft sac, she started again on the other side. When she reached the top and flicked her tongue over his balls. His body arched up from the bench. He muttered, "Powers and Flames, Devonne. Powers and Flames, you're driving me mad."

"Ready to crawl yet?"

He hesitated, then shook his head again.

Damn the man.

She tapped his cock and balls steadily with the crop, not hard enough to jolt or hurt him, but delivering numerous little stings. They should drive him close to insanity. Occasionally the crop diverted to his nipples and slapped them smartly or she would run it down onto his thighs. She continued until he could no longer lie still and he groaned continuously. "Please," he begged loudly. "I can't stand it. Please. Let me come."

"Crawl for me," she demanded.

"Yes!"

She released him from his bonds and watched him shakily get down on his hands and knees. Making no move to help him, she pointed to the shoe that had been left at the far side of dais. "Go get and bring it to me. No hands. In your mouth."

He did it. Grasping the shoe in his teeth, he brought it across the dais to her, crawling on his hands and knees. Though he nearly tipped over more than once, he finally laid it in her lap.

Elation surged through her, ridiculously out of proportion to the silliness of the task he'd just performed.

She smiled and brushed damp hair back from his face. "Stand up."

He trembled so much he had to put a hand on the back of the chair. Devonne stood then turned and pushed him into the chair. Disappointment and irritation crossed his face. She peeled off the leather pants and climbed onto the chair as well, kneeling so that she faced him, thighs spread with her knees outside his legs.

Flames and Stars, he was gorgeous, even with sweat slicking his skin and dampening his hair. Her cunt was so hot and tight. Cream poured from her, mingling with the perspiration on his legs.

She kissed him as she shifted forward and up, wiggling her way over his hard, quivering cock. She sank down, impaling herself on him.

"Devonne," he moaned, burying his fists in her hair as she slid up and down him. Deep, deep inside. Breaths huffed in and out of him in loud bursts, growing harsher each time she impaled herself fully. Her cunt clenched around him, jolting when his penis hit the pleasure spot. It took only a few bounces to bring him to a roaring orgasm. She wound her fingers in his hair and lifted herself again.

A few more bounces, and the spasms of an explosive climax jolted through her as well, making her scream and hang onto him.

Devonne leaned into him, holding his penis inside her like a treasure she didn't want to lose. She rested her head on his shoulder and his arms went around her. Together they gasped and panted their way back to calm.

She couldn't imagine doing this with any other man in the universe. Life would be emptier without him, but she'd have some incredible memories.

* * * * *

On day nine, the lawyer looked very grim when he met her in the dressing room. Devonne's heart lurched.

"What is it?"

"A real challenge today. Possibly a real battle. You and Raje have to fight a corbret. Since it will be totally intent on killing and eating the two of you, you'll have to either kill it or disable it completely. They didn't tell me what weapons you'll have. No special clothes."

"What's a corbret?"

"One of the Creator's most unattractive productions. A big hairy slobbery thing. Cross between a really big, mean lion and a borgez. Not as good-natured as either the lion or the borgez. However they're dumb as posts, so it'll be your brains against its brawn."

"I'd rather it were my beamer against its brawn, but I doubt we'll be that lucky."

She was right. The Sangari guard handed her a sword and a net as he escorted her out to the field. There was no ring or other equipment on the field when she met Raje in the middle.

"You know anything about swords?" she asked him.

"You swing them and hope the blade hits something. Someone's been reading their ancient Earth history."

"Or watching old Earth vids about gladiators. Hell. At least the critter's supposed to not be very bright."

"Advantage us."

But then the gate screeched up and the "critter" lumbered out. All ten feet of length and seven feet of height of it. All six rows of razor-sharp teeth. "Shit," Devonne said. "It doesn't need to be smart."

"But *we* do."

"Yup. Got any really smart ideas?"

"Run like hell?"

"Keep thinking."

The creature had either seen or heard them and was rumbling toward them. It opened its mouth and emitted a roar that would have intimidated a rabid lion. It didn't move quickly but its size meant it covered ground fast anyway.

They slid to the side and ran to the other end of the field. The creature turned and followed. When they sped away it turned and advanced on them again. They let it chase them around for several minutes as they watched it, hoping to see an obvious handicap. Nothing showed.

"I suspect it can outlast us," Devonne said.

"Yeah. But we should be able to out-maneuver it. There are two of us."

"Keep going."

"I was hoping you'd looked at the course chart."

"All that occurs to me is that one of us could distract it while the other…"

"Yeah?"

"I don't know," she admitted. "Search for a weak spot? It worked before."

"It'll be a hell of a lot harder to find one on this thing. I'm thinking more of a hack and slash approach. We take turns with one of us distracting it while the other tries to get in a solid cut or stab."

"I haven't got a better plan."

They spent the next half an hour or so doing just that. One of them would try to lure the beast into paying attention to it, while staying clear of the deadly teeth and claws. Meanwhile the other raced in, stabbed or slashed at it and retreated just as hastily. By the end of that time they were hot, tired and running out of energy. The creature bled from dozens of cuts but it didn't seem to have slowed noticeably. Raje's arm was scratched when he'd failed to dodge one rake of its claws.

"We can't keep this up," Devonne pointed out, while they waited for the corbret to catch up to them again. Her chest burned from the exertion and each breath hurt.

"Eyes," Raje said. "We need to take out its eyes."

"Gotta get past all those teeth to do it."

Raje glanced around the arena. "Can you hold its attention for a couple of minutes, and then draw it over there to the grate?"

He pointed to the barred gate that had slid upward to let the creature onto the field. The Sangari had closed it again to keep anyone from retreating that way. It had about ten vertical metal bars and three horizontal cross-bars.

"Raje, I don't—"

"We're running out of options."

It scared the shit out of her. For the first time, fear that they might not survive roused and shook her.

"All right." She turned and kissed him hard before she moved away and feinted toward the beast to draw its attention to her. Out of the corner of her eye, she saw Raje head toward the grate. The corbret turned to follow him. Devonne stepped toward it and jabbed until she had its attention again.

Maneuvering it over to the grate so that it would be positioned for Raje to make his move proved a tricky business. If she just ran directly to it, she'd end up with herself between the man and the animal. She had to circle around to get it to chase her past the grate.

Quick glances his way showed her when Raje reached the barrier and climbed up to the highest horizontal bar. She continued to tease and lead the corbret, making an arc that took her around the middle of the field and angled toward the wall. One claw caught her shoulder in the process, leaving a burning slash. Finally she reached the wall, ten feet from the grate, turned to her right and led the creature past it. Raje held very still, hoping to keep the corbret from noticing his presence until too late.

Devonne raced ahead. A strange, unhappy roar from the creature told her Raje had made some kind of move. She turned back and sucked in a harsh breath. Raje had leapt onto the corbret's neck, grabbing a handful of fur to hold onto when the creature attempted to shake him off. Her heart stopped beating. Breath clotted in her throat for several long minutes as he battled to stay aboard and position his sword for a downward thrust. She whispered heartfelt prayers to the Creator.

The corbret rose up on its two hind legs, forcing Raje to use both hands to stay on. It continued to toss its head, trying to shake him off. In the process it exposed its chest and underbelly.

Devonne saw the opening. She raised her sword to chest level and wrapped both hands around the handgrip. Holding it pointed out in front of her, she charged into the beast, zigzagging to avoid claws, and drove the weapon as hard as she could into the corbret's chest. It sank deep, up to the hilt. Blood spattered her.

The creature's furious roar grated on her nerves and made her shake as she retreated. Claws groped blindly for the source of its agony. One nearly raked her. She stepped back, out of reach, wiping her eyes.

The corbret swayed back and forth, still emitting that horrible roar. She couldn't find Raje in the mass of waving limbs and flying fur. Her heart clenched and stomach twisted. *Where was he?*

An earsplitting scream came from the creature, then it slowly collapsed into a heap of fur and teeth and claws. Its moans gradually faded. Devonne ran around it and found Raje, half pinned beneath one of the monster's gigantic rear legs. She heaved it up enough to let him slide out and helped him stand.

They held onto each other while the crowd went berserk with cheering and stomping.

"Have I told you yet that I love you?" Raje asked.

Relief made her so weak she almost collapsed. Instead she plastered herself against him. "I'll bet you say that to all the women who slay corbrets for you." The words came out breathy and unsteady.

"Nah, I reserve it for one special one. Devonne, seriously, I want–"

The Sangari guards chose that inopportune moment to surround them.

They watched each other for as long as they could while the guards escorted them out opposite sides of the stadium. She treasured the look in his eyes as they were parted. The love and admiration and gratitude found a permanent place in a corner of her heart. He mouthed the words, "I love you," as he reached the far end.

* * * * *

Both lawyers waited in her dressing room the next day when she arrived for the last of the challenges. She'd been fighting a crushing sense of dread ever since she'd recovered enough from the previous day's challenge to start to wondering what this day would bring. Anything worse than the battle with the corbret would probably defeat them.

It didn't do her nerves any good when she heard the lawyers arguing hotly, and they jangled even worse when the men saw her and lowered their voices so she couldn't hear their words.

She went right to them. "What is it?"

"Not good," Whetlock said.

"Really not good," the other one agreed.

"Another fight?"

Both nodded.

"To the death?"

They nodded again.

"What is it this time? They found something even nastier than the corbret?"

The two men looked at each other. Whetlock sighed. "Not another animal."

"Machine?"

"No."

Devonne's stomach twisted and clenched. "Each other." She forced the words out. "We have to fight each other."

"No."

Relief had just started to settle in when Whetlock said, "Another couple. The couple you had sex with a few days ago.

Chapter Eight

"Shit. They can't be serious. I may barely know them, but we made love with them. Now we're supposed to kill them?"

"You only have to kill one. All four of you fight, until one of the four of you is dead."

"No."

They both looked at her.

"There are limits. I won't do it. I won't kill one of them."

"Raje said the same thing at first," his lawyer said. "Then he thought about it and asked me to give you a message. They wouldn't give him anything to write with, so I'm delivering it verbally. He asked me to tell you he was going to do it and begged you would too. He has a plan. It might not work and there's some risk even if does, but he thinks it will work and you won't have to kill anyone. He asks you to trust him."

Trust him? In some things, maybe, but where his own self-interests were on the line?

Devonne turned away as she struggled with her reaction. Trust him. That was the core issue. She trusted him as a partner in battle or in sex. She knew what he was capable of in those fields. But ever since she'd learned who he really was, she hadn't trusted him to make life-affecting decisions for both of them. He was asking for that now. He'd been a near-perfect partner so far in the challenges, even when it meant doing things he despised. But winning in those had benefited him.

Winning this challenge would be in his own best interest, too.

Could she trust that he understood her reservations and respected them? And if he did, could she trust that he'd act in a way she'd accept? Even if it put his own safety in jeopardy? Did she dare?

"He also promised that he'd let you make the final decision," the lawyer said.

"Word of the Creator, how do I make a choice like this?"

Neither of the two men could give her an answer. The Creator wasn't offering any opinions either. Only she could decide.

"Yes," she said finally. "We'll do it." The Creator help them all if she'd made the wrong decision.

The others nodded, though neither looked happy about the situation.

"No special clothes," Whetlock said. "I believe it's going to be knives again."

The Sangari guard arrived for her. The lawyers both wished her good luck. It would take more than that but a bit of luck wouldn't hurt either. She took the knife from the guard without paying much attention to it.

As usual Raje entered the field from the side opposite her and the other couple on her right and left. For the first few minutes, though, she had eyes only for Raje. Relief and gratitude showed on his features when he caught sight of her then his expression turned grim.

The four of them met in the center of the ring with the Sangari guards standing between them. She looked at Alden and Elissa, catching them staring at each other in a private exchange of love and helpless fury. Her own anger spiked. The next time she looked at them, all she saw was fear and determination in their expressions. She sought Raje's gaze, but she couldn't read anything there when she met his eyes.

The guards stepped back out of their way. One said, "Go, now."

For a moment, they all did nothing but stare at each other and raise their knives into a ready position. Then the other couple moved fast.

The fight was short, fierce and ugly.

Devonne gave Alden and Elissa credit. They had a plan and it wasn't a bad one. They guessed they'd be overmatched and came up with an idea to win quickly. As soon as the Sangari guards pulled back, both of them charged straight at her, intent on taking her down fast.

It damn near worked, too, since Devonne wasn't prepared to have both of them come at her like that. Thank goodness, they underestimated her quickness and agility. She dodged them both while stepping back and away. She parried Alden's feint and pushed Elissa off so hard the other woman almost lost her balance and went down.

It gave Raje time to enter the fray. He took on the more immediate threat of Alden, leaving Devonne to go after Elissa. Alden proved a tougher opponent for Raje than either of them would have guessed, but the other woman was no fighter. After a brief struggle, Devonne knocked away Elissa's knife. The woman continued to fight tenaciously but with no skill, trying to work around Devonne's weapon to scratch or gouge. In one small piece of luck, she knocked Devonne's arm hard enough to jar the knife from her hand and send it flying across the field. With both of them weaponless, the advantage still went to Devonne's quickness and strength. Devonne grabbed the other woman, spun her around and snaked an arm around her throat. Circling Elissa's midsection with her other arm, Devonne pinned her arms to her sides. She struggled but couldn't break the hold.

Give her credit. Elissa realized that since neither of them had a weapon she was in no immediate danger. She didn't call for aid from her husband, made no attempt to distract him. In that assumption, she wasn't entirely correct. Devonne felt sure she could snap the woman's neck if she had to. Or perhaps Elissa did know that, too, and calculated more accurately Devonne's unwillingness to do so.

Raje and Alden were joined in a more desperate battle, bodies close, knife hands locked together over their heads and arms straining for leverage. Their struggle brought them around in an arc that granted both men a view of the two women. Alden broke off the fight with Raje and sped toward Elissa. Raje followed right behind.

When Alden reached between the two women to try to free his wife, it gave Raje the opening he needed. A quick chop across the hand sent Alden's knife sailing away. Raje then pulled the other man backward and sent him rolling to the ground. Alden lay on his stomach, winded. Raje settled a boot on his neck to hold him there. He held the knife in his right hand, poised for a devastating, downward thrust. The crowd roared its approval.

Elissa screamed and started to struggle, clawing and flailing to get out of Devonne's hold to reach her husband.

Devonne held her tight, wondering how she'd feel if that were Raje on the ground about to be impaled.

Time slowed as Devonne held the woman and looked over at Raje. Would he truly plunge the knife down into the other man? The crowd chanted for him to deliver the blow.

Raje stood a moment, catching his breath, then he glanced at the man below and looked up at Devonne. He waited. Waited for her verdict.

She shook her head. Everything else retreated to the background as her awareness centered entirely on Raje. What would he do?

He nodded acceptance.

All but maddened with fury and despair, Elissa clawed at Devonne's arms and tried to bite her way out of the hold.

"Stop!" Devonne told the woman. "Be quiet and we may all get out of this with our lives yet. It's *his* only *chance*." She nodded toward Alden, who also struggled fruitlessly to crawl out from under Raje's leg.

When Raje brought the knife down on Alden's back, Devonne's heart clenched and sudden raging fury stabbed through her.

Before the shock wore off, however, she realized he'd merely pricked the man's shoulder, just enough to draw a bead of blood.

Raje held up the blood-stained knife for the crowd to see, raising it high in the air, pointed upward. He raised his other arm as well.

"You have his blood," he shouted, loud enough for the microphones to pick up at high volume. The crowd screamed and stomped.

"You have his blood," Raje repeated. "Is it enough?" His shouted words held some plea, but more triumphant acclamation.

Elissa and Alden both stopped struggling. The crowd quieted, considering his question. They'd been promised death. Would they settle for blood?

If it worried Raje, he gave no sign as he spoke again. "You've watched us today and these past nine days. You know what we can do. Have we not entertained you well?"

The crowd roared approval. "We have," Raje agreed. "Now you see I have this man's life in my hands. But his blood is on my knife and that is enough for me. We are humans. We may take each other's lives out of necessity, but we do *not* take them for sport!"

The crowd quieted, waiting. Devonne held her breath.

"I ask you again now, have we entertained you well?" The crowd cheered. "Very well?" Again the crowd agreed with a roaring frenzy of stomping and whistling. "Then I ask you this. *Give me my victory*!"

The crowd's noise swelled even further, to levels she wouldn't have believed possible. Her ears began to hurt.

Flames and Powers, the man was incredible. Who else would even try to manipulate a huge stadium full of aliens?

"Hell, no wonder the Gambrian people adore him and the royal authorities don't," Devonne muttered.

In a box that partly overhung the field, a large Sangari rose. The crowd roared again. When the Sangari raised his arms, though, they quieted abruptly. Their leader, she presumed.

The Sangari waited until the place became eerily quiet compared to the frenzy of just moments before. "We agree you have given us good entertainment. You've proved yourself a worthy warrior in battle and in mating. The Sangari salute you and grant you victory."

The crowd went into another orgy of cheering and stomping.

Raje stepped off his opponent and turned. He bowed to the Sangari leader, gracefully and very low. After he straightened, he held up his arms again to request silence and waited for it. "Your Esteemed Majesty, my heartfelt gratitude for the boon. You truly show the greatness of the Sangari spirit in granting this, and my people will long recall your generosity. Because Your Greatness has shown yourself so worthy and so full of all that is admirable and honorable among the Sangari, I dare venture another request. Grant the boon of victory to this couple also. They've fought with courage and determination against odds greater than they knew. They, too, are worthy of victory."

The crowd cheered, though not so loudly as before, while their leader hesitated. Finally he raised his arms again and said, "We grant this also. We beg the Gambrian House will bear in mind our generosity."

Raje bowed again. "We will not forget."

Alden stood up. Devonne released Elissa, who raced into his arms. Devonne went straight to Raje.

They had little time to embrace each other, however, before an award ceremony commenced. Sangari guards, now dressed in rainbow-hued tunics over black trousers, led each of them to a small stool and helped them up. The guards presented each of them with a bright orange leaf the size of her hand, a necklace of rancid-smelling flowers and a piece of parchment paper covered with Sangari script. She hoped it proclaimed her a free woman, quit of all debt to the Sangari.

When the ceremony concluded, the man in the box stood. The Sangari guards on the field retreated and Jason Whetlock ran to meet her. He congratulated her and Raje on their victory and Raje's daring appeal. Alden and Elissa also embraced them and offered profuse thanks. Tears ran freely down Elissa's face and even Alden's eyes showed suspiciously bright.

Raje's own lawyer didn't appear right away, but came in as various Sangari officers and guardsmen were congratulating them. The lawyer's serious expression stood out among the exuberance of everyone else. It unsettled her. The troupe of four other grim-faced men with him added to the gloom.

"Your Highness?" One of those men said, drawing Raje's attention. "Might we have a private word with you?"

Raje looked askance at them, until he met his lawyer's eyes and the man nodded.

"Would you excuse me for a minute?" he asked before he went to them and conferred with the group. It took more than a minute, but not much more. His face, too, was grim, when he returned to her.

"Devonne, I need to go with them back to Gambria, right now. My father died last night."

"Oh, Powers. I'm sorry."

"Me, too," he admitted. "We didn't agree on much of anything and we weren't close, but still… I'll never have a chance to try to work things out with him. Not that it was likely, but…" He stopped and swallowed. "I hate to leave right now, when there's so much we need to say to each other."

"This is more important for now," she said. "Go with them. We'll talk later."

She'd said that to him once before, and it hadn't happened. Her fault, then. Would she have a chance to fulfill the promise this time? A chill of foreboding shook her.

He pulled her to him and kissed her hard before he walked out of the arena with his lawyer and the group of Gambrian officials.

The Sangari arranged for her return to her ship, dropping Alden and Elissa off at a terminus where they could get transport back to their own world.

* * * * *

She didn't see Raje again, but she followed the news vids from Gambria. Reporters informed the universe of the death of the first heir and the return to their world of The Rebel Prince, the former second heir, now first heir. The funeral was a solemn event lasting most of a day and night. Since the Gambrian royals wore face-shrouding gear in public, she didn't get a good view of him. But she listened hungrily to every word spoken about him, and there were plenty of those. Reports on his period of mourning for his father, rehashes of discussions and negotiations with the current regime and finally the newsflash that he'd been granted the council chair normally held by the first heir.

To Devonne, it sounded like a death knell for any future relationship with him.

The news discussions turned to speculation about a marital alliance for the first heir. Those confirmed her belief that any relationship she had with him would be limited to brief, occasional, and likely illicit meetings. Because she didn't think she could take that, she ignored the two messages he sent, some months later, asking to talk with her.

Chapter Nine

Present

Raje emerged from the shuttle bay airlock alone. She'd expected at least a bodyguard or two. He wore plain shirt, tunic and pants, with a pistol at his hip, looking very much as he had the first time she'd seen him. Where were the royal trappings? Had he really argued with his government again and gone back to space piracy with his rebellious friends?

Her heart clenched painfully at the sight of him.

"Your Highness," she said, moving forward to bow. She wanted to throw herself in his arms and kiss him blind but dared not.

"Shit. Can it, Dev," he answered. "I'm Raje to you."

"That was a man I knew a while back. He's no longer around."

"He hasn't gone anywhere." He looked at the rest of her curious crew standing behind her and acknowledged them with a gracious nod. "Can we go somewhere private to talk?"

"It'll have to be my cabin. That's the only private place on the ship."

"It'll do then."

Her small cabin felt crowded with him in it. His presence filled up any space he occupied however big it was. She couldn't help but recall him in the Sangari arena, manipulating that enormous crowd to get what he wanted.

"Why do you want this cargo, Raje? I thought you'd given up piracy. You're respectable now. Acknowledged and accepted as the first heir. Haven't you settled all your differences with your government?"

"All of them? Not by a long shot," he answered. "We still differ on a number of issues. But we're learning how to compromise and work together. Fortunately my uncle's getting old enough to look back and start to consider how history will evaluate him. He doesn't like all he sees in his past and is ready to start trying to put some of it right."

He watched her steadily. The gaze of those beloved yellow-green eyes went straight to her soul.

"Devonne, why do you want this cargo so badly? It's got to be more than the money."

"It is." She paced around the little cabin. Calm. She tried to force herself to it. The combination of his presence and her desperation wouldn't allow it. "I'm at the end of this. The authorities are closing in on me. If I keep it up much longer I'm going to get blasted soon. But my people still need a place of their own. A place they can settle and build homes and communities. A place that will give them a viable future. The Denogrenian treasure is the way to buy that for them. Not the money per se, but what the Denogrenians will exchange to get it back." She stopped and drew a harsh breath. "This is the only way to give my people a real chance at a future. That's why I'm *not* letting you have it. Even if it does cost me my life and my ship."

"I see," he said quietly.

"You'll concede, then?" she asked. "Let me have it?"

"I can't concede. I need that treasure, too."

"Why? Now that you're reconciled to your family, you have all the wealth and gaudy treasure you could possibly want. Why do you need this?"

"As a wedding gift for my future wife."

It hit her like a fist to the gut.

"That was cruel, Raje," she said.

He looked up at her with shock plain on his face. "I'm sorry, I didn't mean it to be." He shook his head. "The lady I want for my wife and consort is being difficult. She refuses to answer my messages or meet with me. She's prickly and difficult and prone to leaping to unwarranted conclusions. She also seriously undervalues what I feel for her. I wanted this treasure to give her, so she'd understand that I'd do anything for her." He paused, watching her face carefully. "It was also a way to get her to talk to me since she's refused to answer my messages or agree to meet me."

It finally penetrated through the layers of her fears and defenses. "Me?" She almost choked getting that one word out.

"Who else?" His expression remained serious. "Who else could there ever be for me? I told you once, the first day we met, that I knew you were the one. I've never changed my mind about that. Everything that's happened since did nothing but convince me even more."

"But... Your government... You're a prince. The first heir. I'm...less than nobody. I don't even have a home other than this ship."

He nodded. "I won't say it's been easy to get them to let me have my way in this. Especially when we're at odds over so many other things. But I finally convinced them I'd be a far better first heir with the most amazing woman I'd ever met at my side, to help me...and to watch my back." He grinned on the last part. "Would you, Devonne? I can function without you if I have to, but I'd rather not. I just feel like more of a man when you're with me. Like you're a part of me that's been missing and I didn't even realize it until I found you. Please? Marry me?"

She had to shake herself out of a daze of disbelief. "I don't know –"

"It won't be easy," he admitted. "Most of the government isn't going to be happy about this. But we can win them over. Together. I'm sure of it. Please? It's going to be a hell of a cold, lonely time if you don't agree. And think of what you can do for your people. You won't even need that treasure to buy them a place. We'll make sure they get justice and reparation of some sort."

"Damn it don't stoop to trying bribery," she told him. "You don't need it. You're enough, in and of yourself. I honestly wish you weren't a prince, but if I have to take the prince to get the man, I'll do it."

"You will?" Disbelief mixed with the elation. "You will?"

"Of course I will. You're a missing part of me, too!"

He grabbed her and danced her around the small space then tipped her onto the bed. In the frenzy of kisses that followed, they managed to get out of their clothes, shedding a few more buttons from her uniform in the process, and then they joined their bodies together in the whole they were meant to be. Months of celibacy left them with a ravening hunger for each other that couldn't wait long for fulfillment.

He pumped into and out of her only a few times before they came together in a furious climax that had them both bucking and shouting.

When it was done, they lay together, panting but fulfilled.

"That was…amazing. For a start. But should we tell your crew before or after the long, sweet loving?" he asked.

"They can wait," Devonne said, reaching for him and holding his face near hers. "I can't."

About the Author

Katherine welcomes comments from readers. You can find her website and email address on her author bio page at www.ellorascave.com.

Also by Katherine Kingston

Binding Passion

Crown Jewels (*anthology*)

Daring Passion

Dominant Boys of Summer

Equinox (*anthology*)

Gargoyle's Christmas

Glimmer Quest: Bronzequest

Glimmer Quest: Silverquest

Healing Passion

Holiday Heat (*anthology*)

Ruling Passion

CONCUBINE'S REVENGE

Arianna Hart

Dedication

This book is dedicated with deepest appreciation for my husband, Paul, who went above and beyond the call of duty so I could get it written. And to the makers of children's videos everywhere, for the same reason.

Special thanks also go out to my wonderful editor, Briana, for working into the wee hours of the night to get it edited on time. I appreciate everything you do for me!

Chapter One

Beta Quadrant, year 2812

Captain Drake Cantor set a course for the pleasure planet Gamoras and engaged the autopilot with a sigh of relief. He was finally getting a much-needed break from patrolling the space around Tramin. Finally getting away from the orders of idiot council members. Ever since the Emperor of Emeraldia got kidnapped, the counselors were scared of their own shadows and afraid to fly without an armed contingent surrounding them.

Like he didn't have better things to do with his time and training than baby-sit some rich bastards as they flitted around space. He should be flying on patrol, not escorting terrified counselors who were afraid of getting kidnapped. It was a good thing he was getting some time to blow off steam. If he had to listen to one more old fart complain, he'd wind up court-martialed for insubordination.

No, going to Gamoras and getting a little wild was just the cure he needed to keep from ending up in the brig. And getting wild was what the pleasure planet was all about. Drake had enough credits to pursue every fantasy he could dream up and maybe find a few more. Gambling, drinking and nightclubs featuring exotic entertainment were only half the attraction. Getting laid as often as possible was the real reason he was zipping through space like his ass was on fire.

It had been longer than Drake could remember since he'd had a nice bout of sweaty, no-holds-barred sex. His last tumble with one of the civilians on Tramin had been something less than memorable. When the lady started pushing for a longer relationship he'd had to cut and run for his life.

Long-term commitment wasn't on his list of things to accomplish any time soon. Drake had too much lust for living—or just plain lust—to confine himself to one woman. Someday he'd settle down but some day was off in the distant future and Gamoras was in his sights now.

"Look out, ladies, here I come!" Drake's dick pressed against the fly of his leather pants as he thought about the variety of women he'd meet and fuck on Gamoras.

He was so busy thinking about sinking his cock into multiple women that he almost missed the alarm alerting him to an unfriendly on his tail.

The blast to his rudder managed to capture his attention.

"What the *feck* was that?" Drake's eyes flew over the control panel to assess the damage to his flyer. The electrical system threw sparks everywhere and the emergency override was already activated. Before he could take stock of exactly what happened, Drake felt the unmistakable pull of a tractor beam drawing him ever closer to his enemy.

Hitting the emergency distress beacon, Drake scrambled to wrestle control away from the beam but it was too late. His flyer lost power by the nanosecond and the more he fought the pull, the more power he lost. If he continued to fight the tractor beam he could very well destroy his ship and spill out into open space.

Drake pulled his oxygen supply over his head and strapped a homing device to his wrist. The emergency beacon would send out a distress call and his superiors should be able to locate his whereabouts from the signal on the homing device. *Should* being the operative word. He'd heard from more than one flyer about the shoddy manufacturing and crappy performance of their equipment.

There was nothing he could do about that now. It either worked or it didn't, in any case he was in a butt-load of trouble and had no one to blame but himself. Drake looked at the ship that drew him into its grip.

The thing was enormous! It was an older model, round and flat with makeshift patches all over it. The ship must be running on stealth mode because Drake hadn't picked it up on his radar until it was too late. Pieces of metal stuck out at odd angles. Those couldn't be part of the original ship. As he got closer he could see puffs of smoke seeping out crevices near the yawning maw of the docking bay. Lights flickered all over the ship in no recognizable pattern.

He'd been captured by a flying junk heap.

* * * * *

"Flyer is secured in the bay, Cap'n. Whadda want to do with the pilot?"

Triona turned from the wires she was splicing together to get the bay doors to stay shut and looked at the nervously shuffling first mate waiting by the door.

"Bring him here and let me interrogate him. If we can get some money out of him we'll ransom him off and if not we'll either drop him at the next station or recruit him. Same as always." This wasn't rocket science. They'd been offering the same choices now for the last five years.

The first mate shuffled his feet a little more. "Beggin' your pardon but this is a little different case, Cap'n."

Finally getting the connection made, Triona tied it off and gave the mate her full attention. "How is it different, Smudge?"

"Well, this is no civilian. This time we captured ourselves a genuine Squad Leader of the Traminian army."

"So? If he doesn't have the money to pay his way free, we'll drop him off and be long gone before he can do anything about it." An idea that held definite appeal. Just the word "Traminian" made her gut clench in anger and remembered pain.

Smudge bobbed his head a few times and swallowed so hard his Adam's apple jumped in his throat. "Ah, it might be too late for that. If he followed procedure he'll have already sent out a homing signal."

"Sparks!" Triona activated the ship-wide intercom on her wrist, "prepare for hyperdrive. Repeat. Prepare for hyperdrive."

The mate scuttled off the bridge of the ship as Triona strapped herself into the pilot's chair. If they didn't hit warp speed soon the homing device would zero in on the ship's ID and their identity would be spread across the galaxy faster than *limfa* hair in an exhaust fan.

Triona's fingers flew over the control panel, plotting a course deep in the Beta Quad. Unless this guy was the Military Commander, no rescue mission would try to find him where she was going.

Drake paced the confines of the tiny cell where he'd been confined. He hadn't been hurt—yet—but that didn't mean he wasn't going to be. He'd felt the force of a hyper-jump and knew they'd hit warp speed some time ago. His homing device was worthless now.

Not that it would have done him any good anyway. The tales of unsuspecting spacefarers who had been captured, robbed and jettisoned into space like so much bilge ran rampant around the Beta Quad. High Command wasn't going to waste valuable resources on some idiot Squad Leader who'd been too horny to pay attention to his own radar.

How could he have been so stupid? Drake kicked at the wall of his pen and swore. If he was lucky he'd just get spaced. If he was unlucky they'd torture him first.

The door opened with a hiss and the twitching pirate who had hauled him out of his flyer came in.

"The cap'n will see you now, boy." He nudged at him with a laser. A second pirate, a gangly redhead who didn't look old enough to shave, stood behind him with another laser. They weren't taking any chances with him.

Drake wisely kept his mouth shut. It wasn't like he could say much in the position he was in anyway. He'd wait until he met this captain and see if he was open to negotiations. Maybe Drake could bargain his way out of this mess.

As he walked through the corridors, Drake kept his eyes open for any possible weapon. He passed by several nasty-looking pirates carrying multiple weapons, all of which were trained on him. Great. For the time being he'd have to remain docile and wait for an opportunity to present itself.

It wasn't going to be a pleasant wait.

Drake followed the pirate's grunted directions until he came to the bow of the ship. He clenched his teeth as the pirate pushed him into the chair. It was all he could do to keep from lashing out as restraints clamped down around his wrists. The only thing that kept him from fighting back was the laser trained on his back. Even knowing he was out-gunned and out-numbered it wasn't easy to keep his temper in check as he waited to meet the pirate that held his fate in his hands.

"Stars help you, boy. You're going to need all the help you can get." The pirate scampered off with a cackle. The redhead followed him silently.

Trapped in the chair with nothing to look at but the ship's console in front of him, Drake tried to get an idea of where in space they were. None of the usual navigational equipment was in sight. In fact, the entire console looked like it had been pieced together from parts of other ships with nothing lining up the right way. The long console had once been white but now looked a rather dismal gray color. The wide vid screen had scratches all over it distorting his view of space and the seat he was strapped into had been patched and repaired several times over.

The restraints seemed to be in working order though.

He was craning his neck to try to get a glimpse of what looked like an Imperial seal on the hyper-drive when boot heels clanked behind him. The tread was slow and deliberate. Whoever this captain was, he was in no rush to get here.

"So what do we have here? Smells like Traminian scum to me." The voice was low and husky but nowhere near manly.

Drake kept his mouth shut. He'd speak with the captain and no one else. With teeth clenched to keep back any hasty retorts, Drake waited for the woman behind him to make her game known.

"What? *Limpa* got your tongue? Don't you have anything to say?" The voice whispered right into his ear, sending a jolt of lust to his cock in spite of the situation.

"I'll say my piece to the captain, not to his doxy," Drake answered, mad at his traitorous body and the game-playing vixen behind him.

"Then let's hear it, Traminian. I'm Triona Fallon, captain of *The Bunny's Revenge*, and you're my prisoner.

Drake's mouth dropped open as the captain came into view and leaned against the console in front of him. Short, jet-black hair that jutted out in spikes caught his attention first. The women he was used to had hair down to their butts. It was almost as if she'd cut her hair as short as possible to remove any traces of her femininity.

If she was trying to look like a man, she failed miserably. Violet eyes stared at him framed by mile-long eyelashes. Her face was as delicate as the porcelain dolls his mother kept locked behind glass. The high cheekbones, slightly upturned nose and stubborn chin didn't mesh with the violent hatred blazing from her eyes.

Her body was more suited for the pleasure houses on Gamoras than flying around in this junk heap. She wore a man's white shirt, long sleeved and laced up tight in front but no amount of male garb could hide the generous breasts under the shirt. Tight black pants drew his eyes to her tiny waist and flared hips, leading down to long legs.

She couldn't have been more than five feet six inches but she had a *feck* of a lot of body packed into those inches. The laser pointed at his chest was so incongruous with the concubine's body behind it Drake was struck dumb.

"Well? Still have nothing to say?"

"You're a woman?" was all he could utter.

"Very observant. No wonder you made it to Squad Leader." She twirled the laser in her hands.

"What are you going to do with me?" His libido knew what he wanted her to do with him. His cock stirred even more. *Feck*! That's what had gotten him into this mess in the first place.

"That depends on you. How many credits do you have?" She practically smirked at him.

"I'm a Squad Leader, not a damn counselor. I don't have much."

"That's too bad," she shook her head but the smirk stayed in place. "'Cause you see, if you can't pay the ransom, you'll have to be spaced." She didn't seem that upset about the possibility.

"Wait a minute! Maybe there's an alternative here." Drake's mind spun in circles trying to figure out a way out of this mess. "Maybe I can earn my freedom in trade."

"That depends on what you have to trade, Traminian."

Drake looked around the bow trying to think of something she'd need. He knew what he needed but somehow he didn't think she'd go for good sex in exchange for his life.

"I know my way around a ship. I can do some repairs for you." Maybe. It would take a lot more than what he knew to make this tub space-worthy.

"I take care of all the repairs on board. Try again."

The laser focused on his head as she moved closer. Anger swelled in his chest and he bit out, "I could trade sexual favors for my life."

Triona's fingers worked furiously on the control board to keep the power flowing to the chair that held the Traminian. She had a feeling if the power died and he was free of the restraints her laser wouldn't be enough to hold him off. She hadn't been paying much attention to his suggestions as she had every intention of getting rid of him no matter how much money he could come up with. He didn't have to know she was going to dump him on a station somewhere instead of in open space. His suggestion of trading sex for freedom had taken her by surprise and she struggled to keep the shock off her face.

"You'd be my concubine?" Tying off the last wire, she prayed it would hold because she needed to get away from his dark-blue gaze.

She strolled behind him to get a better look without being observed. He had hair almost as black as hers but where hers was cut short, his brushed the tops of his shoulders. Broad, muscular shoulders that strained the seams of his uniform shirt. His hands were clenched into fists at his sides and she prayed the restraints held under the force of his anger.

"I was being sarcastic." A muscle twitched in his jaw as she circled him. Stars above he was big! His thighs were easily twice the size of hers and his chest looked hard enough to bounce credit chips on.

"No. I think that idea has merit." She circled him again. The cosmic irony of a Traminian acting as *her* concubine was too delicious to dismiss out of hand. After years of being held against her will, bowing and scraping to the whims of a vicious old man, the chance to be the one in charge was very, very tempting.

Just because he was the best looking man she'd seen in her entire life didn't factor into the decision at all. *Yeah, right.*

"So, you'd be my sex slave in return for your life, huh? I think I need to see a demonstration first."

"A demonstration?" One raven-black eyebrow lifted.

"Yes. I want to know you're worth the effort to keep you around until I get sick of you or you earn your freedom."

"That's kind of hard to do without my hands. If you release my bonds I can show you a demonstration you'll never forget."

His cock bulged impressively and Triona felt a gush of fluid between her legs. What would it be like to have sex because she wanted to, not because it was her purpose in life?

"Oh, I don't think so. There's lots you can do without moving from your spot." She should know. She'd been tied up more times than she cared to remember.

Forcing the revulsion aside, she swung a leg over his thighs and prayed the electrical restraints held. "Show me what you've got, Traminian." She ran her hand over his face and slipped her fingers into his silky hair.

His eyes blazed with fury as she tipped his face up but his cock jumped under her ass as she settled on his lap. He might be pissed as hell but his body wanted her. Her pulse raced as she lowered her lips to his. She'd never kissed anyone of her own volition before.

The first touch of her mouth to his caused a flutter of wings to explode in her stomach. He held his mouth in an unyielding line, his lips flat and tight.

"Come on, Traminian, you're not making a very strong case for your survival here." She licked a line along the seam of his lips and savored the taste of him. Her hips rocked against his erection and sparks shot through her clit at the contact.

With a moan of surrender, his lips softened and pressed against hers. His tongue darted out to taste her mouth. Shock waves swamped her and made her lightheaded. Triona felt her nipples tighten against her shirt as her breasts grew full and heavy. She rubbed them against his chest to ease the ache but the friction only made the need worse.

Every nerve ending she possessed screamed out for *more*! Heat radiated from low in her stomach outward, setting fires in her pussy that burned for him. She tipped her head back and his lips trailed down the column of her throat until the restraints stopped him.

"If you let me go, we can continue this in a much more pleasurable manner," he murmured against the hollow of her throat.

For two heartbeats Triona considered letting him go and exploring this attraction deeper. Luckily good sense reasserted itself and she shook off the urge to release him.

"I don't think so, Traminian. Your kind can't be trusted." She swung her leg off his lap and moved away.

"You think I'd run away? After that?"

"I know you'd say or do anything that would help you get your way. You see, I've dealt with Traminians for a long time. I know what lying bastards you are. The way I see it, you can either agree to be my slave and live or you can choose to go out with the garbage in the next dump run." She leaned back against the console feigning indifference but her hands shook and her pulse raced.

The foundation of her being had been rocked by that one kiss and she wasn't sure if she wanted him to agree to be spaced or be her slave. Part of her screamed with joy at finding a piece of her that had been lost for so long. It argued that she could use him and dump him at the nearest space station. The logical part of her brain told her keeping this Traminian would be nothing but trouble.

His hands clenched into fists and the muscles in his arms strained against the bonds. She knew exactly what he struggled with right now. Was it better to die fighting for your freedom or live and lose your soul? Her conscience lashed her for forcing this choice on him. Was it right to do this to someone who'd never hurt her?

Yes! He was a Traminian! His planet subjugated women like her for centuries. They'd had no crisis of conscience when they stole her from her family and forced her to be a concubine. Why should she regret forcing one of them to do the same thing?

She pushed aside the weakness in her resolve and stood up straighter. This was the best revenge she could ever have and *feck* it, she was taking it.

"So what's it going to be? My bed or the garbage heap?"

Chapter Two

Drake's whole body pushed against the clamps that held him hostage. If he ever got his hands on that violet-eyed witch he'd do more than fuck her. He'd rip her limb from limb! She stood there looking like she didn't give a shit what he decided to do.

Shards, how he wanted to tell her he'd take his chance in space but his instinct for survival wouldn't let him. As long as he lived he could escape. But oh how he wanted to wipe that smug look off her beautiful face.

She stood there looking like she didn't give a *toradal's* ass what he did, even as her chest heaved and her nipples poked through her shirt. His blood still burned from feeling those delicate points rubbing him. What would it be like to have them in his hands or in his mouth?

His cock was so full it was painful. It didn't care that she was using him, it just wanted to sink inside her. Hell, if he'd met her on Gamoras he'd have fucked her in a second and not thought twice about it. Why was this so different? He might even be able to work it to his advantage. He'd been known as a charmer when he cared to exert himself. Maybe he could charm her into letting him go.

Once he was free he'd hunt her down and put *her* in the chair. And he'd do a hell of a lot more than just kiss her.

"Well? I'm waiting?" She tapped her foot impatiently.

A surge of anger flared up but he forced it back down. Patience, he needed to be patient. His turn would come. "I guess it looks like you have yourself a body slave, Mistress." The words tasted bitter in his mouth.

"Don't call me that!"

He could have sworn a look of terror crossed her face before she got herself back under control.

She strolled up to him and ran her fingers through his hair. "We don't have to be that formal. You can call me Captain, like my crew does. In private I'll let you call me Triona, if you're good." She trailed a finger over his chest and unlaced the ties of his shirt.

More blood drained from his head and pooled in his dick at the feel of her hands on his bare skin. "I can guarantee I'll be very good."

"Oh, I'm sure you will be. Your life depends on it, Traminian."

"If we're going to be on a first name basis, you can call me Drake." Fury warred with lust in his body.

"We'll see."

The smell of smoke drifted through his flared nostrils. Drake had a minute to wonder what it was before Triona hit the intercom button on the console. "Smudge! Take our *guest* to my cabin. I'll deal with him personally, later."

"Aye, aye, Cap'n!" came the tinny reply.

The pirate must have been waiting right outside the door because he was there in seconds. Drake forced his muscles to relax even though the laser jabbed him in the ribs.

"Come on, Traminian."

"Oh, and Smudge, make sure he's locked in securely. And set a guard on the door. I'd hate for him to get any ideas he could charm his way out of his bargain."

His eyes flew to her face. A smug grin told him she knew what he was thinking. *Feck!* She'd be on her guard against him now. Time to come up with a Plan B.

Triona watched Smudge prod the Traminian—Drake—out the door and down the cramped corridor. As soon as he was out of sight she pulled the control panel off the overheated wires and yanked them apart. The lights in the bridge dimmed briefly then flared to life again.

With deft skill, she repaired the faulty connection and replaced the panel. Fingers that used to twist her hair into intricate braids now spliced electrical lines and pulled the trigger on laser guns. She looked down at her hands. An abundance of grease sat under the split and torn nails. Cuts and scrapes in various stages of healing covered her knuckles and scattered scars traced all the way up her arms.

Her battered hands were a far cry from the dainty, well-manicured digits she used to have. Triona rubbed her brutally short hair and smiled to herself. The pathetic creature who had hair down to her ass and was afraid to do more than rage silently was long gone.

Good riddance.

Her spirit had been all but broken by the mistress who had trained her and then her master. If it hadn't been for a kernel of strength she carried deep inside she'd never have managed to escape. The world—or at least the Traminian family that owned her—thought her dead and gone. Truthfully, the girl she'd been had died. In her place stood Captain Fallon, owner of *The Bunny's Revenge* and head of a ragtag crew of losers and misfits just like herself.

And now sole possessor of the first male concubine. Would he still be called a bunny? She snickered to herself at the thought of a man like Drake answering to "Bunny". Stars knew she'd hated the term with every ounce of her being.

Flopping down in the captain's chair, Triona watched the stars go by as they cruised through space. Drake's arrival had stirred up memories she'd thought buried too deeply to ever surface again. She wished they had stayed in their graves.

"The prisoner's secure, Cap'n," Smudge said from the doorway.

"Good. We'll let him stew for a while. Any problems?" She busied herself with the navigational system but all her attention was on the first mate's words.

"Not a peep. Lay down meek as a lamb when I told him to go on the bed. I found an old slave collar and strapped it on him. Here's the control for it. I tested it a bit myself to make sure it works. You should have no problem tickling your fancy with him now," he cackled.

Disgust rolled through Triona as she held the tiny remote that would keep her safe from Drake. Just looking at it sent a surge of nausea to her throat. She could practically feel the burning pain shoot through her body as she slipped it in her pocket.

"Where did you get a controller?" They had plenty of collars from the slaves they'd freed over the years. Every time they boarded a ship for ransom the first thing she did was free any concubines or slaves she found. But where had Smudge gotten the remote?

"I picked it from the pocket of one of those dandies in the Beta Quad. He was usin' it to practically kill his slave, so I relieved him of it. Bastard."

Smudge rubbed the back of his neck and Triona knew he relived some painful memories of his own.

"Don't know why I kept it, but it'll come in handy now, won't it, Cap'n?"

"Yes. Very handy." She fought to keep the tremor out of her voice. Could she really use it on someone else? Even a Traminian? She prayed it wasn't put to the test.

"If you don't need anything else, I'm gonna go down to the mess and grab a bite. You want anything?"

"No thanks. I'll stay here and man the bridge. You eat and get some rest." Food was the very last thing on her mind.

"Yes, ma'am, Cap'n."

Triona waited for Smudge to make his way down to the mess hall. It was a grandiose term for a miniscule galley and bench seating for the crew but that's what the former owner, O'Brien, had called it so that's what she called it.

She wondered what O'Brien would think of her dealings with Drake. He'd been a gnarly old reprobate with the heart of a marshmallow. Triona smiled to herself as she remembered the fear he'd struck in his enemies. If they ever knew what a pushover he'd been, they'd deny it to their very graves.

Would O'Brien see the irony in her, a former concubine, keeping a Traminian officer a slave? Or would he be disappointed in her for treating someone else the way she was treated? He'd probably laugh over it at first as long as she let Drake go after a little while. It wasn't like he never kept prisoners.

Hell, she'd been O'Brien's prisoner herself for a little while anyway. With no one to pay her ransom—or at least no one she was willing to call—she'd been given the choice to join the crew or "walk the plank". There hadn't really been a plank but she didn't know that.

She'd run away from her new master the first time he took her off Tramin and had hopped aboard the first ship she could find. Just her luck that it was attacked before she'd even been discovered stowing away.

It was the best thing that had ever happened to her.

O'Brien had given her the first chance at a future that didn't involve selling her soul. She'd scrubbed floors, cooked, done dishes, washed clothes and done all the other dirty work asked of her without complaint. After a while O'Brien began teaching her how to pilot the ship. From there she'd learned the basic electrical work it took to keep the ship in the air. Other crew members had come and gone but Triona had found her spot and wouldn't leave if she had any choice in the matter.

Triona stroked the console lovingly. This was her baby now and she'd protect it with her dying breath. Being a space pirate wasn't the most moral job in the universe but it sure as hell beat being a concubine. Besides, she only took money from those who could afford it and she rarely had to kill anyone. It wasn't like she was evil or anything.

The slave controller fell out of her pocket and stared at her accusingly. "I haven't used it yet!" But the question was, would she?

Pushing out of the chair she paced in frustration. Why did she feel so damn guilty over this? *He* was the one who suggested trading his sexual favors for his freedom, not her. This shouldn't be so complicated. She'd use Drake and let him go at the next space station. He didn't have to know that she wasn't going to keep him forever like his people would have.

Her conscience eased a bit at her decision. She owed the Traminians some payback. She didn't have to tell Drake she was letting him go. Let him sweat for a little while. It was the least she could do after the years they'd stolen from her. That was small enough revenge for what the Traminians had done to her.

She picked the controller up and put it back in her pocket. It was possible she'd need to use it on Drake but stars she hoped not. The electrical shock wouldn't kill him but it would be very painful. Her hands shook at the memory of those pulses sizzling through her. She'd been zapped for the most minor of infractions.

The memory hardened her resolve and she threw her shoulders back. She might not be as heartless as her former master but she'd damn sure make Drake think she was. He'd stirred up all these *fecking* feelings and he could help her exorcise them.

Triona checked the time. Smudge would be relieving her soon. And when he did, she'd try out her new slave.

* * * * *

Drake's fingers felt bruised from struggling with the collar. No matter how hard he tried to pry the thing off it wouldn't budge. A *fecking* slave collar. How many times had he seen the upper classes walking through the market with their slaves attached and felt a surge of envy?

Owning concubines was one of the many perks that came with being rich in Tramin. Only the most beautiful girls were chosen to be concubines and the more money a man had, the larger his stable of women could be. Drake had sworn one day he'd have enough money to afford a bunny of his own.

But that was different! They were raised to be slaves, not captured. There were laws governing the treatment of concubines. Triona could do anything she wanted to him and he had no recourse. He was trapped with her for as long as she wanted, which could be forever.

No! He wasn't trapped forever. Just for now. He couldn't let hopelessness take hold or he'd be screwed. Sure, Triona had caught on to his plan to charm his way to freedom but that didn't mean it wasn't going to work.

Before he could think of another plan, Triona opened the door and strolled in like she was entering a ballroom instead of a rundown, dinky cabin. The room only had the one bunk, a sanitation unit and a storage unit but she acted like it was the ritziest suite in space.

"Have you had a chance to come to terms with your decision?"

She tapped a tiny controller in her hands and Drake flinched. The twitchy pirate she called Smudge had "tested" it on him when he first applied the collar and the pain almost made him wet his pants.

"Nothing to say?" She moved closer to him and ran her fingers lightly over his face and down his bare arm. Anger churned in his gut even as his dick began to harden.

Smudge had stripped him down before he'd locked him in the room. Like he had anywhere else to go?

"I'm afraid I don't know what to say. I've never been a slave before."

"That's okay, Traminian, I can teach you."

She untucked her shirt and stripped off her pants. Against his will, Drake felt desire stir as he watched her bare skin emerge a finger's width at a time.

"First of all, you must never disagree with me. Second, you must obey my every wish. And third, you must act like you enjoy it no matter how much you're dying inside."

Her eyes turned cold for a minute. It didn't take a genius to figure out that she knew firsthand what a slave should do. If the name of her ship, *The Bunny's Revenge,* didn't clue him in than he wasn't quite as smart as he thought he was.

"You sound like you know what you're talking about." Maybe he could play on her sympathy to let him go? She was a woman and they were soft by nature. If he played her right maybe she'd realize how unfair she was being and let him go.

"I was a concubine for a Traminian overlord for six years. I know more than I ever want to about being a slave."

So much for that idea. If he'd been a slave for six years he'd be out for revenge too. Hell, he'd been a slave for two hours and he was ready to rip her throat out.

"So you see, I know exactly what you're thinking right now. You're thinking, 'did I make the right choice? Would a quick death be better than a life of sex on command? Can I go through with this now that all is said and done'? Am I right?"

She looked him right in the eye as she unlaced her shirt and let it fall to the floor. Her breasts were even bigger and more beautiful than he'd guessed and the moisture dried in his mouth. His traitorous cock throbbed and fire burned in his veins.

"Close. Only I know I can go through with it. If you promise not to zap me with that thing, I'll show you."

Triona's eyes widened a bit when she looked at his rock-hard cock.

"I guess you can go through with it at that."

Her nipples hardened into tight little points and Drake knew she was as aroused as he was. Slowly and carefully he got off the narrow bunk and approached her. Her finger hovered over the controller but she didn't back away from him. As he neared her he could smell the musk of her juices along with an undertone of some floral scent. A pirate who wore perfume?

"Is it permissible for me to touch you? Or should I lie back and think of Tramin?"

A ghost of a smile crossed her face and dimples flashed briefly in her cheeks. "It would please me to have you touch me. But just so we understand each other, I'll hold onto the remote."

The thought of the electrical current going through him again cooled his ardor some. If she zapped him while he touched her, she'd get hit too but maybe she figured it was worth the risk to keep him in line. She knew a lot more about the stupid collars than he did. Man, talk about a buzz-kill. He could feel his dick lose some of its rigidity at the idea of her wearing one of the slave controllers but at the first touch of her fingers on his neck he forgot the threat hanging over his head.

"Kiss me, Drake." She pulled his head down to hers and raised herself on tiptoes to meet him.

"Yes, ma'am." Drake wrapped his arms around her waist and let his fingers drift close to the creamy cheeks of her behind.

Her breasts scorched his skin like hot lasers. It had been far too long since he'd felt the smooth skin of a woman against him. His lips met hers and he poured all his frustrated rage and desire into the kiss, telling her without words how much he needed her and how much he hated it.

Hate it or love it, he craved her like no other. His mind screamed at him for offering himself up as a sacrificial virgin but his body reminded him he was *far* from virginal. He may not like the situation he was in but his hormones thought it was a dream come true.

Triona slid a hand along his back, tracing the muscles along his spine. Her touch was almost tentative at first but she soon grew bolder. Drake's blood heated as she gripped his ass and pulled him closer. He could feel the fluff of curls between her legs against his thighs and the friction caused a million tiny explosions to burst in his balls.

"Am I permitted to touch you?" he murmured against her lips.

Her breath came in heated gasps and her eyes glittered seductively behind her long eyelashes. "Please do."

Drake trailed his lips down her throat and over her delicate collarbone. He could feel the heat pouring off her skin as he moved closer to her breasts. He'd been fantasizing about touching those delicious mounds since she first pressed them against him.

Cupping the weight of them in his hands, he gently kneaded them as he admired their shape. Dusky rose nipples pebbled out and just begged to be touched. Drake let his hands drift over her breasts in circles, growing closer and closer to those tempting points with each circuit.

Finally his fingers reached them and he knelt down to get his mouth level with them. Talk about a great view! Drake would gladly spend hours worshiping at the altar of her beauty just to be able to touch her this way. All rational thoughts about resisting his captivity or forming plans of escape went by the wayside as he drew one swollen bud into his mouth.

A sharp gasp slipped from Triona at the first touch of his tongue on her nipple. He smiled to himself as he sucked harder. The musky smell of her arousal drifted up to him, spurring his own desire mercilessly.

With one last lick Drake kissed his way to the other nipple and drew that one into his mouth. He used one hand to gently pinch her sensitized point then smooth the tiny pain away. She moaned as he bit down lightly then laved the sting. Her hips arched against his chest and he knew he had her on the edge.

As slowly as he could with lust pounding in his veins, he nibbled his way down her stomach and over the arch of her hips. Briefly, he rubbed his face against her pussy before moving onto her thighs. His fingers teased her legs at the sensitive spot below her ass.

A quick look up made him draw in a sharp breath. Triona's head was thrown back and her face carried a look of rapture that he'd never seen before. It was like she was experiencing passion for the first time and reveling in it.

He kept his eyes glued on her face as he came closer to her clitoris. When he speared the nubbin with his tongue her whole face tensed in anticipation. Her fingers clutched his head and brought him closer to her slick lips.

Drake needed no further encouragement to give her hot pussy his complete attention. She tasted like the sweetest honey rolling over his tongue. He slipped one finger inside her channel and groaned as her inner muscles gripped him. What would it feel like to have those walls clenching his dick?

More fluid gushed from her as he drove his finger in and out of her sheath. He could feel her body tense as he swirled his tongue around her clit and sweat popped out on his forehead. He was damn close to losing control but fought it back. He refused to come before his cock ever made it inside her body.

Triona let out a wordless cry before her knees buckled and she slumped to the floor next to him.

"You act like this is your first orgasm," he whispered, licking her swollen nub one more time. He kissed his way up her body before pushing his legs between her unresisting thighs.

"It is." Her voice was faint and slightly breathless.

"It won't be your last." Drake didn't have the brain cells left to think about her astounding revelation. His entire being urged him to drive himself inside her until he was sheathed to the very hilt. "Do I have permission to fuck your brains out?" he asked. If she said no he'd lose his *fecking* mind.

"Absolutely." Her eyes glittered at him, full of passion and expectation.

He really hoped he could last long enough to fulfill those expectations. She brought her knees up to encourage him and he groaned as her pussy lips teased the head of his cock. He slipped easily through her slick walls and fought back the urge to let go with all the need driving through him.

Almost hesitantly her legs slid up around his waist. Her hands clutched his shoulders. Drake buried his face in the hollow of her neck and struggled for control. When he thought he could move again without exploding he slowly pulled out. Her wetness made an audible slurp as he drew out and pushed back in again. His sac slapped against her as he increased the tempo and added another goad to his already straining restraint.

Triona's head whipped back and forth on the floor and her hips bucked beneath him. Her short nails dug into his skin but he didn't mind a bit.

"Faster!" she cried breathlessly.

"Yes, ma'am." He gripped her curvy hips in his hands and slammed himself inside her pussy.

She uttered a sharp cry of pleasure and pushed up against him, setting a pace guaranteed to push him over the edge. His blood caught fire as he drove himself into her over and over again. Sweat dripped off his brow as he tried to hold back the orgasm building at the base of his cock.

Suddenly she froze beneath him, unmoving. Her inner walls spasmed against his cock and her body shuddered under him as her orgasm swamped over her. Drake silently thanked the stars she came first because he couldn't hold back his own climax a second longer.

His seed shot from his cock with all the power of an ion cannon. She milked his length drawing out his orgasm longer than he ever thought possible. And still her body shook beneath him.

"Are you okay?" he asked finally, slipping from her with a groan.

"Oh yeah," she said with a smile.

He rolled off her and she stretched languorously. A look of utter satisfaction crossed her face before she got to her feet. With a flick of her wrist she opened a sanitation unit and stepped in. The bright light swept over her and she stepped out a moment later looking refreshed.

Drake got up a little slower, still recovering from the mind-blowing experience he'd had. He'd never connected with a woman like that before. Hell, he'd never experienced anything like that before. There was something to be said for delayed gratification.

"You can have the bunk, I need to get back up to the bridge," she said as she pulled her shirt over her head.

That snapped Drake out of his lust-induced haze. "What?"

"I won't need you again tonight, so you can go to sleep if you want," she said tying the laces of her shirt and hiding those beautiful breasts from him.

What the feck? She was just going to *leave*? Wham bam you're welcome ma'am? Anger at her callous attitude burned in his gut. How could she just pick up and go? She was almost fully dressed and he stood naked, still stunned. He knew she'd had her first orgasm, she'd told him so. Didn't she want to try it again?

Which reminded him of something. "How is it possible that someone who was a concubine for six years only now had her first orgasm? Isn't sex your stock in trade?"

Hurt flashed across her face and he almost felt bad for his sharp words but anger quickly replaced the pain in her eyes.

"Yet another reason to hate your kind."

She strapped the laser to her leg before sauntering out of the room without a backward look.

Chapter Three

Rage burned inside Triona's breast as she stalked to the bridge. She wasn't due on deck for another hour but she couldn't be in the room with Drake a second longer.

"Go get some sleep Smudge, I'll take over for the rest of the watch."

"Huh? I figured you'd be holed up with that boy toy of yours all night," he cackled.

"Well you figured wrong."

Smudge knew when to shut up and get out and that was exactly what he did. Triona ignored his questioning glances and puttered with the console until he shuffled his way out. Her hands clenched into fists and she pounded the arms of her chair.

Damn them! She'd had two masters and neither one had shown her that sex could be pleasurable! At best it hadn't been painful. The worst didn't bear remembering. The bruises from their abuse may have faded but the scars on her soul would never heal.

For six years she'd catered to every whim of her master and his son. In all that time neither one of them touched her pussy except to shove their miniscule penises into her. She'd been expected to obey every disgusting thing they could think of and never once had they bothered to show her that sex could be like *that*.

Since she'd been free she hadn't bothered to pursue a sexual relationship. She'd had none of the desire other women spoke of when they talked about sex. Ha! All this time she thought it was something wrong with *her*. That her failure to enjoy pleasures of the flesh was *her* problem.

Her only problem was having selfish bastards for owners. Bastards who obviously had no idea what to do with a woman's body. A remembered shiver of ecstasy shot through her. Drake knew *exactly* what to do.

She'd never felt like this before. It was hard to remember that it was only a physical act, not a sign of deeper emotion. Drake was still looking for a way out of his predicament. He may have screwed her brains out but that didn't mean he had feelings for her. She had to keep that in mind and not foolishly let down her guard.

But stars above! All this time she'd been denying herself such pleasure and she hadn't even known it. She'd always wondered why women bothered getting married if it wasn't for financial reasons. Now she knew. It wasn't all about humiliation and abuse. The man wasn't the only one who could feel pleasure.

Any guilt she felt for keeping Drake captive she easily pushed aside. Oh no, it was way too soon to think about setting him free. She had years to make up for and he was the unlucky one who would pay the price.

Not so very unlucky though, now that she thought about it. He'd gotten some pleasure from the coupling. The semen running down her leg after he finished was proof of that.

A tiny voice in the back of her mind argued with her that he'd had no choice but to perform, she'd held the controller the whole time. Triona pushed the censoring voice aside. He'd have no reservations about forcing her to have sex with him if the situations were reversed. She'd heard the way Traminian men talked enviously about owning concubines. For some it was the ultimate status symbol.

For her it had been a living hell. Ripped from her home at the age of fifteen, she'd been coached and trained on how to please a man—whether she wanted to or not. She'd learned the complicated dances Traminian men expected, how to bring the ultimate amount of pleasure to her master and how to make herself as desirable as possible. At seventeen she'd been sold to the highest bidder in a sale that still gave her nightmares. All those men looking at her with greedy eyes while she was displayed for their pleasure.

Her breasts had been squeezed, her ass pinched and her teeth examined. Then once she went home with her "master" she had to obey his every command instantly. If she was a second too slow to obey she'd get slapped or shocked from the collar. Endless nights of misery played over in her mind. She remembered sobbing silently while she performed oral sex on an old man who smelled of sickness and disease. Her body ached from the memories of countless beatings that left bruises in places no one else could see.

No one had helped her. There had been no mercy shown her, why should she show any toward this Traminian just because he'd awakened her to the pleasures of her own body?

"Smudge sent me up here. Told me to get you in a better mood," Drake said from behind her.

Triona jumped at his voice and automatically aimed her laser in his direction.

"Don't shoot!" He raised his hands to show he was unarmed. "I've disappointed a girl or two in my past but they never tried to shoot me over it."

He walked closer to her, the overhead light glinting off the dark hair of his chest. Smudge must have only given him his pants in hopes that seeing his naked chest would make her feel better.

She didn't know about better but his well-muscled chest made her feel something for star's sake!

"Does Smudge expect you to fuck me out of my mood?" she asked, holstering her gun.

"I don't know. I'm new at this concubine thing. What should a bunny do if her master is in a foul temper?"

"Anything he wants," she said with a sour taste in her mouth. "Usually she'd dance first to get his attention off his problems then await his pleasure."

"If I were to dance it might very well put you in a worse frame of mind."

He smiled at her and her knees went weak. That sexy grin could be classified as a deadly weapon. It sure as hell debilitated her.

"Seriously, what can I do to help you feel better? I would have thought two orgasms would have been enough but maybe I'm wrong. Perhaps you need more to soothe your temper?"

"Honestly, it was nothing you personally did. I was quite pleased with your…performance."

"Then why did you run out like your cabin was on fire?" Drake moved closer to her.

"Because I didn't want to do anything I'd regret." That was a safe enough answer.

"Meaning?" He came another step closer.

"I didn't want to zap you with the controller because I hate your entire *fecking* race." She slid away from him before he could get close enough to touch her. Her muscles tensed as she fought to keep any expression from showing on her face. She didn't want him to know how badly the experience had shaken and angered her.

"Meaning?" He cornered her against the console.

"You figure it out, Squad Leader." Her breath came rapidly as he loomed over her. She had the remote in her pocket so she wasn't worried about him hurting her. No, she was far more worried about what his nearness did to her insides than any bodily harm.

"I see. You were pissed off because you'd spent six years as a body servant and just got your first orgasm."

"Got it in one. I knew you weren't as dumb as most Traminians."

"Gee, thanks. Don't blame me because you were owned by a bumbling idiot," he said, his hand brushing over her cheek.

"I don't blame you. I blame them but since they are several universes away you're the only one I can get revenge on."

"That doesn't sound very pleasant." His lower body pressed against hers and his hands pressed down on either side of her caging her in.

"On the contrary, pleasure is what this is all about. You, my dear concubine, are going to help me make up for lost time. Starting right now."

"Works for me," he said, dipping his head down to capture her lips in a blistering kiss.

She allowed the pleasure to consume her for a few delicious moments before she broke it off. He'd completely taken over their experience earlier and she wanted more control this time around.

"Stop." She prodded him in the ribs until he backed up. "I didn't get much of a chance to look at you last time. I think I want a more thorough examination of my property."

A muscle worked in Drake's jaw as he stepped back. He didn't say a word but unfastened his pants with jerky movements. When he stood naked in front of her, she let her eyes roam over his body.

He really was gorgeous. His face was rugged with chiseled cheekbones and a strong jaw. He was all man, not like the pretty boy models she'd seen on advertisement vids. Broad shoulders rippled with muscles and well-defined pecs lay under a dusting of dark hair.

Oh yeah, he was all male all right. And all hers—for now.

"You must have those frustrated Traminian wives eating out of the palm of your hand," she said, stroking his slightly erect penis.

It jumped at the touch of her fingers and hardened in her hand. A quick flash of heat shot straight to her pussy. Her pussy lips grew wet and swelled with desire. What had started out as a way to vent her anger at his race quickly turned into a burning need to explore his flesh.

"I try to stay away from Traminian women. They tend to get too possessive," he said, his breath coming in small pants. So he wasn't immune to the heat burning between them either, was he?

"I'm sure you've had your share of women willing to spread their legs for you wherever you go."

He didn't comment so she assumed it was true. The idea caused a slight pang to interrupt her pleasure but she pushed it aside. This wasn't about him. This was about learning his body for *her* enjoyment.

Her first master had been old and fat and his cock had looked like a shriveled sausage. Her second master had been younger but obviously inherited his father's physical attributes. Clearly he'd gotten his pathetic sexual prowess from him.

Touching Drake was a joy to her senses. He felt like velvet over iron in her hands as she knelt down to explore him some more. Triona nuzzled his sac and the musky scent of him drifted through her nostrils exciting her with its earthiness.

With a smile she licked the length of his cock until she could swirl her tongue over the tip. He tasted salty and hot and full of life. She pulled him further into her mouth taking in as much as she could.

Drake groaned above her and thrust his hands into her hair to pull her head closer.

She stopped moving and pulled away from him. "Put your hands behind your back. And don't come."

"You ask a lot, lady."

"Yes I do. And you'll do it too." It felt good to have the control for a change. To be the one calling the shots instead of lying there waiting to see what depravities she'd be subjected to.

Unlacing the ties of her shirt, she pulled it over her head and shimmied out of her pants. When she was as naked as he, she knelt back down and ran her hands over his ropy thighs. His legs bulged with muscle and were thick as *kelee* tree trunks.

She ran her tongue up and down his inner thigh and smiled to herself when she found a ticklish spot. Cream wept from the head of his cock. She licked it off and the salty taste of him filled her mouth. His balls had turned purple and the vein on the underside of his penis throbbed rapidly.

His hands fisted behind him and the muscles of his neck stood out with the strain he was under. Triona felt so very powerful. This was a headier feeling than holding a laser on a man. She had him under her control and her only weapon was lust.

Slowly she rose and rubbed his cock against her wet pussy lips. "Do want to come inside me?"

"Yes!" he barked out. His eyes glittered dangerously with suppressed fury.

"How badly?" she asked, rubbing her slickness over him. Her clit brushed his glans and she felt the shock of it to her toes. She did it again and the sparks of desire almost brought her to her knees.

"*Fecking* badly!"

"Then what are you waiting for?" She could feel the pressure building inside her. There was no way she wanted to wait any longer to feel his cock fill her. Which was a good thing because as soon as her words released him, Drake grabbed her and set her rear end on the edge of the console.

His big hands pushed her legs around his waist and grabbed her ass. With one swift stroke he pierced her to the core. Waves of sensation blossomed along the path his cock took. Her body shuddered with the force of his entrance and she held on for dear life.

Drake pistoned his hips, furiously slamming into her until she had to hold onto his shoulders to keep from flying off her seat. His face was scrunched up in concentration and Triona wondered if he was having trouble holding back his orgasm.

Any further thoughts flew out of her head as he lifted her legs even higher and stroked her clit as he drove into her. Flames of need licked at her with every flick of his fingers and it was all she could do to keep from screaming.

She lost the battle when Drake took her mouth in a savage kiss that mimicked the thrusts of his cock inside her. Her body exploded with the force of her climax, shuddering over and over again as she felt him spurt inside her. Lights danced before her eyes and she gasped at the sheer force of her release.

With two more thrusts Drake collapsed against her, sweat dripping liberally off his face.

"I never knew delayed gratification could feel so good. Or be so frustrating." He kissed her throat and another shock wave rippled through her. His cock was still hard and her inner muscles held him tight.

He groaned and tried to pull out of her but she wrapped her legs tighter around his waist and kept him captive.

"Was the wait worth the outcome?" She didn't know why but she had to know if this was as mind-blowing for him as it was for her. Perhaps it was vanity but she wanted to know she'd given him more pleasure than anyone in his past.

He looked down at her with eyes so blue she could get lost in them. "Yes. As much as I hated it, it was worth the wait. That doesn't mean I want to do it again, though." He kissed her on the nose in a gesture that surprised her even as it sent a strange warmth to her heart.

"But what if *I* want you to do it again?" she asked, dropping her legs and releasing him.

His face hardened and he stepped stiffly away from her. "Then of course I'll do it. Whatever my mistress wishes."

"I told you not to call me that!" Just the word brought back the memory of getting whipped by Mistress Aphrodite.

"Then don't act like one!"

"I'll act however I want and you'll put up with it." The small part of her that wasn't bent on revenge cringed at her words but she ignored it. "Now leave me and don't come back until I call you." She turned her back on him and watched in the reflection of the monitor to make sure he left.

He raised his hand and opened his mouth as if to say something but remained silent. With a disgusted shake of his head he bent down and picked up his pants before walking out. Even angry, Triona couldn't help but admire the male perfection of his naked ass.

She just had to figure out what to do about the rest of him.

* * * * *

How dare she get pissed off because he called her mistress? If she was going to act like a *fecking* overlord then she should expect it! What the hell was her problem?

Drake pulled his pants on and flopped facedown on the bunk. If she wanted to sleep in her own bed she'd have to *order* him to move. Damn woman. That was what happened when a concubine was in charge of a ship. A guy didn't stand a chance in hell of understanding what was going on. He hadn't seen another woman on board, only a motley group of men. How did they handle having a woman as their captain? It would drive him crazy.

One second he's having the best sex of his life and the next she's telling him to leave. No pillow talk, no down time, no nothing. He felt so…cheap.

The slave collar chafed his neck and he ran a finger under it to ease the friction. He deserved this, he supposed. Drake the Rake had finally been laid low by a woman. A woman pirate at that.

If he lived through this he'd make sure to apologize to any of the women he could find. He'd also make sure he never told anyone that he'd been a former bunny's sex slave. If word of his predicament got out he'd never hear the end of it.

Drake rolled onto his back and stared at the ceiling. All he'd wanted was a little rest and relaxation and he'd ended up fucking on command. Well, he'd wanted to have sex. He'd certainly gotten that wish.

Shit, if Triona had been on Gamoras he'd have paid every last credit to have sex with her. He should be happy to be her slave. She was gorgeous, responsive and didn't want any complications afterwards. Wasn't that every guy's dream? And he didn't have to pay a cent for it either.

All the free sex he wanted with no strings attached. Except it wasn't when *he* wanted it. Or even *if* he wanted it. He had to perform no matter what. And that's what bothered him the most. There was no free choice involved. If he had a headache he still had to do what she wanted.

Just like the hundreds of concubines on his planet.

But that was different! They were *trained* for that! He had no say in the matter.

How much say did they have? Their fates were decided by others too.

For the first time in his life he felt ashamed of his heritage. He'd never personally owned a concubine but he knew plenty of men who did. Hell, he'd wanted to own one too. It was an accepted practice on his planet and he'd never thought twice about the morality of it.

Until it was his turn to be owned like merchandise.

Was this what Triona had felt like for six years? Obviously it was because otherwise she wouldn't have such hatred for Traminians. Hell, she probably felt worse. She'd never had an orgasm in those six years. At least he'd gotten a release.

Drake steepled his fingers together and laid them on his chest. She didn't look that old to him, although it was hard to tell with all the regeneration available these days. But she didn't have the mask-like appearance of someone who'd gone through regeneration so he'd assume she was as young as she looked.

If she'd been a concubine for six years that meant she'd been sold when she was still a teenager! That was practically criminal! He knew poor families sold "extra" daughters as concubines when the girls were relatively young. The proponents said it eased the already overburdened families and they were well compensated for their loss.

The girl got an education at a special school and lived a life of luxury as the concubine of a rich master. There were laws in place to prevent the abuse of the women and supposedly they were happy with their lot in life. Instead of grubbing out a meager existence on some mining planet, they lived in gorgeous mansions and had their own servants.

He only now realized it was at the cost of their souls.

How could they live day after day, year after year knowing they had no choices? How could he?

There had to be a way out of this. He'd find some way to escape before he went stark raving mad.

Closing his eyes, Drake tried to force himself to fall asleep. He recalled flight coordinates, star maps and even the multiplication tables but nothing worked. As soon as he'd start to drift off, Triona's violet eyes flashed in his brain.

Something about her drew him even as he resented her. How'd a former concubine manage to become a space pirate? Had she killed her master? Concubines were guarded tightly every minute. When they went out in public it was only with their masters and they were bound to them with chains.

Granted the chains were often made of gold but the impact was the same. A bunny made no move without her master's approval. So how'd she do it?

He'd have to ask her if they could ever be in the same room together without fighting.

Or fucking.

It didn't matter that he hated the situation, something about Triona called to him. And not just to his dick.

Whatever. He didn't have time to ponder stupid emotions. He had to find a way out of here and off this ship.

The first issue was getting his hands on the controller to the *fecking* slave collar. He couldn't do anything if Triona could zap him unconscious from two rooms away.

After that he'd have to either liberate an escape pod or hijack the ship. The only problem with that idea was he had no idea where the hell they were. They'd hit hyper-drive as soon as they captured his ship and without a star chart he was lost.

Wait!

They'd captured his ship too! That meant it was still on board this hunk of junk somewhere.

His ship had navigational equipment. And it also had a laser scalpel that would slice through this collar like nothing. All he had to do was find where they were holding his flitter and he'd be out of there before they had a chance to zap him. If he could outrun their tractor beam, this flying garbage pit would never be able to catch him!

He just had to bide his time until they let their guard down and he could search the ship without alerting them.

No wonder concubines on Tramin where kept chained to their masters—otherwise they'd find a way to escape at the first opportunity. Just like he was going to.

Chapter Four

Triona's body ached with weariness—among other things. She hadn't slept in longer than she could remember and her body had expended a bit more energy than normal. All she wanted to do was crash on her bunk for a few hours and forget about her problems.

Unfortunately, her biggest problem lay sprawled over her bed. She could kick him out and make him sleep on the floor but that would just start an argument she wasn't in the mood to deal with right now. There was no way she was going to sleep on the floor in her own cabin so the only option was to share the narrow bunk with Drake.

As if sensing her thoughts, Drake snorted and rolled to the side. He took the covers with him, exposing his naked ass to her appreciative gaze. Triona shook her head to get rid of those thoughts. Lust was what had her head twisted in knots. She didn't need any more confusion.

It was too late to straighten her thoughts out, she'd worry about it later. Right now she needed sleep and if the only way to get it was to be next to Drake, so be it. Quietly she slipped off her pants and shirt. She grabbed another blanket out of the storage unit since Drake had absconded with hers and slid next to him. When he didn't move she let out a sigh of relief and relaxed.

Stars but she was tired. Between Drake's arrival and repairing the ship she'd been running nonstop for too long. Her body needed a break, if only her hormones would shut off long enough for her to go unconscious.

Like that was going to happen when she could feel the heat pouring off Drake's naked body. His naked body, which was just inches from her. His gloriously muscled, naked body that had turned her brain into so much mush.

Thoughts like that weren't going to help her drift off any time this millennium.

Triona rolled onto her side *away* from Drake and tried to ignore his presence. He certainly hadn't noticed her in the bed. Soft snores came from his mouth as he breathed deeply and evenly in sleep.

Bastard.

Closing her eyes she forced herself to ignore him and think about what she'd do when she got up. They needed to find a space station soon or they'd run out of fuel. The bay door needed to be fixed again and Smudge had said something about cannibalizing Drake's ship for parts.

She thought about what parts were needed and what could be had from Drake's ship. The list hadn't gone past the third item when Drake rolled over and draped a hand over her waist.

Heat immediately bloomed from the contact. His hand wasn't even touching her bare skin and her body reacted to him. This was insane!

"Um, nice," he murmured sleepily and pulled her closer.

Her ass pressed into the cradle of his hips and his hand settled on her breast. Fluid gushed between her legs and her heart rate went into overdrive. He turned her on instantly and he was still asleep!

After a few tense minutes she realized he wasn't going to make another move. Disappointment warred with relief. Her brain was already too scrambled to survive another sensual onslaught but at the same time she was still hot and bothered by his caress.

Eventually relief won and she relaxed against him. She'd never slept in the same bed as a man before. After she'd pleasured her master she'd always been sent back to her own bed. Until the next time he wanted to use her body.

Anger clenched her gut in a tight fist. So many wonderful experiences she'd never known about because of him. Drake's breath fanned her face and distracted her from her thoughts. Her ire couldn't hold out against the pleasure of feeling Drake's chest press against her back. She felt oddly comforted and protected by his big body surrounding her.

Seconds later she drifted off into a deep sleep.

* * * * *

Drake woke up in his favorite way—naked and wrapped around a beautiful woman. For a delicious second or two he forgot how he got that way and just enjoyed the experience.

Then reality came crashing down.

It wasn't just any woman in his arms. It was his owner. He pulled away from her in disgust. He should be thinking about getting off this ship, not about how good Triona's skin felt against his. Maybe he could slip out of the room while she was sleeping? Of course then he'd have to get past the handful of other crew members he'd seen milling around the ship. Even if his jailor was asleep he was still outnumbered.

Pushing thoughts of escape aside, he moved farther away from her. With a sleepy sigh, she rolled onto her back and threw her arm over her head. This position gave him the opportunity to watch her while she slept. She looked so much younger and softer in repose. Those long eyelashes lay like crescent moons on her cheeks and her rosebud mouth looked lush and inviting. Even with her hair chopped off he could see why she was chosen to be a concubine.

Most concubines were sold into slavery by their parents. Every so often he'd heard of an orphan being picked by the slave traders but it was rare. Concubines were picked for their incredible beauty, it was supposed to be an honor to be chosen.

But how could parents willingly sell their daughter into slavery? Even if it meant escaping a life of poverty it wasn't worth it. Did they ever regret their decision? Did they think it was the only option?

He wasn't planning on having a family any time soon but he already knew he'd kill himself before he ever let one of his children be sold. His newly awakened conscience poked at him, reminding him that not too long ago he was envious of the men who could afford to own concubines. Could any amount of money make up for turning your daughter into some reprobate's sex toy?

And did any amount of smooth talking justify taking children away from desperate parents? Shit, instead of buying daughters from impoverished families the upper class should donate the money or give them a job. When he got back to Tramin, he was going to do something about it.

Yeah, *if* he ever got back to Tramin. He had no idea where in the cosmos he was or if he'd ever manage to escape. The door beckoned him enticingly. He could just see if anyone was out there, couldn't he?

Drake tried to slide out from behind Triona but she made a sleepy little whimper and clung to his arm. Her head thrashed back and forth and she flinched away from an unseen threat.

She must be caught in a nightmare or something. Despite himself, Drake felt his heart softening toward her. He reached over to wake her but she shot up in bed with a blood-curdling scream that chilled him to the very marrow.

"No!"

Her chest heaved with ragged breaths and sweat beaded on her forehead. Before his eyes he watched her shoulders begin to shake and her eyes fill with tears.

"Shh. It was just a bad dream. You're okay." He pulled her into his arms and murmured reassurances to her.

She seemed so delicate and fragile now. Nothing like the tough as nails pirate that held him at laser-point or even the sexy vixen that demanded satisfaction from him. His heart bled to see her like this.

"Would you like a package of water?" he asked when her shaking had settled down some. "I can get one out of the unit if you'd like."

Her violet eyes shimmered with unshed tears as she looked at him. She nodded assent, so he reached over her to dial up some water. His naked chest brushed against her breasts and he had to grit his teeth to fight back the surge of lust that immediately pummeled him.

"Why are you being so nice to me?" she asked, her voice husky.

"I don't know. Blame it on a momentary lapse of sanity."

"Th-thank you." She gulped the water gratefully, draining the pouch dry.

"That must have been some dream. You want to talk about?"

"Not really." She pulled the sheet up to her chest and looked down at her lap.

"It might take the edge off it. Talking about a bad dream usually puts it into perspective." Why was he pushing her to bare her soul to him? It shouldn't matter if monsters haunted the dark corners of her mind. Hell, if she had nightmares like this often it could even work to his advantage.

But it just wasn't in him to hit someone when she was down. Maybe that made him weak but he couldn't do it.

He was jolted out of his self-recriminations by her voice, coming low and hesitantly.

"I wish it was just a bad dream. I dreamt about when I got captured." A shudder ran through her.

Drake looked at her blankly. What did she mean, captured? His puzzlement must have shown on his face because she explained further.

"I grew up in a small village in the mountains. I was the youngest of six and the only girl. We never had much but there was always enough to go around. My brothers were overprotective to a fault and used to scare off all the boys."

"Sounds like you were really close." It seemed like they loved her a lot. They must have fallen on some damn hard times to sell her. But that didn't explain why she said she was captured.

"Very close. Like I said, we didn't have many material possessions but we had a lot of love to go around."

"Then what happened?"

Her breathing hitched and she twisted the sheet between her fingers. "We had gone to the valley at the base of the mountain for my brother's wedding. It was a big deal because his bride's family had some fancy relatives from the capital coming. Her parents were worried that we'd embarrass them with our country ways."

"Sound like real winners. I feel bad for your brother." Jerks.

"Oh, he could handle them. Besides, he was taking his bride back to the mountains so he wouldn't have to see them that much anyway." A meager smile flitted around her lips and her hands relaxed fractionally.

"So you went to the wedding…" He was still lost.

She took a deep breath and continued with her story. "We went to the wedding, dressed in our finest clothes and did our best not to mortify the in-laws. Everything was going fine except for one of the guests."

"Let me guess, the cousins from the capital didn't find the wedding up to their standards?" He knew the type.

"No, nothing pleased them. Well nothing except one thing. Me. The man, I forget his name, kept trying to dance with me and corner me when I went to the bathroom."

Drake felt a surge of anger slam into his gut. The bastard probably thought Triona was a country bumpkin ready for the plucking. "How old were you?"

"Fifteen. I'd developed early," she looked ruefully down at her chest.

"I bet. So did this guy trap you in a closet or something?"

"No but not for lack of trying. My brothers kept a close eye on me and made sure I was always in sight. We left and I didn't think anything of it."

A sick feeling rolled in his belly. He could tell by the way her face paled he wasn't going to like what happened next.

"A week or so later a troop of soldiers crashed into our house. They shot my parents and my brothers before they had a chance to defend themselves. Before I knew what was happening they'd stuffed a gag in my mouth and slapped restraints on me."

"What?" She'd been kidnapped? By soldiers?

"I struggled but they drugged me and I passed out. When I woke I was locked in a tiny cell with three other girls. The next day I found out I'd been 'chosen' to learn the arts of a concubine. Two years later I was sold at a private auction. The cousin from the wedding was one of the bidders. Lucky for me he didn't have enough credits to afford my price." She shuddered.

"No wonder you have nightmares." Drake sat down heavily on the bed next to her. He couldn't believe it. Triona had been stolen from her family, not sold by them. Maybe this was some sort of rare occurrence? "So you think the cousin planned the attack on your family so that he could buy you?"

"I'm almost sure of it. How else would the soldiers have known where I lived? Our village is very isolated, that was why my brother had to go to the valley to find a wife. I'm sure no one outside our village even knew I was alive, forget where I lived."

"Have you had any contact with them since that night?"

Tears leaked from her eyes but her voice remained steady. "No. It's been ten years since I've seen them. I don't even know if they're still alive. While I was in training we had no contact with the outside world and when I was in service to my master the only contact I had was through him. It wasn't likely that he'd let me write to my parents so they could come rescue me. Since I've been free I've been on the run. I didn't want to bring danger to their doorstep."

"What about the other girls? Where were they from?"

"All over but mostly poor villages like mine."

Drake tapped his knee with his finger trying to think of the best way to phrase his next question. He didn't want to anger her but he had to find out the truth. Could his government have been covering up for slave traders all this time?

"We'd always been told that concubines were sold into slavery by their parents. That impoverished families sold their daughters to keep them from starving to death. It doesn't sound like that's what happened in your case but what about the other girls?"

"Ha!" Her face twisted cynically. "Is that how they justify their depravity? By saying parents sell their children? And you believed it?"

"Hey, it's the way I was raised!"

"Well it's wrong! Not one of the girls I met had ever been sold. Soldiers took all of us in almost the same way. I never heard of anyone getting sold."

"That doesn't mean it didn't happen..." he trailed off. He just couldn't imagine something this sinister had been going on right in front of his nose all this time.

"Believe what you want. I have things I have to do." She pushed away from him and reached for her pants.

"Triona, I'm sorry." He didn't know if he was sorry for what happened to her or being part of the race that did it. Or both.

She looked at him but didn't reply. Drake searched her eyes for any clue to what she was thinking. After endless seconds she nodded her head once and turned her back on him.

Drake didn't know what to say so he just watched as she pulled her clothes on and left the room. He was no closer to escape than he was when he went to bed. And twice as confused.

Triona pushed back the tears that threatened to fall as she marched to the docking bay. Damn him! *Fecking* Drake had stirred up way too many memories, both good and bad, for her to handle. She could almost take his disbelief easier than his sympathy.

It was time for him to go. The next space station they came to, he was gone. She climbed down the hatch to the bay and pulled her tools out of storage. This time she'd fix that sparking door for good.

O'Brien had always said working with your hands was the best way to straighten out your head. She'd have to rewire the entire ship to get her head back on straight. Ripping wires out with a vengeance, Triona muttered curses under her breath.

What? Did he think she made up her story because the truth was too boring? Just because he was stupid enough to believe the lies his people fed him didn't mean she was a liar too. It was ridiculous to even think that parents would sell their children into a life like that. Well, maybe some parents might but hers never would.

And they weren't that poor anyway. Compared to her master they weren't exactly well-off but they'd been rich with love and that mattered a hell of a lot more than material goods.

Would Drake think the way they lived had been underprivileged? Would he look down on them too? A wriggle of sadness twisted in her gut. Could he think that she'd been "saved" by becoming a concubine?

Who cared what he thought? She was beyond that now, it didn't matter what some stupid Traminian pilot thought about her. He wasn't one to talk anyway since he was a slave now himself.

At least until she could jettison him on the nearest station.

Sparks flew from the control panel and she jumped back to avoid getting singed. A movement out of the corner of her eye snagged her attention and she spun around looking for the source.

"Who's there? Smudge, is that you?"

No one answered her. She was about to chalk it up to her imagination when Drake stepped out into the hall.

"What are you doing here?" she asked. A shiver ran down her spine as she watched him come closer. He moved with a panther-like grace that did strange things to her body. It was probably a good thing he was fully dressed. She didn't need to get distracted by his muscular chest when she held electrically charged wires.

"I got to thinking about what you said and wanted to apologize."

She raised her eyebrows in surprise. That certainly wasn't what she'd expected.

"It's not easy for me to admit the country I dedicated my life to serve and protect could allow girls to be taken from their families and sold."

Triona didn't say anything. She could see where it would be hard to hear that something you'd believed in turned out to be corrupt but that wasn't her problem.

Drake leaned against the wall next to her. "If I ever get back to Tramin I'm going to petition the Council to abolish slavery."

"Easy enough to say when we're across the galaxy." He'd say anything to get her to let him go. Just because he'd been nice to her earlier today didn't mean he'd stopped trying to escape.

"I know there's no way to prove I mean what I say but it's the truth. I *will* fight to free the rest of the concubines. You have my word on it."

He took her hand and placed it over his chest. Triona felt his heart beat under her fingers. Part of her wanted so badly to believe him. To finally have someone on her side who was willing to fight for all the sisters she'd left behind. The other part of her scoffed at her näiveté. He wasn't here to help her he was just looking for a way to escape.

And she'd practically gift-wrapped it! The docking controller was ripped to shreds. If he made it to his ship he could escape before she had a chance to stop him.

"How'd you get out of the cabin anyway? There should have been a guard outside the door." Slowly and carefully she pulled her hand out of his grasp and reached for the remote for the slave collar.

"I didn't know I couldn't leave the room. No one stopped me."

"Well they should have!"

"Fine. I'll just go—" Before he could finish his sentence an explosion rocked the ship.

"Get down!" Drake threw himself over her and rolled them away just as debris crashed down where she'd been standing.

"Get off me! I need to get to the bridge." Triona scrambled up the ladder to the main part of the ship and bolted for the bridge.

Smudge vacated the captain's seat as soon as she burst into the room. "I don't know where they come from, Cap'n. One second we're motoring about in space, the next some crazy bastards hit us with an ion bomb."

"Don't worry about where they came from, let's focus on getting away. Go man the rear guns." Triona flipped on the ship-wide intercom. "All hands man your stations. Repeat, all hands man your stations." Her crew knew what to do in this situation.

The old pirate took off like a shot and Drake sat down in the copilot's chair. "What've you got for weapons on this tub?"

"Ion cannon is on your right. The blue button on the left is for the front guns and the red buttons are for the sides." Triona didn't have time to question his willingness to help. She had to concentrate on outmaneuvering the enemy using them for target practice. Her fingers flew over the console trying to identify the threat.

"Got anything yet?" Drake asked searching the view screen.

"I'm working on it." *Come on, come on. Show yourself you piece of space crap.* "There! Eleven o'clock and closing fast. Get them with the port guns."

"No shit!" Drake swiveled in his chair until he got a read on the attacking ship.

Sweat made Triona's hands slippery on the controls as she fought to avoid the next assault. *The Bunny* was a fast ship but this close up she needed agility more than speed.

That could be a problem.

"They must have shields up. I hit them dead-on but they didn't so much as spark."

"When I give the word, hit them with the ion cannon."

Triona pulled the ship into a spin, flipping up and over the enemy ship. She could feel the shudders as *Bunny* took heavy damage.

"Get ready." Her voice was calm even though her insides had turned to water. This trick would work if they managed to stay in one piece after they came out of the flip.

"Ready."

She didn't dare look over at him. "On three. One. Two." They were at the apex of their loop and Triona could see the target she wanted to hit. "Three!"

Drake hit the cannon and the enemy's nuclear converter took a direct hit.

"Yes!" Triona screamed as she fought to keep from spinning into the explosion. It only counted as a victory if you lived to tell about it. She put on a burst of speed and *Bunny* shot out of range.

And not a moment too soon. The shock waves from the exploding ship pushed them forward end over end for more rotations than she could count. By the time she had everything under control again several wires popped and hissed around her.

"Smudge, you okay back there?" she asked through the intercom.

"Right as rain now that those bastards are gone."

"Good. Get me a damage report ASAP."

"You got it, Cap'n."

Her heart still pounded furiously and she knew her knees wouldn't support her. She'd been so caught up in Drake she'd been taken totally off guard by this new threat. He was making her weak.

But he'd also saved her ass. Smudge wouldn't have been able to handle the cannon while in the middle of a spin. He was a great pirate but his reaction times left a little something to be desired.

"Who was that?" Drake asked when they smoothed out some.

"I don't know. Another pirate probably."

"You don't sound too upset about almost getting blown to smithereens."

"Occupational hazard."

"Lady, you need to come up with a safer occupation!" His eyes opened wide and he wiped at the sweat on his brow.

"Beats having sex with a man old enough to be my father. I'd rather take my chances here in space where I have a choice in what I do than be coddled in a silk-lined cage."

Drake opened his mouth a few times but nothing came out. "I guess you're right. No matter how bad the job is, if it's your choice that makes it better than being a slave."

Triona looked at him in amazement. Did he actually get it? Her heart lurched at the rush of hope that shot through her. Could he be serious about seeing an end to slavery?

"Why didn't you escape when we got hit? I couldn't have stopped you from sneaking out and running with your ship. The bay doors were wide open. Instead you helped me. I don't get it?"

"I don't know. I guess I just didn't think about it. Besides, flying out of a ship under attack is a sure way to get blown out of the stars. If I'm going to run I want to have the best chance for success possible." He fiddled around with some of the dials on the console.

"I'll keep that in mind."

Chapter Five

Stars! He was too stupid to live! Drake wanted to pound his head against a wall, maybe that would knock some sense into his addled brain. What the hell was wrong with him? He'd given up a chance at freedom to protect Triona and her blasted ship.

Now he'd never get another opportunity. Stupid, stupid, stupid! He let a pair of dewdrop eyes and a curvy body screw with his mind and now he was stuck on this ship for stars knew how long.

But he couldn't have let her get blasted out of the sky. He'd instinctively protected her when the ship got hit. When she'd taken over the flying it had felt natural to help her out. She'd done a damn fine job of getting them out of a tricky situation. He'd put her flying skills up against anyone on his squad and she'd probably win.

Which made him feel a little better about getting caught unawares by her. Not much but a little. It also magnified his missed opportunity. Unless they conveniently got attacked again she wouldn't be distracted enough for him to grab his flitter and go. Damn it, he'd been so close.

He'd managed to slip away from the dozing guard and find his way to the docking bay. His ship was pretty beat-up but still looked operational. He wouldn't know for sure until he got a closer look. What were the chances that Triona would be working in the bay the one time he slipped out of the room unnoticed? And that the ship would get attacked before he could knock her unconscious and escape?

Drake paced the tiny confines of the cabin and tried to sort out his muddled thoughts. His recon wasn't a complete failure. He knew where his ship was stored and that it was still in one piece. Plus he knew they were flying out of Federated Space because he'd gotten a quick look at the flight plan after they escaped the enemy ship.

It made no sense for him to try to leave until they got closer to protected space. He didn't know his way around out here in the back of beyond and his flitter only held so much fuel. Triona would have to get repairs done after the attack and refuel. Maybe that would be his best bet. Wait until they hit a space station and slip out. He just had to make sure she didn't fry him through the slave collar while he made a run for it.

Yeah, that was it. He'd bide his time and try to get more freedom on the ship. When they docked he'd make his move. In the meantime, there were worse "punishments" than having sex with Triona.

His heart gave a little double thump at the mere thought of her. If the situation was different, he'd chain himself to her and never let go. But there was too much between them. She hated his whole race and he couldn't really blame her for that. But neither could he forgive her.

The collar chafed his neck and he ran his fingers under it to ease the pain. Had she worn one of these too? Had her master zapped her with it? Smudge had only tested it out for a second and the pain had been incredible. Drake was a grown man and the pain had brought him to his knees, how could a seventeen-year-old girl survive that?

Not without some serious scars on her soul, that's for sure. Drake swore to himself that he wouldn't stop petitioning the Council until they abolished slavery. It would piss off a lot of people but he had to do it. He owed it to Triona and all the other girls like her.

The door opened and a weary-looking Triona walked through. "Oh! You're still awake. I thought you'd be asleep by now," she said looking at him rather shyly.

"No, the adrenaline rush is keeping me up. How about you?"

"I could sleep standing up. Smudge just gave me the damage report. Listening to that was enough to exhaust me."

"That bad, huh?"

"Worse. Luckily we have enough fuel to limp our way to the nearest space station on half power. It'll take forever but we won't starve to death or suffocate."

She passed him and collapsed on the bed, pulling her pants and shirt off and slipping under the covers. Drake's nostrils flared at the scent of her and his cock stirred with interest.

Down boy! Not now! She looked worn out. Dark circles ringed her eyes and she looked paler than usual. "If you want, I can sleep on the floor. It wouldn't be the worst bed I've ever had." But it wouldn't be anywhere near as nice as sleeping next to her delicious body.

"I-I'd rather if you slept next to me. W-we don't have to have sex but I'd like... Oh never mind. Do what you want." She rolled on her side and brought the covers up over her shoulder.

Drake stared at her silent form for a minute in absolute shock. Did she just want him to hold her after the day she had? A glow of warmth infused his heart as he considered it. Could she be developing feelings for him?

Quickly he stripped down and slid into the bed next to her. She held her body stiffly but didn't move away. Daring to be a little bolder, Drake pulled her into the cradle of his body and held her close.

"Good night, Captain," he whispered against her glossy, black hair.

"Good night, Squad Leader," she whispered back and relaxed against him. A few minutes later her breathing slowed and evened out and her body went limp with slumber.

The tiny ember that had begun when she gave him the choice of where to sleep settled into his heart and smoldered there. Triona might not be the only one developing completely illogical feelings.

* * * * *

Triona woke first and immediately felt the press of Drake's cock against her back. He'd held her through the night and kept the nightmares at bay. She felt refreshed and ready to take on the universe.

Or at least a stubborn, debilitated relic of a ship.

It would take every trick O'Brien had ever taught her to keep *The Bunny* going long enough to reach a space station. She didn't even know if she'd have enough credits to pay for repairs. Pirating wasn't all it was cracked up to be.

Maybe she could sell Drake's flitter for the credits she needed? But then how would he get back to Tramin? She'd promised herself that she'd release him when they hit the next space station. He'd need some way to get off it.

Her heart ached with sadness. They'd reach the station at the Beta Quad in two weeks and then Drake would be gone like a rocket. It was the right thing to do but it left her feeling miserable.

When he'd slid into the copilot's chair it had felt so *right* to have his help. They worked well as a team in and out of bed.

But in a team everyone is equal. Drake's your slave, not your equal, the annoying little voice in the back of her head reminded her.

It didn't matter how she felt about him, if she could even figure that out. She'd enslaved him, forced him to have sex and stepped on his pride. He could never forgive her for that. All his talk of petitioning the Council would fall by the wayside as soon as she let him go.

As would his kindness toward her. She had no notions otherwise. Once she set him free he'd forget about her in seconds. The thought depressed her viciously because she knew she'd never forget him.

Her dismal thoughts were interrupted as Drake's hand caressed her breast. His fingers teased her nipple and sent bolts of pleasure straight to her pussy.

"Good morning," he murmured, kissing the back of her neck.

Shivers shook her to the core at the feel of his hot lips on her sensitive nape.

"Good morning to you too." She arched her back to give him better access.

He took it without any further invitation.

Fluid pooled between her pussy lips as they swelled. A long, slow pull of desire came from her gut and grew bigger as his hand drifted lower. Her breath held as his fingers teased the top of her pussy.

Triona squirmed in anticipation, silently urging him to touch her clit and end this torture. When he skipped her nubbin and traced her wet lips instead she almost whimpered.

"Something wrong?"

She could hear the smile in his voice.

"Not at all," she said breathlessly. When would he touch her?

"Oh, then I can move back to your delectable breasts."

He made to move his hand but she trapped it between her thighs. "Don't you dare!"

His laugh rumbled through her body setting off explosions in its wake. She could feel his cock brushing the cheeks of her ass and she reached around to grab it. "Touch me, Drake!"

"In good time."

His fingers continued to tease and torment her pussy, slipping over and around her swollen nub but never touching it. Her head twisted as she tried to hold back the moans of desire rolling through her. How much longer could she go on like this?

Finally, when she thought she'd scream if he didn't stroke her clitoris, his finger pushed into her slippery channel and his thumb brushed against the engorged bud. Faster and faster he thrust inside her while circling the center of her pleasure. The pressure he'd built inside her sprang free with an eruption that rocked every atom of her being.

Triona's hips bucked against his hand. Her pussy spasmed in pleasure and stars danced before her eyes. When the tremors finally stopped she could have sworn she'd been blasted across the universe and back again.

But Drake wasn't done with her yet. Lifting her leg, he wedged his thigh between hers and drove his cock to the hilt. Triona's eyes sprang open at this new position. She couldn't move against him or he'd fall out. His hand squeezed her breast while he slowly rocked against her back.

The nest of hair surrounding his cock brushed against her ass with every stroke, adding a new caress to her overloaded senses. He moved so slowly she wanted to shout in frustration. Sweat dripped down her face as the pleasure built into a new crescendo.

Drake's hand pinched her ass making her jump. The pain faded fast to be replaced by a definite heat that pushed her desire even harder. His other hand moved down between her legs and teased her curls. When he pinched her behind again, she was ready for the slight pain but not for the increase in heat.

His finger lightly tapped her clit, bringing more blood to the nerve ending-packed area. Spots swam before her eyes as she tumbled headlong toward oblivion. Drake stroked her clit and thrust furiously inside her. Pleasure assaulted her from every angle but when he bit her lightly on the neck it was too much for her to handle.

Her climax tore through her with all the force and heat of a nuclear explosion and did just as much damage. Tremors shook her as she clenched her inner muscles and milked Drake's cock. His hands gripped her hips as he continued to pound away. In seconds she felt his cum spray inside her and heard his hoarse shout as he reached his own oblivion.

Their breathing came in gasps and Drake's heart beat as rapidly as hers.

"That was incredible," she said in awe. That he did it with no prompting from her made it even more amazing to her.

"Tell me about it. You're going to be the death of me, woman." He slapped her ass lightly.

"I'm going to be the death of you? As I recall it was *your* idea," she said indignantly, rolling over to face him.

He wore a satisfied smirk and stroked her cheek. "I know. I can't help myself. Every time I'm around you my dick takes over all thought processes. Once I see you all I can focus on is getting back inside you. It's a good thing I'm not one of your crew or I'd have to be blindfolded to get any work done."

He kissed her forehead lightly. The sweet gesture brought tears to her eyes. She was getting way too emotional with him. It was idiotic to let her heart soften toward him now when he'd be gone in a few weeks.

But if that was the case, shouldn't she enjoy every minute she could with him? The idea of spending all day in bed with him and exploring his body held definite appeal. She almost considered suggesting it until the power in her cabin dimmed and went out.

"Sparks! I've got to get moving or we'll never make it to safety."

"Hold on, I'll help."

Surprise held her motionless for a moment while he climbed out of bed. "You'd help me?"

"Sure. What else have I got to do around here if you're going to be busy keeping this tub running?"

Triona looked at him warily. He could be looking for a way to sabotage the ship instead of fixing it.

"What? Don't you think I know my way around a toolbox?"

"It's not that..."

"You're afraid I'll booby trap the ship, aren't you?" His face hardened.

"Well, the thought crossed my mind. You can't blame me for worrying. The lives of my crew members depend on me keeping this ship running. I have to put their safety above my own needs."

He relaxed slightly from his defensive stance. "You're right, I can't blame you for thinking of your crew first. I vow I'll not harm your ship or do anything to put it in jeopardy. Okay? After all, if the life systems crash I'll suffocate along with the rest of you."

"Okay." Triona bit her tongue. She wanted to add a warning about attempting to escape or use the tools on his slave collar but her courage deserted her. They'd had such a wonderful morning she didn't want to say anything to ruin what time they had left. She'd just have to trust him for now. "Come on, let's get something to eat before we get to work. It's going to be a long day. Hell, it's going to be a long week." She got up and grabbed clean clothes out of the storage unit.

"As long as we can start every day off like today, I don't mind how long they are." Drake gave her bare butt a little slap and climbed into the sanitation unit, whistling.

Triona shook her head and dragged her own clothes on. It wouldn't bother her any to start every day off in Drake's arms. Too bad that pleasure wouldn't last.

Drake couldn't believe the condition of the ship. He didn't know how much damage came from the attack and how much was there before. The thing was held together with prayers and wire ties for star's sake! It was a *fecking* miracle that they hadn't crashed in a fiery ball long before now.

And Triona had managed to out fly the attacking ship in it too. He could only imagine what she'd be able to accomplish if she had a top-of-the-line speeder. As the day went on he had more and more admiration for her abilities. Her meager crew was fanatically loyal to her. He'd found out that some of them had hired on with the old owner of the ship but most of them had been rescued from slavery as had Triona.

Even if he didn't promise not to damage the ship, he'd never have had the opportunity anyway. He didn't know if Triona had passed the word that he was to be watched or if the crew had taken it upon themselves but either way he was never alone for a second.

As much as it frustrated him to be kept under such scrutiny he supposed he couldn't blame them. If he were in their shoes he'd be watching the prisoner pretty damn closely too.

Since when did he start empathizing with the enemy?

And did he still see them as the enemy? They'd fought together to escape a common threat and had worked together for their mutual survival. That didn't sound like people on opposites sides to him.

But they held him captive! His logical side protested. *They'd taken away his freedom!*

Wouldn't you have done the same given the circumstances? His heart responded.

He couldn't maintain the anger no matter how much his brain pushed. His feelings toward Triona had changed and nothing could make them go back.

Stars this was a mess! This morning he hadn't thought about Triona as the enemy. He'd seen her as a desirable woman who lay soft and willing in his arms. No one had forced him to make love to her. He'd done it because that was what he wanted.

Hell, he still wanted her even now when he was dead tired. It went far beyond the physical needs of his body too. He wanted her to turn to him when she was upset or emotionally needy.

And if that wasn't enough to scare the life out of him he didn't know what was. Drake the Rake *wanting* emotional ties from a woman. Stars above this was an insane situation.

"You gonna tie that circuit off or shred it?" Smudge asked over his shoulder.

"I'm tying it off, old man. Keep your pants on."

"Woo hoo! Not me that needs to keep his pants on, boy. Seems to me yours have been off more than on." He cackled at his own wit while he closed up a circuit board.

"Isn't that what I'm here for?" Drake didn't need to deal with the twitchy old fart when his head was already messed up.

"That it is. And just you remember that. Don't go hurtin' the cap'n."

"That would be pretty hard to do since she holds the controller." She hadn't been holding it yesterday. And she sure as hell hadn't held it this morning.

"Yep. And if she doesn't use it on you I will. Bet on it, bucko."

Drake took one look at Smudge's squinty eyes and realized the pirate meant every word. He might look as old as dirt but he wouldn't let anyone hurt his captain. "I believe you."

He'd just have to make sure Smudge wasn't around when he made his break. Somehow the prospect of escape didn't seem quite so urgent any more. Drake arched his back to ease some of the kinks and finished repairing the circuit.

At a nod from Smudge he headed back to the cabin. There was no doubt in his mind that Smudge would drop him in a second if he tried to escape. The old bastard probably wanted him to make a move so he could zap him.

Well Drake hadn't made Squad Leader because of his good looks. He was no idiot and wasn't going to make a single twitch that would give Smudge an excuse to fry him. Nope, he'd play the docile little captive and go quietly back to his cabin.

After the day he'd had he was too tired to try to escape anyway. How did Triona manage to do this day after day and not drop? Granted, the ship wasn't always in this bad condition he imagined but even before the attack it must have needed constant maintenance to stay in one piece.

And how had a former concubine learned about electrical circuit repair? That was something he'd have to ask her if he ever got the opportunity.

Smudge let him into the cabin and made sure a guard was posted before he left him with a warning scowl. Drake snickered to himself as he pulled off his clothes. He'd probably disappointed the old man. Too bad. His body hurt enough without sending a surge of electricity through it.

His thoughts drifted a bit as he stepped out of his pants and into the sanitation unit. The bright light felt good against his aching muscles. Cleaning off the sweat and grease didn't hurt either.

A few minutes later he stepped out feeling refreshed, just in time to see Triona stumble in.

"What happened to you?" he asked. Her face looked red and bruised and a long scrape ran down her cheek. "Did you get into a fight?" Had one of her crew hit her? He'd kill them with his bare hands!

"Only with the reverberation converter. I had to overhaul it and the cooling cylinder fell on me. It's no big deal. At least I got the stupid thing fixed."

A slow burn of anger coiled in his gut. "I don't suppose you could have asked anyone else to do it for you? Those *fecking* cylinders weigh almost as much as you do!"

"Hardly. Don't you think you're exaggerating a tad? I'm fine and that's one more thing off the list. Besides, no one else knows how to fix the converter."

"I do. You could have asked me."

"How could I know that? I'm sorry I didn't ask you for help but you were plenty busy elsewhere on the ship. Next time I'll ask you before I do something you consider to difficult for my pretty little head." She stripped down and stepped into the sanitation unit with a huff.

Okay, now he felt like a jerk. He hadn't meant to make it sound like she couldn't take care of herself. She'd captured him and managed to keep this flying junk heap afloat, he should have realized she knew what she was doing.

As soon as she stepped out of the unit he went to her and took her hand in his. "I'm sorry for doubting your abilities. You're a damn good captain and I apologize for inferring otherwise." Any discomfort he might have felt eating crow vanished when she smiled at him.

"You're forgiven. I didn't mean to sound so defensive. I'm tired and achy and there's still so much more to do. I *should* have asked for help and I shouldn't have bitten your head off. Why don't we call it even and go to bed. I'm beat."

"I have a better idea. Why don't I get you a massage?"

"I'm not really in the mood…"

"Just a massage, not sex. Not that I'd be opposed to that idea, mind you but right now you need to relax more than I need relief."

"In that case a massage sounds like a great idea."

Drake led her to the bunk and bundled up the pillows and blanket for her to lie on comfortably. When she positioned herself he wisely covered her derrière with a sheet. If he wanted to keep his promise not to press her for sex he'd need to avoid temptation.

"Do you have any lotion or oil around?"

"I have some lotion in the storage unit," she mumbled sleepily.

If he didn't hurry up she'd be asleep before he could get started.

Snagging the lotion he rubbed it in his hands to warm it then poured a generous amount on her back. He straddled her legs and carefully kept most of his weight off her. She really was a delicate thing. It was hard to remember that when she was in motion—which was constantly.

Her skin felt silky smooth under his hands and his cock stirred to life. So much for hiding temptation. He could look at her little toe and probably get aroused at this point.

Triona let out a moan as he rubbed out a tight knot in her neck. "Stars, that feels good. I always knew you had great hands."

"You ain't seen nothing yet."

"Oh, I think I've seen plenty. But don't let that stop you." Her voice was muffled by the pillow but he could hear the smile in it.

An answering smile lifted his lips and warmth filled him. He loved bantering with her. That was a little surprising. Drake couldn't remember any other women he enjoyed spending time with if it didn't involve sex. Sure he had female co-workers but they mostly talked about work and went their separate ways. He didn't think he had any female friends or women he just enjoyed talking to.

It was a development he didn't really want to think about.

The overhead lights shone on her ivory skin, making it gleam. Her skin was soft as silk and felt just as smooth under his hands. His gaze moved down her back and he noticed very faint scars crisscrossing her lower back just above her ass. They were thin and white and looked very much like tiny whip marks. But if she was whipped, why in such an odd place? And why hadn't he felt them before?

"Triona?"

"Huh?" she mumbled sleepily.

"Where did you get these odd scars on your back?"

"Oh, those." Her body tensed. He ran his hand lightly over the marks. They weren't raised like other whip marks he'd seen. If the light hadn't hit them just right he'd never had noticed them. What the hell were they? Would she tell him?

Triona let out a shuddering breath before finally answering him. "Mistress Aphrodite. The 'trainer' at the school for concubines. She carried a thin belt that she'd use as a threat if we balked at our lessons."

Anger gripped him as he thought about her being whipped. There were several lines there, all very faint but they'd had to have stung. "But why way down there?"

"So if she left marks they wouldn't show when potential buyers came to view us."

"I can't believe they'd allow her to damage their future property," he said, the words tasting bitter on his mouth.

"They wouldn't have, which is why she used such a thin whip. It looked vicious so she rarely had to use it. But I was stubborn and she had to make an example out of me. It worked." Her voice grew husky but she continued on. "After one particularly bad class she staked me out in front of the entire group and whipped me."

Drake swore violently.

"It wasn't as bad as all that. She wasn't stupid. She kept the lashes light. The noise was enough to frighten most girls into obedience. I happen to scar easily so it looks worse than it actually was."

"I'm sure it was a walk in the park," he growled under his breath.

She gave a snort of laughter. "It wasn't that easy, no, but I've seen worse done by owners. At least I didn't have one that enjoyed pain."

He felt her shudder all the way through him and it strengthened his resolve. No human should have to endure such brutality and have it allowed by law.

"This conversation isn't helping to relax you, I'm afraid. I'm sorry I asked."

"Don't be. That's part of my past and I'm over it now. Lately it seems like I've come to terms with a lot of my past and gotten beyond the old pain."

Drake rubbed her arms in silence, considering her words. "Does this mean you no longer hate Traminians?" he asked finally.

"Well, I don't think I'd like to move there any time soon but there are definitely some Traminians that I wouldn't mind spending time with."

He bent over and kissed her nape lightly. "Good thing."

Chapter Six

Two weeks later

Triona sat in the captain's chair and stared at the vid screen. The enormous space station was visible even from a day out. The sight of it should thrill her. It meant they'd made it safely and *The Bunny* would live to fight another day.

Instead her heart felt like it was breaking in little chunks.

Tomorrow she'd set Drake free to do as he would. Even though it would kill her inside. A lump formed in her throat as she thought about life without him. Over the last two weeks she'd come to depend on him for far more than physical urges.

Though he'd handled urges she'd never known she had. But besides the sex he'd comforted her when she had bad dreams, which were much less often now that he held her in his strong arms every night. He'd done his fair share of work around the ship, helping her to contain the damage and even fixing some things she didn't have the expertise to repair.

And the man gave a damn good massage too.

After tomorrow that would be all over. She debated telling him her plan tonight but something held her back. Would he still want to make love with her if he knew she was letting him go? Or worse yet, would he sleep with her out of thanks?

What was she dithering about? Who cared if he had sex with her out of thanks or lust? He'd been sleeping with her because she forced him to since she met him.

But had he? More than once she'd woken up with him caressing her into arousal. She hadn't demanded his attention, they had been purely his actions. Could he want her on his own?

Triona pounded her hands against the console in frustration. What the hell was wrong with her? This had been so simple at the start. Since they couldn't ransom the Traminian she would get her revenge by using him as a sex slave and then set him free.

It wasn't supposed to get this complicated. Her feelings most definitely weren't supposed to get involved. But boy were they. In spades.

And it was killing her.

After all this time being consumed with hatred and distrust for men in general and Traminians in particular she fell in love with one. And she had to let him go.

The lump in her throat dropped to her stomach and settled there with a sickening thud. How could she let him go? But how could she not?

"You look awfully serious for someone who should be celebrating," Drake said as he ambled into the room.

Her heart did a slow flip in her chest and her blood pounded in her veins at the sight of him. He leaned against the door looking far too sexy for words. They'd made love in almost every position imaginable and still the mere sight of him made her mouth water.

"Someone has to steer the ship. I owed Smudge so I let him celebrate with the rest of the crew." The knowledge they were docking tomorrow didn't exactly put her in the mood to party.

"You want some company? Smudge may like me a bit more now that he's seen I won't destroy the ship but he's not about to let me drink with the rest of them."

"Have a seat. I wouldn't mind having someone to talk to." She'd much rather do something other than talk but she wouldn't push him on their last night together. Even if he didn't realize it was the end of their association.

Drake dropped into the chair next to her and reached for her hand. He idly stroked her palm with his thumb as he looked at the vid screen. "That's a big station, all right."

"Uh huh," she said vaguely. Her attention wasn't on his words but on the feel of his hand on hers. For the last two weeks he'd held her hand or wrapped an arm around her every time she was in touching distance. She should be used to it but it made her pulse thrum in her veins every time.

"You're awfully quiet tonight. Something on your mind?" he asked, bringing her hand to his mouth and drawing her finger inside.

"Lots of things," she said breathlessly. Heat flew from her finger straight to her crotch. His tongue teased the pad of her finger and reminded her of him licking her clit. Fire rushed to her pussy and her labia swelled with need.

"Anything I can help with?" His teeth bit into her flesh as he smiled wolfishly.

Her nipples sprang to attention under her shirt as he stood in front of her. "You're the problem."

"I guess I'll have to find the solution then." He pulled her up and captured her mouth in a steaming kiss.

Triona attacked his lips with all the pent-up desire flooding through her. If this was to be her last night with him she was going to make enough memories to last a long time. Her hands dove into his hair and held him still so she could ravage his mouth to her heart's content.

While her tongue and teeth were occupied, Drake's hands got busy untucking her shirt. His fingers stroked her breasts through her clothes. "Stars, you're a handful," he murmured against her mouth before loosening the ties of her shirt. "And a mouthful." He ran his mouth down until he could bite her nipple.

Words escaped her as molten lust boiled inside her. His tongue laved her sensitive bud as his hands kneaded both her breasts. Triona arched her back in ecstasy as cream flooded her pussy.

His rock-hard cock rubbed against her pussy and sparks seared her to the core at the contact. She released his head and pulled at the fly. She wanted to feel his erection. To stroke it and taste it until he cried for mercy. She ripped off his shirt and yanked his pants down.

With a laugh of pure lust, Triona knelt down and licked the weeping head of his gorgeous cock. The vein along the underside of his erection pulsed violently and his balls felt full and heavy. She fondled his sac as she sucked his cock into her mouth. The taste of him was honey on her tongue and she wanted to show him how much she enjoyed pleasuring him.

Still cradling his balls, she pressed her thumb against his perineum and lightly stroked the nerve bundle there. His sac was tight and ready to explode. Good. Just wait until he felt what she was going to do next.

With a secret smile, she moved her hand and grasped the base of his cock. Filling her mouth with saliva, she slid it over the length of him and pulled him deep into her throat. When his entire cock was wet she slowly drew her lips up his erection. As she slid back, she twisted her hand slightly until she reached his weeping tip.

Reversing the process, she twisted her hand back down and brought him as deeply into her throat as she could. His hoarse moan was music to her ears and she hummed in satisfaction.

"Mother of the cosmos! You're killing me!" He pulled her head away, breathing heavily.

"Didn't you like it?" she asked with a smug smile on her face. She could feel his balls tense in anticipation of coming and knew he was close to losing control.

"You know I did. Too much. I'm not coming until I can do it inside you."

Drake hauled her up against his chest and fumbled with her pants one-handed. He was clumsy and his fingers brushed repeatedly against her clit in the process. Triona's eyes almost crossed with frustration but he finally yanked her pants down around her ankles.

Before she knew what he was doing he spun her around and bent her over, bracing her hands on the console. Her ass stuck up in the air and her pussy lay wide open to his gaze.

"Oh Triona, you are a beautiful sight," he whispered against the cheeks of her ass. His hot breath caressed her wet pussy lips.

"I hope you plan on doing more than looking," she practically whimpered.

"Oh yeah." His finger drove inside her, rasping along every nerve of her sheath.

While his finger thrust inside her, Drake nipped the sensitive skin where thighs joined her butt. The fire he started with one kiss raged through her like an out of control inferno. The very atoms of her being were consumed with need for him and she couldn't wait much longer.

Luckily for her neither could he.

He stood behind her and maneuvered his cock inside her with ease. Triona clenched his throbbing cock with her inner muscles. Stars, how she loved the feel of him filling and stretching her.

Drake wrapped his arms around her waist as his hips rocked in and out slowly. She could feel his breath on her neck, his chest against her back and his sac slapping against her. One of his hands drifted up to squeeze her breast while the other slid down and tapped her clit.

Triona bit her lip to keep from screaming. Fire exploded from her swollen nub and grew as it traveled through her body.

"That's it, my sexy pirate, come for me." Drake pinched her nipple as he increased the tempo of both his finger and his hips.

Her whole body clamored for release and with one final stroke of his rough finger it was hers. Stars swam before her eyes in a dizzying ballet. Through her orgasmic haze she barely registered the sound of Drake's ragged breathing in her ear and his hands gripping her hips as he drove himself home.

She was still struggling to come back down to Earth when he erupted inside her, filling her with his seed. Triona milked him and his tremors echoed her own.

Drake lay in the chair completely boneless. Triona had slipped down to the cabin to clean up a bit and check on the crew. They must have talked her into sharing a pint of ale because she'd been gone for a while.

He'd lied slightly when he'd come in before. Smudge had grudgingly told him he could party with the crew, that he'd earned the right with his blood and sweat, but Drake had turned him down. It was his last night on the ship and he wanted to spend it with Triona.

His gut clenched with guilt and something else. He shouldn't feel guilty for planning his escape. It was a prisoner's job to escape, damn it!

Then why did he feel like he was betraying her? Why did the sight of her beautiful violet eyes make him want to confess everything and beg her to stay with him forever?

Because he was an idiot, that's why. Sure, he might have come to enjoy being with her but he couldn't spend the rest of his life on this flying junk heap being her sex toy. He had a job to do, a squad to lead and people who would be worried about him.

Plus, he had to get back to Tramin so he could petition the Council for Triona. Nothing short of death would stop him from that task. Any lingering doubts about his course turned to ash after seeing her scarred back. No one deserved to be treated like that and he was going to make sure no one else ever was.

He'd managed to find out his flitter was in working order, including the navigational systems. During the past two weeks he'd been allowed the run of the ship and had worked out a flight plan to get him home quickly. All he needed was a chance to slip out.

And that would come tomorrow morning while the crew prepared to dock. A ship this size was a bitch to land safely. Everyone would be focusing on getting into the space station without any more damage. They'd never notice him leaving. By the time they figured out he'd escaped he'd be too far away for the collar to zap him.

Yup, he had it all figured out and ready to go. So why did he feel like he was losing his best friend?

"Drake?" Triona's voice came from the door and he jumped up with a guilty start.

He turned to face her and his jaw dropped to the floor. Triona stood in the doorway wearing a traditional concubine dancing costume. Her gorgeous breasts were bound with a filmy scarf that looked ready to fall at the slightest breath. More scarves knotted around her waist made up the skirt.

With every step she took toward him her long beautiful legs flashed for his awed gaze. All the moisture in his mouth dried up and the blood rushed from his head to his cock in a heartbeat.

"I thought I'd gotten rid of this when O'Brien rescued me but I guess I kept it." She looked slightly embarrassed. She'd draped a scarf over her head and it trailed out behind her. "I guess I don't look much like a pirate in this get up."

She seemed to be waiting for some reassurance from him and he struggled to make his brain function enough to form words.

"You look amazing. I'm honored that you'd do that for me but it wasn't necessary. I—" He'd almost said he loved her no matter what she looked like but he bit the words off. "I don't have words to describe how lovely you look but I find you just as beautiful covered in grease and in your pirate garb."

"In that case I'll go change," she said with a cheeky grin. Her dimples flashed and her eyes glittered with mischief.

Guess he'd said the right thing. She no longer looked nervous. Suddenly she looked like a tiger on the hunt. And he was her prey. His cock pressed insistently against his pants as he watched her move around the bridge. The lights were dim since they operated at half power and gave the room a dreamy quality.

Triona fiddled with something on the console and soon smoky music surrounded him.

"I thought I'd give you a break tonight and be the slave for a change."

"Triona, you don't have to do this."

"I know. I want to." Her eyes glowed with something he couldn't identify but as soon as she started moving he lost his train of thought.

Truth be told, he'd lost every brain cell the minute she called his name. It didn't look like they'd be returning any time soon either.

"Sit."

Drake landed in the chair heavily. The music floated through the air and cast a spell over him. Triona's body moved to the beat, her hips gyrating sensuously. With every turn he got glimpses of her legs, her ass and the deep valley of her cleavage.

She shimmied around him, her scarves brushing over his bare chest and setting him aflame. He couldn't take his eyes off her as she transformed from the Triona he knew to some mysterious seductress who carried the secrets of endless pleasure in her eyes.

The tempo of the music increased and she spun faster and faster, her skirt flaring out around her. He caught glimpses of her pussy and groaned in frustration. Even though they had just made love his balls turned blue with agony.

Finally, the music ended and Triona stopped spinning. She'd ended with her hands on his knees, her face inches from his. Drake couldn't move for fear he'd break the spell. Her breasts heaved with exertion and sweat popped out on her brow.

Without a word he slid his fingers in the deep V between her breasts and pulled the scarf free. Her bounty spilled into his hands and he pressed his face between them, licking and kissing the creamy mounds feverishly.

Triona climbed on his lap and straddled his thighs. Her scarves parted as she spread her legs leaving her pussy bare. All that separated him from ecstasy was his pants but he wouldn't release her breasts to free himself.

"What do you wish of me, master?" she asked, licking the shell of his ear.

"Fuck that! I don't want a slave. I want you however, whoever you are."

"Then how do you want me, lover?" She bit his earlobe and rubbed against him.

"As fast as possible."

She reached down and pulled his aching cock free. In seconds she slipped him inside her hot, wet channel and he almost wept in relief. Her tight walls surrounded him and pleasure shot along every inch of his length.

Drake suckled a nipple hard against the roof of his mouth and was rewarded by a cry from Triona. She had a look of fierce concentration on her face and her beautiful eyes glowed with passion.

Taking his head in her hands, she pulled his face up for a kiss that stunned him with its intensity. Her breasts pressed against his chest and her thighs gripped his as she pumped up and down on his cock.

It was too much for him to handle. Drake grabbed her hips and thrust up into her as she came down on him. Both of them strained to reach the pinnacle of desire. He felt his orgasm begin at the base of his dick and stroked her clit frantically to make sure she came too.

As the shudders of release overtook him, he felt her body spasm around him. Drake shook as his body continued to pulse into hers. He closed his eyes as his muscles turned to water inside him. He couldn't move if the entire United Federation army marched through the room.

Triona cuddled against him sleepily and he knew he didn't want to ever move again.

* * * * *

Morning came far too soon for Triona's heart. She and Drake had made love through the night and her body still hummed from his attentions. They were like two possessed. Neither could get enough of the other and the slightest touch turned into frenzied coupling.

She leaned over the bed and pressed a kiss against his sleep-slackened lips. It was time she headed to the bridge to prepare for their docking. Getting *The Bunny* into a space station was never easy but on half power it would take all her concentration and skill.

Yet another reason she couldn't linger ogling Drake's naked form. Even if it was the last time she'd see it. She sighed and slipped out of the room. Damn it, she was doing the right thing. It shouldn't hurt so badly to do the right thing.

Integrity sucked.

The bridge was already bustling with activity. Her crew looked a little green around the gills after last night's party but they moved smartly enough when she appeared.

"This is gonna be a stone bitch, Cap'n," Smudge said as he got out of the captain's chair.

"I know. I'm going to need everyone in position and paying attention. We don't have the credits to pay a fine if we bump something. Understood?" She raised her voice so everyone could hear.

There were a few winces at her volume but they all nodded in agreement.

"All right then. Let's dock this tub."

Anxiety rolled in her gut as she waited for the security drones to read her serial number off her port side. She'd been assured this number was guaranteed legit but that didn't mean squat. If the number had been reported stolen the authorities would investigate further and they'd see pretty quickly *The Bunny* wasn't the space scavenger she pretended to be.

"Proceed." The mechanical voice came through the speakers and the entire bridge let out a collective breath of relief. They were in no shape to escape pursuit from the authorities.

The path to the docking bay was littered with obstacles to prevent ships from speeding in out of control. It was a good idea that prevented serious crashes but moving a ship on half power around them was nearly impossible. Triona was sure she'd see gray hair in the mirror after that docking.

A cheer went through the crew as the station's tractor beam picked them up for the short trip into the bay. Triona fell back in her chair, the tension washing out of her shoulders at last. Taking a look around she noticed everyone heading for their cabins to gather their belongings. It wasn't often they got to get off the ship and they'd want to blow off some steam.

Good. That would give her time to free Drake without an audience or interference.

She joined the departing mob and slipped to her cabin. It was empty. Her gut clenched in dread. She ran to the docking bay and prayed she was in time.

Skidding to a stop, she saw Drake climbing into his flitter. At the sound of her footsteps he stopped and faced her.

"Leaving without even saying goodbye?" A lump clogged her throat but she refused to let her emotions show. She knew he would escape at the first chance. She'd been a fool to think otherwise.

"I have to, Triona. I can't stay here and be your sex toy."

"Go ahead. I'm not stopping you."

"What? You're not going to zap me as soon as I step foot in my ship?" He laughed harshly. "Somehow I doubt you came here to see me off."

Triona pulled the controller out of her pocket and tossed it to him. "Here, you can have it. I took the batteries out of it after the first day anyway."

She watched the surprise flash across his face but he quickly covered it. "I have to get back to Tramin. I can't stop the abuse of the concubines if I don't."

It was her turn to laugh. "You don't have to blow sunshine up my tailpipe. I was going to let you go as soon as we docked anyway. I'm no Traminian who would keep someone enslaved forever." Her voice cracked with unshed tears. She dug her nails into her palms to keep from letting those sobs spill out.

"I'm not lying. I'll petition the Council until they're so sick of me they abolish slavery. I have friends in high places. I can do this." He lifted a hand toward her but dropped it back to his side.

"Just go." She didn't want to hear any more of his excuses. All her agonizing over setting him free was for nothing. She didn't know why she was so damn surprised that he'd been planning to escape all along. Just because he acted like he cared about her and tried to help her didn't mean he'd want to stay with her. Hell, just because she developed feelings for him didn't mean he returned them. The hurt of betrayal tore at her heart and she couldn't hold back the tears any longer.

"I'll get your flight clearance from the station so they don't blow you or us out of space. Happy flying, Traminian." She was proud that none of her agony showed in her voice. Slowly she turned on her heel and walked out.

"Triona! Don't leave!"

She kept walking and slammed the door shut behind her. Hopefully he'd get the hint and leave because she couldn't handle it if he came after her. After endless minutes she heard the roar of his flitter.

He was gone, forever. And her heart would never be the same.

Chapter Seven

Two months later

Drake kicked back in his chair and ordered another beer. Doing the right thing blew chunks. Even though he'd managed to find an underground society of abolitionists, he wasn't any closer to ending slavery. Hell, things were getting worse instead of better. He'd lost his commission as Squad Leader because he refused to stop fighting to end slavery. Death threats had started coming on a regular basis and he'd only barely won enough support to get the bill up before the next session of Council.

Unless he could get some more support behind the bill it would never pass. All this work for a whole lot of nothing.

And he missed Triona. He pulled a filmy scarf out of his pocket and ran it through his fingers. It was one of the scarves that had made up her skirt. He'd used it to tease her pussy during one of their last times together. It might be his imagination but he could swear he could still smell her scent on it even two months later.

Shards, it had been two months and what did he have to show for it besides a major case of blue balls? When Triona had turned her back on him he vowed he'd show her he wasn't lying. Visions of bringing her back to a concubine-free Tramin played out in his mind. He thought of millions of pleasurable ways for her to show her gratitude when he told her she would never have to be a slave again.

Unless she wanted to put on the costume and dance for him that is.

It had been two months since then and he hadn't accomplished jack. Who was he kidding? He'd never be able to convince the Council to abolish slavery. Half of them probably had concubines! He should just get in his flitter and go find Triona.

Except he had no idea how to find her again.

The serial number she'd given the space station had been a fake so he couldn't trace her through that. Not that he hadn't tried.

He downed the rest of his beer and slipped a credit chip into the automated slot. Getting drunk wasn't going to help him tonight. Maybe in the morning he could try and find a signature ion trail and follow that from the space station.

There was a slim chance there'd be something left of the trail. Slim was better than nothing and it would give him something to do while he waited for Council to get back in session.

Drake pushed his way out of the bar around a group of burly soldiers. As he cleared the mob he did a double take. One of those soldiers looked damn familiar. He had only enough time to recognize Smudge through his disguise before the old bastard hit him with a tranquilizer dart.

* * * * *

Triona paced the confines of her cell and bit what was left of her nails. The last thing she remembered was getting hit with a tranquilizer dart five minutes after they docked.

Damn it, she knew better than to get this close to Tramin! If she hadn't been pining after Drake she wouldn't have gotten caught by the Feds. She'd told Smudge it was risky landing on one of Tramin's satellites but he told her she worried too much.

Now she didn't know what happened to her ship and her crew. Some of them had some serious arrest warrants out. Others were freed slaves like herself. Most of them couldn't afford to get caught by the authorities.

Stars, she hoped Smudge had seen her get hit by the dart and taken off. The worst that would happen to her is that she'd have to go back to her old master. Fear lodged in her gut. She wouldn't be killed but that was almost worse than death.

The tread of several feet thudded down the hall and Triona tensed as they stopped at her cell. The door slammed open and a body was thrown in. The door slammed shut again before she could get a look at her captors.

Triona rushed over to see if her new cellmate was all right. She rolled the body over and almost passed out when she saw Drake.

He looked bad. His hair was even longer and his face hadn't been shaved in days. The smell of beer oozed from his pores and his clothes were none too clean. He was a sight for sore eyes.

But why was he in jail? And with her? Had he gotten blamed for not turning her back in? Oh no! She couldn't let that happen! She'd confess to kidnapping him and turn herself in before she let him take the rap for her.

She stroked his face and smoothed the hair back off his brow. If she had even one brain cell left she should be dancing for joy that he got arrested for something too. The old Triona who lived for vengeance would have been glad to see him brought low but not now.

No. Something had happened to her in the time she'd spent with Drake. Maybe she'd grown up or maybe loving him had helped her to let go of the past. Whatever it was, she'd changed. And she'd do anything to save Drake, even if it meant becoming a slave again.

His eyes fluttered open and she stared into his beautiful blue orbs.

"Triona? Am I dreaming?" his voice was raspy.

"Afraid not. You're in jail with me."

He grabbed her hand and held it tightly as if worried she'd run away. Where exactly was she going to go in a cell, she couldn't guess.

"Jail? Why would Smudge put me in jail?"

"Smudge? What are you talking about? I got nabbed on Satellite Nine. When I woke up I was here. I figured the Feds caught up with me finally."

"No, I saw Smudge outside the bar in the capital. He hit me with a tranq dart."

"What? You're sure you saw him?" Triona pulled her hand away and jumped to her feet.

"I'm positive. He's rather distinctive you know."

She ran to the door and banged on it furiously. "Smudge you rotten son of a space whore!!! Open this cell!"

Rowdy laughter sounded from the other side. "Not until the two of you make up or kill each other. I don't care which either. Just so ye aren't pinin' away anymore!"

"And to think I bit my nails to nubs over worry for you!" She kicked the door for good measure and crossed back to where Drake sat on the floor.

"So. You were pining for me?" Drake asked, taking her hand back.

"Don't flatter yourself. I was just mad you escaped before I could be magnanimous and release you." Her heart fluttered at the touch of his hand and her stomach flipped with nerves. Now that she was with him she felt anxious.

"Oh really? Well I was miserable without you. Actually, I was on my way to the space station to see if I could trace your ion trail."

"You were?" Her voice was faint. Hope flared in her heart but she quickly squashed it down. She didn't dare believe him again. He could be saying that because he wanted a quickie and she was available.

A little tingle stirred in her pussy. A quickie might not be such a bad idea…

No, no, no! She would not settle for just sex ever again. If she'd learned anything since he'd been gone it was that she loved him and wanted him in her life, not only in her bed.

"You bet. I have nothing to do until Council is back in session anyway so I figured I'd go looking for you and beg you to take me back."

"What about your Squad?" Against her better judgment her heart swelled with joy at his words.

"I lost my commission when I wouldn't stop pestering the Council to abolish slavery."

"Oh no!"

He really did it! Stars! Triona couldn't believe he'd petitioned the Council on her behalf. And it wasn't just a token gesture either. He'd lost his commission over it.

"Oh yes. And I couldn't care less. All I want is to be with you. I've been miserable these last two months. If I didn't have to be present at every public forum to fight for my bill I'd have been searching high and low for you."

Tears of happiness or love or relief slipped down her cheeks as she threw herself into his arms. So many feelings stirred inside her she couldn't sort them out. The only thing that mattered was Drake was back in her life and wanted to be there.

"I've missed you so much. You can probably tell I've made Smudge crazy. I couldn't concentrate on anything and didn't want to eat or anything. I'm sorry I didn't tell you sooner that I planned on freeing you. I was afraid you'd want to leave immediately or only sleep with me out of thanks." Her words tumbled over themselves in the rush to get out.

"Honey, I'm thankful that I'm the lucky bastard that gets to sleep with you but I'd never fake my feelings for you." He gripped her shoulders and stared her right in the eye. "I love you. I want to be with you forever, as a team."

More tears leaked down her face. "I love you, too. So very much I thought I'd die without you."

Drake pulled her close and crushed her to his chest. "You're too tough to die but I'm glad you think you would. I was really afraid you'd refuse to see me if I ever found you. I guess I should thank Smudge for interfering."

"Yeah, I guess we should. But let's not tell him that yet. I say we let him stew out there for a while wondering if we killed each other." She rubbed her sensitive breasts against his chest and felt his cock harden beneath her.

"He probably wouldn't believe a stubborn pirate like you would give up the fight so easily anyway." Drake pulled her shirt over her head.

"Me? Stubborn?" She wanted to protest further but Drake had pulled a nipple into his mouth briefly and all she could do was gasp.

"Yes. You. But I love you anyway."

Triona pulled his head up to hers and kissed him hard. They fell over backward until she lay on top of him, his erection pressing into her mons. "Good. Because now that we're a team I'm never letting you go."

"I dare you to try." Drake pushed her pants over her hips and trailed his fingers up the backs of her legs.

Heat pooled in her core and cream wet her thighs. She tore furiously at his clothes, ripping his shirt in her haste to get him naked. When he finally lay bare to her gaze she crawled between his legs to make love to his gorgeous cock. It pulsed there, red and throbbing for her.

She nuzzled his sac and the familiar musky odor assailed her senses. Sliding her lips up his length she let her tongue curl around him, wetting him with her saliva. With a shiver she pressed her breasts around his cock and rubbed it between them.

Drake's face looked almost pained in his ecstasy. With every glide up his cock she licked the weeping eye in his glans. Her hands cupped his balls lightly and she pressed her finger along the nerves near his anus.

She slipped her tongue around the soft head of his cock again and lapped up the pre-cum that dripped there. His taste rolled over her tongue and she couldn't get enough of it.

"You taste so good. I've missed it."

"Not half as much as I have." In a move too fast for her to follow, he flipped her over and pressed his face into her pussy.

It was his turn to taste her juices and her body shuddered in pleasure. His lips and tongue teased her clit while his finger speared her channel. Triona arched up against his weight as the pleasure swamped her. His cock brushed her cheek and she took advantage of the position.

While Drake drove her to distraction playing with her nubbin, she sucked his length as deeply into her throat as she could. Her whole body was on fire for him, straining to meld with him in any way possible.

When his thumb pressed against her anus, surges of pleasure slammed into her and rocked her to the core. Her body convulsed with forgotten pleasure and still he licked her.

"No more! I want you in me!"

"Works for me!" He rolled over and hauled her on top of him. His lips and tongue slid over her torso and captured her mouth in a devastating kiss.

More fluid gushed from her pussy as their tongues dueled. Love and lust swam through her veins making her glow from within. Drake's fingers fondled her clit as he slipped his cock into her welcoming warmth. Sharp bursts of pleasure exploded wherever he touched and she almost wept at the feel of him filling her.

"Stars I missed this," Drake groaned in her ear. His hands kneaded her breasts as she reared up above him.

The position rubbed her clitoris against his pubic bone and increased the heat building inside her. She didn't know how much longer she could contain the sunburst within her.

Drake arched up and bit lightly on her nipple as he grasped her ass in his hands. The sting of his teeth on her sensitive tip, the feel of his cock hot and hard inside her, and the stroke of his body against her nubbin was too much for her to take.

The orgasm hit her like a supernova and swept her away. There was no way she could ever recover from this. She collapsed against him as he drove up into her two more times and reached his own release.

"I don't know if I can handle you, woman. You make me crazy with lust."

"Same goes. And I wouldn't have it any other way."

He kissed her brow and cuddled her close. She loved how his arms made her feel safe from the world. She'd love to stay wrapped in his cocoon of protection forever.

But it wasn't possible.

"Would you mind if we didn't live on Tramin? I'm still a fugitive there."

"Not for long. The bill might not pass at this session but I'll keep putting it up every chance I get. If I could get your testimony it would help."

"And maybe if I told my story, other women would find courage in that and come forward. You bet I'll do it," she said, excitement coloring her voice.

"And until then we can travel through the stars when Council isn't in session. That is if your ship is still running."

Triona smiled down on him and stroked his face. "I'm afraid not. *The Bunny's Revenge* is no more. We stripped her down and sold her for parts. Her reputation had gotten a little too infamous so we went into retirement."

"You mean you're not a pirate anymore? Forget it then, the deal's off," he teased.

"I'm still a pirate at heart." She mock punched him in the arm. "But now I'm a respectable entrepreneur. With a new ship and everything."

"Oh really?"

"Yes, sir. You're talking to the captain of *Bunny Love*, space scavenger extraordinaire."

"*You* are my bunny love and I'm never letting you go."

That was slavery she could live with.

About the Author

Arianna Hart lives on the East Coast with her husband and three daughters. When not teaching, writing, or chasing after her children and the dog, Ari likes to practice her karate, go for long walks, and read by the pool. She thinks heaven is having a good book, warm sun, and a drink in her hand. Until she can sit down long enough to enjoy all three, she'll settle for the occasional hour of peace and quiet.

Arianna welcomes comments from readers. You can find her website and email address on her author bio page at www.ellorascave.com.

Also by Arianna Hart

Behind the Enchanted Door

By Honor Bound anthology

Convince Me

Ellora's Cavemen: Legendary Tails III (*anthology*)

Federation Chronicles: Lucy's Lover

Federation Chronicles: Rebel's Lust

Federation Chronicles: Sloan's Heart

Sable Flame

Screw Cupid

Silver Fire

CRASH COURSE

Dawn Madigan

"Ladies, gentlemen…when it comes to combat, think of a good fuck… There is no such thing as a simple in-and-out operation."

~ *"Naval Strategy and Tactics" opening lecture,*
P.G.A. Navy Academy

Prologue

The Ambrosine, Captain's bridge
Charted deep space

ᘓ

The *Ambrosine* quaked from deep within, jarred brutally by another direct hit. Navy Commander Blade Steele had been exceptionally lucky over the last few Galactic-hours.

Which was more than could be said for the Ambrosine's captain.

"Fuckin' military bastard!"

Starship captain Chiliad-Kai Jayrt'ian smashed a large fist against the flashing navigation board as all hell broke loose around him. Shrill bleeps and buzzes joined the ominous flickering lights illuminating his bridge.

"*Ambrosine*, kill the *fuckin'* alarms!"

"Alarms deactivated, Captain," his ship acknowledged with a sultry voice, swiftly deactivating the cacophony of warning signals. That breathy, on-the-verge-of-an-orgasm voice had been programmed into the ship's computer by Chiliad himself. It had helped pull him through some of his darkest deep-space moments.

"Much, much better," he grunted at the sound of blessed silence. Steele's battle cruiser was gaining fast on his battered ship.

Hell, this was supposed to be a clean, in-and-out job! Load goods aboard ship at Kintha's lesser moon then take off like greased lightning.

Only, somewhere between "lesser moon" and "greased lightning", Chiliad's neat little plan had gone brilliantly awry. Being hotly pursued by a fully armed battle cruiser clearly wasn't listed on the day's schedule. For the last couple of hours Chiliad had been sweating blood, tweaking the *Ambrosine's* performance to the max, trying to convince his light trader it could beat a third-class battle cruiser. And right now, his persuasion skills were failing miserably.

Someone had tipped off Steele regarding his whereabouts, Chiliad was sure of that. That lesser-moon wiseguy, maybe. The sleazy crook *had* flashed him quite a nasty smirk when the goods had been safely tucked into the *Ambrosine's* belly. Chiliad made a mental note to run a little private investigation at a later, more leisurely time, and grill the two-timing bastard's ass. Assuming he wouldn't get his own ass grilled first by the cruiser's DEWs—Directed-Energy Weapons.

Dammit, he had to bail out of here, *fast*!

"*Ambrosine,* give me the closest leeway estimate on a hyperleap."

"Leeway estimate unavailable. Navi-system malfunction." His ship sounded like she was about to climax at any moment.

"No shit." He cursed roundly as another fiery line emanating from the cruiser's DEWs seared through his view screen.

And missed.

Chiliad forced out a slow breath. The last direct hit that had rocked the *Ambrosine* had been a damn close call. Commander Steele was hardly dropping the chase. First of all, the military bastard *was* winning. Second, the Naval senior officer had a bitter, three-year-old grudge against the rogue pirate—one of Chiliad's smuggling operations had cost Steele a long-overdue promotion. In the Pan-Galactic Alliance's Navy, you missed one promotion and all you had to deal with was the bad rep—you missed two in a row and the P.G.A. politely kicked your ass out the door.

The unremitting shower of heavy artillery clarified whose ass was in immediate frying danger, though.

Chiliad growled at his view screen. He was done picking his brain for smartass evasion maneuvers. He'd already tried every damn trick in the book. Every damn trick, except for a semi-suicidal one… Leaping naked into hyperspace, without his Navi-system's cushioning computations. There was no telling where such a leap would land him. It might plant him right inside the heart of the nearest supernova, for all he knew. On the other hand…

Chiliad raked his fingers through his wild chestnut mane. His deep-blue gaze scoured the view screen with one last assessing glance. Was he insane enough—no, desperate enough—to try it?

Apparently, he was.

"*Ambrosine,* bypass leeway. Perform hyperleap in ten. Commence countdown now."

"Commencing countdown at ten," the *Ambrosine* breathlessly obeyed. *"Performing hyperleap in ten…nine…eight…"*

Chapter One

Chebrri, Dyad Star System
Uncharted Territories

"Val, don't you *dare* touch him!"

"Why?"

"His kind is an abomination!" Aello spat, tightening her fist on her sheathed *sheko*. Strands of night-dark hair, loosened by the wind from beneath her head-wrap, swirled around her anxious face. She stared from a safe distance at their oversized, unmistakably masculine catch.

"Since when are *you* the expert on men?" Valasca ignored her companion's indignant, sharp gasp at her taunt. In truth, she'd meant naught more than to play for time. The twin suns danced prickly heat against her skin, and yet she had no wish to rise from her crouch.

She'd just found a true, flesh-and-blood man!

How could she so easily discard such an enticing, rare capture? She swayed closer to the hefty, motionless male, her hair bathing her shoulders in starless black. The lengthy, light blue tails of her head-wrap dangled from her neck, twirled by a warm desert breeze.

The man *was* huge… Big hands, big feet. Big everything-in-sight. Too bad he was slumped on his face, his fascinating front buried in hot sand. The way he was turned, she couldn't make out his face, veiled by a wild tumble of chestnut hair.

She'd never encountered anyone like him before. Usually such a treat was reserved for the priestesses alone, while she, as well as Aello, were trained to lead the warring life of a trader. As much as she hated to admit it, her patrol-companion was right—they had no business dealing with his kind. Their pressing duty was to report their find to the Temple. But the pulsating auroras had broken off radio communication, which meant they had to make their way back to the settlement—about a day's flight, no stops included—to get their message across.

Val's thoughts moved to a subject far more fascinating, one sprawled almost within an arm's reach.

Was the man truly out cold? Might he already be dead?

No, the steady rise and fall of his expansive torso could hardly be missed. Val's heart pounded. She extended her left arm, her saber-arm, aiming her *sheko*'s knob at the impressive, sand-caked man. The sticklike weapon throbbed faintly, not yet fully activated.

"Will you quit being such a total *putanah*?" Aello squeaked in her nervousness, her voice breaking on an involuntary high note. "Val, *listen*. We d-don't have the Temple's permit for this! We should be heading back—"

"He'll die if we leave him here."

"Then the Dyad will care for his soul, if he owns one! Besides, if *he* made it here, there might be more like him. Let's fly."

"We saw none from the air besides this one," Val insisted.

Her curious hazel gaze caressed the man's large, still form. She bit her bottom lip in thought. There were forbidden stories running around the cadet traders camps about *things* done in the Temple's innermost chambers. Mysterious rites performed by the priestesses alone with the captured males brought by Chebrri trader crews from faraway worlds. Worlds she'd never been to. She was about to venture off-world on her first journey as a trader, joining Lyssipe's crew. Knowing she'd finally *see* men—live ones, not 3-D displays—on her upcoming journey, Val had been wondering what, exactly, men were *about*.

Did all of them look like this one?

Her eager gaze roved over the white fabric that clung to the man's broad back. Val's assessing eyes skimmed over the man's bared shoulders, the burnished swell of his powerful arms. His honey-tan, muscled forearms were dusted with dark, curly hair.

Val was fascinated by the sight. His upper arms boasted no hair, their flesh smooth and golden.

How would it feel?

A ludicrous notion hit her.

Maybe he wasn't that different from her, after all…

Or was he?

Val dared a glance lower. A search for *some* kind of concealed weapon was warranted, surely? Her gaze found none in plain sight, but she glimpsed lean hips and the black-swathed curves of the man's backside. She took a hard swallow as her eyes gulped their fill. The sleek material of his breeches seemed molded against the solid hardness of his thighs. He wouldn't last long in the heat, wearing such a tight-fitting garment.

Val's sable brows bunched together in a quizzical frown as she surveyed the man's intriguing physique all the way back up again.

He looked like…like…

Trouble.

Aello had had enough. "By the Dyad, Val!"

Val startled, her cheeks burning at her brazen thoughts. Her trembling hand gave her *sheko* a light, inadvertent squeeze. Before she could stop it, the weapon ignited with a soft hiss, its dull point blushing to an angry red. A burst of biting current shot into the man's unwavering flesh, swathing it with leaping bluish sparks.

Val sucked in her breath.

"Dammit!" Starship captain and space-outlaw Chiliad-Kai Jayrt'ian was *done* playing dead. His head had already been pulsating with the baking heat and the strain of listening to the ongoing, melodious gibberish being spoken above him. Being shot at was just an added bonus. Lucky for him the damn thing had been set to a low energy level.

He erupted from the sand with a savage groan, tossing a shock of chestnut hair off his chiseled face. His eyes shot open with startling abruptness and almost instantly squeezed shut again, unaccustomed to the stark light.

Val's mouth gaped as she stared in horrified fascination at the otherworldly sight before her.

Aello screamed in terror, stumbling back over her own feet. Scrambling up again, she darted toward the hovering *wingless* and pressed a palm against its gleaming alloy surface. The patrol craft's doors flowed open silently.

Val shot an alarmed glance in the direction of the *wingless*. Her taut thigh muscles bunched as she readied herself to pull up from her crouch.

The man moved with a power and speed she hadn't foreseen. His large, sand-encrusted hand clamped on her left wrist like a steely manacle.

"Stay, honey," he growled in hoarse command, his eyes ablaze. "I fear I must insist."

The man's throaty accent was alien to Val's ears, but she could make out the words fine enough. The man was speaking *Hub-Nemean*, a language taught as part of her training.

What was he doing on Chebrri?

The vibrant potency of his grip briefly stunned her. Her *sheko*'s knob wasn't in intimate contact with the man's body, but a powerful enough energy arc could still bridge the narrow gap. A full-force charge would also fry a big, nasty hole in him. Something vague kept Val from doing just that. Instead, her right hand shot to her weapon's shaft. She flung her full weight into the man, jabbing her *sheko*'s tip into his ribcage with brutal force.

She took him by surprise. He toppled backwards, his breath wheezing out in an agonized hiss.

He took her down with him as he fell. She raked a hard, single-handed blow over the side of the man's head, hearing him groan—more with rage than pain.

She twisted against the sand and him, her light-blue head-wrap slipping down her neck. Kicking both her feet hard into his stomach, she finally wrenched her left forearm free from his grip.

Panting, Val scrambled up to a crouch and staggered toward the hovering *wingless.*

Unluckily for her, the man was determined and much, much stronger than she.

Val cried out as he plunged after her and seized her ankles, dragging her back down. She fell hard, facedown in the sand.

With a rough oath the man climbed atop her, almost wrenching her right arm out of its socket with a sharp, painful twist.

The air rushed out of Val's lungs with a ragged scream. Her numb fingers let go of her *sheko* and it dropped to the sand. An isolated, cool part of her mind prayed her leather canteen wouldn't go the same way, spilling its precious water. She gasped as the man flipped her on her back with ease. His powerful hands captured both her wrists, forcing them against the sand, high over her head. Grinding his pelvis against her, he sank heavily between her thighs, pinning her down with his weight alone. They were both breathing hard now, awash with sweat.

"Don't…fuckin'…fight me," the savage commanded with a thirst-abraded voice.

Dizzy, Val struggled to make out his words.

Sweet Dyad, what was he doing on top of her?

Panic hit her in a blinding, violent surge. She howled like a caged animal, straining against her captor as wild terror swept over her entire being. Why hadn't she shot him while she was able to? She had never had a man above her…had never had one touching her, had never seen one that wasn't a lifeless hologram. Outside the Temple's boundaries, men were a banned species on the world of Chebrri-Taj. For once she should have listened to Aello…

Speaking of whom, where had her trusty companion gone?

Val struggled to look for the *wingless,* writhing beneath the weight that was crushing her against the hot sand.

"Fuckin' stars, I'm not going to hurt you— Will ya relax? *Shit!*"

Chiliad swore as the thrashing girl's white teeth dug a set of double crescents into his right arm. Her dark limbs were slick with sweat, making it harder for him to hold her down. There was a huge ache where his head should have been, and his sunburned skin still prickled with the energy charge from the girl's odd weapon. *Stars, who else was hearing the girl's screams?* He had to put an end to this madness, now!

Val managed to crane her neck to a painful angle, gasping aloud and spitting out sand. Most of it found the man's face. *Good,* she thought with frenzy as his expression soured. The edge of her visual field caught a white blaze streaking the low sky, the *wingless* making a swift escape across the arid dunes.

"*No!*" Val cried out with a torn breath. "Aello—you scared little piece of—"

Her screams were sharply cut off as the man's large hand clamped over her mouth. Val's free hand wrapped weakly around his wrist then sagged to the sand. Her world slowly dimmed.

"Shit," Chiliad grunted, staring down with a deepening frown at the passed-out hellcat beneath him.

He swiftly withdrew his hand from her mouth with another curse. Dammit, he'd miscalculated his own strength—and now the little demon was out cold! Alive, though, he noted with relief. All he'd wanted was to break that raging fit of hysterics…

Chiliad's sour gaze lifted to arch about the landscape. The sky's unusual brightness made him wince again before his eyes managed to take in the view.

Sand, sand, sand!

And just to make sure he got the message—more sand.

But the scene wasn't totally monotonous. It had a bunch of rocks in it too.

Chiliad gritted out an inventive oath. His aching brain tried to remember the *Ambrosine's* last position just before she'd made that flashy plunge through the planet's atmosphere. A hell of a fireworks show too—he'd been wondering who else might have witnessed it besides the two wildcats who'd found him.

His battered Navi-system had cast the *Ambrosine* out of hyper dangerously close to the broiling heart of a binary star system. Suddenly the twin suns of this cursed system had been filling his view screen.

The pair hosted a complete set of seven planets. The third one had seemed uninhabited, and Chiliad had swiftly decided it was as good a target as any to crash on.

Right now, he wasn't so sure.

"Of all the shitholes in Nemean charted space," Chiliad growled with feeling. He reconsidered. Dammit, he was probably off charted territories altogether! Rephrasing, he again ground out with menace, "Of all the *shitty*, gods-forsaken places in the fuckin' unknown universe—"

A soft, breathless moan beneath him drew his gaze back down. The girl's head turned to the side, her lean muscles taut against the sweat-slick prison his body made. With all the harshness drained from her face, she had a fresh, true beauty—an untamed, natural look that stacks of artificial enhancers couldn't produce. He knew all there was to know about beauty enhancers—he used to smuggle tons of the stuff, among other things of a less benign nature.

She was the most gorgeous thing he'd ever laid eyes on.

Her hair fanned against the golden sand in midnight-black abandon. He could tell exactly how the silken strands would feel sifting through his fingers… Better yet, he could vividly imagine the dark splendor spilling over his ribcage as she rode him.

Chiliad groaned, shaking his head.

Water first, wet dreams later!

Still, he couldn't stop staring at her.

Beneath the sand, her skin was a dark olive. Her eyes were shut tightly, their long, thick lashes painting dark crescents against her high cheekbones. He remembered her slanted hazel eyes, alight with a heady blend of daring and terror. There was something vaguely familiar about her looks…

Maybe it would come to him later.

Chiliad's gaze dropped to the girl's full, rosy lips. Her mouth was a sweet candy asking to be licked. Unable to quench the urge, he bent low and ran a slow tongue over each lip, moistening it to its rightful dewy lushness.

A tiny protesting moan slipped from her mouth into his own.

Chiliad couldn't help a roguish grin, his mouth still a hairsbreadth from hers. He rather liked the lush womanly curves hugging his hard thighs, and he just *loved* the full, rounded ones pressing taut against his chest. She boasted a form more curvaceous than that commonly seen—and felt—in Nemea-Hub.

Not that he'd recently paid a visit to his home solar system. Too many kind souls were lurking there in hope he might be thickheaded enough to show his face again. *Idiots, the whole lot of them,* he thought without much rancor. For a long time now Jayris, the planet of his birth, had ceased being home. Home was within the *Ambrosine,* in the emptiness between the stars. But he needed help to get back up there, and his delicious little captive seemed the closest one to give it—

He felt her tensing beneath him and readied himself for a second round.

The long, sooty lashes stirred. She was staring straight up at his face, her eyes misty, as if she'd just woken up from a dream. So darkly angelic and beautiful that Chiliad was almost tempted to ease his harsh hold…

In an instant her eyes cleared and sparked golden fire.

Her lovely mouth flew open.

And *screamed.*

Chiliad gave his pulsating head a savage shake. That *scream* was the most horrible sound he'd heard throughout the passing Nemean-year, even counting his unfortunate clash with a bunch of hydras in the Jorrani swamps. Groaning, he clamped his hand over the beauty's mouth.

Somewhat more carefully this time, though.

"If you want to breathe again, honey," he grunted, "*don't* scream."

Her eyes grew wider above his clasped hand, but she seemed to warm to the idea.

Chiliad cocked a cautious brow. Slowly, he withdrew his hand, ready to go through the same drill all over again if the need arose.

She kept quiet, a dark flush tinting her cheeks. Her nostrils flared with each quick, shallow breath.

One corner of Chiliad's mouth shot up in a wicked grin. "Smart girl," he whispered. "Women never scream because of me, honey…unless they're screaming for more."

"That's probably because you gag them!" the girl lashed out in crude *Hub-Nemean*, struggling to regain her breath.

Chiliad froze in surprise. He let out a low, humorless chuckle. "You're a true bundle of joy, aren't you?"

"Why don't you take your big paws off of me and find out?"

He cocked an amused brow. "Fine by me, but play nice…or we'll be doing this all over again. I wouldn't mind that, wildcat…I wouldn't mind that at all."

She spat in his face.

Chiliad didn't even blink. Slowly, he lowered his mouth to his captive's delicate ear, his unshaven jaw brushing her silken cheek. She instantly froze beneath him. She started to tremble against his body, her hands balling into small fists. His hold on her sweaty wrists tightened. Very softly, he drawled into her ear.

"What's your name, honey?"

"V-Val," she stammered in a thready voice.

"Keep in mind that I mean business, Val," Chiliad murmured, an unmistakable undertone flaring in his voice. His strong teeth captured her earlobe and tugged gently, then let go. He felt her ample breasts pressing tauter against his chest as she reacted with a sharp breath.

She was scared of him.

Good.

Just to make his point clear, Chiliad ground his pelvis against her rounded hips. Grinning into the rich darkness of her hair, he sent his tongue swirling around her ear.

She trembled silently beneath him and held her breath, not daring to move.

"I don't give second chances…Val. Understand?"

"Y-yes."

Chiliad's sultry grin broadened as he pulled up, releasing Val to scramble away from him, panting. She'd been easier to handle than he'd first feared.

That line of thinking didn't last long.

Free at last, Val's head snapped in the direction of her fallen weapon, and she leaped toward the darn thing like the wildcat she was.

Chapter Two

Val was through screaming, and she was clearly in no position to struggle. She settled for pursing her lips until they hurt as she lay facedown against the sand, the barbarian on top of her. *Again*. She shuddered, remembering how he'd wrenched her *sheko* from her grip and cast it with violent force into the far sands. Her waterskin bore into her right hip, adding to her discomfort. Val could only pray to the Dyad that this would be over with quickly—whatever punishment he'd planned.

She had to credit the man—he *had* given her fair warning.

Straddling her ass, he easily forced her hands behind her back.

Cool metal locked around her wrists with an unmistakable, wicked *click*.

Val screamed again in frustrated rage, straining against the restraints. The overbearing barbarian had cuffed her!

"I thought you were done screaming, honey," the man growled from above, hardly amused.

Then his weight abruptly eased as he leaped to his feet and nearly in the same furious movement yanked her up by her loose-fitting wrap-blouse. He seized her shoulders in a rough grip and spun her around to face him. The movement almost sent Val tumbling over. Almost. Her captor's strong, sure hands had been quick enough to steady her.

Her feet still struggled against the sand as he held her. Dizzy and breathless, Val gazed up, taking her first true look at his face. And for a brief instant, she stopped breathing…

His blunt gaze surveyed her face, hungry and sharp, then slid lower, giving the whole of her a leisurely, sizzling once-over. She could *feel* his look as if it were a tangible caress. As the man's eyes took a slow trip back up her body, Val's cheeks caught fire. His grip on her arms was close to bruising as he bowed his head down to hers and crushed her lips with his own.

His mouth took her utterly, frightfully unprepared. His domineering lips eased her yielding ones wider apart without the slightest resistance. He felt soft, dangerous…*alien.* Dazzled, Val gasped against the exotic creature's mouth, his raspy, low chuckle singing her lips. His expert tongue breached her, penetrating her moist depths. He was white-hot velvet and sharp flavors, branding her with the sweet tang of untried spices. Her eyes trembled shut as his mouth left her no choice, robbing her of her deepest, darkest secrets. Taking it all. Making her fight for her breath. Making her…*wet.*

Someone was moaning aloud…

Val let out another desperate moan and the man's ravenous mouth took that away from her too. Her chafed wrists strained in vain against the restraints. The barbarian was torturing her…pleasuring her…showing her *exactly* who was in charge. Her body sagged against her captor's unwanted support as he drank from her lips.

Chiliad pulled out of Val's mouth as abruptly as he'd entered. Almost gently, he eased her away from his body. He watched her face as her eyes fluttered open and gained focus, shock and wonderment battling over their hazel depths. *Fuckin' stars…* He'd just planned to give the wildcat a little lesson—he'd never meant to go that far with her. She was obviously inexperienced. Kissing her that way just wasn't—

Damn.

When Chiliad was sure she was steady enough, he let go of her arms.

Val stumbled away from him, her tongue flicking over her bruised lips.

The sight of that quick, pink cat-tongue made Chiliad want to ravish Val all over again. He wasn't about to do that for now.

He'd wanted to get his message across, and it seemed like he'd managed it pretty well.

"The name's Chiliad," he softly intoned. "Chiliad-Kai Jayrt'ian."

The wildcat pulled herself back together quickly. A speedy recovery, considering the game he'd been playing. She lifted her narrow chin in defiance, squaring her shoulders. It made her lush breasts jump to sweet attention, an effect Chiliad was somehow sure she wasn't aware of.

"Chil-EE-ad Kah-EE Jay-AR-tee-an?" Val snapped, her eyes ablaze. "Sweet Dyad, your name must be the only thing bigger than your ego!"

Chiliad shot her a devilish grin. "Hardly the only thing."

Her eyebrows drew together in a curious frown.

His own dark ones arched in amusement. "Dammit, you really don't have a clue, do you, honey?"

"I'm not your honey, you...*beast*!"

"I've been called that a few times." Chiliad's fiendish grin broadened as he added, unable to resist, "*Honey.*"

Val snorted her contempt and turned her back to him.

Chiliad watched her petite form, his thoughts racing. His eyes followed the gleaming, black cascade of her hair all the way down to her cuffed wrists, then moved to her derriere. Her dark blue, loose-fitting slacks hinted at her tempting, curvy silhouette. The flowing garment bared slender, olive-toned ankles and small, leather-sandaled feet. An ankle bracelet of minute indigo beads reflected the sunlight, catching Chiliad's eye. For some vague reason, the pirate's calloused heart clenched. Surely it was nothing more than the damn heat messing with his mind! Chiliad bent down anyway, picking up Val's abandoned light blue scarf.

"Turn around, Val."

The sudden rigidity of her shoulders was the only proof she'd heard him. She turned to face him, a slow, reluctant movement.

"Come over here," he commanded.

Her eyes ignited with a brief, angry flame. She took a couple of steps closer then halted.

"Closer."

"*No.*"

"No?"

"Kill me if you want, barbarian," Val muttered. "Why not use my own scarf to do it?"

"Oh, I *am* about to use your scarf," Chiliad assured her as he took that last step, placing his body in a heated proximity to her own.

Val stilled as he raised both his hands to her throat. She closed her eyes, her lips moving in a silent prayer.

She actually believed he'd strangle her!

Not that he hadn't been tempted earlier.

Chiliad shook his head with a low laugh as he lifted Val's hair, draping the scarf on the back of her neck. Her eyes popped open. He surveyed her face, loosely grasping the scarf's long tails.

"You dropped this," he whispered, gently tugging on the cloth.

"I—" She fumbled for words. Her eyes dropped briefly to his mouth, and she blushed. "Chiliad," she finally managed.

One of his brows slightly raised in question.

"Undo me," she asked.

"What?" He gave her a slow-simmering smile. "Honey, you're confusing me with someone who gives a damn. If you want the cuffs off, you'll have to pay up first."

Val's face heated even more. "H-how?"

He grinned. "Easy, honey, I won't lay another finger on you. I've never had to beg for a woman."

"Sure," Val mumbled. "You're more the kidnapper type."

His hand let go of the scarf, trapping her chin instead. "Don't tempt me," he said softly.

Val swallowed nervously. She spoke again, her lower jaw moving against his fingers. "Wh-what do you want me to do?"

"Mmm." He had several ideas, actually. Holding the girl's jaw captive, he lowered his head above her own, fully aware of her inadvertent squirming. "I meant nothing too hard, honey... Just help me find my way back to my ship. You and your friend, the other screamer, surely saw it from your little toy-craft."

Val's eyes widened. Her mouth gaped yet wider. "You want me to..." Still caught in his grasp, she broke into laughter. "Oh, sweet Dyad...you lost your own ship! And you said that *I* didn't have a clue?"

Chiliad squinted his eyes, slowly letting go of her face. *What was so damned funny?* "After I crashed I took an aircycle out to explore," he growled. "I lost connection with my ship. *And* my fuckin' cycle is down too."

Val nodded slowly, failing to keep her deadpan expression. "Your connection wasn't radio-based, was it?"

"Yeah," Chiliad muttered. "The homing signal *was* radio-based."

"Oh, well..." She hesitated. "Relying on radio communication with those wild auroras out there isn't the best move."

Chiliad watched her in deathly silence. Hell, he should have figured it out by himself. He'd been acting greener than a thumb-sucking rookie... It should have occurred to him there'd be a problem with radio-based signals on a planet orbiting a close binary!

Chiliad swore and pounded his fist against his spread palm. He swiveled away from Val, his mind humming.

The suns were so close to one another, they were interacting *a lot. Damn, just look at the egg-shapes the two were stretched into due to the monster tidal effects!*

He remembered noticing their auroras from space, draping the planet in shimmering snakes and swirls. He'd chalked the view up to a demented view screen, sure at the time that his display unit had been damaged. The auroras covered *far* more than the planet's magnetic poles, interfering with radio signals...keeping the poor excuse for a planet in and out of eternal static.

Chiliad tunneled his fingers through his mussed hair. His eyes snapped to the sky, searching for the auroras pulsating lights.

"You can see them much better at night," Val said.

He nodded vaguely. "I can hardly wait."

"I can take you there, you know," she whispered.

Chiliad's surprised gaze whipped to her. "Take me where?"

Hands cuffed behind her back, she flashed him a forthright stare. "Uncuff me and I'll take you back to your ship," she repeated in a steadier tone.

"You will, huh?" Chiliad said softly, his sharp blue gaze surveying her face. "Just like that?"

"Got any water left, hotshot?" Her voice held only the slightest of trembles. She gestured to her waterskin, still miraculously secured against her hip. "Dyad knows, I have none on me besides this. All was left in the *wingless*. So unless you're planning a double suicide—"

"How far?" Chiliad broke in. "How far to the *Ambrosine* on *foot*?"

Val hesitated. "Your ship's about a day and a half walk from here."

"We won't last that long, wildcat." He shot her a feral smile.

"I know an oasis on the way—it's a couple of hours walk from here—if you just—"

Who was she kidding?

In the blink of an eye Chiliad once more towered above Val, hauling her up against his body. She stifled a cry, her toes barely skimming the sand.

"Are you pulling a number on me, honey?" he whispered, his eyes scouring her face. "If you can find water at the oasis, there's no reason for you to help me get back to my ship."

The wildcat was trying hard not to tremble. Keeping her eyes locked with his she said, voice shaky, "Guess you'll just have to take my word for it, *barbarian*."

She'd done it again. Made him freeze in surprise, the second time that day.

Slowly, Chiliad lowered Val the few inches back to the sand, his fingers still twisted around her blouse. A tiny smile tugged at one corner of his mouth.

"Guess I'll have to trust you then," he whispered.

His grip on the cloth tightened as he pulled Val up against his body, his head dipping to meet hers.

Chiliad let out a pleased groan as the wildcat's lush lips opened for him, hot and willing. He decided to take this one slower, much slower... He rubbed his lips against hers, a circular, unhurried touch, and she gasped, straining to get their mouths tighter together. Grinning slightly against her mouth, he pressed harder, forcing her lips wider apart with his own. He felt her answering tremble...sharp, violent, wanting.

His hands slowly left her blouse and climbed up her neck to cradle her face. Her hair spilled over his wrists like hot, dark silk. He tipped his head to nibble at those sweet candy lips, testing their softness with a skilled tongue.

She moaned around quick, shallow gasps for air, instinctively pressing her lush breasts against the hard plains of his chest. The innocent little wildcat wanted him...*badly*. Only he wasn't sure the girl knew *exactly* what it was she wanted from him.

Chiliad's plan to "take it slow" was already crumbling to desert-dust. He was achingly hard. Angling his hips against Val's lush softness, he stroked his caged erection against her full curves. She didn't shy away from him. The feel of her, hot and supple against his throbbing cock, made Chiliad's pulse hit light speed. His long fingers molded against Val's delicate jaw, stroked over her sculpted cheekbones. His tongue caressed her burning lips, sweeping over the gap in between.

He was hungry for more—he couldn't get enough of her sweet-pungent taste. Pressing his mouth harder against her softness, Chiliad deepened his kiss, lashing his tongue into her wet heat.

She was burning inside…

Both of them moaned together as their tongues joined and melted into one seething, liquid flame. She was a quick study, his desert wildcat… His tongue started to tease her mouth with soft thrusts, telling her exactly where else he wanted to thrust himself right this very second. He wasn't sure how much she knew about the other kind of thrusting. Wasn't sure she knew how much he wanted to fuck her right then and there, to fill each and every of her secret hollows with his throbbing self. His tongue in her mouth. His cock in her cunt. His fingers dimpling those sweet, rounded ass cheeks…

Chiliad groaned with true physical pain, tearing his tongue out of Val's welcoming, moist depths. He would have exploded in his breeches if he hadn't.

Her eyelids trembled open, baring that otherworldly, dazed hazel gaze. A dark flush infused her cheeks. She took in a quick, shuddering breath.

"Chiliad? I…" Her words faltered. She gazed up at his face with big, beautiful, *clueless* eyes.

"Turn around," Chiliad barely pronounced, his voice husky.

When she didn't respond right away, he roughly spun her about. His hands slid down her arms to her slender wrists.

The handcuffs sounded another *click* as he released her.

Val took another deep breath. She was free… Wasn't she? Her back facing the man, she kept rubbing her chafed wrists. Even though he'd released her from the restraints, he hadn't stepped away. She was acutely aware of his overpowering presence. His body heat edged into her flesh. His expelled breath stirred tendrils of her hair. She sensed him at her back, hotter than the desert's own breath. Val shuddered and raised her gaze to the simmering, dusty horizon. Her eyes squinted at the unexpected, ominous sight.

"There's a storm coming," she said.

Chapter Three

Val led him straight into the storm. Toward the darkening wall of golden sand that would surely bury them beneath its hellish blast. Hair and face tucked beneath her blue wrap, her sweaty little hand secured firmly within his own, the young warrior was leading them both into sure doom.

Chiliad was having serious second thoughts about trusting the little wildcat. He kept expecting her to pull a fast one on him, taking the first chance she had to split. His ruthless handholding was a trade-off for removing the handcuffs.

Obviously, it was too late to change his mind.

The pulsating air heralding the storm's front was thickening with hot sand, charged with electricity. Visibility was swiftly nearing zero. As he raised his painfully squinted eyes skyward, he could now actually *look* at the distorted suns behind the vibrating veil of sandy haze… Make out the two egg-shaped orbs, stretched toward each other in an endless attempt to touch.

Chiliad's eyes dropped from the hellish sight to Val's small, dark form bobbing in front of him. His arm shielding his unguarded face, he could hardly see anything besides her, could hardly breathe. His mouth tasted of sand. Every chance he'd ever had in this damn universe narrowed to his hold on her small hand.

He hated it.

He loathed depending on any other soul besides his own.

And right now he hardly had a choice in the matter.

Val's hand suddenly twisted within Chiliad's, signaling him they were taking a sharp turn to the right. Missing the sandstorm's full impact by mere minutes, Chiliad's heavy boots were abruptly treading upon something hard. His broad shoulders bashed into a framing of rocky outcrops. The sheer surprise of it made him lose his grip on Val. He drew in a hasty breath then dealt with the consequences, a bout of violent coughs.

Fuck… The wildcat had the perfect chance to–

"Chiliad, over here!"

He squeezed his way through the rough slabs of limestone toward that sweet, muffled sound. She had to scream at the top of her lungs so he'd hear her over the mayhem. The air was heavy with sand. With a rough oath Chiliad wended his way through the crowded, jagged protrusions of rock, a path obviously not made for a big man such as himself.

Val was crouched in a small clearing amid the stone. Chiliad nearly stumbled over her small form. She lifted eyes almost completely shaded by her wrap.

And pointed *down*.

Chiliad knelt beside Val at the edge of a dark pit, an irregular, narrow crack in the stony floor. He bent over its rim, scouring the hole's empty blackness. His stung, reddened eyes hardly made out the metallic gleam of a slim ladder stretching deep into the darkness.

He lowered his mouth over Val's ear, tugging aside the blue, sand-dusted cloth. "You want me to go down *there*?"

"Yes."

"Honey, I'm a big man. This hole might be just your fuckin' size, but—"

"You'll fit."

And with those words she slipped away from his side and down that damn pit.

"*Hey, wait*!" Chiliad leaned over the dark opening, catching a dimming view of her draped head. "Can this damn thing carry us both? Do I need to wait up here until—"

"It's a strong ladder," came her fading response.

And then she was gone altogether.

Chiliad did the only thing he *could* do under the current circumstances.

He bit out a long, vile curse.

And then he tried that ladder-into-hell, finding the wildcat had been right. It was a damn tight opening, but he could make it through. And now he was able to form a solid idea how a cock felt when it was squeezed inside a really tight pussy. The bawdy image made Chiliad's thoughts drift to the way Val's soft body had been pressed against his hard cock earlier…

The very likely virginal Val.

Chiliad groaned.

At some point the constraining walls around him had disappeared, and the ladder swayed more profoundly beneath his weight. Finally his feet touched rock.

"Told you you'd fit," Val's soft voice sang beside him, echoing hollowly.

"Smartass." Chiliad's head snapped to where her face should be, seeing nothing but solid darkness instead.

Val sighed. "How about some light?"

Only then did Chiliad discern a faint, bluish glow around Val's left ankle. Her beaded ankle bracelet was glowing. He could trace her movements as she inched her way behind the ladder he was still grasping. Her bracelet illuminated a neat stack of spine-covered spheres.

Bending low, Val plucked one of them up, wrapping her small fist about a random spine. A soft *snap* resounded as she cracked the thin shaft. A burst of light followed, spilling from the wounded sphere cradled in her hands.

"Shit!" Chiliad squeezed shut his irritated eyes.

"Oops. Sorry. Forgot to warn you about the glowstone." Val's lips twitched in a slight smile. "Welcome to *Sen-Halya,* Cave of the Winds." Elevating her glowing orb, she turned away from him.

Sen-Halya. The words lilted in the wildcat's odd, melodious tongue. As he followed Val out of the entrance chamber and into a narrow passageway, Chiliad shook sand out of his hair, slapped it out of his clothes. His gaze skimmed over the reddish-brown bedrock walls then skipped up to the slanted ceiling. The sphere's soft glow danced over stalactites' dripping long crystals and ghostly clumps of feathery filaments.

Chiliad grinned. "Gotta love the decoration."

"You'll love the comforts, then," Val giggled.

Her laugh surprised Chiliad. He liked how sweet it sounded.

The passage fanned out into another natural chamber. Val paused at the bottleneck entry, her back to Chiliad.

"Something wrong there, honey?"

Val swiveled to face him—a sharp, decisive movement. She gazed up at him, her face painted into a lattice of light and shadow. "When you get back to your ship tomorrow…you must leave straight away."

A grin curved his lips. "Tell me something I don't know."

"No, you don't *get* it. Promise me, Chiliad. You'll…"

"Take my sorry ass and get the hell out of here, yeah." *Only, the Ambrosine didn't have any hyperfuel left to go on.* Chiliad didn't tell Val that. Instead he stared with a deepening frown at her, the glowing sphere clutched tightly against her lovely bosom. "There's something you're not telling me, Val."

Val turned away from Chiliad and stepped into the chamber. The subterranean cave was a geared-up shelter. "Enjoy the comforts," she muttered offhand, refraining from looking Chiliad's way. She settled the glowing sphere within a low-hung sconce rigged into one of the chamber walls, wondering why she cared enough to warn him.

The pirate followed her in, watching the orb's light as it flickered around the dark waters of a small underground lake.

With a few long steps Chiliad was crouched by the water's edge, dunking his head deep inside.

Val watched the barbarian downing the water, pouring shimmering handfuls over his face, over his untamed, tangled hair. With a wild, carefree howl that echoed off the chamber walls, he gave his mane a savage shake. Water dripped from the soaked chestnut locks, painting wet lines down the back of his thin shirt.

He tore the dirty garment off his chest and yanked it over his head.

Val couldn't take her eyes off him. She bit her bottom lip as she watched muscles rippling in the man's naked back.

Her barbarian sprang to his feet, his large hands slicking back his dripping hair as his eyes shut in ecstasy. His sculpted torso expanded with a deep breath.

He looked like…

Trouble.

Val's lips curled in a bittersweet smile. Her mouth burned with a sudden dryness, a craving fiercer than thirst. A different kind of need was scorching her insides, a compulsion as yet unknown to her.

Chiliad turned from the lake, his eyes cracking open into blue slits. His slick chest boasted dusky hair on it, the dark fuzz dusting his pectorals arrowing to a trail that led beneath his breeches. Right to the distinctive bulge straining against the snug fabric…

Sweet Dyad, the barbarian was watching her right back!

Val's startled eyes snapped to the man's amused face. He'd caught her looking, saw that intent, downward glance… Her face flared with a heated blush.

Chiliad dropped his arms. He gave Val a devilish, sultry once-over.

"Come over here, Val."

Val recognized *that* line. She shot Chiliad an uncertain glance. Her feet made the decision for her, taking a couple of steps closer to the man.

"*Cloooser…*" Tension sizzled in his teasing voice.

"No."

"No?" His eyes flashed with a roguish grin. "You'll end up dehydrated."

Oh. He was just offering her a drink. Val's jumbled feelings swayed between an overwhelming relief and an odd tang of disappointment. She stumbled over to the water's edge, kneeling by the murmuring lake, a safe distance from Chiliad. Dunking her waterskin, she filled it anew. The modest leather container had somehow maintained them both through their hike among the dunes.

All thoughts escaped Val's mind as her mouth touched the canteen. *Slow. Take it slow.* She struggled with an unhealthy compulsion to pour it all down her burning throat. When she finally lowered her waterskin, swiping her forearm across her dripping mouth, her eyes locked onto the pirate's sharp, blue gaze.

She hadn't sensed him draw near, watching her silently as she drank. Val's breath faltered as Chiliad dipped into a crouch before her, his slick hair and torso dripping water. Reaching out, he rescued the forgotten canteen from her unresisting grasp. Her eyes fell to his powerful forearm extended her way. The man's subtle, tangy aroma of untried spices thrummed over her sensitized skin. Her stiff muscles began a fine, irrepressible trembling.

Chiliad steadied the canteen against the cave floor, his eyes not leaving Val's face. In silence he reached for her again, trapping a lock of her hair in his fingers. He smoothed the silky tendril behind her ear, his warm palm lingering against her cheek.

"Tell me you don't want me, honey."

His rough voice stroked over her skin. Val gazed back at Chiliad, spellbound. "I-I can't tell you that," she whispered.

One dark, masculine brow raised. A hint of a smile tugged at the corner of the man's full lips. His large hand sank beneath the silken midnight hair at Val's nape. He leaned over the short gap between their bodies and kissed her.

Val closed her eyes with a muted sigh as his masculine lips branded hers. Her tentative hands climbed to Chiliad's tousled hair, glided through his damp locks. His soft, raspy chuckle slipped into her mouth. Settling his other hand against her cheek, he nudged her lips wider apart.

Val's answering tremble was stirred by something other than fear. The man's lips felt so soft, yet their touch bordered on bruising… He plunged into her mouth, hot and velvety, stroking her tongue with a sizzling welcome. Sweet Dyad, she had never guessed something could feel like this…had never known. She gave in to his deepening explorations with a hunger that tore through her small form like a desert storm.

Val's response only incited Chiliad. He reacted like quicksilver, his hands steadying her head against his as he drank from her mouth.

His wild, intoxicating kiss saturated her senses, crumbled her thoughts to dust. Val moaned into Chiliad's mouth as the deep ache inside of her grew. Something feral and ancient awakened within her, gushing up to surface. A sense yet untried stirred to life, recognizing this rugged, incontrollable man for who he was… Her would-be mate.

Val hardly noticed as Chiliad gathered her closer, settling her atop his lap. Her breasts pressed against his damp chest. She felt his hands roving all over her back with simmering, slow caresses. His fiery mouth sipped from her lips, wanting, coaxing, demanding. Giddy and breathless, she let his sure hands guide her splayed legs around his waist.

Something long and hard prodded her right between her spread thighs.

Val's eyes shot open. Chiliad's hands were cupping her naked shoulders. She didn't recall her blouse slipping so low down her arms, baring her to the urgent heat in his eyes. Her peaked nipples lifted with a rushed breath, pebble-hard, their points teasing his hard muscles. She shivered with the raw sensation of the male flesh rubbing hers, of the coarse hair chafing her satiny skin. Her nipples tingled and ached, jutting from engorged, dark areolas. Moisture was soaking the cloth between her thighs. Val whimpered, struggling against Chiliad's mouth. Her sweaty hands shoved hard against his chest with a sudden panic.

The pirate groaned, tearing his tongue out of her mouth. His hands cupped her face, his whisper rough and hot on her lips.

"Val, honey…you need to decide what you want."

Val's small fists clenched against his damp skin. "I don't—don't know what it is that I want," she bit out, her voice thick with unshed tears.

"Easy, honey, it's okay..." Chiliad's soft murmur rasped against her swollen lips. His hand captured one small fist, gently opening it. He lightly pressed her palm against his chest. "Touch me, Val," he coaxed. His other hand slipped from her face, mirroring the same movement against the smooth valley between her breasts.

Chiliad's skin was still cool from the water. Val liked how it felt. Her lips curved in a slight smile, twin dimples popping into her cheeks.

Chiliad's eyes flashed with a matching grin. He walked Val's trapped hand lower, taking her on a slow tour down his bunching abdominal muscles. Down that enticing, arrowing line of dusky hair. His other hand emulated a similar trail down Val, over the subtle curve of her tummy. He paused, his heated gaze surveying her face.

She returned a wondering look...an expectant one.

Chiliad guided her hand lower down his body until it rested over his caged erection. Her light, hesitant fingers stirred white-hot electricity up his groin. Stars, it hurt. He needed...

Employing restraint he hadn't known he possessed, Chiliad's hand splayed over the delta between Val's spread thighs, waiting, watching for her response. Her immediate tremor throbbed beneath his palm. He captured her other hand as well, guiding both her arms over his shoulders.

"Put your arms around my neck, Val," he whispered in soft command, pulling her tightly against him.

His rough cheek brushed her velvety one as his mouth sought her neck, kissing the hot, pulsating skin. His hands fell to her hips. He started to rock her slowly against him, rubbing her sheathed pussy against his imprisoned cock. His hips thrust up softly in a matching rhythm. Chiliad hoped he wouldn't burst right then and there.

Val gasped, her eyes trembling shut. She tightened her hold on Chiliad, her fingers burrowing into his upper back as he slowly rolled her body against his own. A sweet ache built between her thighs, where his hard, throbbing bulge was kneading her flesh through the damp slacks. She felt his hands easing her away, letting go of her hips. His quick fingers undid the laces cinching her pants, finding bare flesh. With surprising tenderness those long, masculine fingers slid deeper into the humid heat between her thighs, parting her pussy's delicate petals.

"*Chiliad...*" Val shuddered violently, a loud moan tearing loose from deep in her throat. Her taut fingers bit into his back.

"I have you, honey."

His fingers kept playing over her flesh, his mouth seeking her damp neck once more. His wildcat was soaking wet, just as he'd expected. She was ripe and ready, even if she didn't know it yet. His fingers traced her tiny, engorged clit. He brushed against the slick nubbin then started a slow, gentle massage.

Val groaned. Her fingers bore into Chiliad's strong shoulders, her back arching sharply.

"Yeah, Val...that's it," he whispered.

Chiliad gripped her ass, forcing her closer against his moving hand. He watched, riveted, as she started to move, her body intuitively seeking more pleasure. Eyes shut, she went from slow, hesitant sways to sensuous undulations that pushed her flesh against his moving fingers. Her ripe breasts jiggled with her body's dance, heaving with each quick, shallow breath.

"Gorgeous..." Chiliad mumbled against the salty hollow at the base of Val's throat. One finger trailed deeper between her pussy lips, dipping into her hot, wet opening. She gave a half-sob and moved against his finger, an innocent attempt to take him deeper inside her.

His hand abandoned her ass and touched a hidden fastener over his crotch, unclasping his breeches. His rampant erection burst out, free at last.

Val's eyes popped open as she felt something very big and very hard against her groin. Her gaze dropped to Chiliad's throbbing cock, thrusting up at her from a nest of dark hair. She stared in fascinated shock at the thick rod. Its shaft was long and smooth and oddly beautiful. Her eyes traced a snaking vein. The broad head looked even smoother, blushed to an angry purple. The very big, very hard *thing* flexed beneath her eyes and she yelped in surprise.

Chiliad's subtle grin broadened. His hands clutched Val's hips again, lifting her with ease against his body.

A wild notion hit Val as to what *exactly* the man had on his mind.

"*Sweet Dyad, wait*! It's too big! Chiliad, it won't—"

"It'll fit."

And with those words he lowered her down on his cock.

Val screamed.

Chiliad cradled her trembling body against his own. "Honey, I'm sorry..." His rough whisper ruffled her hair. Buried to the hilt in her tight, honeyed heat, he kept himself still, allowing her to adjust to his size.

Val buried her face in his powerful shoulder, her breath coming in quick gasps. She was trying to deal with the very big and very hard *thing* that was suddenly wedged deep within her, stretching her virginal passage. It didn't exactly hurt anymore...she'd been very wet when he'd penetrated her. Her body yielded to Chiliad's lingering caresses as her cunt molded around his cock. She felt his hands stroking over her partly clothed thighs, stripping her pants off her legs.

"Val...squeeze your legs around me. Yeah, like that, *tight*."

Chiliad shifted up from the rock, his hands supporting her buttocks. Crouched on his knees, his muscled thighs slightly apart, he pulled her body to his own with a sure grip. "Give me your mouth," he whispered. "I want to taste you."

Val raised her burning face to Chiliad's low, husky voice. He captured her lips with a long, hard kiss that cast aside all needless thought. His tongue deep in her mouth, he started to move her against him, slowly rocking her, shifting her up and down his slick shaft. *A few inches up...a few down...up...down...* The rhythm was both sharp and hypnotic. Val moaned around his tongue, shaken. She hadn't thought there was room left down there for any kind of movement! Yet that big, hard rod of his was slipping in and out of her tight passage, oiled with her own juices.

And it felt downright incredible.

The sweet, rough friction intensified, sending a wave of heat through her entire body. Val tore her mouth from Chiliad's with a strangled moan. Her head fell back, eyes squeezed shut. An added sensation poured in, the feel of a hot mouth on one taut nipple. Val gasped, swaying in Chiliad's hold.

"Chiliad…I *can't…*"

His mouth released its treat with a loud *pop*. Val's deliciously abused nipple was peaked to a glistening hardness.

"Just let go, wildcat."

Chiliad's sultry whisper pulsed through Val's core, made her skin bloom with goose bumps. She sucked in her breath as he closed his mouth on her untouched nipple, his trained tongue working magic on her flesh. His hips thrust in a wicked, matching rhythm as his hands moved her on his cock. The hot mouth on her breast grew more ravenous. He started to take her harder, faster, undulating her up and down his shaft. His sheer size stretched her taut about him, his kneading movements built up a blazing, urgent pressure. Unable to stop herself, Val cried out, her impassioned scream bouncing off the chamber walls.

Chiliad let out a savage groan, his face buried against the dark cream of his wildcat's breasts. It still wasn't enough. He needed to take her harder…*deeper…* He carefully lowered her to the smooth stone floor then crouched low above her.

Val's eyes trembled open, passion-dazed, wondrous. "Chiliad…what…?"

Propped up above her, Chiliad locked his fiery blue gaze with Val's. "Just squeeze me tight," he whispered.

Then he took her just the way he needed, just the way he'd wanted when she'd lain beneath him against the burning sands. He pounded into her drenched cunt with sharp, long strokes. He pressed his weight against her pelvis, rotating his hips, shuddering. Something wild, intoxicating and bright gushed through him with a ruthless force, an unbound pleasure, consuming and intense.

He'd never experienced something like this in his life, and he'd experienced plenty.

As Val's ecstatic screams echoed off the cave walls, as her sweet honeyed desire bathed his hard, pulsating cock, sensations mounted within him 'til his stunned senses dissolved into pure sensation.

And then the universe exploded inside him in a myriad of colors. For a fraction of a second existence became pure pleasure itself. Orgasm hit Chiliad with a violent, mind-blowing intensity. He tautened and shuddered against the small, sweet body that writhed in pleasure beneath him. He burst deep inside Val's tightening cunt, shooting hot semen deep into her womb…crying out raggedly…calling out her name, over and over again.

When the storm inside had abated, Chiliad's stunned gaze fell to Val's face. Her eyes were closed, those long, thick lashes shading her cheeks. Her sweet candy-pink lips were loosely parted as she struggled to ease her wild panting. She was trembling roughly in his hold, still caught up in the throes of her first orgasm, her arms hooked about his neck.

She was the most gorgeous thing he'd ever laid eyes on.

He was lanced with an unforeseen stab of pain, a knowledge that she'd never be truly his.

Chapter Four

*"Mmmm...*what are you doing?"

"Enjoying the comforts." His mumbled words tickled her neck, low and rasping and warm.

Val stirred from a light sleep into complete wakefulness. It was dark—the glow-stone's light had long since died away. She found herself warmly spooned against Chiliad's naked body beneath a rough cover of *sooka* wool.

Naked.

Val groaned, not sure whether she wanted to wake up to this new reality. A reality where she'd so willingly, so foolishly given herself to this man. What they had shared was wild, achingly beautiful, something beyond her wildest imagination...

Something utterly forbidden.

She had broken the Temple's law. She was a traitor to her own race. Sweet Dyad, mere hours ago she'd wallowed in pleasure, not even once thinking about Aello—had the storm hit her companion? Had she made it out of there alive? Disgusted with herself, Val shifted beneath Chiliad's arm, trying to break the intimate contact between them.

"Something wrong, wildcat?" His grip tightened on her waist.

The sensation of his powerful arm subduing her bare flesh, of his rough hair grazing her skin, pierced her core with a sharp pang of desire. Val bit her bottom lip. She was about to become trader, to go out into space. She wouldn't give in again—to this man, to the mysterious awakened force within her that demanded more of his touch. She would lead the man back to his ship and watch him leave then drive his existence forever out of her mind.

"Nothing's wrong," she replied, her voice tight. "We should get ready to go and find your ship, Chiliad. The suns will rise soon. We should use what little time that we have, while it's a bit cooler—"

"We don't need to leave *now*, do we?"

"I think we'd better—"

He flipped her over to her back, swiftly trapping her body beneath his.

"Better what, honey?" he drawled lazily.

She heard that roguish tone flashing in his voice. It felt somehow *right* to have him above her in the darkness. The hard steel of his chest pressing against her breasts, his muscular thighs snug between her legs. Which was probably why she flattened her hands against those firm pectorals and pushed as hard as she could.

"Get off me, barbarian!"

He hadn't budged, hardly affected by her rough handling. "Aren't we past this 'barbarian' bullshit by now?"

She stopped pushing, but her hands tightened against his chest. "It changed nothing...*nothing*. You can force me to do it again, but—"

"Whoa, lover, *force* you? You were practically begging for it!"

Val stiffened, hissing out through her teeth, "Just so you know, I *hated* every single second of it!" Which wasn't the smartest thing to say.

Chiliad commented wryly, "That bad, huh?"

"*Yes.*"

"Hmmm."

He still hadn't raised himself from her body, and his voice had taken on a mischievous undertone she wasn't sure that she liked. That low, husky "*hmmm*" trailed pleasant vibrations over her chest, a sensation she desperately struggled to ignore. She was also straining to disregard that big, hard *thing* of his pressing against her. Val gazed up warily, striving to guess the exact expression on Chiliad's handsome, shaded features. All through the exchange she had sensed his face in the dark, hovering intimately above her own… So close that his scent washed over her, warm, with his unique spicy tang.

"Chiliad, will you get off…*aaaahhh*…what…what are you doing?"

"A little research." His fingers moved against her already moist pussy lips, expertly pressing the right spot. Val almost reared up from the ground as he whispered most slyly, "See, I'm trying to find out which part *exactly* you didn't like earlier. So that I won't ever…*ever*…put you through that again."

The "*ever, ever*" was whispered right against Val's burning ear. His skilled mouth skimmed up her cheek, drawing an unintended sigh from her. His lips brushed her own before slipping to the madly beating pulse in her neck. He was all fire and movement, leaving her gasping for air and hungry for more. And throughout it all, his fingers kept playing a wicked game deep between her thighs.

She felt him diving beneath the coarse *sooka* wool, his nakedness sliding against her own. A ragged moan tore out of her throat as his mouth laved one jutting nipple, his tongue circling the moistened peak. His teeth bit the taut flesh and let go just as his fingers massaged her clit *exactly* the right way…

Val tightened with a hoarse scream, her cunt convulsing on Chiliad's fingers in tight, violent waves. She arched up from the covers and strained beneath him, his weight pinning her down.

His head popped up above her own, his voice a soft, coaxing whisper. "So, was that it, honey?"

"Wh-what?"

"What you didn't like."

"I—"

Chiliad chuckled against her mouth.

And then she sucked in her breath as he caressed his erection against the pouting, glazed petals of her pussy. Her arms crept up to encircle his neck. Her legs clamped around his strong thighs.

"Chiliad…" Val mumbled, her heart beating wildly against her tightening throat.

She didn't know what, exactly, she was asking for…but he had a rough idea. Chiliad's response wasn't a verbal one. His thighs gave a subtle thrust that nestled his cock head within the slick embrace of her cunt. Val's breath quickened as she heaved her hips, straining to take him deeper inside. She discovered it was impossible to make the man move when he didn't *want* to.

"Slowly, wildcat." His fingers burrowed into her hair. "We'll take this one nice…and…slow."

His warm breath teased her lips. He had her gently restrained, his hands holding her head and his hips pressing her body down. She couldn't raise herself to meet his mouth, couldn't bring his cock deeper inside her. A swift curse slipped from her lips, uttered in her own tongue.

"I love it when you talk dirty," he murmured.

She could hear his grin in the dark—right before he lowered his head and finally sealed her lips with his own. His kiss was languorous, slow, simmering. He tasted her leisurely, savoring each expelled moan, every secret flavor. His cock sank further into her silky heat, taking her inch by inch.

And she let him in.

As her tentative fingers made a slow climb up his bunching back muscles, as her thighs tightened on his slow-moving body, she let him inside her in every possible way.

They rocked together in the darkness, slowly, the deliberate friction of flesh against flesh kindling a growing flame between their bodies. Val groaned as the dark, vague feeling inside of her awakened once more…taking on the fiery colors, the pressing heat of the man above her, augmenting them, infusing them right back. A cycle flared up between them, an electrifying, sweeping force enhanced with each quick breath, with every burning touch.

Val curled around Chiliad as he moved inside her, his thrusts growing urgent and sharp. His hand tangled roughly into her hair, pulling her head back so he could kiss her again, breathless and hard. Her scream of release pressed against his mouth. Her teeth sank into his lower lip. She dug her fingers into his back as her cunt squeezed his cock over and over again in tight waves of rapture. She felt his deep groan against her neck, felt him shudder, pulsating within her…felt his hips jerking in her tight embrace as he found his own release.

And suddenly only their heavy panting was breaking the silence of the cave.

Val's eyes cracked open. She couldn't discern Chiliad's expression in the darkness. His fingers were still snagged in her hair as his whisper, aching and rough, scorched her lips.

"Stars, girl, what the fuck are you doing to me?"

"I don't…" she mumbled, puzzled and utterly at a loss. "I didn't…"

His fingers slowly unclenched, releasing her hair. His weight shifted above her as he silently slipped out of her and rolled over.

She suddenly felt empty and cold. Val gathered herself into a ball as she sat up, tugging the *sooka* wool over her naked breasts. What had she done wrong? He sounded so angry with her. She struggled with a foolish, unwarriorlike impulse to cry. *Crying was a careless waste of water*, her favorite tutor, Lyssipe, used to say. Well, at least the man would be leaving soon, and she'd never have to deal with him again. For some vague reason, the notion of him leaving didn't bring the expected relief. Val shrugged off this oddity. Forcing her tense fingers loose from the coarse wool, Val sighed and stretched in the darkness, allowing the coverlet to slip down to her waist.

"I hated *every* single second of it," she informed Chiliad again with a frosty tone before making a swift escape from beneath the covers.

"Sure, honey, the way you were screaming just now, I bet everyone up top heard *just* how much you hated it," was his lazy response.

The bluish radiance of her beaded ankle bracelet guided Val toward the nearby stack of glowstones. She snatched one up from the heap and clamped her fist on one of its spines. Imagining it was the barbarian's big, hard *thing*, she snapped the thin rod sharply near its base with an acute sense of satisfaction. Cave air touched the exposed core, igniting a chain reaction within the orb—instantly light burst out, flooding the chamber.

"Nice view," Chiliad teased from beneath the covers.

Val gritted her teeth as she placed the glowstone within its sconce then decisively headed for the lake for a quick, cleansing wash.

Since Val refrained from alerting Chiliad there were better, warmer breakfast options stored in the shelter, the two of them shared a cold, brief meal of water and *kved,* a precooked desert bread. The food, nicknamed "warrior's bread", was a lightly cooked paste of ground *esma* grains and concentrated *vishi*-beast's milk. It was known for its great nourishing and preservative qualities, and for having one hell of a nasty taste.

Chiliad's strong teeth tore out large chunks of the stiff loaf as he chewed in silence, downing it along with generous swigs of water from his newly supplied waterskin.

Val did her own silent chewing, making a big production of not giving a damn. After breakfast she beat the hell out of the slept-in covers in the name of aeration, neatly re-tucking them into storage. She thrust a few loafs of *kved* and dried *mashta* fruits into a couple of knapsacks, but the real life and death issue was water. They had to have enough of it for nearly a day's walk. Crouched by an assortment of waterskins, Val shot Chiliad a calculating glance.

The pirate was bent over the lake with naught but his breeches on, holding a straight blade to his face. Where had he hidden *that*—not to mention the handcuffs—with that tight outfit? She watched hypnotized as his steady hand ran the knife down one damp, chiseled chick. Sensing her gaze, he paused and tossed her a look, arching a brow.

"What, never seen a man shave before?" And then, in a voice threaded with mischief, "Damn, forget I asked that."

By the Dyad, but he was exasperating! Swift anger flashed in Val's eyes. "I'll be adding that to my things-to-forget list," she snapped.

He slowly rose to his feet, tucking the blade away. Quick hands. Val's cheeks blazed as she recalled these quick, apt fingers of his moving against her…inside her.

"So, you already have a list?" Chiliad grinned. "I'm flattered."

She retorted with something rather nasty in her own tongue.

He didn't speak her language, but curses seemed to share a common sound everywhere. "Fuck you too, sunshine."

Val snorted. The morning was getting better by the minute.

The slim metallic ladder was bathed in a golden shaft of sunlight as the two of them stood in the cave's entrance hall. By the mere look of it, the storm was over. They crouched and laid the two roughly bundled packs holding their food and water supplies near the ladder—the bags would have to be transported separately through the narrow entrance in the cave's roof.

Chiliad slanted Val an impish glance. "Tie me up, honey."

"Sounds like you've said that before."

"That transparent, am I?"

Val couldn't help a soft grin as she hooked the hauling cable around his hips. She did her best to ignore the other nicely packed bundle straining against the man's tight breeches.

As for Chiliad, he did *his* best to ignore the wildcat's light fingers stroking over his upper thighs, hips and abs.

Val glanced up his chest and straightened, clasping the rest of the light harness. "Bend over a bit. I need to strap you up a little higher."

He obliged, kneeling in front of her. His eyes sparked with a blue smile. "Now, why didn't you try this line on me a while back when we—"

"Cut that out!"

He threw back his head with a low, husky laugh. "Hated every second of it, my ass," he whispered.

Val's olive cheeks ignited. She fastened the harness against his ribcage with a vicious jerk. "The rolled cable is secured right *here,*" her fingertips fluttered over his right hip.

Chiliad blew out an unintended breath as she scarcely touched him.

Val fought back a satisfied smile at his knee-jerk reaction. "When you're finally out—"

"I'll roll down the cable so you'll start hooking up the goody bags," he grumbled. "Will ya fuckin' relax?"

Her eyes flashed and she slid a step away from him.

He felt like a bastard.

Chiliad jerked himself back up to his feet. Stars, he must be losing his touch. Fine, so the wildcat was a beauty. She was a rare, sharp-sweet blend of jagged and soft. She was…

Chiliad's jaw tightened.

She was here now, but she wouldn't be tomorrow. He couldn't allow himself the privilege of giving a damn.

He gripped the ladder and heaved himself up towards the morning heat.

The third time Val stumbled, Chiliad caught her before her knees hit the searing sand. He hunkered down, cupping both Val's elbows in a sure, steadying grip.

"Tell me what's wrong, wildcat."

"N-nothing. Let me go."

She was swaying even as he held her. Chiliad cocked a doubtful brow. "You'll nose-dive if I do, honey."

"I can still…still go on for a while."

"Oh, yeah?" His hands gave the slightest of pulls and she dropped into his arms like a ripe fruit. He loosened the sweat-drenched scarf from her face, touching her feverish skin. Ignoring Val's frail protests, Chiliad started to disentangle her from her knapsack. "Still think you can argue? What is it, heat exhaustion?"

Shivering in his hold with quick, shallow gasps, she still managed to look insulted. "H-heat exhaustion? I've lived here all my life… I've never…"

"First time for everything, I guess."

She missed his snappy retort, which made him realize there *was* something seriously wrong with her. An unexpected twinge of concern sliced through him.

"I just feel so tired," Val mumbled. "Like...an uncharged *sheko*."

Damn. Maybe he was the one to blame for this. Take an innocent virgin, make love to her all night long, then take her on a hike in the desert. What did you get?

Yeah. This.

Chiliad groaned. "Fuck, there's never an M.U. around when you need one." He uncorked Val's waterskin, pressing it to her lips. "Got a good quality Medical Unit back on the *Ambrosine*. It does the basics—primary workup, first aid."

She cried out in dismay as he poured the rest of the water over her burning face and scalp. "Are you insane? Wasting water while on patrol—it's an automatic death sentence—"

"Damn, just committed another felony." He grinned down at her. "I've lost count."

A brief answering smile flickered over her lips. It quickly faded. "Chiliad, your ship… I c-can't guide you back." Her hazel eyes looked huge with distress. "Try your homing device. It might work now. Radio connection comes and goes…"

One arm supporting Val's back, Chiliad unhooked a thin metal square from his belt, snapping it open with a flick of his wrist. His quick fingers played over the gadget's delicate controls. His eyes lit up. "Whaddya know," he hummed. "It works."

"You should go now," Val whispered. "Move fast, as long as you have a good signal."

"Yup, *we* should move fast." Chiliad re-hooked the homing device to his belt and shifted Val in his hold, about to haul her up.

"Wait…" Val's thready voice was rough with anxiety. "You shouldn't carry me. The suns… You'll never make it."

"Val, I'm not leaving you here."

An odd smile played over her scorched lips. "Funny," she whispered. "If I wanted to…back then, I could've put a full charge though you… I could've…left you in that sandstorm."

"I know."

"Could've vanished within the passages of *Sen-Halya*...and you...never would've found me..."

"I *know*," he said, his gaze unreadable. "Don't you think I know that?"

She fell quiet save for her rough breathing, those big eyes of hers trained on his face.

He bundled her into his arms, straightening to his full height. A sudden incredulous smile curved Chiliad's full lips as he softly added, "I could've pulled my blaster on you too, wildcat...or used a blade. I didn't."

* * * * *

The SpaceHound, Captain's Quarters
Charted Deep Space

"Captain Steele! I think I've finally got it figured out, sir!"

Commander Blade Steele didn't take well to the interruption in his private chambers. He'd just been thinking of inviting Lieutenant Commander Kimi in for a quick drink. And a quick fuck. Instead he lifted a weary gray gaze from the light-dotted starmap to the young science officer's face. "Ensign Denarro," he observed, voice flat. He smoothed a large hand over his blond crew cut. Seeing the man still stretched into a jittery salute, he added, "At ease, Ensign."

"Captain Steele, yes, sir!"

Damn scientists. Steele scanned the young officer with a dark glare. When a number of seconds had passed in silence he pointed out dryly, "You were about to tell me what you've got figured out, Ensign."

Denarro blushed again. "I meant Jayrt'ian, sir."

There was an added sharpness to Steele's voice. "What about him?"

"I think—I mean, I *know* a way to uncover his location, sir."

"I'm listening." Steele squelched an urge to grab Denarro by the nape and whip some spunk into him.

"The informant said Jayrt'ian left Kintha's lesser moon loaded with hyperfuel," Denarro stumbled on. "We were on his tail ever since, so we can calculate exactly how much he had left when he'd made that hyperleap. I went over Jayrt'ian's visual recordings with Engineering, sir. It looks like we hit his Navi-system's sensors. He wasn't able to control his hyperleap, sir. It must've burned all of his hyperfuel. We can estimate his leeway's magnitude—"

"Ensign Denarro," Steele cut in tersely. "Even if you can tell exactly how *far* Jayrt'ian leaped, you can't tell *where* he aimed. He could've ended up in endless alternate points."

"Well..." Denarro swallowed, sweat beading on his brow. "There are actually only eight possible end-points, sir."

Steele's brows lifted. "You have my attention, Ensign."

Denarro wet his lips. Winning Steele's undivided attention was unnerving. "I had the computer scan the entire calculated perimeter. I then programmed it to eliminate the dead-end leaps. *Then* I checked what was left." The Ensign's eyes gleamed. "Couldn't believe it myself—it gave me only eight possible sectors, sir, some in Nemea-Hub, some in Frontier. One's in uncharted territories."

"Let me see those." Steele extended his hand. His quick gaze browsed through the listing of datum points. "What you're suggesting is that we personally comb through each and every one of these sectors. Of course, for this to work, we'll have to assume Jayrt'ian is still alive."

"Well it *is* Jayrt'ian, sir," Denarro said gravely. "Besides, I figured that if he's dead, then you've got him, anyway."

The scientist had a point, there.

Steele considered the young officer's unusual scheme. It demanded he believe the SOB *was* alive somewhere...and he *could* believe that. He refused to accept the man's demise unless he, himself watched him disintegrate into infinitesimal specks of stardust. And if Jayrt'ian *were* alive, Steele had to believe he'd left some kind of a trail behind him. He'd have to rely on the various sectors' cooperation with the PGAN. He already foresaw problems coming from Frontier sectors Romalli and Morenne, and scanning through crowded Hub sectors was a whole different kind of headache.

Was he insane enough—desperate enough—to try this long shot?

Apparently, he was.

Or maybe he just hated Jayrt'ian's guts that much.

"Let's start with the one located in uncharted territories," he sighed. "That portion of the galaxy is supposed to be barren, right? A simple in-and-out operation..."

Chapter Five

"Ninety-seven point five two degrees and stable."

Val's eyes shot open. Her throat felt gritty, as if she'd been screaming. Where was she? She couldn't remember. She needed to get up.

She couldn't move.

Swift panic washed over her blurry mind as she writhed against the *thing* that was holding her.

"Val, stop tearing my M.U. apart. *Relax*."

That voice… She recognized its rough, low timbre. She tried to turn her head towards it, discovered that she couldn't. A desperate sob escaped her lips.

"Ninety-seven point six four degrees and – "

"*Ambrosine*, shut the fuck up and deactivate the M.U."

"M.U. deactivated, Captain."

The Medical Unit's top raised and slid into the wall. Chiliad bent down and draped a blanket about her as she started to shiver. His hands ran over her limbs, kneading stiff muscles. "Tell me your name, honey."

"V-Val." She peered up into his concerned gaze.

"Good girl. Now, say my name."

The word slipped with ease into her mind. "Chiliad."

The pirate grinned. "Guess you didn't fry your brain, after all."

Val quieted beneath his touch. "The woman…is she your companion?"

"My *what?* Oh, that's no woman, that's only the *Ambrosine*. My *ship*. I programmed her to talk that way."

Val smiled. Her eyes fluttered shut. "You found your ship."

"Yeah, the homing signal broke again just when I had her in sight," he softly responded. "First thing I did on boarding was pop you into the Medical Unit. It went crazy, flashing a list of diagnoses 'til my head started spinning. I got the dehydration and hyperthermia part, but I ain't no doctor. I just let the M.U. fix you up."

"I need to…need to get back…"

"Easy, wildcat, I won't hijack you into hyperspace. The *Ambrosine* is still grounded."

She didn't answer, already fast asleep, tucked into his loose embrace. Her full breasts rose and fell beneath the blanket in a steady, relaxed rhythm. Chiliad stroked the mass of tangled, dark tresses away from her forehead.

He snatched back his fingers. Their tips tingled with the need to touch the supple olive skin once more. Damn, he was in way over his head, though he'd sworn to never again… He released Val to sink against the padded platform, cautious not to wake her. His gaze kept clinging to her, though his arms had already let go. He rubbed his unshaven jaw.

"What am I to do with you, wildcat?"

Her only response was a soft, oblivious snore.

A couple of hours later he found her wandering wide awake and wide-eyed in the cargo area, clutching the comforter to her bosom. Her eyes snapped his way. He paused, tilting his head sideways with an appreciative glance. She whirled to face him in a flurry of dark hair.

"I think I'm lost," she mumbled.

"Hey, nice to see you up on your feet." Chiliad indicated the columns of sealed crates. "See anything to your liking?"

"What's in there?"

His face split with a broad grin. "Oh, just some dangerous toys for big girls."

"Toys?" Val echoed, mystified. "What would I want with toys?"

"I'll have to show you later. It's one of those cases where actions speak louder than words." Chiliad's mind sifted through the variety of smuggled sex toys stashed in the *Ambrosine's* cargo hold. Which one would be right for his innocent wildcat? The *Supernova Blast* was obviously out of the question. *Taurus* might be a bit intimidating for a first-timer. *Vega-Vibes,* maybe? Chiliad heaved a mental sigh. Commander Steele had to know, of course, that the sex toys were nothing more than bogus cargo, a shallow cover to the *Ambrosine's* real baggage—"toys" of the lethal kind.

"I want my clothes back."

Chiliad looked away, tunneling long fingers through his mussed hair. "No can do, honey."

"What do you mean?" Val clutched the comforter tighter against her breasts.

"Let's just say I wasn't too careful about your clothes when I got you into the M.U." Chiliad's thoughtful gaze toured the cargo space. "I think I have just the right outfit for you though."

About half an hour later, Val pounded her fist against the galley table. "This is hardly funny, Chiliad!"

"I have to agree with you on that one." His hungry gaze roved over Val's ample curves. Her new attire made her look more appetizing than ever. "You look *mean* in black, honey."

Val tugged at the tiny, snug miniskirt then rolled her shoulders within the tight vest. "Well, I don't like it. Don't you have anything…uh…longer?"

"A long outfit after a case of heatstroke? Nope." His eyes couldn't let go of her enhanced cleavage. The tawny, delicious domes of her breasts were packed into that tight vest. He felt a stirring in his loins.

Val drew in a deep breath, obviously about to voice a protest.

Stars, she'd almost popped out of there! For his own mental sake, Chiliad broke in before she uttered a single word, motioning at the elongated seat facing him. "You must be starving. How about a snack from the *Ambrosine's* kitchen? Today we're serving a great selection of synthetics."

"Fine, but we're not done yet." Val sagged to the edge of the offered seat, plucking at her skirt. She watched Chiliad as he punched her request into a small console. Tousled chestnut locks brushed the pirate's broad shoulders. The sheen of sweat had already dried off his muscled, bare chest. Val's gaze was drawn once more to his large hands. She swallowed nervously.

A sealed canister popped up onto his side of the table. He snapped the lid open with a lithe thumb, sliding the steaming dish toward Val. "*Voila.*" He next sent the disposable utensils skating her way across the platform.

Val sniffed at the canister's unfamiliar contents, shrugged then stuck her fork inside. "When will you be leaving?" She stuffed a pulpy chunk into her mouth. *Mmmm, not bad!*

"Yesterday, if I could have my way," he softly replied.

She froze, the fork halfway to her mouth. "What's wrong?"

Chiliad's sharp blue gaze scanned her as he chewed. He took a slow swig from a glass of clear liquid. "I still have to figure out how to leap into hyper without hyperfuel," he said at last, lowering the glass from his lips. "I've got only basic, non-crystalline fuel left, so I can move the *Ambrosine* around a bit, but that's about it. Hell, nowhere interesting to go, anyway. Can I offer you a drink?"

When she didn't respond, staring at him with wide, startled eyes, Chiliad punched another request into his console and handed Val a drink. "What are you not telling me, Val?"

She shook her head. "Nothing. It's nothing."

Chiliad nodded, surveying her anxious features. Something feral and dark flashed in his eyes before fading away.

Val sipped from her glass, the sharp bite of the liquid shocking her taste buds. Sweet warmth dissolved into her muscles. Deciding that she liked the concoction, she took another, larger sip.

"Go easy on the *Wassuki,* wildcat, the stuff might be a bit strong for you."

She stuck out a pink tongue at him. "But I really, *really* like it."

Chiliad sniggered, rising from his seat. Circling the platform, he snatched the glass from her loose grip. "No more *Wassuki* for you tonight."

She peered up at him, hazel eyes misted. "Not fair," she mumbled. "I almost never, never have any fun. It's…it's a waste of training time."

That minute amount of *Wassuki* had already loosened her tongue. Chiliad crouched beside Val, his hands pinning her thighs against the padded seat. "Fun is no waste of time," he whispered. "Who told you such a thing?"

"Lyssipe." Val frowned, struggling to shape her fuzzy thoughts into sharp sentences. "She's my…my tutor. She'll be my commander soon. I'm going to…going to become a trader. Travel off-world."

Something unfamiliar knotted the pirate's innards. Was that where his conscience resided? Here was his perfect chance to milk the girl for information he desperately needed. Yet, he couldn't go through with it. Chiliad cursed softly. Knowing he'd regret it later, he placed his large hand over the girl's mouth. "Val, stop. Stop, honey, right now. Don't say anything else, okay?"

"But…" she mumbled against his hand.

"Wildcat, you're telling me things that you don't really want to. You're not used to strong drinks."

"Oh," she uttered beneath his palm.

She opened her mouth to talk some more, but Chiliad pulled her from the seat into his embrace and covered her mouth with his own. Val moaned, clinging to Chiliad's bare shoulders. Her lush, warm lips parted for him, inviting him in. She tangled her fingers into his hair, gasping out his name.

Chiliad groaned, seizing a handful of her midnight-dark locks. He pressed down harder on his wildcat's sugary lips, deepening the kiss. She still tasted of sharp *Wassuki*. His ravenous fingers trailed over the soft globes that strained against her tight vest. A slight tug on the zipper and her magnificent breasts burst out, bobbing with her quickening breaths. His fingers squeezed one supple mound, teased around the wrinkled areola, rolled the sensitive, hard nipple. He tore his mouth from Val's lips and pulled back so he could take a look at her again.

Her fingers slipped from his hair, trailing down his rough cheek. Her long, knotted locks draped his arm, spilling to the floor like a dark waterfall. In the quiet that had dawned a single bead of sweat melted at the base of her throat, painting a slow, shimmering line down the deep vale between her breasts. Chiliad touched Val's throat, following the sweat along its tortuous course.

"What am I to do with you, wildcat?"

There was a faraway look in her hazel eyes. "Put your mouth on mine again," she whispered.

"Think it's that easy, huh?" A brief, savage flame flickered in his blue eyes. "Well, maybe you're right."

He bent low and stroked her lips with his own, his tongue outlining the gap in between. Her quick breaths heated his mouth…her heartbeat rushed beneath his palm. She sighed as his tongue invaded her deeper, stroking inside her with leisurely movements.

Chiliad lowered Val to the floor, her head still pillowed against his forearm. He lavished her small body with slow, hungry caresses, his fingertips branded with the intimate memory of her flesh. Her eyes clung to his face. She yielded to his touch, spreading her legs wide for him, the tiny miniskirt riding high upon her thighs. Chiliad smiled at her innocent eagerness, welcoming her fresh response. He stroked over the dark, moist curls shading her mons, feeling her skin throb with an answering tremor. Her hips bucked as his fingers slid along her nether lips, circled her hot opening, climbing back to pleasure her clit. His mouth came down on hers to claim her again. She half-sobbed into his mouth as he rubbed his thumb along her clit, writhed against the floor as his finger drummed a vicious rhythm against the engorged nubbin. His mouth stifled her cry as she shuddered beneath him with a rushed, soft orgasm.

He chuckled against her lips.

"Mmm…we should try this at least once with a big, soft bed beneath us." He scooped her up into his arms and rose, yanking a surprised cry out of her. "But first there's this other fantasy I just *have* to try..."

"You just want to wash my *hair*?!"

An amused smile curved Chiliad's lips at Val's unmistakable note of disappointment. After he'd carried her to the shower and peeled the scanty black outfit off her skin, he'd stepped in himself. The wildcat had obviously expected a bit more than a shampoo. "I have this hair fetish, see?" Chiliad's voice whispered in Val's ear as his muscled chest pressed against her naked back. His palms cupped and kneaded her bare shoulders, infusing her flesh with heat.

"Fetish?"

"Hmmm," he hummed against her cheek. His hands skimmed down her arms, trapping her slim wrists. "And we could both use a shower, don't ya think?"

"I...I guess..."

He guided both of her hands up to the shower's smooth partition, his large body wrapping her from behind. His erection throbbed against her back. Val drew in a shuddering breath, her hands clenching against the wall. The thought of his hard, steely rod pulsing inside her made her wet and aching again.

His fingers drew fiery lines up her arms, cradling her shoulders. Val swayed against him, yearning for him to cradle her breasts the same way. Her nipples knotted into hard points, conveying her desire. Chiliad's hold on her tightened, responding to the tension oozing from her flesh.

"Spread your legs for me, Val."

Arousal clouded her mind, dousing her thoughts with a bittersweet haze. Val shifted against the man behind her, the back of her thighs brushing rock-solid muscles and coarse hair. Her own muscles tautened in burning anticipation. She felt Chiliad's hands slipping down her back in a soft caress, closing firmly on her hips.

"Oh, sweet Dyad!"

He was suddenly inside her, filling her with one long, clean thrust. Her breath caught at the swiftness of his actions, at the abrupt, incredible sensation of his cock sheathed in her cunt. It felt breathtaking to be stretched around his hard length, around his broad girth. To be so completely full with him, unable to escape his touch. He flexed inside her and she cried out again, bracing herself against the wall. She half-heard him at her back mumbling a soft command, his voice sultry and low, and an obedient spray of water lashed at them from above in a warm, steady drizzle. Val closed her eyes against the soft spatter, leaning further into the partition.

"You're so hot inside," Chiliad whispered, buried to the hilt in her tight, soaking pussy. "You feel like silk, wildcat...like the finest silk..."

"Chiliad..."

He slipped his hands up her narrow waist, thrusting inside her with long, controlled strokes. His fingers traveled up her ribcage and found her breasts, heavy and water-slick. He hefted the twin globes, pulling her body against his own as he kept pumping into her. Val arched back to him, her eyes shuttered. The movement made her breasts rear up into his palms. She felt amazing in his hands, around his cock. Her soft, rhythmic moans mingled with the patter of water, with his own throaty groans. Water cascaded down her dusky skin in shiny rivulets, soaking her midnight hair.

Chiliad slid one of his hands down her stomach, over her soaking mound, slipping into the wet heat between her thighs. His fingers remembered exactly where that tender nub of hers was hiding. She almost jerked away from the wall, crying out as he started to tease her clit. His body locked her in place. "Stay with me, honey."

His cock speared her with deep, hard thrusts. Her hips were moving with him. With each fierce movement he slid with ease into her tight, well-lubed pussy. She beat her fists against the slippery wall, mumbling in a tongue he didn't know. Then her back arched sharply and she screamed, a rough, violent shudder racking her lean muscles. Her cunt tensed on his shaft, convulsing about him in tight, swift waves. Scorching fire sped through her loins. He thrust once more and exploded inside her in a burst of sensation that stole her breath…and for a brief instant nothing else existed but pure pleasure.

Soaking wet and still tangled within each other, they collapsed to the floor of the shower. Chiliad turned Val in his arms, pulling her over his lap. He embraced her beneath the water's ongoing beat, pressing his lips against her dripping brow.

"What are you doing to me, wildcat?"

Val looped her arms about Chiliad's neck, enjoying the solid, damp feel of his flesh. "You asked me that a while back…in the cave, after we…" She hesitated, straining to ease her rough panting. Back then, he'd seemed angry with her for some reason. "I did nothing then—or now—besides…besides…" Her cheeks caught fire and she buried her burning face in his chest, groaning.

"Besides fucking my brains out," Chiliad offered, a boyish smile playing on his lips.

Val dared to raise her eyes to his face, meeting his humorous blue gaze. There was not a shred of anger within that deep cerulean. A sudden flood of emotions choked her chest, chasing the air out. She *wanted* this man. Wanted him more than anything else, his mind and his heart and his flesh. Yet she couldn't have him. The knowledge crashed through her very soul, swelled in her mind until stinging tears squeezed out. What she'd allowed, what she'd done with him, meant enduring the Temple's wrath. No greater sin existed, no greater treachery. There was no hope for her. But she could still save his life…

"What's going on behind those big eyes of yours?" He smoothed his finger down her moist cheek.

Val shook her head, a stubborn, desperate jerk. "Chiliad, please…you must leave these lands. If you're out of *Mankha* fuel—"

He stiffened at her words. His eyes narrowed, suspicion and anger rushing in once more. He turned her in his arms so that she fully faced him, his gentle grip at odds with his harsh stare.

Val blinked against the steady spray of water, staggered at the sudden coldness of his gaze.

"I asked you once before," Chiliad said softly. "What is it that you're not telling me?"

Chapter Six

Val swallowed over the lump in her throat. Chiliad's hold on her arms was tender, but the look in his eyes—it was as if he'd just truly seen her. His assessing gaze pierced her insides, hurt her more than any biting grip could.

Chiliad stared at Val in silence a moment more. He uncoiled from the shower floor and yanked her up to her feet, muttering another soft command under his breath. The rhythmic drizzle above them stopped, replaced by a swirl of warm air. The soft gusts tugged at Val's hair and lapped at her damp skin. She watched the brooding pirate as the coiling air currents whipped his hair around his handsome face, dried the water off his gold-toned body.

"*Mankha* fuel," he said at length, his low voice barely carrying over the wind's hum.

Val gazed up at him in confusion. "What about it?"

"That's what you just said, honey. *Mankha* fuel. I've heard the term a few times before." Chiliad surveyed Val from her toes up to the roots of her hair, a speculative gleam in his eye. "The only ones who call hyperfuel *Mankha* are the Amazons."

"Amazons?" Val's confusion grew with each of his hard words.

"That's everyone's favorite nickname for their kind, since no one knows where the hell they come from or where they're heading." Chiliad's gaze was unreadable, his stance rigid. "You know them quite well, I bet. Women warriors, always traveling through space in small, tight groups. Trading top-grade hypercrystals, mostly for basic supplies. Will kill you without even blinking if they *think* you're after their ass."

Val sucked in her breath, not knowing how to respond to this. She hadn't been off-world yet… Had never heard of this particular epithet for her kin. Yet Chiliad's description matched Chebrri's rough trader crews. It was a known fact there were things spoken of only within the intimacy of the trader crews themselves, a world of secret knowledge not shared with the cadet warriors. Of course, the young trainees had often heard bits and pieces, but they had only served to add to their confusion. Joining a trader crew, maturing among its crewmates, learning as you went, were considered essential parts of a warrior's training.

She hadn't gotten there yet.

Val tensed as Chiliad's hand clamped on her left wrist.

"Now that I think of it," he bit out, "they do have your coloring. Dark hair. Dark skin. Those big, fiery eyes. So *this* is the Amazon planet, is it?" Chiliad marched out of the cubicle, tugging Val with him through the unlatched portal. "Damn, when I go looking for trouble, I sure hit it big time!"

"But this is *Chebrri*," Val snapped back, anger rising like bile in her throat. Her thoughts whirled in confusion. She wrestled against his grip on her forearm. "This is Chebrri," she repeated desperately, "and its *traders* are its heart, its blood and its breath. I'm not *worthy* to be one of them."

Chiliad glared at Val. The wounded look on her face tugged at his heart, briefly overriding his qualms that she'd played him all along.

Maybe she was truly innocent? Maybe she hadn't known. Likely she'd never been out of this hellhole in her life, had never journeyed with the others to the stars.

His gaze softened.

"Why aren't you worthy, Val?"

"I gave myself to a man," she lashed out, raising her narrow chin.

"Yeah, we had sex, so fuckin' what?"

"I've violated the Temple's law."

For a brief instant Chiliad seemed too stunned to speak, trying to make heads or tails of her words. "Since when is sex a felony?"

"It is *sacrilege* here," Val whispered. "I was trained to be a trader. I should trade. I should fight. Instead, I performed a priestesses' rite with you." She drew in a shaky breath, her hands balling into fists. "At least, I *think* that's what I did."

"You—" Chiliad lightly squeezed her shoulders. "Why didn't you tell me this before?"

"I don't know." Puzzlement flickered over her features. "By the lake, when you placed your mouth on mine, I wanted…" The rest of her words got lost in a trembling, rushed intake of air.

For another stretching moment Chiliad regarded her face in silence. "My mouth on yours," he finally echoed. "You mean, like this?" He bowed his head, murmuring against her half-parted lips. She stood very still, swaying slightly, and he trapped her face in his hands. His bare skin molded her soft curves. Val sighed her surrender into his mouth, the subdued sound igniting each and every one of Chiliad's nerve endings. He was hard and heavy again, as if they hadn't just spent eternity fucking in the shower. His hand snagged a handful of her hair as he pulled her head back.

"How about violating that law again?" His voice was rough with promise and need.

"Yes…"

Before the word quit her mouth he hoisted her up to his waist, sliding with ease into her snug, silken embrace. Her breath hitched in her throat. She squeezed her arms and legs around his body, clinging to him like she'd never let go. Chiliad's rumbled groan tickled Val's neck. His fingers bit into her ass cheeks as he steadied her against him.

Val closed her eyes and embraced her pirate as he carried her the short distance through his ship's softly illuminated passageways. He was so deep inside her. Each of his long strides rocked his cock within her, tenderly kneading her flesh. Short moans of pleasure escaped her mouth, one after the other, even though she bit her lips trying to lock them inside.

Her eyes fluttered open at the feel of slight friction as Chiliad pulled out of her. He laid her against a spacious mattress, handling her as if she were something fragile. The springy material molded against Val in a welcoming caress. It sagged further beneath their combined weight as Chiliad climbed atop her and crouched between her thighs.

Val struggled to speak, her heart pounding in her throat. "Is this your bedchamber?"

A broad grin split his face. "Yes."

And then he sank inside her once more and she screamed, hardly able to take his slow penetration, the delicious, raw sensation of his broad cock head breaching her cunt. Her short nails bit into his bunching arms as he kept filling her. And then, at last, all of his length was nestled inside her and he rotated his hips and gave a slight thrust. Val threw back her head, gasping for air.

"Sweet starfire," Chiliad groaned.

Val's eyes flew open at Chiliad's low, husky voice. He was propped on his hands above her, elbows flexed, his arms bulging in golden perfection. His blue gaze sizzled with a dark fire, sweeping the length of her. Her face heated beneath his ravenous stare.

A roguish smile sparked in his eyes. "Don't be shy," he whispered. His hips started to thrust inside her, rocking her body with slow, steady strokes.

Val moaned into his breath.

"Mmm...Chiliad...*yes*..."

He retorted by sealing her mouth with a hard, probing kiss.

She locked her legs high on his back as he slowly fucked her. His steely thighs pressed against her ass. He plundered her moist, dark depths with his cock, with his tongue, each of his deliberate movements demanding her complete submission. A familiar, blazing pressure started to pulse low in Val's stomach. She writhed beneath Chiliad, squeezing her legs harder on his taut waist.

Sweet Dyad, she wanted more of him. Wanted to give it all *to him.*

They were both breathing raggedly, their bodies awash with sweat. Propped on his hands and knees, Chiliad increased his pace, pounding between Val's splayed thighs. He pressed his weight down on her pelvis, grinding upon her clit. The way her legs were wrapped around his back, he could go deep.

"Wildcat," he groaned.

She cried against his mouth with each hard stroke, her fingers boring into his arms. The pain invoked by her fingernails blasted Chiliad's last shreds of self-control to stardust. He growled into the damp crook of Val's neck, ramming into her with a ruthless force. He didn't know what had come over him. A burning need to fuck her, to please her, to claim her as his own, body and soul, had incinerated any functional brain cells remaining. He wanted to come inside her. He wanted to make her come.

Val was breathing hard, barely able to scream anymore. She couldn't handle this man. Couldn't handle herself. Her immediate universe became his touch, his scent, his breath. An abrupt shudder raked her entire body and her cunt tightened on him in a shattering climax.

Her pussy's quick, tight squeezes drove Chiliad over the edge, setting fire to his loins. With one last guttural groan, he burst inside her.

"Chiliad..." she mumbled, her eyes still closed. "Oh, *Dyad...*"

He sagged against her small body, burying his face in her neck, inhaling the sharp perfume of sweat and sex and Val. He couldn't believe the rough treatment he'd just given her. Dammit, each time with her—each fuckin' time—he'd spiraled out of control. He breathed in the warmth of her throat, sampling her salty flavor...realizing with a start that there was no other place he'd rather be, no other thing he'd rather do, no other woman he'd rather be with.

Come with me.

The unexpected words formed on Chiliad's tongue, but he didn't voice them.

Pushing himself back up to his hands, he again looked at her. Her tousled hair fanned about the rumpled bed in a rich, black spill. Her eyes popped open, the golden fire in their hazel depths thawing him down to his icy core. Damn, she looked so young. She *was* so young. He'd done enough to her already. How could he even consider it—muscling her into coming with him? Even if she agreed, what kind of a future could she have with him?

Unaware of his glum thoughts, she grinned up at him, dimples popping. Her left hand sought his cheek, trailing gentle fingers down his stubbly jaw. "I know of an untended mine close by," she whispered. "It's more of a natural cavern, really. Un-reaped. Cut out as much *Mankha* crystals as you can carry and leave."

"Val, are you sure?" Chiliad surveyed her face. "I've got you into enough trouble already."

"I'm sure." Val returned his forthright stare, a smile still tugging at her lips. A bit more trouble wouldn't matter… What she'd already done with him had condemned her beyond hope. She was willing to accept her own death, but rejected the fate awaiting this rough, untamed man should he stay on her home world much longer. It was a wonder the patrols hadn't hit upon his ship by now. The thought of the Temple gaining hold of Chiliad wrenched Val's heart, stole the air out of her lungs. She couldn't bear the thought of a priestess touching him the way she was touching him now. Of him, doing *this* with another. Her shaky fingers slid down his chest, converging possessively over the arrowing line of dusky hair. "We should go to that crystal cave right now," she offered, her throat tight.

Chiliad held his breath as her fingertips moved over his flesh, leaving fiery trails in their wake. His abdominal muscles tensed in renewed hunger. What the fuck was wrong with him? He was wearing the poor thing to exhaustion! He made a formidable effort to quench this new upsurge of desire. "You want to go out there in the middle of the night?"

"Night?"

"Yeah." Chiliad rolled over to his back, shifting Val up to straddle him. "Your auroras are out there, lighting up the sky."

Her face softened. "Have you seen them?"

"Only on the bridge's view screen," he murmured, caressing her thighs. This new position, with her riding his lap, did little to soothe his arousal. He wanted her to spill that gleaming cascade of hair all over his chest…

She socked him right in the stomach.

"Ouch!"

"That's no way to watch auroras, barbarian!"

Chiliad grinned. "Show me the right way, then."

Moments later his gaze was riveted to the naked night sky as the aurora pulsed above him, an infinite drapery of light bursting into the darkness in iridescent yellows and greens. The surreal glow raked over the far-off dunes, delineating the remote skyline.

"You were right," Chiliad mumbled. "This *is* the only way to watch auroras."

"Sometimes the colors are different." Val curled her toes against the cool sand. "And sometimes, I swear that they *talk*. Hisses, snaps…crackles." She grinned up at the sky. "I always try to guess what they're saying behind the static."

Chiliad's gaze dropped from the fiery sky to Val's raised face. That beaming, childlike smile made her look even younger than he knew she was.

Come with me.

Once more, the words burned on his tongue, but he didn't utter them. Tomorrow it would all be over and done with—she'd take him to the mine, he'd grab as many damn crystals as he could carry and be on his sweet way. He'd leave her his remaining aircycle, so she'd be able to—

His fists clenched at his sides. Who was he fooling? He couldn't bear the thought of losing her…of leaving her behind. But what could someone like him offer her? He was bound to get his ass fried, one way or another. She deserved better.

Cut it now, clean and sharp—it was best for them both.

Chapter Seven

"There…*yes*…right there!"

Chiliad swerved the aircycle forty-five degrees eastward, complying with Val's shouted instructions. Her keen, almost mystical senses never ceased to amaze him. How, dammit, did she know her way unerringly around this brutal landscape? After the aurora show last night she'd even guided him as he'd taken the *Ambrosine* into a low hover above the dunes, moving his ship to a new, more appropriate shelter. He hoped that stunt hadn't drawn any undesired attention.

He imagined Val's eyes squinted into golden slits against the wind and the suns, her heavy, dark braid lashing the air. She tightened her slim, steady arms around his waist, and he reveled in the firm squeeze of her thighs as she rode behind him.

"Drop altitude," she warned.

"Backseat driver," Chiliad growled, and Val giggled against the back of his shoulder.

"There!" she suddenly yelled. "Can you see it?"

Chiliad's gaze caught a sharp glitter within a clutter of rocks and sand, like sunlight bouncing off a shard of glass.

Val's would-be crystal mine.

"Hold tight!" Chiliad let out a howl and squeezed the aircycle's controls, shooting toward the sparkling mine in a blazing downward course. The vehicle touched ground in a perfect landing, scorching a dusty trail through the sand.

Val leaped from the aircycle, her dark braid swinging. Chiliad dismounted, reaching for the backpack secured against the vehicle. He turned, watching Val hesitate before the grotto's gaping mouth. Her left hand did a slight jerk toward her hip—

where her weapon would have been, he supposed, had he not cast it into the sands.

"Val?" His blaster eased into his right hand in less than a heartbeat.

"I just..." There was an added tightness to her shoulders. "I thought I saw a movement in there. Guess it's nothing."

He paused by her side, scanning the murkiness within. "Looks as quiet as it gets."

Val's stance eased somewhat. "Let's get this over with," she muttered and stepped into the dusty maw, swiftly engulfed by its soft shadows.

Chiliad strode in after her, re-holstering his blaster. Standing by the entrance, they'd made pretty easy targets for anything armed and dangerous. If something inside there wanted them dead, it would've gotten the job done by now. If something wanted them alive, however...

His gaze lifted to the low ceiling, bounced off the rough walls. The luster of sand-crusted crystals showed through the dull bedrock. He'd never hit upon such a wealth of hyperminerals in any of his infamous escapades. He shifted his backpack on his shoulder, drawing out his handy cutter. It was lightweight, boasting a powerful laser-knife—nothing less would even nick the hard crystalline.

"Wait," Val whispered, ill at ease with raising her voice. "Don't waste your sweat on these. The top-grade ones are a bit deeper inside."

"The *top-grade* ones?" Chiliad grinned in disbelief. "Stars, most of what I see around here already rates over ninety-nine percent pure. You're saying it gets even better than this?"

"Sure," she said, a subtle tension threaded in her voice. "Take out your beam. I'll show you."

The white shaft of light fanned out, painting a bright circle against the crystal-studded slabs of serrated rock.

"Chiliad, try these here." Val halted, caressing the jagged stone.

"You were right, honey. This *is* top-grade." Chiliad surveyed the rock with a smuggler's assessing eyes. These crystals could make him a fortune on the black market. Damn his luck, finally he was surrounded by undreamt-of wealth, and all he could carry was…well…all he could carry. In truth, he'd settle for making it off this world in one piece. Chiliad dropped the backpack and surrendered the flashlight to Val, readying his laser-cutter.

The crystals wouldn't be all he'd leave behind, though.

The sudden thought of leaving her took him utterly, frightfully unprepared. Chiliad froze against the bedrock, cutter in hand. His gaze snapped to Val's shaded features, catching the gleam of her eyes. He just *had* to tell her before logic paralyzed his tongue again.

"Val, I—"

An abrupt flood of light washed over them both.

"Drop the knife, handsome. Do it nice and slow, so I can see your hands."

Beside him, Val stiffened.

The cold, even voice, as well as the slash of light, came from the syrupy darkness ahead. Chiliad didn't have to see that voice's owner to know there was a blaster pointed at him with a steady hand. He sensed a familiar, hot tingling right between his shoulder blades, a feeling slightly sharper than having someone's eyes trained on his back.

Chiliad stifled a curse and dropped the cutter, the metal clanging coldly against the stone. He had a pretty good idea what was coming next.

"Good boy. Now place your hands high against the wall and spread your legs. Do it, *both* of you."

Familiar with this type of dialogue, Chiliad gritted his teeth and propped his hands against the rough stone. He glanced toward Val, catching her frightened gaze as she leaned against the rock, his glowing flashlight still clutched in her fist.

"Keep your eyes on that wall, handsome. Thraso, Clete!"

Someone behind him kicked his legs wider apart. He heard the soft hum of a handheld scanner run over him. Then practiced, lithe hands ran over his body from his tangled hair down to his heavy boots, relieving him of his lucky cuffs, his homing device, his pocketknife, his blaster and his four-inch boot-knife. The cutter had been kicked from between his legs and vanished the same way. Luckily the homing gadget was code-locked—any decoding attempt would erase all existing data. From the corner of his eye Chiliad glimpsed Val enduring the same rough treatment in dogged silence.

The searching hands withdrew.

"Turn around," the icy voice commanded. "*Slowly*. Keep your hands behind your heads."

They did, squinting against the glare.

The tall figure at the edge of the light balanced her weapon over the compact floodlight, her aim easy and flawless. The ricocheting glow barely illuminated her face in the darkness. Even so, Chiliad discerned the hard glint of her eyes, the stone-etched quality of her features, and knew her for who she was…one of the trading Amazons, and a cold-blooded specimen at that. Damn his capricious luck. He glanced sideways, noting the four additional warriors who were guarding their sides, blasters trained. Their outfits were dark and loose, matching the one he'd first seen on Val. He could well imagine these lethal beauties packed into the typical black catsuits in which they'd commonly traded.

Their chieftain spoke again, this time addressing Val. "I pleaded before the High Priestess that it would be me who came for you, Valasca."

"Lyssipe-Taj." Val gave a reverential bow, an apprentice acknowledging her tutor. "Then Aello has made it back safely."

Lyssipe lingered a fraction of a second before responding. "Your patrol-companion arrived unharmed," she confirmed at last, a hint of disapproval in her tone.

"I thank the Dyad, then."

Lyssipe paused one instant more before shifting her sharp attention to Chiliad. "You took her as your own," she abruptly bit out. Her raw, terse words had by no means been phrased as a question.

Val's cheeks scalded beneath the floodlight.

Chiliad's surprised gaze snapped to Lyssipe's stony features. "She put up a good fight. I won. I raped her, Chief. She's done nothing wrong—hasn't broken any of your damn laws."

Val gasped audibly beside him. "Chiliad, don't—" She cried out as a well-aimed kick to her shin from Thraso tumbled her to the rough ground. Her desperate gaze darted around the surrounding shaded faces in search of help. Clete, Derinoe, Thraso, Alkaia. She knew each one of them by name. The blank-faced warriors who were now holding her at blaster-point were to have been her crewmates.

"There's no need for that!" Chiliad started toward Val and froze as a blast from Lyssipe's weapon took out part of the wall behind him in a cloud of shimmering dust.

"Next time it'll be your pretty head." The chieftain edged closer, handing the floodlight over to Alkaia. "Now, don't try to fool me, handsome. You didn't rape her. She willingly gave herself to you."

The pirate regarded her in acerbic silence.

Lyssipe stalked closer to his motionless form. "Do you know what you've done?" With a rough movement she thrust her blaster beneath his jaw, forcing his head up.

Val sucked in her breath, her eyes wide with fear. Her fists clenched into aching knots against the cave floor.

Lyssipe spoke again, her low tone edged with fury. "When you gave Valasca her first pleasure, an *Udo*—a *priming*—occurred. Every fiber of her being is now *tuned* to your *foul, selfish* pleasure. Her body will scent your want, and like a beast in rut, she'll come to you. And you'll want to take her, again and again, for the body of a female bonded by *Udo* secretes an aphrodisiac each time she beds her mate. This beastlike submission is the ancient curse of the female *Neryandi*."

"You are wrong," Val cried out. "It doesn't have to be like that—"

"You know shit, Valasca," Lyssipe hissed. "In forgotten times, when the *Neryandi* men still ruled over Chebrri, they bonded their women by *Udo* and enslaved their will. Our oldest records claim a singular, rare virus wiped out all our males, but was this truly a mishap of nature? I think not. Who knows. The truth is buried deep beneath the sands."

Chiliad cocked a disbelieving brow. "Come on, Chief. Now that sounds plain crazy."

"Is it? You should know who you're taking to your bed, handsome." The chieftain gave him a dark smile. Her eyes then shot back to Val, still squatting against the rough rock. "That is why only our priestesses handle off-world men, Valasca—for the Mothers are the only ones trained to protect themselves against the *Udo*. They are the only ones allowed to perform the Rites, giving birth to new *Neryandi* daughters."

The blaster was now boring into Chiliad's flesh. He swallowed. "If you want to put a hole in me, just squeeze the trigger, Chief."

"Make no mistake, I'd love nothing more than to blow your brains out." The chieftain gave him a smile sauced with dark promise. "Unfortunately for you, my immediate orders are to deliver you to the Temple in a functional state. Seems they have other plans for you." Lyssipe stepped away from him, the weapon abruptly removed from his flesh.

"Up on your feet, cadet," she barked at Val. "Start walking. Both of you."

Chiliad shifted further away from the rock, his movements cautious. "Where are we going, Chief?"

"*Move*," she snapped, gesturing with her weapon in a way leaving no room for argument.

To the Temple, no doubt.

The unspoken answer to Chiliad's query hummed in Val's mind as the two of them were marched back toward daylight. To the Temple, where the High Priestess, Toxaris, would decide their fate. Val's pounding heart clenched for Chiliad. The Temple's clandestine actions could only be guessed at outside its innermost chambers, but this she knew—male captives who had been brought there were never again seen.

Outside, they cuffed their hands behind their backs. As their grim, small group waited by the grotto's mouth, a standard patrol craft rose from hiding in the surrounding rocky terrain, drifting to a halt mere feet away. Designed to hold a crew of eight, it could travel across the dunes far faster than the compact *wingless.* They'd be back in the settlement within hours.

Sweet Dyad, her time with him had narrowed down to hours…

Val felt as if ice had settled deep in her bones. Her eyes shot to the motionless pirate. Hands cuffed behind his back, he still managed to appear at ease. Chiliad caught Val's look, rewarding her with a puckish wink.

The warriors shifted about them, preparing to board the craft.

Chiliad winced at the sight of his beloved aircycle in the belly of the beast.

They entered the craft.

Chapter Eight

The part of Chebrri-Taj that lay above the sands was like the tip of an immense iceberg. The Temple set its roots beneath the surface of the sand and stretched upwards towards the sky's painfully bright dome. Chiliad likely would have been disappointed at the sight if he weren't blindfolded, for the Temple was no more than an austere keep of ruddy, bare stone.

After a journey lasting too long, in a seat too tight, he'd been shoved down the landing platform and marched along a tortuous trail in the unsavory company of several of the warriors. At some point they got him into an elevator—he felt the downward acceleration at the pit of his stomach. Through it all he'd strained to listen, searching to no avail for some hint of Val around him. Then their small party had halted, and something blunt poked at his chest. He heard the scanner's soft hum as they ran the device over his body.

"Kneel," a woman's rough voice commanded behind him. His knees buckled with a sharp, well-aimed kick.

They tore off his blindfold.

Chiliad fought a bitter, dark rush of disappointment.

Val wasn't there.

The warriors guarding him weren't the same ones who'd captured him. These ones wore the black catsuit uniform he was familiar with, a silvery crest of twin suns embroidered atop their left breasts. Chiliad had never seen the emblem before. *Now what?* he mused darkly. *Off with my head?*

"I am Eriobea. I am here to give you pleasure."

Pleasure? Chiliad's dark brows rose a notch. His gaze snapped up to see the owner of the sweet, silvery voice. It almost sounded like Val but was wrong, somehow. The olive-skinned beauty gazing down at him wore nothing but the shimmer of a gossamer caftan cinched at the waist with a wide sash, itself an elaborate weave of minute golden beads. The gauzy cloth caressed her well-rounded hips and her full breasts, enhancing their lush, nude curves. She had a soft, rounded stomach, only adding to her charms. A golden thong stretched over her mons, and flat, golden-strapped sandals graced her small feet. Likely she was one of the priestesses Val had talked about.

"I figured you were about to blow my brains out," Chiliad said wryly.

Eriobea surveyed him with slanted hazel eyes. "Hardly," she murmured, a subtle smile curving her lips. "Not with a blaster, anyway."

She leaned down to him, her hair spilling over him in a rush, and nestled his face in her hands. Her flowery perfume engulfed him. He glimpsed exquisite, long fingers and golden, honed nails. Eriobea's soft lips caressed his mouth like silk stroking skin. The tip of her tongue followed, sketching the inside of each lip in a sensual promise of more. She rose, her sweet aroma deserting his senses.

The priestess gazed down at the captured man, briefly silent. When she had touched her mouth to his lips, she had also stroked her sensual aura against his own. Exploring the vibrant eddy of his colors, she tried to learn what barrier would block a possible *Udo* between them. Only, she sensed...*something*...from him. Or maybe it was nothing. This captive's raw sexuality made it difficult for her to discern any subtleties.

"Of course, I can give you back to our warriors...if that is your choice," she whispered at last, her dark eyelashes lowered demurely.

Chiliad's lips twitched with a faint grin. "Nah, I like you better. You're a hell of a lot nicer."

One of the warriors let out a nasty chuckle above him.

"It is decided, then." A minute, silvery gadget popped into the priestess' hand, and she touched it to his upper arm.

Chiliad felt a slight needle-sting. *What the hell?*

Eriobea surveyed her gadget's display. "You're using a long-term contraceptive," she stated. "Nothing that can't be fixed."

The priestess swiveled with a soft rustle and a flurry of gold, sashaying somewhere outside Chiliad's visual field. She was quick to return, carrying a compact hypodermic, and touched it to his arm.

This time he'd seen the needle coming. The chieftain had mentioned delivering him to the Temple in a "functional" state, and now he figured out what kind of a function she'd meant. He was beginning to feel like a mobile sperm bank.

Eriobea stood erect once more, a tantalizing smile on her face. "Now let's get to the pleasure part," she murmured. "Uncuff him."

Chiliad flexed his chafed wrists. He accepted her proffered hand and rose to his feet, his guards drawing back a step. He let the lady lead him to the huge canopy bed occupying a generous portion of the chamber. The spacious, comfortably cool space brimmed with luxury. It felt close to indecent to stomp his boots against the rare Romallian carpet of bushy white fur that graced the floors. That alone must have been priceless. His smuggler's eyes skimmed in disbelief over hand-woven wall rugs and heavy furniture costing ridiculous amounts. He doubted Val had ever gazed upon such lavishness in her life. Dumbstruck as he was, his eyes hadn't neglected Eriobea's shapely buttocks swaying before him, nude but for the thong's scanty golden thread and the sheer caftan.

Eriobea let go of his hand by the bed, glowing with satin and velvet. She swiveled to him, her heated gaze trained on his face, and shucked her sandals.

"Are they going to watch?" Chiliad gestured toward the two warriors.

"I'll make you forget that they're there," Eriobea whispered. Her full lips ignited with a sultry smile and she started to unwind her sash, her movements a slow, sensuous flow. On and on the ornate band of cloth coiled about her feet, until she was left empty-handed. Her dark nipples were peaked beneath the loose caftan. She drew in a soft breath, aware of the gaze riveted to the rise and fall of her breasts.

One corner of his mouth shot up in a half-smile. "Mine to play with?" he whispered, not waiting for a confirmation. His hands glided over the dark globes, rubbing against the hard points. He lightly pressed the supple flesh through the gauzy barrier. Eriobea's skin throbbed beneath his fingertips. She trembled, drawing in a shaky breath.

"Undress me," she purred, leaning into his muscled, hard chest.

"I was getting there." Chiliad slipped his palms beneath the caftan, splaying his fingers over Eriobea's naked skin. He climbed his hands up her heaving chest, parting the caftan until the rich fabric slid completely off her shoulders. It dropped down her body like a soft caress, spilling about her feet in a golden puddle.

With a moan she wrapped her arms about his neck and pulled herself up to his mouth.

He closed strong arms about her softness and invaded her mouth with a crushing kiss, knowing it was what she wanted of him. Tangling his fingers in her silken hair, he locked her head in his grip, not releasing her even as she struggled for air. There was a muted commotion behind his back—their lethal chaperons, no doubt, alarmed at his rough love play. Chiliad tore his mouth from Eriobea's lips a bare second before the warriors got *truly* upset.

"Dyad," the Priestess mumbled, licking her swollen lips. She would have to work extra-hard blocking this man's aura... His was a powerful one. "If that is your kiss, I wonder how a woman feels when you bed her," she murmured.

As Chiliad had hoped, the woman's gaze sizzled with an added heat. His grin broadened. He took her mouth again. She clung to him, her body pulsating in his embrace like an explosive about to detonate. He caught the sweet-sharp whiff of her arousal and knew she was already soaking wet for him. He seriously doubted the warriors would be as hospitable after the lady got what she wanted from him.

His quick hand drew out his bio-blade.

"Too bad," he mumbled against her lips. "I don't feel like donating right now."

Eriobea squealed as Chiliad wrapped her long hair around his fist and spun her in his hold, pressing the blade's jagged, bony edge against her throat. The blade was the recent product of bioengineering, made completely of bone, tendon and muscle. It was a rare, unpopular weapon—pricy, ugly and not easy to handle. Most scanners, however, couldn't pick out its kind, and most body searches missed it.

The warriors leaped towards them with rough curses, blasters aimed.

"That was really stupid." Chiliad flashed them a feral smile. "You should've pulled your stunners. Now, one more step and I cut the lady's throat. Fuck, I'm so pissed right now, I might do it anyway." Eriobea writhed and he pressed the blade deeper into her soft flesh, forcing out a crimson bead of blood. She went stock-still in an instant, not even daring to scream, her breath wheezing out in an agonized rush.

Both warriors glanced at one another then glanced back at the show at hand. Eriobea was a priestess—and a high-ranking one, at that. She had already mothered two daughters for the *Neryandi*. Injuring her—or causing her harm by inaction—would be rewarded by a death sentence, or worse. Whatever the guards did, their fates had already been sealed by allowing this little incident to take place.

Chiliad had hoped they would react exactly as they had. "Ladies," he growled. "Drop your blasters, *now*." The warriors hesitated. He dug his blade deeper into Eriobea's neck, and this time she screamed.

Both blasters dropped to the thick rug with a muted thud.

"Good girls." They looked anything *but* good. Chiliad pulled the naked, shivering priestess against his chest with a steely grip that squeezed the air out of her lungs. He considered how the blasters could make their way across the rug, but quickly decided against it. "Now, both of you put your hands up—high. Don't even *think* about touching your stunners. If you do, she goes. Now back away from those blasters. I want to see your backs hit the wall. Yeah, I meant you too, sunshine."

Both warriors withdrew 'til their backs met the wall, their gazes intent on Chiliad. Lucky for him, a look couldn't kill.

"Turn around and face the wall—I want to see your mouths kissing it! I ain't kidding, ladies!" He advanced toward the discarded blasters, dragging Eriobea with him, his bio-blade etching a red line into her throat. Silent tears rushed down her cheeks, dampening Chiliad's forearm. He paused by the blasters. Crouching to pick one up would be too risky as long as he had to restrain Eriobea. Besides, his hands were kinda full. He dragged the priestess further along with him toward the warriors, who faced the wall in rigid silence. Speaking softly into the priestess' ear, he hoped the words got in past her terror.

"If you want to live, do exactly what I tell you. Do you get that, Eriobea? Say yes if you do. *Do you understand*?"

"Yes."

"Good. I want you to pull that stunner from the back of her belt, right there. I know it's a little hard for you to see right now, but you can do it. *Stop*. Keep the stunner in contact with her body, or my blade goes deeper."

The warrior's back grew even stiffer as she realized Chiliad's scheme, but she didn't dare move. Her sweaty fists clenched against the wall rug.

"Keep it against her back," Chiliad ordered calmly in Eriobea's ear. "Now squeeze the trigger. Don't worry, it won't kill her, she'll just sleep for a while."

Eriobea obeyed, her hand shaking badly, and the stunned warrior sagged against the wall to the soft carpet.

"No sudden movements, now. Keep your arm away from your body." Chiliad hauled the priestess the short distance to the remaining warrior. Already knowing what to expect, the guard uttered a soft, venomous curse of impotent rage. Within less than a minute she was down as well.

"Drop the stunner," Chiliad said softly.

The priestess unclenched her trembling fingers and the stunner hit the carpet.

He withdrew the blade from her neck and spun her around, pinning her against the colorful wall rug. She gulped air, her body erupting with loud sobs. She struggled to contain the sounds, not having much luck. Chiliad flinched at the sight of blood on her refined, soft neck. He'd rather deal with armed warriors any day than terrorize this dainty creature. However, they'd left him no choice, and his life wasn't the only one on the line here.

"Now tell me," he whispered, his tone lethal. "Where might I find the young cadet named Val? She was brought here with me."

And Eriobea suddenly realized what it was that she'd sensed earlier beneath his untamed aura. When he said the young cadet's name, it was loud and clear. *The man was bonded to the girl.* "The one that was taken with you," Eriobea mumbled, half-dazed. "I'm not sure—"

"But?"

"If they haven't tried her yet, she should be in the Temple's detention chambers, a level down," Eriobea blurted out. "Please…"

"Get dressed. You're taking me there."

His tone, accompanied by the steely look in his eyes, convinced her not to argue. He walked her over to the bedside, collecting the stunners and the fallen blasters. Then he watched her as she donned her caftan and wrapped the beaded sash about her waist. The jittery movements of her hands were a far cry from their initial flowing grace. She slipped her feet back into her sandals and lifted big, hazel eyes to him, suddenly looking very much like Val.

"Where's your restroom?" His voice was rough with a bad mix of anxiety and anger. "I want you to clean yourself up a bit before we go out there."

She pointed with an unsteady hand and he took her there, amazed at the generous dimensions of the room and its lavish decor of pink-white marble. Eriobea stumbled over to the gilded washbasin and pressed a damp, white towel against her neck.

"Let me have a look at that." Chiliad tilted her head back with a gentle grip. The mild bleeding had already stopped, leaving a jagged red line and an ugly, swelling bruise. "D'you have some kind of scarf?"

"S-scarf?"

He sighed. "Forget it." Arranging her long, rich hair about her shoulders, he hoped it would be enough to conceal the mark.

"Here's the deal, Eriobea. You take me to Val, and I will let you live. I'll be close behind you at all times. If someone, *anyone*, suspects something is wrong, than I will take that someone out with my blaster. That someone's life will then be on *your* conscience. Do we have a deal?"

"Yes," she whispered. "You need not take any of my daughters' lives."

"Good."

They walked across the dense, white fur to the sealed entryway. Chiliad put another stunner-charge through each of the warriors, noting by the subtle twitching of their muscles and the cadence of their breathing that the initial effects had started to wear off.

They paused by the door.

"After you," Chiliad said softly.

Chapter Nine

They were coming for her.

Val's eyes darted towards the entryway. Her heart jolted in fear of what awaited her behind the door. She had prepared herself over and over for what was to come, still, her breath hitched at the sight of the high-ranking priestess who paused at the entrance of the room.

The priestess stepped into the detention chamber.

And Chiliad slipped in behind her, sweaty and tousled, a stunner clutched in one hand and a blaster gripped in the other.

Val had never gazed upon a sweeter sight in her life.

"Stars, honey, do you need a royal summons to get your ass over here?" He chucked the stunner he'd held, muttering something about *second-rate useless weapons*, and tossed her another one he had tucked in his belt.

Val snatched the weapon from the air with sure hands, bouncing to her feet. The standard cadet weapon was the short-range *sheko*, and she dearly missed hers, but she'd been trained to handle most firearms. How had Chiliad enlisted the priestess' aid? An abrupt stab of dismay lanced her as she realized the priestess hadn't joined him willingly. She caught sight of the ugly bruise swelling on that divine, velvety neck. *Chiliad surely hadn't –*

"Val, honey, start breathing," Chiliad growled. "Go out there while no one's shooting at us and put on a guard's uniform. We're going to play guard and prisoner, you and me." He shot her a wayward grin that made her core sizzle even in these circumstances.

The couple of stunned warriors sprawled outside the chamber were Temple's Guard, by the look of the silver embroidery atop their left breasts. The still-smoking control panel affixed to the wall told Val exactly how Chiliad had broken her cell's entry-code. Her chamber was the only one occupied within the short, lustrous row of doors—Chebrri's Temple rarely needed to illustrate its penal system.

To Val's overwhelming relief, she didn't recognize any of the guards. Crouching by the one closest to her size, she struggled to disrobe her. Dyad, whether she knew her face or not, she still was her kin! She uttered a soft *Neryandi* curse as her trembling fingers fought a disobedient fastener.

"Help her." Chiliad gave Eriobea's shapely derriere a slight encouraging pat.

She jolted.

Val paled, aghast. "Don't! She's a priestess—"

"So what? A little exercise will do her good."

Eriobea had already knelt opposite Val, straining to wrestle a limp arm out of a tight, dark sleeve. "Daughter," she whispered in *Neryandi*. "Do not distress yourself over me."

"Hey," Chiliad snarled. "I said *help* her, I didn't say *talk* to her!"

Val sensed the pirate's eyes touching her back with heat as she tugged the suit up her hips. She swiveled to face him, quickly fastening the snug fabric over her breasts. "Aren't you supposed to watch the hallway?"

"I can multitask," he said, one shoulder propped beside the empty mouth of the access corridor. "Put on one of the belts, wildcat, or it'll look funny."

She sent him a fiery gaze, remembering that he could indeed multitask quite well, and bent down to grab the guard's duty belt.

He returned a look packed with the same amount of heat. "Do you think you can get us out of this hellhole?"

Val shifted with unease. "I know my way around most of the ground level, but I've never been this deep before."

Chiliad nodded. "We'll play it by ear, then. Let's move." He recoiled from the wall and aimed his stunner at the comatose guards. Val flinched as he fired two quick, consecutive shots.

"First you'll have to give me your word you won't use the blasters," she demanded. "And the Mother is free to go." Val motioned at Eriobea's crouched form. The priestess had unwound her sash and was working to cover the naked warrior.

Chiliad stared at Val. Whenever he heard that tone coming from her, it promised trouble—and delivered. "I might need to use this blaster," he said coolly. "And she's our ticket out of here. I'll let her go as soon as we get our hands on some kind of transportation."

"Then I won't do it." Val's stance was rigid, her stunner lowered to the floor.

Chiliad knew a lost cause when he slammed into one. Muttering something incomprehensible, he shoved the blaster into his belt. "I know I'll regret this," he growled, "if I live long enough. No blasters. But *she* still has to come with us."

"I don't know where the underground docking is located," Eriobea responded in a reedy voice. "I've never needed to— " She stumbled into silence, her voice too shaky for words.

"There's a landing area at ground level for brief stopovers," Val intervened.

"Forget the underground docking then, Eriobea," Chiliad bit out. "Just take us up to the surface. Can you do that?"

The priestess nodded.

Their small group rushed down the corridor, spilling into a quiet hall of modest dimensions. Val's eyes widened at the sight of two more warriors lolling unconscious against the sealed elevators. She bit her bottom lip as Chiliad's stunner sent them into a deeper slumber. Eriobea cringed at the weapon's soft hiss, her refined hand flickering over the wall console. The door slid open, revealing the elevator's hollow interior, and tension partly seeped out of Chiliad's and Val's rigid stance. They all stepped inside. The door slid closed.

Stunner gripped in each hand, Chiliad turned to Val and gathered her into a rough embrace, covering her mouth with his own. She tensed, surprised, then sagged against the warm, solid feel of him. She hadn't dared hope he'd ever hold her in his arms again. They kissed open-eyed, open-mouthed, each hanging on to the other. They savored and drank and inhaled, intoxicated with each other, the lift's upward acceleration fizzing in the pit of their stomachs. The snatched seconds slipped into some hidden place beyond time, a place where only bittersweet tastes, feverish touches and sweat-mingled scents existed, and it was theirs and theirs alone.

They tore their mouths and bodies apart at the hint of subtle deceleration and jerked back to Eriobea's side, standing hot and winded. Chiliad concealed both weapons behind his back, hoping whoever glanced his way would assume he was handcuffed. He shot Val a sizzling look over Eriobea's head, and she returned one full of promise.

Eriobea expelled a breath, her own gaze intense and unreadable. Her own misgivings clouded her mind and clutched at her heart. What she'd just sensed between the two was the most powerful *Udo* she'd ever stumbled upon. Such a bond couldn't have formed without the Dyad's consent!

They stepped out of the elevator into the disciplined turmoil outside.

"Is this usual around here?" Chiliad inquired in a muted tone, his wary gaze scanning the organized mayhem.

"No," Val whispered back. "Something's going on. Think maybe they found out about us?"

He was about to reply when a dark figure detached itself from the flowing bustle and breezed their way. Val made out the golden embroidery atop her chest, recognizing her as one of the Guard commanders. Unlike Guards, the trader crews never donned such indications of their internal rank hierarchy. Val forced her breathing to ease, making a show of training her own stunner on Chiliad.

"Mother," the commander graced the priestess with a courtesy bow, then lashed out at Val. "Where is your partner?" she demanded. "Why isn't the prisoner blindfolded? Give me your commanding officer's name!"

Chiliad hadn't understood the specifics, but he caught its drift well enough. His sweaty fists tensed around both stunners.

Val opened her mouth to answer, not sure what words would come out.

"This guard was acting at my urgent request," Eriobea's silvery voice cut in. "I instructed her to escort me and the prisoner up to the surface. I need the Dyad's full guidance before I perform the Rites with this man."

"You were placing yourself at an unnecessary risk, Mother." The commander surveyed the pirate with distaste. Chiliad tried his best to appear harmless, aware that he was probably doing a lousy job at it. To his relief, the lady's acerbic attention focused back on Val. "Don't delay outside," she bit out. "A foreign battle cruiser has just breached our immediate space. I don't want the Mother's life in needless danger." Someone motioned her from the distant hall; not waiting for a reply, the commander turned and hurried back.

Val blew out a held breath. She couldn't fathom Eriobea's unexpected help, nor could she believe their luck. Lyssipe would have never allowed such negligence. Her chieftain would have probably insisted on getting a much more thorough explanation, and a foreign battle cruiser wouldn't have sidetracked her quick mind from her other duties. She would have understood the "prisoner" was not only bare-eyed, but uncuffed and armed, as well.

"I thank you for your help, Mother," Val whispered.

"There is a powerful *Udo* between you two," Eriobea replied in *Neryandi*. "I have felt the Dyad's blessing upon this bond. Maybe I am wrong, but I shall not be the one to break it. I do not know, daughter, if the High Priestess would've granted you the same pardon. She has the benefit of the whole of Chebrri-Taj to consider."

Val's cheeks flushed at the priestess' impassioned words. "Move, barbarian," she commanded Chiliad aloud, shoving her stunner in his back.

"Barbarian?" He fought back a smile, obeying her slight poking.

Val grinned behind his back. "Go that way," she added more privately. "It'll take us to the Temple's ground-level landing area.

Can you tell me anything about a battle cruiser touring these territories?"

"I can think of only one man who hates my guts enough to try and dig my ass out of the galaxy's shittiest holes," Chiliad snarled, not caring to elaborate. "No offense," he added.

Val snorted.

They were moving through the spacious hall at a swift pace again, picking their way through the rush of warriors, priestesses and cadets. No one else had bothered stopping them, thanks to Eriobea's steady company. A short distance from freedom Chiliad's own sixth sense—what he called his smuggler's sense—awakened. He'd learned never to question that vague prickle between his shoulder blades. With a quick backward glance, he caught a subtle commotion starting at the back of the hall.

Their shaky cover must have been blown.

Seemed like no one had made them out within the crowd yet. *Thank the Stars for the busy hall!* Chiliad tightened his fists on his stunners, tossing a terse whisper over his shoulder.

"Val, we're bailing."

She gave him a brief, intense look.

The warriors stationed at the entryway shifted blank gazes to the threesome, about to wave them through, when something hijacked their attention. Chiliad caught the subtle shift in the guards' stances. Their slight hesitation worked in his favor. His stunners reacted quicker than his mind, taking both warriors down in a deep-rooted reflex.

"*Run!*"

Leaving Eriobea behind, they both burst outside. Intense sunlight hammered at their unguarded faces and baking heat attacked their skin. Half-dazzled and panting, they tore through the landing area. The field was dotted with the sharp gleam of parked crafts. Val's squinted eyes darted about, honing in on a somewhat battered glider.

"Move aside," Chiliad breathed. "I bet I can get this garbage pile open!"

Mere seconds later he slipped into the pilot's seat.

Val slipped beside him into the navigator's station. She'd wanted to fly the glider herself! Sadly, the man was too big to be wrestled out of his chosen position. She frowned. "Are you sure you can handle this craft?"

"A fuckin' craft is a fuckin' craft is a fuckin' craft," he shot right back. His quick fingers were already fluttering over the control board, swiftly taking the glider into a light hover. "Let's split before they discover *exactly* which junk pile is missing." Chiliad grinned at last, his blue eyes flashing with pure malice.

Val could swear he was enjoying himself!

"Better pray your pals haven't come across my *Ambrosine* yet!" he roared, taking them to a higher altitude. "First stop, that damn crystal cave. Point me in the right direction?"

She did.

The glider bucked and zoomed toward the golden sands that lapped at the city's edge.

Chapter Ten

The SpaceHound, Captain's bridge
Uncharted territories

"They're still giving us the silent treatment, Captain."

"Instruct Communications to redispatch the usual crap, Lieutenant." Steele sighed. "You know—we come in peace, take us to your leader, don't fuck with us."

"The polite version," the bridge communications officer concluded. "Affirmative, Captain."

Steele paced in front of the ship's display. Their unwanted escort consisted of stealthy, speedy crafts, odd crossbreeds between a trader and a light cruiser. He'd recognized them as Amazonian trader vessels, and Information had just confirmed it.

"We could always zap one to stardust if they get too cuddly," Lieutenant Commander Kimi suggested. Her slanted coal-black eyes narrowed with subtle amusement. She poked a burgundy fingernail into the holographic display, whispering, "*Boo.*"

"Bitchy." Steele cocked his brow at his sexy Executive Officer. Whenever she displayed that kind of attitude, it meant great sex later. "XO, there's 'handle with care' written all over this one. We found something we weren't supposed to find. Let's give our hosts a little time to swallow the idea that the Navy is swimming in their pond."

"You have a point, Captain," the XO said, sending him a subtle smile.

Great sex later, Steele mused again as he watched Kimi's expression. He imagined her mocha skin stretched against the white linen backdrop of his bed. Aside from the prospect of steamy sex, the unexpected development appeared more than promising for him. While exploring the uncharted sector, he hadn't come across his favorite SOB, Chiliad Jayrt'ian yet—instead he'd stumbled upon the home base of the enigmatic Amazons. Their elusive, rough trader crews seemed to have a surplus of top quality crystalline mineral to trade all over charted space. If he sweet talked their top dogs—or rather, bitches—into conversing with the rest of the Nemean galaxy, then maybe he'd finally get that damn promotion he'd been robbed of years before.

"What's this? A new boy wants to play?" The XO pointed at a new bright dot flickering over the display. "Damn, sorry. I meant, a new girl."

Steele felt an odd stirring in his stomach. "No, this one isn't Amazonian. Ops, get me a full visual," he roared.

"We've got him on screen, Captain," the Operations lieutenant replied. "Information just gave us a positive I.D. on him—"

"*Jayrt'ian*!" Steele growled, eyes affixed to the *Ambrosine's* insolent image on the viewscreen. "I want him in my immediate fire zone, *now*!"

"You said subtle diplomacy is needed here," the XO commented. "If we fire, than our escorts might think we're firing at *them*. Which will lead, of course, to *them* firing back at *us*. Not that I'd mind a bit of mud-wrestling..."

"I want to see that bastard bite the stardust." Steele's tone was quiet, lethal. "Lieutenant Yan?"

"We've got him within DEWs range, Captain," the combat operator responded. "Stations five to nine, sir."

Steele grinned. "Zap the bastard. Do it before he achieves leaping distance. Fire at will all in-range DEWs."

The SpaceHound spat out an abrupt, dense energy cluster, searing through the vacuum toward the receding *Ambrosine*.

* * * * *

The Ambrosine, Captain's bridge
Charted deep space

Chiliad surveyed the iridescent output of datum points traversing his Navi-system's display. Hot damn, for once a hyperleap had landed him right where he'd intended! Not to mention, two points in his favor, zero in Steele's. He'd scarcely managed to leap before he got his ass fried. Talking about a narrow escape! Grinning to himself, he switched navigation control over to the *Ambrosine*.

"*Sweet Dyad.*"

Chiliad turned away from the controls at the sound of Val's voice. Stars, the wildcat actually looked pale! She was staring wide-eyed at the star-dotted darkness of space rushing by on the view screen.

"Now, *that* was a close call, honey," he said, rising to his feet.

Her head snapped his way.

Chiliad shot her a smug smile. He moved closer, swiveling her chair and propping his hands against both her armrests. "Easy, wildcat," he whispered. "We ain't dead yet." His gaze stroked over her face and much lower, moving like a hot caress. The last few hours had built adrenaline inside him that had to gush out *somehow*.

Val gazed up at Chiliad's face, giddy and short of breath. She was having a hard time deciding if she should blame it on their narrow escape from death or on the man's sheer proximity. Chiliad made that decision easy for her. He leaned low, sealing her mouth with his own. His sexual aura, eager and raw, blasted into her senses. Her lips opened under his burning need. She moaned aloud as his fiery tongue lashed at her own, setting her mouth ablaze. He cradled her face in a hot embrace so he could taste her better. She tunneled her fingers through his hair, pulling him deeper inside.

At some point they both had to go up for air.

"Mmm, honey…" Chiliad breathed over his warrior's candy-sweet lips. "I can't resist a woman in uniform. It makes me want to…" He let his fingers drop down the curve of her neck. "Take it right off."

She gasped beneath his curved lips. The man's expert touch had already loosened her catsuit's front fastener, allowing his hand to slip beneath the fabric. Then, slowly, he pulled back from her. Val murmured a soft protest as his palm withdrew from her hot skin.

"Stand up," Chiliad coaxed with a husky whisper, trapping her small hand in his large one.

Intoxicated with his scent, aroused by his voice, she obeyed.

He pulled her close against his chest, claiming her lips in another hungry kiss. His hands started to undress her, and she felt the slow advance of his hands as he peeled the tight uniform off her skin. Whenever his fingertips touched bare flesh, she trembled, needing his touch so bad that it hurt.

Val's fists clenched against her thighs as those rough-soft male lips claimed each and every patch of bare skin exposed by his fingers. He kissed, licked and nibbled from that salty dip at the base of her throat to the shaded vale of her breasts. She dared not move as he loved her with his lips, his tongue, his teeth…for fear she'd miss the lightest of his touches. He licked a hot trail against the lush underside of one breast, and she shuddered in his arms… His tongue teased tightening circles about her areola, and she moaned, swaying, her head falling back.

The full heat of his mouth engulfed a jutting, dark nipple. So sudden, so powerful, it made her scream. Val's eyes wrenched open, her fingers twisting into Chiliad's untamed locks. She dropped her gaze to his face, watching him with ravenous eyes as he sucked her hardening flesh.

"You're driving me crazy, barbarian," she groaned.

He looked up at her, still holding her in his mouth, those wicked lips of his curving into a knowing smile. He let go then, leaving her nipple rigid and gleaming, and kissed a scorching path down to her bellybutton. Val's knees almost gave way as he dipped his tongue into her navel. She felt like a grain of sand about to be swept away by a desert wind.

"Chiliad…"

"Tell me what you want, Val," he whispered against her. "Tell me what you *want*, wildcat."

"You," she breathed, pulling his head taut against her flesh. "I want *you*."

It was the right answer. His eyes ignited and he dug his fingers beneath the dark fabric that still clung to her hips, giving the uniform one last, sharp pull. His look devoured her from her slim ankles up to the roots of her midnight hair. Her raw beauty stunned him. Draped in hair down to her waist, watching him with gleaming hazel eyes, she was like a desert mirage come to life. She was still wearing her beaded blue bracelet about her left ankle, and somehow, this small piece of jewelry only played up her nudity in Chiliad's eyes. He sprang to his feet and scooped her into his arms. Val's naked, hot curves against his clothed torso were a devilish turn-on. Chiliad's already hard cock was about to burst out of his snug breeches.

In a surprise move, Val looped her arms around his neck, pulling herself up to his mouth. Pressing her kiss-swollen lips against his, she stroked her tongue between his lips in a gentle, tentative movement. Stars, she was trying to kiss him for the first time! In her own sweet way, his Val was finally demanding entrance.

An entrance he gave her.

Mumbling a low, pleased moan of encouragement, Chiliad parted his lips before her questing tongue. She sank deeper inside and he welcomed her in, playing with her. The wildcat bit. Chiliad chuckled at the soft nip she gave him. He sucked her tongue deeper into his mouth for payback.

Val moaned in response and squeezed her arms tighter about Chiliad's neck. She opened her mouth wide against his own, clashing teeth and twining tongues. Tossing conscious thought out into the vacuum of space, she delved into Chiliad's mouth with uncurbed hunger. Obviously, the last few hours had caused a build-up of adrenaline. Hours? Sweet Dyad, *years*! Years of wondering. Years of wanting. Years of pining and not knowing for *what*. Well, now she knew, and she was determined to have it.

Chiliad's blood hit the boiling point as she took his mouth. He *loved* a strong-minded woman! His fingers bit into supple flesh as their mouths engaged in wild combat. Blindly he stumbled out of the *Ambrosine's* bridge and into the narrow passage, his precious load writhing in his embrace. He was so into her, so deep in her mouth, that he couldn't recall how, exactly, he made it to his private chamber.

With a rough groan Chiliad tossed Val on his big, empty bed. She propped herself up on her elbows, gazing at him through her tumbled hair. Her thighs were loosely parted, baring her moist curls and the glistening, swollen lips of her cunt. Chiliad's eyes clung to this display of naked feminine beauty. He ripped his shirt off as he dived for the bed.

"Open wide," he growled, grabbing her thighs and dragging her pussy over his mouth.

Val yelped, her back hitting the bed. She arched with a sharp gasp as she felt his hot breath caressing her wet flesh. An excited tremor coursed through her body. He'd never done *this* to her before. Was he truly about to—

"Aaahhh...Dyad!"

She shuddered all over as his tongue laved her from her ass to her downy mound. She sensed him pull back a little. His breath rasped ruthless heat over her drenched pussy. Val groaned at the sensation, digging her sweaty fingers into the bedcovers.

Chiliad glanced up from between her thighs, his tongue sweeping her sharp, rich taste off his lips. She was delicious, and he wanted more. He'd never have enough of her. His smoldering gaze dropped to her sweet pussy, giving it the thorough inspection it deserved. The scent she gave off hammered at his senses, and he was like a drugged man. Releasing his rough hold on her thighs, he splayed her nether lips apart with feverish fingers and fully bared her clit to his eyes. The tiny nub, coaxed out of its hood, pointed shiny and swollen towards his mouth.

Val cried out as air skimmed over that raw hub of her pleasure. Writhing against the rumpled bed, she raised her hips, straining to get herself to his mouth. A desperate, soft plea escaped her lips.

Chiliad couldn't help a soft grin, hearing her unknowingly slip into the *Neryandi* tongue. Yet he understood perfectly. A wicked mood overtook him and he withdrew from her cunt to dine on the sensitive flesh of her inner thigh, kissing and sucking her skin into his mouth.

Val moaned at this cruel neglect of her pussy, twisting against the bed. She flung her head sideways, burrowing her taut fingers deeper into the mattress. "*Please*," she panted.

Enough torture. Chiliad planted one last teasing kiss on the damp inner fold of her thigh and got down to business. *Stars, her honey was pouring.* He licked around her opening, circling the empty slit that longed to be filled. He heard her—felt her—sucking in her breath. Her hips jerked. Dipping his tongue inside her, Chiliad lapped at her juices, ravaged her cunt with an intimate, hard kiss. He went deep, he went shallow, he swirled and stabbed in a languorous motion.

Val's breathing roughened. Her hips were moving on their own in a slow, rhythmic rocking. Chiliad's fingers on her clit gave her what she was missing. She arched up from the bed, the heady blend of his tongue and fingers almost sending her over the edge.

Chiliad himself was dealing with a bad case of hard-on. Val's innocent, raw reactions almost made him burst against the mattress. He withdrew his tongue from her cunt, replacing it with a finger. She moaned, moving against him, her breathing ragged. It was time to relieve her from her sweet misery…time to make his wildcat come. Chiliad honed his tongue to a hard point and sliced up through her moist cleft, teasing her engorged clit with a light flick. She reared up from the bed with a sharp gasp, her fists clenching. *Ultra-sensitive…* He'd have to go carefully. He licked her swollen, sensitive clit while slipping a second finger inside her hot cunt. She was throbbing, burning hot like a supernova. Gently drawing her between his lips, Chiliad gave her a soft suck.

Val's hips bucked at the delicious sensation. Her pulse ran amok and her breath wheezed as the man's talented mouth dined on her flesh, as his fingers—those quick, clever fingers—plied their craft. His tongue drummed a soft, quick beat against her captured clit.

Val exploded.

She screamed her release at the top of her lungs, her cunt convulsing around Chiliad's fingers in rich spasms. He watched, spellbound, as naked rapture spread over her features, lighting her up from within.

"You look gorgeous like this," he murmured, gently withdrawing his glazed fingers when the tight contractions had abated.

Dazed and still trembling, Val watched him climb to his knees between her thighs, wrestling his breeches open. Her eyes heated up. She was hardly an expert at what a satisfied cock should look like, but this man's erection looked *painful*. His hard, steely rod pointed proudly towards his abdominal muscles. A pearly drop lingered at the tip of its swollen head. Chiliad crouched low between Val's thighs, his weight pinning her lower body against the mattress. Her eyes locked with his. The raw need she saw there stunned her. Her breath faltered as she felt his cock head push against her opening.

"Wait," she whispered.

"Honey?" The man looked like he was in a serious pain.

"This time, *I* want to do it," Val murmured. "*I* want to take *you*."

"Mmmm." He let out a guttural groan, barely able to speak, then rolled over to his back, sweeping her along with him. Val squealed in surprise, finding their positions switched. She stared down at Chiliad's hard cock.

"*Sit*," he growled, pointing. "And do it quick before you kill me."

Val grinned. So this was what true power felt like! She sat down. Slowly. She recalled that first time she'd given herself to him, how she'd cried out in panic that he was too big. It had been mere days ago, and already she couldn't fathom not knowing this man. Truly, he was almost too big for her tight passage, but she loved the aching delight he gave her as he filled her. She loved his mouth on hers. Loved the changing light in his eyes as his gaze shifted from cool to smoldering. The edgy undertone in his voice.

How his skin felt—the blended sensation of coarse *sooka* wool and the Temple's finest velvet.

As she took him inside her now, inch by inch, Chiliad hissed out a sigh of pleasure that made her core sizzle. Taking him was easier than she'd feared…as if all their parts matched in just the right way. At last his hard length was wedged in her tight passage, stretching her to a wonderful, aching fullness. It felt like she'd just connected with a missing piece of herself.

"Chiliad?" Val whispered. "Help me move."

His eyes sparked with a blue fire. He shifted up from his elbows, slipping his hands over her damp hips.

"It's easy," he said, a subtle amusement flaring in his voice. "Go up and down and around, wildcat, and it'll get the job done." Still, his hands guided her initial, tentative movements. "Try leaning back. Grab my legs." In next to no time she had him clutching the sheets and fighting for breath.

It was like nothing she'd ever felt before. Val bobbed up and down the large cock inside her, swirling her hips. Her eyes squeezed shut. She leaned back for support, clutching Chiliad's legs, and let her innate *Neryandi* senses guide her. She felt the pirate's rapt gaze on her, knew he was watching her move up and down on him, over and over. It only served to boost her excitement. Back in the crystal cave, Lyssipe had said that she was primed for this man…*tuned to him.* Each time he'd touched his body to her own, each time he'd penetrated her with his tongue, with his fingers, with his cock, a vibrant, vaporous part of him had taken control of her too. Their sexual auras melded into one, his unique colors merging with her own, bringing their rhythms to a perfect match.

"Val, I can't hold back much longer," he rasped.

Val came on a moan, her cunt tightening around the throbbing cock inside her. With a final, ragged cry, Chiliad grabbed her hips and pulled her down hard on him. Blinded with hot rapture, he thought her cunt's milking would be the end of him.

"*Sweet Dyad.*" Val collapsed against his chest, trembling.

Chiliad wrapped muscled arms about her narrow ribcage. His own chest was heaving. *What a ride!* Then, suddenly, it hit him.

"Oh, *fuck.*"

Val's eyes popped open. She struggled to push herself up. Propping herself against Chiliad's glorious, sweaty chest, she gazed down at his face. His handsome features took on a painful expression.

"Chiliad?" she queried, shaken. "Have I done something wrong?"

"No, no, honey. It's nothing like that." His voice was husky with anger. Anger at himself. "It's me. I'm not protected anymore. *Dammit!*"

"Protected?" Val was utterly at a loss.

Chiliad's voice softened as he took in her hurt expression. "Val…when we did this before I was on a long-term contraceptive. Then, at the Temple, Eriobea neutralized it. How could I fuckin' forget that?"

"Contraceptive?" Val stared down at him.

The wildcat was reduced to single word sentences, and she was giving him that big-eyed, clueless look again. *Dammit, hadn't they taught her anything besides hand-to-hand combat?* Chiliad heaved out a morose sigh. "Val, when we had sex before, I'd already taken care of any possibility of…uh…babies. There wouldn't be any. I was *protected.* When we had sex just now, I wasn't protected anymore."

"Oh." *Babies.* Val considered that new, tantalizing notion. For the first time since he'd fallen from the sky into her world, the man appeared seriously ill-at-ease.

One of his dark brows was cocked in doubt. "Wildcat, you *do* know how babies are made, do you?"

"*Yes,*" Val blurted out angrily, then added, "I think."

"We need to have a *very* long talk," he growled, yanking her up from his lap. "In twelve Galactic-hours we're hyperleaping to see a good friend of mine. She's a real doctor, with real instruments, nothing like the lousy M.U. I have in here. If you are pregnant—"

"Then I don't mind," she snapped back, crossing her arms over her naked breasts. Her narrow chin lifted in defiance.

Chiliad smoldered, staring at her determined little face. Whenever he heard that tone coming from her, it promised trouble—and delivered.

Epilogue

Quoted with permission from the PGA House of Representatives, 69th Congress, 1st session, report 103-54:

...following the discovery of Chebrri by Pan-Galactic Alliance Navy Captain—at the time of the recorded event, Commander—Blade Steele, the *Neryandi* consented to host a PGA scientific delegation. The mission's report stated it likely that several hundred Galactic-years before, the *Neryandi* male population had indeed grown extinct due to an infection by a lethal sex-linked virus. The exact circumstances of this exceedingly rare, singular event are not clear. The *Neryandi* refuse to be genetically tested. The past shall therefore remain, as always, shrouded. The *Neryandi* strongly deny the rumors of alleged male abductions motivated by race procreation purposes.

Primary negotiations have been initiated between the Pan-Galactic Alliance's representatives and the *Neryandi* Priesthood leadership. Word is, the PGA is willing to cease further investigations into the mysterious disappearances of thousands of able-bodied young males as long as the *Neryandi* agree to share ownership of their *Mankha* mines. The exact nature of the crystal-mine possession has yet to be defined.

Notorious space outlaw Chiliad-Kai Jayrt'ian and his companion, *Neryandi* cadet-trader Valasca, have been declared officially missing by a PGA-appointed commission. The ruling was based upon the written and oral testimony of PGA Navy Captain Blade Steele.

* * * * *

"Missing" or not, Chiliad and Val run a successful smuggling business, mainly centered around various Frontier sectors. They still can't keep their hands, as well as various other body parts, off each other. Their favorite game is "Guard and

Prisoner". Besides an assorted collection of sex toys, the *Ambrosine* currently carries in its belly a reserve of contraceptives…several brands. Chiliad claims that one little space brat with sky-blue eyes and midnight-dark hair is more than enough for him to handle. Val hasn't had her last word on the subject…yet.

About the Author

Dawn is a hopeless romantic and a Gemini, a tricky combination to handle. During daytime she's moonlighting as a medical doctor, but at nights...oh, at nights...at nights she's fervently hammering steamy scenes on her moaning keyboard.

A secret identity…sort of like Catwoman, right?

Simply put, Dawn finds penning Erotica/Romance for EC so much more stimulating than writing boring medical articles! After all, daydreaming of alpha werewolves, sexy, dark vampires and muscle-bound futuristic warriors is by far a more invigorating pastime than listening to your patients complaining!

Dawn welcomes comments from readers. You can find her website and email address on her author bio page at www.ellorascave.com.

Also by Dawn Madigan

Celtic Charms: Destined

Ryality Bites

Things That Go Bump In The Night VI (*anthology*)

Enjoy an Excerpt from:

HUNGER'S HARMATTAN

"Welcome, Captain Bartlett," Tariq said, coming toward them with his hand out. As he grasped the captain's forearm in a strong grip, his eyes slid playfully to Shanee. "And a most gracious welcome to you, Lieutenant Colonel Iphito."

As soon as his hand gripped her arm, Shanee could feel the strength of power that ran through this man. He was intensely sensual with his handsome features and all-seeing eyes, but it was the undercurrent of authority that passed from his body to hers. She knew this man would make a formidable opponent.

"There is no conflict here, Colonel," Tariq said. "You and I will become good friends."

Shanee blinked. "You believe so?" she asked, casting a quick look to the stunning woman at the Prime Reaper's side.

"I know so," he said. "Your fate lies here on Theristes." He looked down at his wife. "Doesn't it, beloved?"

Bahiya nodded. "It does." She stepped forward and stunned Shanee by embracing her as a sister or mother would. "Welcome, sister."

Shanee had never been hugged by anyone except in a moment of careless passion. Her own ken did not behave in such a fashion and it embarrassed her for a moment before she realized that the friendship offered by Bahiya and her mate was genuine and extended without expectation of anything but its return in kind.

"You have come to speak to Ailyn," Tariq said.

Once more Shanee was taken aback. She hadn't known word had been sent to Theristes in preparation for her arrival.

"Reapers know these things, Shanee," Tariq declared then lifted an eyebrow. "May I call you by your given name?"

"Aye," Shanee said, lost in the golden sparkles flashing in his kind eyes.

"I am Tariq and this is Bahiya, as you know, and these are our people."

Shanee nodded to the beautiful crowd who was gathered around them.

"So he *is* here?" she asked to hide her embarrassment for her recalcitrant glance had dipped to Tariq's very well-endowed package.

"He is and he knows you have come to see him. His abode is beyond Mount Korak and the way is perilous after nightfall. I suggest you stay here for the remainder of the day, meet our people and eat with us. Tomorrow I will have someone lead you to Ailyn."

She turned to the yeoman who had accompanied her from the ship. "Tell the captain to let General Strom know Lieutenant Harmattan is here and that I will be speaking to him tomorrow."

"Aye, aye, Ma'am," the yeoman said. He turned to head back to the ship.

"You will be spending time with us, Shanee?" Tariq asked. "A month of rest?"

"Aye," she said, staring into his eyes.

"You will call to that man and tell him to bid the captain return in one month's time. Tell him you will send a report on Ailyn then."

Shanee found herself nodding, agreeing with Tariq, intrigued by the golden glints in his amber eyes, and did as he said. His voice was soothing, mellow, sensual, and what he said made perfect sense. There was no disagreeing with his words. It would only be later as she lay upon the soft mattress in his and Bahiya's hut that she would realize he had been using subliminals on her as easily as taking a breath. By then it was too late for the LRC had left and she realized with shock that she was stranded on Theristes without a vid-com link.

"How did you do that?" she snapped at Tariq. "You made me forget about all contact with my superiors and…"

"All Reapers know how to do these things, Shanee," he told her that next morning.

Be careful when you meet Ailyn Harmattan then, she warned herself as she trekked through the jungle behind her guide, a very shy and gangly youth named Barat. Out of consideration for her, Tariq had bid the young man to clothe himself and it was evident with every step he took that Barat was chafing under the fabric he was unaccustomed to wearing. He was carrying her compact travel bag and for that she was very grateful.

The jungle was lush and green and smelled—not of fecund earth—but of exotic flowers and fresh spring waters. Extraordinary birds of every hue under the rainbow flitted through the overhanging branches of the tallest trees Shanee had ever seen. Unusual animals swung from vine to vine or leapt from branch to branch, keeping pace with the two humans walking through this striking domain. Strange sounds wafted through the air—some comical, some unsettling.

"How much farther?" she asked.

"Less than one hour," Barat replied.

They were skirting a meandering stream into which a fan-shaped waterfall cascaded. Large white flowers grew in lush abundance on the banks of the stream and lent a heavenly scent to the already sweet, intoxicating air. Thick grass covered the banks and with the rippling of the stream over sparkling boulders in the water, it was a serene place, an astonishing little piece of heaven set down in the midst of the jungle.

Shanee was not used to the intense heat and humidity. No wonder the people of Theristes preferred to go "sky clad" as Bahiya called it. Already perspiring heavily in this tropical climate, she armed the sweat from her forehead and stopped long enough to take out her bottle of water. Tipping it up, she drank deeply.

"I will take it from here, Barat."

It was not the softness of the voice speaking but the sultry quality of it that washed through Shanee as though the water she was consuming were iced and not tepid. She slowly lowered the bottle and turned her head to take in the speaker.

Rory Quinn had not been Shanee's first man nor had he been her last when their brief interlude ended. She had lain with enough males, enjoyed her romps with them, but not even Quinn had ever made her womb clench and her juices flow as did the man who had suddenly appeared there in the jungle.

Handsome did not adequately describe the tall, muscular male who wore only an abbreviated breechclout over his hips. His long legs—like the rest of his spectacular body—were deeply tanned and so perfectly formed his creation had to be at the hands of the goddess Herself. Gleaming black hair in the form of a thick braid lay over his shoulder but tendrils had escaped the careless plaiting to curl gently around his face. Eyes the color of topaz gems were framed behind long, sooty eyelashes and sexily arched thick brows. His lips were full, perfectly shaped, and his nose was in perfect proportion and size for his face. With high cheekbones, a deep cleft in his chin and—by the goddess!—dimples when he smiled, he was a living, breathing god himself come to earth.

Shanee became aware of Barat hurrying back the way they'd come, stripping off his offending clothing as he walked. "T-thank you, Barat," she managed to say, her gaze never leaving the man in front of her.

Reluctantly her attention went from his faultless form to the tall spear he carried as though it were a natural extension of his powerful physique. She was reminded of tales of ancient legendary warriors from such places as *an Éigipt* and *an Ghréig*

"Ailyn Harmattan?" she asked, picking up her travel bag.

"Aye. Come, little Amazeen," he said, and held out his hand.

Almost as though in a trance, she dropped the water bottle and moved toward him. "You know who I am?" she asked as she slipped her hand in his. The moment her flesh touched his, she knew she was lost.

"I have been reading your thoughts since you crossed the stream near the Rain Tree," he replied. "Is your bag too heavy for you to carry? If so, I will carry it for you."

"No," she mumbled. "I'm good."

He glanced down at her. "Not always I would imagine."

Enjoy an Excerpt from:

MADE FOR TWO RIVALS

ꟾ

Her eyes were pure crystalline fire as she glared up at him. Jeezis, she was a hot little package. Riled and naked. What a provocative combination. She might not know it but she was about one inch from getting nailed to the wall.

He released her wrist reluctantly and watched as she backed away from him toward the narrow bed tucked against the wall.

Jed's gaze smoothed over her ass as he drawled, "You might as well let her tease, Hammer. She has to be marked before we go to the tearoom anyhow."

Velvet turned and gave Jed a wary look as she dropped the towel and reached for her black thong. Gray's large handprint glowed across her bottom in a splash of deep pink. It looked good on her. If it weren't for Jed's presence, he'd have gone down on his knees then and there, gathered her legs into his chest and pressed a kiss of penitence onto her adorable little ass—right there where his hand had heated her skin into a warm blush.

"Marked?" she asked.

Gray answered her before Jed could open his mouth. "We're about to go into a tearoom full of Tauran males. You can't go in there unmarked. You're a blonde. They'll tear you apart trying to claim you."

His jaw tightened when she didn't even turn to acknowledge his explanation. Instead, Velvet kept watching the Cajun as she stepped into her thong and pulled it up her legs. A narrow black line split her cheeks as she leaned over and snagged her knee pants. Gray rubbed a hand into the spray of dark hair on his chest, growling as he watched Jed's eyes follow the light bounce of her breasts.

"The Hammer's right," Jed told her, rolling to sit on the edge of the bed. "Taurans can't resist a female with fair hair. One of us is gonna have to mark you."

"One of us?" Gray exploded with a rumbling snarl. "Don't get any ideas, Cajun. In this case, one of us means me!"

But Velvet continued to ignore Gray, her gaze fixed on the Cajun as she pulled her regulation pants up over the sweeping line of her hips. "What do you mean by marked?"

"The Taurans won't touch you if you're carrying the scent of another male."

Velvet just stared while Jed put her bra in her hand.

"If you smell like you just had sex," Jed explained bluntly. "If you're wearing another man's..."

Why an electronic book?

We live in the Information Age—an exciting time in the history of human civilization, in which technology rules supreme and continues to progress in leaps and bounds every minute of every day. For a multitude of reasons, more and more avid literary fans are opting to purchase e-books instead of paper books. The question from those not yet initiated into the world of electronic reading is simply: *Why?*

1. ***Price.*** An electronic title at Ellora's Cave Publishing and Cerridwen Press runs anywhere from 40% to 75% less than the cover price of the exact same title in paperback format. Why? Basic mathematics and cost. It is less expensive to publish an e-book (no paper and printing, no warehousing and shipping) than it is to publish a paperback, so the savings are passed along to the consumer.
2. ***Space.*** Running out of room in your house for your books? That is one worry you will never have with electronic books. For a low one-time cost, you can purchase a handheld device specifically designed for e-reading. Many e-readers have large, convenient screens for viewing. Better yet, hundreds of titles can be stored within your new library—on a single microchip. There are a variety of e-readers from different manufacturers. You can also read e-books on your PC or laptop computer. (Please note that Ellora's Cave does not endorse any specific brands. You can check our websites at www.ellorascave.com

or www.cerridwenpress.com for information we make available to new consumers.)

3. ***Mobility***. Because your new e-library consists of only a microchip within a small, easily transportable e-reader, your entire cache of books can be taken with you wherever you go.
4. ***Personal Viewing Preferences.*** Are the words you are currently reading too small? Too large? Too... *ANNOYING*? Paperback books cannot be modified according to personal preferences, but e-books can.
5. ***Instant Gratification.*** Is it the middle of the night and all the bookstores near you are closed? Are you tired of waiting days, sometimes weeks, for bookstores to ship the novels you bought? Ellora's Cave Publishing sells instantaneous downloads twenty-four hours a day, seven days a week, every day of the year. Our webstore is never closed. Our e-book delivery system is 100% automated, meaning your order is filled as soon as you pay for it.

Those are a few of the top reasons why electronic books are replacing paperbacks for many avid readers.

As always, Ellora's Cave and Cerridwen Press welcome your questions and comments. We invite you to email us at Comments@ellorascave.com or write to us directly at Ellora's Cave Publishing Inc., 1056 Home Avenue, Akron, OH 44310-3502.